Angel Hair

Angel Hair

Margot Griffiths

Library of Congress Control Number:		2013911918
ISBN:	Hardcover	978-1-4836-6302-9
	Softcover	978-1-4836-6301-2
	Ebook	978-1-4836-6303-6

Rev. date: 07/29/2013

To order additional copies of this book, contact:
Xlibris LLC
1-888-795-4274
www.Xlibris.com
Orders@Xlibris.com
136452

"Thou art thy mother's glass and she in thee
Calls back the lovely April of her prime."

William Shakespeare

Chapter One

·❧❦·

Our simple childhood sits upon a throne
That hath more power than all the elements.

William Wordsworth

1958

The house was a different planet at four in the morning. In that blurry moment when night gave up and dawn took hold, when shapes were shrouded and corners soft, the house was veiled in mist, like Venus. Alien, unknown, mysterious Venus.

Maffy crept through the back hall. Alien, yes, but this ghostly light could make the house normal, hiding the things that made it different. What you had to face head on in daylight could be anything you liked at four in the morning. What was that big mummified thing by the back door? A three-speed bicycle with spoked wheels and thin black wires that wound from the rear wheels to the handle bars, so you could brake with your hands and not your feet? No. It was an English pram. Another baby was on the way. Another way they were different. This baby would have a pram, just like royalty. The aunts had seen to it. The pram's navy blue hood hung importantly over spoked wheels that overlapped each other, the small ones in front fitting behind the big ones at the back so they looked like an optical illusion when the buggy was moving.

How would things change with the new baby, now showing in her mother's stomach? Neither she nor the three others still asleep could know. Just as well. Best not to know. But the little fox in Maffy's stomach kept gnawing. Sometimes just a flutter, sometimes sharper. Now when no one else was up, and she could pretend they'd wake up smiling, the fox was only nibbling.

She crept through the back hall, where she knew without seeing, shoes would be scattered next to the cat's litter box, and coats would be piled on the counter by the laundry sink. In this light, shoes could be stowed in the big wooden box by the door, and coats hung neatly on hooks that her father, in this light, could have gotten around to mounting on cedar walls. Into the kitchen now, all open to the den, one big room, so big she could walk through it whirling her hula-hoop. To the right of the den, through the big sliding door, was the dining room and beyond it, down two stairs, was the huge living room. She reached out her toe, feeling for the first stair. Another place that made them different. The living room was sunken, with sheets of glass sweeping from floor to ceiling. Window walls. The side of the house that looked out onto Uplands Park was all window. Straw matting covered the floor. Everyone else in this perfect part of Victoria called the Uplands had broadloom, according to her mother. Straw matting had its strengths. When a square got scruffy, around the door or by the marble hearth, her father would cut it out and sew in a new square with a big curved needle and thick ropey thread. The matting was dry and coarse and creaked under her feet. The house smelled of new hay. She liked it, but her mother didn't. It made them different.

She knew they were different. Denise Green made sure of that. Denise always had a reason when she asked you over to read movie magazines, and when she asked, you didn't say no. She was big, almost thirteen. Yesterday she'd been wearing a tight turquoise cardigan buttoned up the back and black slim-jims, not looking so slim. Maffy knew she'd been asked over so they could listen in on Mrs. Green's bridge club. Denise had herded her into the den, right off the living room where the bridge club held court, and they had heard every word the bridge club said.

"Hugh Morgan built their house, you know . . . yes, really, the Morgans'."

"His own design?"

"It drove Eleanor just about crazy at first. All those windows yawing at you. With her pride, she'd want a doll's house."

"Hugh thinks he's the next Eichler!"

"He never finished it, the bathroom off their bedroom is—"

"Do they really have hemp on the floor?"

"It sets off her antiques, that Chinese screen. You have to admit, Eleanor is artistic."

"Who's Eichler?"

"Oh Nancy—he's famous! That California architect. Open space, glass."

"She's so highly strung, I can't believe she's having another baby."

"What! Is she crazy? Her favourite child is the cat."

"Where've you been? She's five months pregnant."

"She'll never be the same."

"If we're lucky."

Big laughs. The Moron Quartet was hilarious all right, voices jangling like nails in a tin can. *Yakety yak. Don't go back.* They hadn't known she was in the den with Denise, who smiled as she fiddled with the black, knife-pleated scarf knotted around her neck. Or had they? Maybe Mrs. Green had known all along, and had kept it up till she was sure the damage was done. Grownups thought kids were a different species, one that couldn't hear. Yup, Denise's mother had known Maffy could hear every word and it didn't matter. It put the fun in it for her, pointy nose picking up the smell of weakness.

It wouldn't have been half so bad if Denise's sister had been home. Donna was fifteen but she was still a scared rabbit, not at all like Denise. Even when one of the Morons called her mother "artistic," Denise had found a reason to smirk. It had been said grudgingly.

Artistic had been a good word once, for a few weeks last year. When her grade four teacher had announced, "Your daughter shows artistic talent," the art lessons at the Victoria Art Gallery had started. When the art teacher and her mother enjoyed a little laugh over the self-portrait assignment, the art lessons stopped.

The house was silent except for the dog snoring from his bed
under the hifi. There was a heat vent down there and every once
in a while Bosun whinnied in his sleep. In the quiet she could
think of all the things she'd like to say to Denise Green's mother.
Hear the toilet flushing on all that hilarity. The best conversations
were the ones you had in your head, at four in the morning,
when your enemy was safely tucked away. Her parents had those
conversations out loud, in broad daylight, the way only really old
people were supposed to.

"Bridge on the River Cry," her mother said of Mrs. Green's
Moron Quartet.

"Finally it will be a bridge too far," her father said, giving the
theme song a little whistle.

"It takes her forever to play a hand."

"Like ordering a nightcap on the Titanic. A waste of time. You
know she's going down."

Her parents were unbeatable when they were both rowing
in the same direction. That had been last summer. Now it was
summer again and they weren't even in the same boat.

The windows in the living room were covered with heavy
curtains, the murky colour of swamp water. Wool, to keep the
cold out. It was always cold, her mother said. Even in summer, the
mornings were cold in Victoria. In winter, the rain would seep in
at the base of the windows. Denise Green's house had "sheers"
that blew around during the day, in a creepy horror movie way,
and pink brocade drapes that sealed them in at night.

She pulled the curtains open and felt her way to the
chesterfield. She could curl up on one cushion, without
overlapping onto the next. She was thin, with acorn brown
hair and freckles that emphasized the bump on the bridge of
her nose. But sometimes it was good to be a runt and not to be
noticed. And anyhow, she wasn't in a hurry to grow up, not if it
meant turning into a mother.

Growing up. It wasn't tempting. It would have been different
if she'd been a boy. When she'd been a little kid, she'd snuck
Owen's old brown pants out of the jumble sale bag and worn
them one whole, hot summer. Her mother probably wished
Maffy had been a boy too. Maybe they had something in common
after all. That and the piano. She could see its promising outline

against the wall to the left of the fireplace. They were both hopeless. Even with lessons, swirling more money down the drain than his rum did, according to her father, she and her mother were hopeless. The big upright her mother had painted green had suffered a lot of insult. Only her father could coax out everything a piano had.

The straw matting rustled. Bosun was awake. He padded over and licked her hand. She patted the cushion beside her on the couch. He had to be sure he was invited. He was a gentle dog, except when welcoming them home. Then he couldn't hold back his yelps of joy.

"Come on, Bosun. It's okay."

The dog clambered up. He was seven now, not quite so nimble. He circled clumsily on the couch and settled into a heap next to her.

"Good boy."

He nosed at her arms which were wrapped tightly around her shins. She lowered her legs and Bosun's head found its way onto her lap. She wrapped her arms around him now.

"Do you know what day this is?"

The dog lifted his head and licked her chin.

"The Summer Soltice. It's summer's birthday, Bosun, the longest day of the year. When the sun is born today, we'll see it. Summer is here. Let it be good."

Bosun whined a little prayer of his own.

They waited. A clear day was a good sign for the first day of summer. Today was her mother's birthday too. Would it be good? She watched the sun touch the sky in the east, then eased Bosun's head off her lap.

"Back to your bed, boy."

She turned down the hall, past her parents' room toward her own. She could just make out the family photograph on the wall. At this time of day they could be the perfect family. They had the makings. Handsome son and two perfect years later, the girl. They were all tricked up. A picture couldn't be counted on to let you know who people really were. Frozen smiles didn't have anything to do with what was going on before or what would keep going on after the camera clicked.

Sometimes though, in the afternoon light, the picture seemed to have gotten at the truth after all. Stuff that went by too fast in life was clearer in that one second that would always be the same. Like the way everyone's smile was different. Owen's smile was firm. Serious. You could tell he knew when things weren't right. Her father's smile was sweet and sad. Dreaming of being the next Eichler? Her mother's smile looked worried, just a breath away from, "That tears it!" Mothers. Making you feel like you were coming up short. You, and the whole rest of the world, coming up short. Long suffering mothers, the only ones with no place to go.

Her own smile. She'd said cheese and still her mouth had that turned down look.

She had done a circuit of the house. It was square, sunken in the front corner where the living room hunkered down. In summer she and Owen would lie on its flat roof and look way into Uplands Park, to the Hawthorne bushes and the gnarled oak trees growing grey, corduroyed bark.

Uplands Park wasn't like other parks, with swing sets and sandboxes and goal posts, with smooth-skinned trees in prim rows sticking out of perfectly mowed grass. Uplands Park was wild and tangled, with secret paths winding through yellow broom and thick-branched oaks writhing out of the earth wherever the ancient acorns had fallen. Choked in spring with white fawn lilies and purple shooting stars, it was the most beautiful place on earth, after Twin Coves.

The house was perched on the edge of the park at the end of a small lane. It was good they weren't out in the open with other houses, seeing as theirs was different. Other houses had two stories and small windows divided into little squares, covered in filmy curtains. Other houses were painted green or white and had shingles on the roof. Their house was the colour of red cedar with tar and pebbles on the roof. The reason they could afford the glorious Uplands was because her father had built the house.

She was back in her room. It was cold. The window was open in case the cat needed in. Her mother insisted. *Put out the dog and let in the cat. Yakety yak.* She slid into the bed that her father had built, planks of knotty cedar hammered together to make an oblong box. Her mattress lay on a piece of plywood that fit into the box. The white Hudson's Bay blanket, with stripes of red, green, yellow and navy, was tucked in all around. Her eiderdown was the colour of a new acorn. Donna and Denise slept under canopies, the frilled nylon of party dresses, cotton candy pink, with pink poodle dog pillows yapping on pink bedspreads.

She could pretend in her bed. She was in the Alps, in a bed like Heidi's. Up in the mountains with no grownups. Just goats and clouds. She pulled the eiderdown up to her chin and felt its paper thinness. The feathers were all down at the bottom. She sat up in bed, shook it, and sank back under its warmth.

Chapter Two

Earth turned in her sleep with pain.

Robert Browning

Eleanor Morgan eased out of bed, swollen legs poking from under the sheet like downed tree trunks. She'd lost her ankles and it was only June. The baby wasn't due until October. A Halloween baby.

A sigh winnowed through her lips. Owen and Myfanwy would be on their way to school by now. One more week and they'd be home for the summer. She leaned on the night table and pushed herself upright. She couldn't avoid the mirror over the dresser. Her hair was flattened by sleep. Today was her birthday. She was thirty-nine.

She'd forgotten her past pregnancies, but then it was ten years. She'd forgotten how her legs ached, how her stomach mooned, how her shoulders arched to stave off the knife in her lower back. How her mind clouded. Pregnant again. Everyone was talking. She'd given them something new to chew on.

Their neighbourhood was like an English village. They knew each others' secrets but everyone kept their distance. Oh, they'd socialize, it was all very civilized, but lines were drawn in the sand. The Uplands. This was what they'd aspired to. What she had aspired to, Hugh liked to remind her. It didn't faze him that the house was never going to be finished, that he'd never get a move on, especially now when they needed the spare room done up. She'd loved irony when she'd studied it in novels, star English student at the University of Victoria, on scholarship no less. Now, irony consisted of being married to an architect and living in an unfinished house. Yet she wanted to hold on, and so, another baby.

The phone rang in the kitchen. It would be Daphne Green. Let it ring. She'd seen Daphne yesterday in her new Plymouth Fury. The car cruised silently, yellow stripe bisecting its creamy, low-slung body, tail fins flaring out like a great white shark swimming through the undercurrents of the Uplands. Daphne had waved furiously, on her way to the Ladies Auxiliary, no doubt. Turn back, Daphne. Go home. Turn on your new television and watch *This Is Your Life*. Those folks at Lux Soap want you washing your whites, buffing your linoleum in your high-heeled shoes. This Is Your Life.

The phone wouldn't stop. It had to be Daphne, calling to brag about her new car. Yesterday Eleanor had waved limply from her algae green Hillman, crabbing along in the wrong gear as Daphne had glided by. The Plymouth Fury had a push button transmission—a real trendsetter. Daphne never would know where to draw the line.

The phone wouldn't stop.

"Hello."

"Eleanor, Happy Birthday. How *are* you?" It was Daphne Green, all right.

"I'm fine, how are you?"

"Oh, all is well here. But I'm wondering about you, after I saw you yesterday, driving home, you looked *so* tired. I just couldn't *imagine* being pregnant, at this stage in life, and now with the weather getting so warm."

"Best not to strain your imagination, Daphne." What could you say to someone who only wanted bad news?

"Denise and I would love to have Myfanwy over to visit again. Even though Denise is older, and more mature, they had a lovely afternoon. She's a quiet little girl, isn't she?" There it was, the edge, masquerading as concern.

"Thank you Daphne, I'll let her know. I'd better be off, I've got a pie to bung in the oven." The lie popped out so easily.

"You're not having a birthday cake? What kind of pie? I'm planning a lemon souffle for dessert tonight."

"Well . . . it's raspberry, Hugh's favourite. The raspberry patch is early this year, the warm weather and all. I really must go, Daphne."

"Bye-bye then, and *do* take care of yourself. I'm off to the Literary Society. We're planning a fund raiser for the—"

"Bye for now." Eleanor hung up. Literary Society? Daphne could never just say something, she had to *say* something, her tone suggesting—screaming—that the subject of her commentary bordered on bizarre.

It was worse for Lily Miles. The way Daphne made up to Winton Miles was disgusting. Poor Lloyd Green was the one who really looked tired. Daphne had been his legal secretary before she'd married him and launched her meteoric rise in fortune. Now a real estate lawyer wasn't enough. She was after a softer cushion.

And that dig at Myfanwy. Well, good for Myfanwy. Obviously she hadn't given Daphne and Denise the information they'd hoped for. But the truth was, Myfanwy was unusually quiet. Denise was never at a loss for words, but Eleanor didn't like the girl any more than she liked her mother. Donna, mercifully, was tall and slim like Lloyd. Though two years older than Denise, she was sweet and humble, in all features just off the mark of memorable. Denise was Daphne; florid, obvious. Denise would only have Myfanwy in to play if she was the plaything.

Eleanor dialed Lily's number. Lily Miles was Eleanor's best friend, and Lily's daughter, Janna, was Myfanwy's. It seemed so perfect—bosom friends, like *Anne of Green Gables*. Thank God the Miles were home from Seattle, and God alone knew what those family events were like for Lily. She rarely let on. Five rings, she was probably in the greenhouse, no wait, it was being answered.

"The Miles residence. Janna speaking. Who is calling please?"

Winton had his women trained. "Hello, Janna. It's Mrs. Morgan. How are you?"

"Just tired from the birthday. I'll go to school this afternoon."

"Did you have fun?"

"Well, you know . . . I'll get Mummy. I think she's in the greenhouse."

Eleanor stared at her feet as the line hummed in her ear.

"Hi Ellie." Lily's voice was breathless.

"How was it, Lily?"

"Like food poisoning."

"That good?"

"It crept up on me, all innocent at first. You know it's a bit off, but you eat it anyway. You can't help it, even though you know you'll pay later. In the moment of eating it's worth anything."

"Lily, what happened?"

"We danced. Isabelle's annual dinner at the Seattle Club. Winton's mother keeps the membership, although Charles has been gone for years. Died in his forties, his heart, and maybe better off for it. At any rate, off we go to the Club for her seventieth birthday. After dinner a rather attractive fossil comes over and asks Isabelle to dance. She's puffed up in that way of hers, always the belle of the ball. So now everyone else must dance around her, put a frame on her performance."

Eleanor broke in, "Lily, what happened?"

"Oh Ellie. We danced. Alistair and I danced."

Eleanor stifled her response, afraid Lily wouldn't go on.

"We got up and found ourselves moving toward each other. It was like I was watching myself in a mirror, from a long, filmy distance. I saw his arm became part of my back, his palm grazing the lowest part of my spine, fingers moving invisibly down my hip. His touch, so light—I was overcome. It took all I had to give up his rough, callused hand without pressing my face into his palm and breathing him in for one last moment."

"Lily, what came over you?" Her throat was tight, the knife in her spine a jealous stab.

"I don't know, Ellie, we were both—well, crazy. He could see my unhappiness and he responded. We're only human. I don't know how Winton and Alistair can be so different. They have the same mother. Oh Ellie, that mother."

"A mother is a different mother to each child, Lily. You don't know how it feels to mother more than one." Eleanor's hand rested on her swelling stomach. What was it that made her go at Lily, who had wanted more kids?

"Are you defending that woman?"

"No, no—oh Lily, I know Isabelle, the way she fawns on Winton. She's a nightmare. Sounds like a hellish weekend."

Lily sighed. "With a few moments of bliss."

"How did Winton react to you dancing with his brother? They've been competing all their lives haven't they?"

"Mmmm, I think Alistair stopped competing years ago, when he realized who his brother was. And of course, he took himself out of Winton's sphere, creating as different a life as he could on the ranch. Anyway, Winton's too arrogant to let on if he suspects Alistair could ever be more appealing than he is."

"Winton must be blind!"

"The self-absorbed usually are, but he's not blind enough. He knows, somehow, that Alistair is the high road. I thought I'd get away with it. Was willing to risk it. But I can feel him seething, Eleanor. It's brewing again. He doesn't care about me; it's his pride. He's so disdainful of Alistair, but underneath, he's jealous."

"What's brewing?"

"That black part, the part he hides so well. A frightening . . . it's hard to explain. An inhuman part of Winton."

"It'll blow over," Eleanor said, but she knew. She'd seen it in those cold eyes. "He's got his latest development to elevate his pride. Hugh's hoping the lots will sell to those who want an avant garde architect, if only we can keep them from seeing this house."

Lily laughed her lovely, low chuckle. "I love your home, Eleanor. What Hugh's done is important. We may not grasp modernism, but it's his passion. And your instincts for decorating—it's beautiful and different. I find myself wandering around this house, thinking I should be more creative and daring, like you. I'm lost here. I don't belong. It's all Winton's taste."

Eleanor could see Lily giving her shrug of defeat. "It's no wonder you're down. Go back to the greenhouse. That always relaxes you. Try not to worry about Winton."

"If only I could stop thinking about Alistair. You're right about the greenhouse. Daphne's bridge club needs a fourth tomorrow. I said I'd sit in. They're coming here. I'll see if I can get the phalaeonopsis to bloom for them. That ought to motivate it."

"Bridge club? I thought you'd quit coming forth for them."

"I did."

"When?"

"Well . . . it was, uh, right after I invited them to play here—just one last time—so I can quit with impunity."

"Right, Lily, that's telling them."

"I'd give anything to be more like you. It's always been about appearances with me." A pause. "Oh, Ellie, I didn't even ask how you are. And it's your birthday. Happy Birthday!"

"Thank you, Lily."

"How are you?"

"I'm fine." She'd phoned to complain about Daphne but that wasn't safe, not now that Lily was hosting that bridge club. They would spend at least some of their time talking about Eleanor.

"I'll come right over. I'll bring a coffee cake for your birthday breakfast."

"Well, truthfully, I'm a little tired. Could we make it lunch?"

"Of course. I'll make my crab au gratin."

"That sounds lovely, Lily. See you then."

Eleanor hung up for the second time and felt the cloud around her head thicken with envy. Delicate Lily, in love with Winton's brother. Again. Perhaps she would have him this time. Alistair—remote, romantic—living on a small island off Seattle, owner of a horse ranch, of all unlikely things. He'd been smart, buying when prices were low. It would be worth something now. Winton wasn't the only one with the Midas Touch. Who was this Alistair of the Island that Lily was self-destructing over? Did she have any idea what she was doing? As bad as Winton was, he provided well and Lily had a lot to be grateful for. Her home was perfection, her daughter an exquisite reproduction of herself, save for Winton's deeper blue eyes, without the ice. Lily wanted for nothing and had time for bridge games. It was that bridge club!

She put the kettle on. A cup of tea and raisin toast, then back to bed. Her feet were puffing up like rising dough. Tomorrow she'd see Dr. Gregson. She'd have to watch her blood pressure. Only one more week and the kids would be around all the time. Owen would mow lawns, and there was the paper route, until August when they left for their three weeks at Twin Coves.

Owen was happiest outdoors, running, always moving. As for Myfanwy, she'd drift into that world she shared with Janna. Their friendship didn't waver with jealousies and fights. They were kids. Their lives were simple.

She steeped the old Brown Betty teapot and got the sugar out of the twelve-inch high cupboard, with the sliding doors built in all along the length of the kitchen counter. Another of Hugh's ideas for the ultimately convenient house. Most kitchens have stuff cluttering up the counters, he said. This way everything can be neatly stowed behind the sliding doors. Garages, he called them; that would house the toaster, marmalade, peanut butter, and whatnot, then the garage door would slide shut, Bob's your uncle. What he hadn't bargained for was the garage stowed with a thousand other things, and the car hanging around on the counter after all. Where was the tea? He would have had his, then put it away. Only where? Ah, next to the coffee, which they rarely drank. There was only loose tea in this house. God forbid it be neatly stowed in teabags. She had Hugh's Welsh family to thank for that.

The phone rang again. She stood on swollen legs and let it ring. It would be her mother. Her mother, who knew a woman's place was in the home. An honours English Degree didn't mean she should get above herself. "Don't be ridiculous, Eleanor. Think of your children!" There would be no teaching of poetry in the University of Victoria English Department. There would be another child. The phone rang on. Let her mother think Eleanor was off to an early start on her birthday, gardening, volunteering, shopping for lemons for a planned souffle. She couldn't let her know how this pregnancy was dogging her. Balancing her tea and toast on the straw tray, she pushed her loaf-shaped feet back to bed.

Chapter Three

———◆◆◆———

You must still be bright and quiet,
And content with simple diet;
And remain, through all bewild'ring,
Innocent and honest children.

Robert Louis Stevenson

"Maafawnwheee, is so scraawneee."

Her mother frowned. "Just ignore them."

She had picked her up after school. Only two more days of school left. They were going downtown to buy her first pair of toe shoes. The shoe store had a machine you could stick your foot into, and see the bones of your feet. Her excitement had a sick feel. Being "en pointe" meant so many more ways to make mistakes. What she really wanted was a pair of moccasins. They'd already tried two stores, but moccasins were hard to find.

"I know a store we can try," she said. Joanne's mum saw—"

"That's enough!"

They drove in silence. The aunts on her mother's side were coming for dinner tonight, and so was Grandmaf, on her father's side. The aunts took the ferry from Vancouver, where they lived with Grandmother in a huge house on a shady, tree lined street. Grandmother was too tired to come this time. A weak excuse according to her mother, who didn't want her around anyway.

Aunt Alice and Aunt Bea were sitting on the horsehair chesterfield that looked out at the park.

"The wildflowers are over," said one to the other. Their voices were so much alike you had to be watching them to know who was speaking.

Maffy was looking down, counting the daisies on her favourite dress. Her mother had made it. The field of flowers lined up perfectly at the seams.

Owen slumped into the room in time to open their presents. Every time they came, the aunts brought things to improve you. You could never tell how you needed improvement. The aunts were tricky that way. Maffy opened sky blue tissue paper to reveal a white bathing suit. She held it up. It had a flouncy skirt that looked like it would hit about the middle of her thighs. She looked at the aunts. Aunt Bea watched her with what might be pity. Aunt Alice looked stern. Would this bathing suit stand alone, or was an explanation coming? An explanation that was really a lecture.

"You know, Myfanwy, a lady shouldn't be seen in a bathing suit without a skirt. It's simply, well, it's not ladylike."

"Did you bring one for my mother?" Would she ever look like her mother did in her black bathing suit? Until the baby, her mother had looked very good in a bathing suit. "Thank you, Aunt Alice. Thank you, Aunt Bea."

Owen was smirking with what definitely was pity. He pulled the blue wrapping off a small black leather wallet with a zipper that went around three sides. He unzipped it.

Aunt Alice started in. "A manicure set, with fifteen pieces, two sets of scissors, one for cuticles."

He made for his room to get an immediate start on good grooming.

She heard her dad's car crunching on the gravel driveway. It took a long time for him to come in the front door with Grandmaf. She was old, over seventy. She seemed to have lost track of all the years she'd been on earth. Her face was carved with deep, heavy lines. Her thin white hair was pulled into a bun that let lots escape. She was beautiful in a shoes-off way people got when they were comfortable being old. Grandmaf didn't have money to buy them things like bathing suits, but she won in the gift department. A Life Savers Sweet Story Book for her, and for Owen, a plastic Flying Space Ship, that she'd got from sending off three box tops from Malt-O Meal.

Her other grandmother, who insisted on Grandmother, not Granny or Grandma or Nana, wasn't comfortable being old. She wasn't comfortable with much, especially when it came to family. Family was where the shoe began to pinch. If it wasn't perfect, where did that leave her?

"We're waiting, Myfanwy. Make your grand entrance!" Her mother was showing off the toe shoes, and calling for her to start her dance. She had a real audience when the aunts came for dinner. It would have been easier to be a tap dancer, like Karen and Cubby on the Mickey Mouse Club, but her mother said it was common. With ballet you had to be perfect. Miss Grimshaw would call out the steps in French. "Pas de chat, relevee, pas de chat, bouree. Repeat." But she had beautiful arm positions. "Hands like the dying swan," said one of the aunts.

Tonight she'd asked her father to put on the music from the Dances of King Henry the Eighth. Grandmaf said King Henry had written the music himself, sitting around a smoky peat fire in his castle, feather pen flying. The first dance was already over, but she couldn't get the ribbon on her left slipper tied.

"Myfanwy, where are you?" Her mother laughed. "She's a perfect ballerina—a face like a horse and a figure like a needle."

They couldn't see her. She was in the hall off the living room. The second dance had started, her slipper was tied, but she stayed rooted in her spot, looking at the family photograph.

Her mother coaxed. "We're waiting!"

"Is the child shy in front of us, Eleanor?" Grandmaf's voice was wispy, like dry leaves scuttling along a sidewalk.

"Well, she's a cool little thing. Moody like Hugh, I never know what gets into her."

She slid silently into her room. The mirror over her dressing table leered at her. She stared at her long, freckled face, at eyes even greener when her eyelids turned red.

Her bedroom door opened.

"Hello, Little One, you're not asleep are you." It wasn't a question.

"Hi Grandmaffy."

"Your toe shoes are very fine. Are you excited, child?"

"Mmmm."

"Bare feet may be best. Bare feet bring freedom. You're a beautiful dancer."

She felt the warm, scratchy hand on her head. "You make me feel special, Grandmaf."

"You are special, Myfanwy."

Light was coming in from the hall and she could see the outline of Grandmaf's hodgepodgy hair. Her hand was rough and dry and Maffy's hair got caught in one of her torn nails. Grandmaf worked in her garden all summer. Dirt was worn into the grooves of her skin.

"Would you like a story?"

"Yes, please."

"Which one tonight?"

"The Spartan Boy."

"The Greek myths tonight, Little One?" Grandmaf settled on the bed. Maffy's body rolled into hers. She curled around the warm bottom and smelled lavender in Grandmaf's clothes.

"Hundreds of years ago in the country of Greece, not grease as in the drippings from a turkey, but Greece, the glorious home of the most fine and literate of the ancient civilizations . . ."

She told it the same way each time, using words Maffy at first hadn't understood.

"Hundreds of years before the birth of Christ, there were two city states. One was Athens, the other, Sparta. Athens was a seat of great learning. There lived the great philosophers and playwrights. Aristotle, Plato, Socrates and Sophocles. The Greeks worshipped many gods, this being before the time of Christ. Athena, Apollo, Zeus and Poseidon, the god of the seas who lived under the waves.

"The other great city state in Greece was Sparta. And the people who lived within her fabled walls were known as Spartans. Now while Athens was a place of culture and learning, Sparta was a place where great warriors were born. Where courage was revered above all things. Young boys were taken from their mothers at six years of age. Taken to live in barracks and learn the ways of war. The Spartans were a warring people. The Athenians, as the people from Athens were known, were a learning people.

There was a baby boy born in Sparta who should have been born in Athens. There were many little boys and girls in Sparta who should have been born in Athens. This little boy, when he left his mother at six years of age, did not want to go. He was a dreamy little one, but he was born in Sparta and his job was to become a brave soldier. And so the boy turned his dreams to the development of courage. Little Spartan boys were taught that as courageous soldiers they must never betray their whereabouts."

Wear a boots. Maffy could see the little boy pulling on his boots, and not letting anyone interfere with that.

"They were trained to be silent, when in hiding or when creeping up on the enemy. Nothing was worse than to give away a hiding place and to be taken prisoner. The glory was in courage.

"When the little Spartan boy had reached ten years of age, he had learned many fine skills. He had learned to hunt and he had learned to snare. One day he snared a small red fox. The fox was angry and snarling, but the little Spartan boy was able to get him into his leather sack and pull the drawstring tight. Then he put the sack inside his tunic, which was also leather. He admired the bravery of the fox, and hoped to tame it as his pet and his friend. He had traveled a long way from his barrack to snare the fox, and on his way back, he heard enemy noise. A long column of soldiers in the colours of the Peloponnesus, was surging down the slope ahead of him, like a snake writhing downhill. The little Spartan boy darted into a dense thicket to wait for the enemy to pass by. But it would soon be dark and the enemy was looking for a place to camp. The little Spartan boy realized in alarm that they were beginning to camp all around his thicket. He crouched silently. To move a muscle, even to release the fox, would alert the enemy. The little red fox was stirring. The Spartan boy had held him firm for a long time. His arms were tired. The fox was winning purchase of movement, his small muzzle was gnawing through the leather sack. Gnawing through the leather jerkin of the little Spartan boy. Without a cry, or a movement, the little Spartan proved himself that day in the thicket. He died in the thicket, as the fox gnawed into his stomach. He died rather than be caught by his enemy, rather than lose his courage."

She was gliding into the kitchen to make a peanut butter and marmalade sandwich. The lights were bright but no one was there. The peanut butter was in the sliding cupboard that ran the length of the kitchen counter. She put her finger in a hole the size of a fifty-cent piece—instead of knobs, there were holes—and slid the wooden slat back along its grooves. There was a scrabbling noise. Was something alive in there? Suddenly the fox leapt out of the dark hole that the cupboard had become. It leapt at her face, fastening its sharp little claws around her neck. She couldn't get it off. Its pointed teeth were in her ear, and she heard the growling getting louder and louder, then a high pitched screaming as she shook and shook, trying to free herself, but it hung on tighter, and tighter.

"Maffo, it's okay, you're okay."

The room was dark and she couldn't see his face but she hung onto Owen's voice.

"You're dreaming, Maff. It's okay, don't cry. You'll wake them up."

*

Maffy measured the water carefully. Too much and the porridge would be runny, too little and it would be sticky. Goldilocks, her father teased. Goldilocks, who wouldn't get out of her bed that was just right, who could stir the porridge until it was just right. Once the porridge started to thicken, she added the raisins. She hated raisins, but Owen loved them. He'd be sloping into the kitchen pretty soon now. His bedroom was farther away from theirs than hers was. Even so, he'd have heard the fighting in the night. It wasn't possible not to, but he wouldn't let on.

Today was the last day of school, the day of the big picnic that lasted all afternoon at the Junior High School. Maffy would be off school at noon. The elementary kids had their picnic yesterday. She'd won three ribbons for sprinting.

Owen was coming down the back hall. He looked good, but who knew what was behind those half-closed eyes? The color of them could tell you something. They changed, like the top of a wave—turquoise when the sun was on it, grey blue when a thundercloud was overhead. Everyone noticed Owen's eyes. She could see it in her friends' eyes when they were around him. It made her something because he was her brother.

His eyes were hooded now, and Maffy had to concentrate on the porridge, the last pot she'd have to make for two whole months. In the summer they ate Shreddies with raspberries. She would slip out to the raspberry patch and pick eight. Always eight, that way they'd last longer, and she wouldn't take away from the possibility of a pie. She liked an even number.

"Porridge ready, Maffo?"

"Just about. Your lunch is by the phone."

"I don't need a lunch."

"But it's the picnic. I put in extra stuff. Two packages of Dad's cookies and cupcakes."

"We won the track meet last week so old man Harrison is bringing hot dogs, making us all promise to turn out next year so we can whip Vic. High again." He gave her ear a flick with his thumb and forefinger to remind her he'd told her yesterday.

She was getting off at noon and wouldn't need a lunch either, but took his anyway when they rushed out the door to the bus stop. That way her mother wouldn't find it and the cellophane package of Hostess cupcakes. She had peddled over to Estevan store after school yesterday to get them. They were her favourite, but according to her mother, they were appalling.

The bus roared up and Owen gave her a bus ticket. He shoved ahead and went to the back of the bus with the other big kids. Denise Green would get on at the next stop so Owen looked for a seat with someone—anyone—so she couldn't sit next to him when she made her big entrance. Now that Elvis was in the army, Denise was turning her eyes on him. Maffy was afraid to tell Denise how Owen felt about her, but it helped knowing it inside. Maybe it was having that big bust that made Denise mean. She just figured she could be.

Janna was sitting in the middle of the bus. She patted the seat next to her, and Maffy sat down. Janna was great in the morning. She'd never ask why Maffy had Owen's lunch kit. Janna didn't add anything or take anything away, and Maffy knew she'd get to school with nothing new to worry about. It didn't get more complicated than trading hopscotch charms. Janna didn't ask questions, like Denise did. Questions she already had her own answers to.

It took ages to get to school. Fifteen minutes to daydream. In just over a month she would be at Twin Coves again. They went every year for the last three weeks of August, and stayed until the last swim on Labour Day. Swimming was what she loved most, and each hot day, the water got warmer and warmer. She'd wade into the hot tide through armies of crabs and bullheads darting frantically out of her way.

Tiny crabs smothered both coves at the summer cabin. When you walked in the water, each step an earthquake, they'd race under rocks, down holes in the sand. When you turned over a sandstone slab on the beach, they'd scrabble for new cover. Some were green, some the red of dried blood. She'd find the smallest, shell marbled grey, legs pure white. On her palm these tiny legs tickled. Soft as a spider web across her lips. When she walked out deeper, bits of seaweed caught in her fingers, leaving a slithery film.

When she got ducked, seaweed wrapped around her ears like mermaid earrings, green and salty smelling. The Japanese seaweed, brown and lacy, hung like a bridal veil down her shoulders. Rolling onto her back, she watched the clouds puffing through the sky. Salt stung her lips where she'd chewed them, and the smell of the sea filled her. She frog kicked over to the sandstone shelves where the water was warmest and crawled onto the hot, flat rocks. Spread-eagle on her back like a starfish, she willed her bones to remember this warmth, memorize the periwinkles that bit into her thighs. She lifted her head and looked at the sea. The water was aquamarine, like Owen's eyes. Like the Caribbean, her mother said, because the sand underneath the water was white. White shell beaches were common in the Gulf Islands, her mother said, because the Indians dug clams and left their shells to be beaten down into coarse white sand by the waves.

Who could believe her? How many Indians would it take to make those beaches?

They'd gone to Twin Coves every summer since that first one when Maffy was three. The summer they'd gone exploring. They'd driven up the Malahat Highway, so winding and narrow it made Owen sick. They'd had a picnic along the Yellow Point Road near Nanaimo, then taken the ferry to Gabriola Island. Along the dirt road that wound around the island was a sign, *Larkspur Lane*. According to her father, only her mother's eagle eye could have spotted it. At the foot of the lane sat Larkspur Lodge. Fanning out on either side, amid arbutus trees and Douglas Firs, was the Lodge's family of cabins. One in this litter sat off by itself, musty, uninhabited for years, its dank, mildewed outhouse mysteriously equipped with two holes, in case the need arose for a social moment behind the rickety door with the crescent moon carved in the upper left corner. The Moon House.

"A cabin fit for trolls," her mother had said. "We loved it at once."

"We couldn't rent it to you," the tiny Larkspur lady said, a flower herself, cheeks soft as wilted petals.

"Just for one week," her mother said.

"Oh, we can't, it's not fixed up. We don't rent, you see. We can't possibly—"

"Yes, you can."

Larkspur Lodge was now a going concern. A resort by the sea, thanks to her mother. Seven years later, five cabins still fit for trolls, pot bellied stoves belching out heat on late August nights. Trips to the outhouse in the black. There were ghosts lurking. The adults didn't believe in the ghosts but the kids did. When it was dark the phosphorescence in the sea glowed and they'd swim then hang over the campfire, water sizzling into the flames. Then she and Owen would race back to their cabin for hot cocoa. And last, the best part, the climb up the small wooden ladder to the top bunk under the knotty roof she could reach up and touch.

She lived through the year waiting to get back to Twin Coves. She'd loved the name Larkspur Lodge, but after it became a going concern, the little flower lady wanted a more seasidey name. The whole west coast of the island was dotted with little white coves. Twin Coves had two, one facing south and one facing north, only the coves weren't really twins at all, because they were completely different.

Janna's family stayed a few miles down the coast at a resort, but for Maffy, nothing was better than their tiny cabin. The whole of Twin Coves was haunted. There were spirits, she could feel them. And she liked them.

Fifteen minutes went by fast. The bus stopped at the red brick school. Her last day of grade five at Willows Elementary School.

"I'll meet you here at noon," Janna said, stepping off the bus. "We'll go bike riding—we'll be free!"

School wasn't really school that morning. It was cleaning out their desks, filling their brown paper bags with pencils, erasers and rulers. Taking the nibs out of their red wooden pens so they wouldn't stab themselves on the way home.

Of the things going home that day, most important was her planet. All but nine of the forty-six kids in her class had taken their planets home at Christmas. The teacher had picked the nine best for the solar system on display on the top of the cupboard at the back of the classroom. First there was Eddy Thompson's Mercury, easy, because it was just a golf ball. Then Venus. Maffy's Venus. They'd worked on their planets all through October instead of making Halloween masks like the other grade five classes. She'd started with a balloon blown up to seven inches in diameter. She'd covered it with six layers of paper mache. Each layer had to dry before another was begun and the ball was strong as a rock. A straightened coat hanger was anchored into the second layer of newsprint, its other end stuck into the wooden base her father had made. She'd painted her Venus with gold and silver paint, using her fingers to blend the colors till it looked misty and mysterious. But the important thing, the reason it was chosen, was the angel hair. She'd taken it home to finish it so no one else would steal the idea for the clouds whirling around Venus. It was hard to find angel hair in October, but Owen had helped her drag out the Christmas stuff one night when their parents were at a party. They'd found enough to drape around the ball—just enough so you could still see through to the planet. All the other Venus planets, there were five of them, had blobs of cotton batting stuck to them. She knew where she was going to put it. On top of her dressing table next to her lamp, where the light would shimmer around it.

She ate the cupcakes in the toilet. In grade one she'd been afraid to go to the toilet. Too embarrassed to put up her hand with her forefinger and her middle finger sticking up, to let the teacher and everyone else know she had to go. She'd wet her pants in grade one, rather than put up her hand. It had been just before lunch. She'd almost made it. She'd slunk out of the classroom when the bell finally rang, leaving a puddle under her desk. It was raining but she'd spent the whole lunch hour walking around the schoolyard. No one else was out there, and she got wet enough to disguise her skirt. It was the smell that worried her though. Owen had come out in the rain and found her. He'd come to take her back to her classroom, prepared to wait around till she stopped crying. When she couldn't, they'd begun the long walk home. He'd left the bus tickets in his desk. They took the short cut through Uplands Park and got even wetter in the long wild grass. He'd made her put on dry clothes and played Hangman with her until Howdy Doody. Their mother wasn't there to sweet talk about how they'd go blind sitting too near the TV.

Next morning he'd waited with her till she went into her classroom. When she couldn't, he'd gone in with her and hung around, smiling at the little kids. The grade one teacher let him even though he was late getting to his own room. No one had whispered about her. The puddle was gone.

Now she wasn't afraid to put up her hand, and ate both cupcakes. Eating in the toilet was no problem. It was eating in front of others that made her nervous. Table manners were important as the rising of the sun in her mother's universe.

Janna was at the bus stop first, carrying her brown bag and her pink skipping rope. The trip home was slower than in the morning, but finally it was Janna's stop.

"I'll be over in an hour, I'll wait for you outside," she said.

Maffy managed to get her bag and Venus into the back hall. It was dark. The light had burned out. She dropped her brown bag on the floor next to the litter tray, put her planet on the counter by the sink and sat down to take her shoes off. The house was quiet. She didn't call out. Better to wait and see. Sometimes quiet was good but not always. It was the never knowing.

"Did you take off your shoes?" Her mother's voice startled her.

"Yes, and I brought Venus home."

"Venus?"

"My planet, the one on display."

Her mother stepped into the back hall and bent over the litter tray in the dark. Maffy could smell it. It had been her turn to empty it.

"Your last day of school. A sunny day to start summer with." Her mother straightened up slowly, then arched backward, litter tray in one hand, the other reaching behind to hold her lower back. The litter box swung toward the counter. Maffy couldn't see the sink, but she could hear the splash.

"What have you left on the counter?" The litter tray had knocked her planet into the sink, where something was soaking. "My stockings! What is this wretched thing?"

Her mother dropped the litter tray and yanked open the back door. Light flooded in. Dirty cat litter dotted the counter and dribbled into the water. She dragged the planet out of the sink, by its wooden platform.

"My stockings!" A long silk stocking was caught on a rough ridge of paper mache. "That tears it!"

Her mother hurled the planet out the back door, swung her arm back and smacked Maffy on the side of the head. Maffy stumbled and the smell of alcohol blew in her nose. Her father's empty rum bottles crammed the wooden box, sitting, always sitting, by the back door, like he couldn't bear to throw them away even when empty. She was on her feet and out the door before her mother could swing again.

She headed for the carport. The back door slammed. She squatted down beside Bosun, who licked her face. She stayed there, head throbbing, watching little stars dance on the dog's black coat. She stayed there a long time, staring at her father's boat, kneeding Bosun's neck. Her father had wanted that name. It was really spelled Boatswain, he'd explained, but pronounced Bosun in sailor talk. A bosun was a naval rank, held by a highly experienced practical seaman, he'd said.

She crept into the backyard, and spotted her planet. She ran toward it in a low crouch. The angel hair was plastered to the gooey paper mache. She ran back to the carport and slumped behind the stack of lumber waiting to become part of her father's boat. The angel hair had swirled in the breeze coming through the window at school, the way real clouds would swirl around Venus. The planet was protected from the heat of the sun by its glorious, vaporous clouds. She pushed the ruined planet under the tarp covering the lumber pile in the carport.

She got on her bike and rode down the long winding driveway. Bosun followed. You couldn't see the house from the end of the driveway; it was hidden in the oak trees. There was a holly tree too, a volunteer, her mother called it. No one knew who had planted it. She sat with Bosun under the tree farthest from the house. Janna should be coming up the street pretty soon, red hair flying like a flag. Like in the mornings, Janna wouldn't ask a lot of questions even if she noticed pink-lidded eyes and hiccuping sighs. Sometimes the only two she could count on not to talk were Janna and Bosun.

The dog prodded her with his paw. His eyes watched her face for a smile. She managed one and he panted his reply. Then he began rustling under the prickly holly tree where he knew no one would go. His treasure chest. First he brought out a ball that squeaked when he chewed it. He dropped it at her feet. Then he went back for his secret bone. Dropped at her feet. Then his special throwing stick. All for her.

"Thank you, Bosun." She put her arms around his neck and burrowed her face into its soft folds. The dog whimpered, full of wordless feeling. He would always match his mood to hers.

The afternoon was warm and they decided not to ride their bikes after all. They stashed them under the oak tree and followed the main footpath into the park. They knew all the little paths that wove around oaks and led into pockets of bush that no one else knew about. The broom pods snapped like pistols in the heat. The park was huge and a lot of backyards in this part of the Uplands looked out on it. Janna's house didn't back onto the park. It took up almost half a block all on its own, down near the beach. But Denise's did. Spying was easy, lying in the broom's cover, staring unseen at the Greens.

They wandered through the park. It felt like a good day for one of their make believe games. It felt like a good day for The Lady Robbers. Maffy had gotten the idea from the Lone Ranger, who was always helping people, and bringing to justice the outlaws who were robbing stagecoaches. She and Janna weren't interested in helping. They were interested in robbing, and no one ever brought them to justice. They ran over to the big rock mound, almost completely covered in soft, thick moss. On top of the rock a new oak tree was starting up. She had watched it for a few years now and it was doing okay. The stagecoach would be rumbling along the path anytime now. They lay flat on top of the rock, and when they could hear it, they drew their legs up beneath them, ready to jump down in front of it, guns waving, trigger fingers itching to shoot. But they didn't have to shoot this time. Just their being there got everyone in line due to a lot of hollering and threatening. People willingly gave up their jewels and money because The Lady Robbers were terrifying. There were a lot of stagecoaches that day and by the end Maffy and Janna were tired out from yelling, and having to beat up the odd stagecoach driver who put up a struggle. It had been a good afternoon of crime.

They wandered toward Denise's for a little spying. Denise would still be at the Junior High picnic but her mother might be entertaining in the backyard. She had new garden furniture, Denise had told everybody, as if they cared. It was only two-thirty. It felt good when she and Janna were on the loose pretending to be someone else. It was ages till she'd have to peel the potatoes.

They ran over to the back of Denise's. Maffy got too far ahead of Janna, and stopped to wait for her. The closer they got the slower they went. The best way to stay hidden was to creep. They saw the back of the Greens' house and looked for laundry on the line. They saw Denise's white bras sticking out like traffic cones. She'd bypassed training bras altogether. The sun was shining so brightly it was hard to see into the rooms of the house. No one in the Uplands pulled their curtains in the day since everyone wanted to look out at the park, but the curtains were moving now in Mr. and Mrs. Green's bedroom, like an unseen hand was getting ready to pull them. Denise had bragged about the bedroom after Mrs. Green had redecorated it but Maffy wouldn't be bragging if there was a room in her house that looked like that. A bedspread of fine ivory lace, all the way from Ireland, and Mrs. Green had dyed it pink. A picture of a fat naked lady lolling on a couch, and Mrs. Green had hung it over the bed. The wallpaper was flocked. Denise hadn't missed a detail.

There was Mrs. Green. She was pulling the curtains across the window. Was she going to take a nap? How could she be tired?

After her cleaning lady sterilized the house each morning and hung out the family underwear, Mrs. Green's afternoons were occupied with her bridge club or gin parties, not naps, according to Maffy's mother. Maffy saw two people in the bedroom now. Someone tall. Why would Mr. Green be home at two-thirty in the afternoon? Mr. Green had no hair. This man had a lot of hair. The hair reminded Maffy of someone. She turned toward Janna, who was looking into the kitchen, where she expected to see Mrs. Green. Maffy grabbed her arm.

"Let's get out of here."

"Why? It could get good, if Denise comes home and starts to suntan in the backyard."

"She won't be home for an hour; it's only two-thirty. Let's go."

Janna didn't argue. She would go along, and Maffy was counting on that. The curtains in the bedroom were fully closed now. Maffy stood up and headed back into the park, veering toward the main path. They could follow that, go clear across to the other side of the park, and come out only seven blocks from their school. They could see if Joanne Reynolds was in her yard and if they could play on her swing set. Janna jogged along, asking no questions. Good. In ten minutes they were on the other side. Janna looked red and hot.

Joanne wasn't home. Maffy remembered she'd gone shopping with her mother that afternoon to get a special treat because she'd finally got an A on her report card. If things went as planned Joanne would be coming home with a Mouseguitar. Maffy's own report was in the brown bag on the floor of the back hall. It was good except for the part about not concentrating and not listening.

"I think I'd better go home," Maffy said. She didn't want her mother hurling anymore stuff. She might put her brown bag in the garbage without remembering the report card.

"Can you play after dinner?"

"Yeah, I'll come down to your place and we'll go to the beach."

They headed back slowly. The day hadn't turned out like she'd planned. As they plodded through the park they heard a long whining sound getting louder and louder.

"There's a siren," Janna said. "It's coming from Lansdowne Road. Hurry, Maffy. Maybe it's a fire!"

Janna was running now, out in front for a change, and much as she wanted to stay away from Lansdowne Road, Maffy followed. When they burst off the path onto Lansdowne they saw the ambulance in the Greens' driveway. Two men in white were carrying a stretcher out the front door. Mrs. Green was standing on the grass, wailing and tugging at the poppet beads around her neck. Maffy pulled on Janna, who shrugged her off and raced over to Mrs. Green. A mound lay on the stretcher covered in white. Mrs. Green stumbled over to the mound and took its hand. Maffy looked sidelong at the mound's head. It had no hair. Mr. Green was on the stretcher.

The ambulance drivers levered the stretcher into the long ambulance, yelling at Janna and Maffy to stop loitering and go home. Mrs. Green was being helped into the back with Mr. Green. The siren was screaming again. The ambulance was backing out of the driveway, then it was turning, then it was racing up Lansdowne Road.

"What's wrong with Mr. Green?" Janna gasped. "His face was all bluey. His eyes were open, but he wasn't moving."

Maffy hadn't taken that much in; she hadn't wanted to see the face. Only that quick look and then that strange feeling of relief.

"My mother's out, let's go get your mother," Janna said.

They ran up the long winding driveway. Bosun met them half way, tail wagging frantically. They dashed past without a word or a touch, and in the two seconds she could spare to look, she saw his eyes were disappointed. They went to the back door and rushed in past the pram. Janna looked at it, distracted for a second. It was quite a pram.

"Mum, Mum!" Maffy shouted. "Mr. Green was taken away in an ambulance."

*

She lay in her Heidi bed thinking about Donna and Denise. What had happened when they got home and found the new Plymouth Fury in the garage, but no mother? How had they found out that their father had died that afternoon? It was all over the neighbourhood by now. Heart attack, her father had said. What was he doing home at two-thirty her mother asked? The sixty-four-thousand-dollar question, her father said. Probably came home because he wasn't feeling well. But wouldn't he have called, her mother said, and asked Daphne to pick him up? She always had that car.

On and on it went. They'd be able to talk about something this big for ages. Poor Mr. Green had patched up things between her and her mother too. Her brown bag was on her bed when she finally sank down on it, after Mrs. Miles had come for Janna. Janna had taken a long time to settle down.

"She's so sensitive," Mrs. Miles had said, like it was a good thing.

The first time she'd heard that word was back when she was six. Her father had woken her up earlier than usual. Her mother made her take a bath and put on a dress. Her father held her hand as they walked to the green car. They went to his office and she met his secretary who said she was very pretty. That was a lie, but she liked her saying it. The secretary gave her some tea and a raisin scone. Maffy didn't eat it but she liked her giving it to her. Her father's secretary really was pretty in a dark way. But mostly, she was nice. So nice you didn't notice thick legs and ankles that weren't there. Then her father took her to the doctor. Her father said there were times he didn't feel like eating either.

The doctor smiled at her and said, "Hello Sunshine." He pressed her stomach and asked a lot of questions. She got a new coloring book and a set of crayons.

"This little chair is just your size, Nuffer," her father said. "I'll just be a few minutes." Her father went into the office with the doctor and closed the door.

After that they went to the petting zoo in Beacon Hill Park where the baby calf followed her around the yard chewing on the hem of her new blue dress. Her father smiled. "The calf thinks you're its mother." If she'd been its mother, wouldn't she have turned around and smacked it on the head? They went home.

She hadn't gone back to school that afternoon. She was told to rest in her room where she'd coloured more pictures. When she got bored she'd snuck through the back hall. Her mother had been in the kitchen, talking on the phone.

"Yes, he took her this morning . . . no, nothing's wrong. Dr. Gregson said she's just sensitive. Yes, Lily, of course . . . lots of advice. Does he think he's a psychiatrist?"

Chapter Four

Full many a flower is born to blush unseen,
And waste its sweetness on the desert air.

Thomas Gray

The church was full. Eleanor turned slightly in the pew. It wouldn't do to gawk but funerals gave you a chance to take everybody in. Later there would be those awkward moments before the liquor hit. Moments of looking somber and searching for something to say. Lloyd Green's funeral was no different except no one was prepared to bury someone so young. Someone their own age.

It had been over a week since Lloyd had died. It had taken the family that long to pull themselves together. Lloyd's old Victoria family filled the church. Poor Lloyd. He would never have drawn this crowd if he hadn't died an untimely death, leaving a grieving mother who could still rally her troops. She was a staunch supporter of the Salvation Army, as good a person as you could hope for. The funeral should have been conducted by the Army.

Daphne came down the aisle with her girls. She wore her widowhood well. Black veil falling from the brim of a wide straw boater, black bow in the back. Smart black dress, three-quarter sleeves and two tiers in the skirt. She was obviously not too distraught to spend a decent amount time and money getting ready. For God's sake shut up, Eleanor commanded the little voice. It's a funeral. Her husband's funeral. She concentrated on the music. Uninspired and predictable. If she heard *Jesu Joy of Man's Desiring,* one more time . . . did the organist know only one funeral piece? Apparently not, for now she'd wheezed into, *What a Friend We Have In Jesus.*

"Lloyd loved old time religion," Daphne had sobbed yesterday when Eleanor had taken her a chicken casserole. Jesus probably would be a good friend to Lloyd. He'd been the best of them.

The Miles were sitting in the pew two up on the other side. Seeing them separately was stunning enough, but together, they ascended to another level. The most striking thing about all three of them was their hair. Lily's was the softest red-apricot—grazing her shoulders in a lush pageboy. She was a Renoir—shimmering translucent skin, wide set blue eyes, fine-lipped mouth bracketed by the faint premature smile lines of the red haired. On her they were beautiful.

Winton's hair was also red, but deep, almost copper. The way it swept straight up from his forehead was most unusual. Like an old fashioned pompadour, thick and high in the center, cascading off to the right, a waterfall frozen into submission. It would shine even if the sun weren't touching it through the stained glass.

Janna was most striking of all. She sat between her parents, hair full down the back of her forest green organdy dress. Her delicate feline head could scarcely be seen in between her parents' heroic ones. Lily usually tamed that extravagant mass into thick braids but today she'd allowed the ringlets free reign. While her mother's hair was tempered with blonde and her father's with brown, Janna's was full-blown glorious red.

Eleanor sighed from somewhere deep, and felt her daughter's eyes on her. Myfanwy had once asked what she was thinking when she sighed. Mind your own bees wax, she'd answered. What kind of picture did the Morgans paint?

George and Jean Baker were settling in to the pew directly in front of the Morgans. Both overweight and prematurely grey. Jean was only a few years older than Eleanor but even with all George's money she was too down to earth to dye her hair.

A painful rendering of *How Great Thou Art* sparked a memory. Last time she'd sung it at Art Hames' burial she'd been hard pressed not to lose control, standing in the Ross Bay Cemetery where arrogant old Art had been planted. *How Great Thou Art,* Art.

Then there was Mrs. Dunlevy's funeral. The old lady had insisted, in advance of course, on *Home, Home on the Range,* when she finally passed over Jordan after one hundred and four years. Those shanty Irish could go on and on. She'd insisted on an open casket, one last outing. Her transition to corpse had been smooth. She'd always had a waxy complexion.

Lloyd's brother was going on and on. He was like Lloyd, only less, which was saying something. Wisps of baby fine hair plastered over his dome, soft brown eyes, just like Lloyd's. Soft voice to cap the overall effect.

"A man who tried his best to do his best. A man given to giving his all."

A man who'd lived his life from a crouching position. He'd given his all, all right, given it to Daphne and she'd worn him out. Daphne's grandmother had always said, "Lloyd will wear well." Apparently not. Now they were standing for *Till We Meet Again at Jesus' Feet.* Eleanor felt tears build, but held them back the way she always did, by digging her fingernails into her palms. If anyone got to sit at Jesus' feet, it would be Lloyd. He'd been a good father to his girls, and Donna had adored him. She was like him, gentle and unremarkable. He'd given Daphne everything he could and must have known it would never be enough. Dead of a heart attack at forty-three. Brand new car sitting in the garage and how many times had he driven it? How would Daphne pay for it now? Hugh said they'd have insurance. Lloyd would have made sure she was taken care of just like she'd taken care of him. Daphne had seen him coming and set her sights. A lawyer. It had sounded good until she'd realized he didn't have the imagination to take her where she wanted to go.

The service ended and it was time for the hollow words of comfort. The church hall was crowded, and she fought her way over to Lily and Winton.

"Lily, Winton, hello." The air around them was toxic.

"Eleanor, great to see you!"

Winton was always a hail fellow but she knew he didn't like her. Did he blame her for contaminating Lily with unhappiness? Bring it home, Winton. Look to yourself.

"When are you up to bat?" His voice boomed.

"I beg your pardon?"

"The bun in the oven—you look wonderful when you're pregnant!"

Funerals brought out the best in Winton, reinforcing his personal mythology. He was invincible. Another person's frailty emphasized his strength. He didn't wait for her comeback—she was out of comebacks—and strode off to talk to someone more interesting.

Lily took Eleanor's arm. "Hi, Ellie. The girls are doing well, aren't they? I was worried about Janna but she's resilient. Tougher than she looks."

But you're not. "Are you all right, Lily?"

"It's been a bad few weeks, that last day of school—horrible—" She began to cry silently. Eleanor knew better than to push it. Lily valued her composure too much to pursue this.

"Come on, Lily, you need a drink. Here's Hugh—get us a drink, Hugh."

Hugh put his arm around Lily and kissed her cheek. "Lloyd's final boarding call. A sad farewell. Yes, let's have ourselves a nip." He waved then toward the back of the hall. "There's food and drink set up. The good ladies of Christ have outdone themselves—cucumber sandwiches that will make you cry, brownies so brilliant they'll break your heart."

"For God's sake, Hugh, she's already crying." He was well into his first nip.

Daphne was near the entrance and Eleanor knew they had to get over there and greet the family first. She called to the children. Hugh, with Lily in his grip, led the way across the room. There was no sign of Winton. Eleanor's lower back was screaming. She could use a drink and a chair to swill it in. A dose of Jean Baker would go down well too. Jean would capture this whole scene in a few pithy sentences. Where was she?

Lloyd's mother looked stricken, face crumpled around the mouth like she wasn't wearing her dentures. Life didn't dish out worse than outliving your child.

They fought their way across the church hall, uttering banalities to grieving neighbours. The bereaved family had positioned itself under the large wooden cross, draped in black crepe, hanging over the hall's entrance. Daphne's daughters flanked her, forming a medieval tableau.

"Daphne, Donna, Denise. You have our deepest sympathy and all our support." Daphne's perfume hit like the blast of a blowtorch.

"Thank you, Eleanor, you've always been such a wonderful friend, we're going to need you more than ever. I don't know how I'll cope. Who will be there to call me Sugar Cheeks? But my girls will be such a comfort. They'll be there at the end of each day to tell me I am loved."

Sugar Cheeks? What about Lloyd? Aren't we sorry he's dead at forty-three, overworked and worried to death? She took each of Lloyd's daughters by the hand. Who would be there to tell them they were loved? Donna looked shrunken, shoulders caved in. Her dim light was now out. Denise was darting glances over Eleanor's head, no doubt hoping Owen would appear next. And he would. Her children would do their duty. Lily greeted Daphne next. She was mistress of her emotions with a presence that could hide anything, but Eleanor had never seen her so sorely tried.

Chapter Five

———— ·◁◈▷· ————

Was it a vision or a waking dream?
Fled is that music—Do I wake or sleep.

John Keats

Lily walked through her greenhouse to the wicker rocker in the corner. The ceiling fan sent down currents of moist, perfumed air. The orchids had no scent but the gardenia was intoxicating. She turned on the green Tiffany lamp sitting on the garden table by the rocker. It was still dark and the lamp wrapped her in warmth. She had made her green house a home, furnishing it for comfort. She could sit here in earliest morning with no chance of being disturbed.

Her thoughts hovered briefly, reluctantly, on the funeral. Eleanor's concern, Hugh's kindness. And Daphne. Batting her eyelashes at Winton during her husband's funeral. Lily sat in her rocker and realized she no longer cared. The fury and helplessness she'd felt at the funeral were gone. The penny had dropped. At this point, Daphne might actually be of some use.

The gardenia smelled of heat, of freedom, of a life anywhere but here. Her thoughts settled, as always, on Alistair. She'd known he would be at the birthday party. He would never miss their chance and of course he was too loyal to miss his mother's seventieth. But knowing hadn't prepared her for seeing him.

She'd told Eleanor more than she should have about Isabelle's birthday. Not that Eleanor would tell a soul. It wasn't that. It was Eleanor's unhappiness that made you want to hold back. It didn't take much to provoke her bleak side, and yet, people were drawn to her. Eleanor was difficult but you always knew who she was. Strong as an oak and constant in her way.

The dream told the story, the dream that had woken her this morning. Two ragged women skulked in a squalid lane hawking their wares in some strange medieval fair. Each had a wooden leg, and in the way of dreams, it seemed perfectly normal. The first woman was vital, vigorous, careering through the lane, her flapping skirts revealing the wooden post that served as her leg. The other woman was weak, unable to fend for herself, or sell any wares at all.

She was handicapped by unhappiness. Eleanor wasn't. Eleanor would survive marriage somehow and Lily relied on her. It would never be the other way around.

She hadn't told Eleanor about the dream. It was enough to tell her about the waking fears. And that last moment of dreaming—when the weaker woman attacked the stronger, trying to disable her one good leg—that part she wanted to forget.

The waking fears. She was no match for Winton. He knew. He must. His brooding anger was worse than any fight Eleanor could describe. Eleanor fought and Hugh fought back. Winton seethed and Lily cowered. And when Winton wasn't seething he was smug and self-satisfied, hiding something, just like she was.

She got out of the rocker and stuck her finger into the moss that nurtured her prized orchid. Not moist enough. She walked to the entrance of the greenhouse where the hose snaked under the door. Apart from Janna, these plants were her life. But Janna was getting too old for Lily's constant care. She needed attention from a father but Winton could scarcely drag his attention off himself and left the reins of child rearing to Lily. She carefully soaked the exposed roots of the orchid, then it was back to the rocker.

What had attracted her to Winton? It was sixteen years since that first spring at the University of Washington. Her parents had already been gone. Her father's Seattle cousins were the only safe port.

The campus was hung with cherry blossoms. She looked up from where she sat on the grassy southern slope outside the administration building. He was all confidence and thick auburn hair, on the run to his financial seminar. I could marry a man like that, she thought. And wasn't that why women were on campus? To get their MRS degree? With the sun in her eyes she squinted at his lean body and strong-jawed face. He spotted her. She looked down quickly at her psych text. She was reading Freud. She looked up again from under her wave of hair, saw him hesitate, then head toward her. He sat down, the picture of success—sloping blue eyes, the right touch of colour in his cheeks from the first sun of spring. Underneath a perfect nose was a smile that widened at the smallest provocation. He bowled her over with enough certainty for them both.

She'd once thought he had hesitated that day out of fear she'd disdain him. But he'd only been making sure she was worth his time. She'd passed his test and he had sat down to charm her. What she didn't see till later, but not much later, was how his wide mouth could thin in disapproval and how his blue eyes could narrow to slits. How his interest in her would be circumscribed by who he expected her to be. Freud. How prophetic. She could write the book on narcissism now. He thought he'd found the perfect little wife. She'd been needy and insecure and he had needed her to be that. But then she'd grown up and he'd found new niches of need to fill.

In the beginning she'd known very little about Winton. It had all happened too fast. He was graduating from business school that spring. She'd just completed her sophomore year in psychology. He was sure enough for both of them that no time was to be lost. His life was beginning. He had avoided service—some slight irregularity in his heartbeat—and was ready to go. She didn't need a degree he argued. They married that summer in Seattle. Her father's cousins had done their best for her and now she had someone else's name. It was at the wedding, made modest by the war, that she'd had first seen Alistair. Home on leave. The shock of that meeting had never left her. The confusing recognition. Winton had never told her, so self absorbed it hadn't even occurred to him.

Why had she allowed herself the joy of Alistair? The creak of the rocker was steady and hypnotic. Could she have resisted him? No, it wouldn't have been possible—not last weekend, or the bitterly brief time before. She could smell him, loamy with earth. She could feel him holding her, his work-hard arms weakened with wanting. She could see his hands, reddened and nicked with scratches from the hay stubble. His touch was tentative, nothing assumed. She watched as if suspended above it, watched the dance unfold, their bodies swaying like whispering wheat.

She started awake, aching with memory. She had dared to look into his face. Eyes the same deep blue as Winton's, but soft, with a hopefulness he couldn't escape. Her own hope nipped doggedly at her heels.

Chapter Six

————⬦⬥⬦————

In which she had a cok, hight Chauntecleer,
In al the land of crowing nas his peer.

Geoffrey Chaucer

Winton Miles woke and looked to his left in bed. She wasn't there. He looked in the direction of the steady ticking. The illuminated face showed three forty-seven. No matter what time he woke these days, Lily was gone. Sleep was the one thing she couldn't fake. She drifted through the motions most of the time, but at dawn she woke up and went to the greenhouse and the tepid company of her orchids. He'd once prided himself on knowing everything about his wife. What if she became a problem?

He'd managed to get through the funeral. Sweat slid down his armpits onto the sheets. Think about something else! He had learned to discipline his thoughts but there was no discipline at four in the morning, and now his mother's birthday party stormed into his mind. He could count his heartbeats, they pounded so hard. Pain tightened behind his eyes. Did Lily think she could humiliate him?

She had Janna. He had provided a daughter that hot August night she'd seduced him. That one incredible night. No time to get ready, no time to ensure there would be no child. There would be no more children. No chance of a son to compete with him, judge him.

He awoke again at four forty-nine, alert now, ready to go. He'd get the proposal to City Hall by eight o'clock. Leave time to do some handshaking before the meeting at ten. "The Uplands is underdeveloped, folks. That's why we're here—to explore how these subdivisions are going to proceed." Not if, but how. He had a way of choosing his words. He'd had a way since he was a kid. And when words weren't enough . . .

The narcotic of an old excitement filled his veins. There were ways to deal with an irritant. To lay a plan, to stay in control. Ways to get what you deserved. And so easy when you weren't afraid of anything. She was not going to humiliate him.

Winton stretched. The sore muscle in his groin twinged. It was two weeks now and the injury was no better. Winton made a point of staying in shape. He was down at the Y every day after work, the only man who could chin himself fifty times. He'd have to nurse this groin for weeks. Lily hadn't even noticed his limp. Once she'd noticed everything about his powerful good looks.

Two weeks ago he'd been stepping off his boat, reaching for the dock, just as Hugh Morgan stepped onto the dock. The floats at the marina had no buoyancy left. The whole dock had sunk under Hugh's weight so Winton's reach was off and the groin muscle had been pulled painfully as he'd struggled to regain his balance. Hugh didn't even have his own boat, unless you considered what was perched on stilts in the Morgans' driveway, right in the middle of the Uplands. It wasn't enough that he'd built that house. Winton's own boat was a Chris Craft. The best. Lily had loved it for a while. He lay there one last minute massaging the inside of his left thigh. Hugh had been on the dock that day to look at John Peterson's sailboat. To check on the boom. He must be close to finishing his boat if he was getting ready to rig her. Choosing a mahogany mast and boom was getting close.

Chapter Seven

And young and old come forth to play
On a sunshine holiday,
Till the livelong daylight fail:
Then to the spicy nut-brown ale.

John Milton

After Mr. Green died her parents couldn't talk about anything else. According to Mrs. Green, Mr. Green had come home from work early that day to surprise Donna and Denise on their last day of school. But they weren't there. They were at the picnic at the Junior High. Wouldn't their father know that? The last time until September that Mrs. Green would be able to have a tea party. Tea party? Her father wouldn't know if she and Owen were at a picnic but Mr. Green would have known.

Maybe now that they were at Twin Coves she'd stop thinking about it. Maybe they'd all stop thinking about a family with no father. Saturday nights around the TV with no father. Would they ever watch *Do You Trust Your Wife* again?

The sun was beating on her face and the best part of the year was beginning. The sandstone slabs warmed her bones. Twin Coves didn't change and the way they were when they were here hadn't changed. She stretched and felt the itch of salt. Time for her annual ritual. After the first swim of the summer she slipped around to all the special spots to see that nothing had changed. The water in the first of the small coves was tinged the lightest green, shimmering over its bed of white shells. Here and there the water was darker, bluer, where the shadow of the arbutus tree fell on it. Bouquets of yellowy-brown seaweed clung to the sandstone rocks, waving up and down in the lapping tide. Beds of kelp with light bulb heads and amber hair drifted by, hiding spider crabs in their rubbery tangle. Where the white shell beach ended a grassy slope began and led up to the big picnic table.

She ran from the first cove which faced south to the second cove which faced north. The second cove was very different from the first with its mysterious bottle green water. The sand was muddy grey. The Indians hadn't been potlatching here. The second cove was long and thin, set between rocky walls that rose up on both sides, its seaward wall forming the small peninsula that separated the two coves and reached north like a pointing finger. Arbutus trees found a foothold on the rocky cliff. Their copper trunks were smooth, with bark so thin you could peel it back and see the bright green of new bark underneath, like caterpillars poking through rusty skin. An oak tree, old and stunted, gnarled its way around caves carved in the sandstone rock by waves breaking century after century. Barnacles crusted like spittle on the lower lip of the cave. Lime green moss clung to the cliff pushing up pink shoots and green succulents sent out long stems of yellow flowers. She'd named this cove the lagoon. A musical word, and wasn't it nearly a lagoon with its rock walls almost completely surrounding the long inlet of deep green water?

Her mother had taught her the names of the plants. Queen Anne's Lace, waving white canopies, was really a weed. Last summer her mother had woven it into a garland for Maffy's hair, and laughed and said she looked like a little fairy princess. Tansy was similar, only yellow. The salal, sounding so much like salad, dressed in deep shiny green, had round leaves that hid white flowers hanging on tiny stocks like fairy bells. August would turn them into purple berries with a dusting of grey. Oregon grape looked like holly; prickly green satin. Autumn would turn it red.

Voices floated over from the first cove, then their mother's unmistakable laugh, one loud shriek followed by soft rippling.

She ran back and saw them on the white beach. Her mother under her yellow straw hat with the huge brim, long legs arranged on the dark blue picnic blanket, back propped up against a bleached log. Her father stretched out on the rough shell sand, one arm under his head, the other thrown lazily on her legs. Owen, already fishing in the yellow and red kayak. Trying for rock cod that swam around the reef. He'd throw them back, but not before studying their gills, feathering in, feathering out. Maffy stood still as an Indian behind the big arbutus tree that arched over the front cove. She could smell the baby oil on her mother's legs and the hint of sweat on her father's back. The whiff of Owen's bait. She smelled the bitter scent of arbutus leaves crackling under her bare feet. Let it be good. Let every day stay the same. Please God! Let it be good. When they were good, they were very very good.

A soft whooshing and an eagle sailed overhead, laughing like a madman. A laugh so close to a cry. Its white head gleamed in the sun. She watched it glide down and hover over the sandstone rocks, its tufted legs floundering until it settled near a tide pool. It was tearing at something in the seaweed, using the strength of its neck to wrestle with dinner.

"Owen, look, the eagle!" her mother shouted.

He trained his binoculars on it. He carried them everywhere, even in the kayak. Maffy ran down to the picnic blanket where her father was sitting up to watch the eagle.

"How about a scavenger hunt?" he asked. "First thing, an eagle feather."

The other August families were settling in, kids hanging around their cabin doors, watching the Morgans on the beach.

Her mother saw the Johns family and laughed. "The annual stand off. In two hours they'll be inseparable."

Maffy's father took her hand, and they walked toward the group of cabins sprinkled like monopoly houses along the path.

"Hi, Henry," he said to the youngest of the Johns boys. "Think you can find an eagle's feather on your first day back at Twin Coves?"

"Maybe, Mr. Morgan." Henry looked shyly at Maffy, and when she smiled, the creases evened out in his small, brown face.

"Get your brothers and let's go then." He turned and called to Owen. "Come on in now, Owen, and show these kids how to find an eagle feather."

Owen was way too old for Henry, who was only nine, but Henry's brothers were eleven and thirteen, and would have been perfect for Owen, if he'd been a run-of-the-mill twelve year old.

"Jimmy, Lawrence," Henry called to his brothers. "We're gonna play scabenger hunt. C'mon now or they'll start without us."

Henry was a worried little kid. Maffy ran at his speed as they headed down to the beach to get Owen.

The McLeans were still unpacking. They lived in Duncan and Mr. McLean had to make two trips to bring all they needed for three weeks. They had a stroller and a jolly jumper that was already hanging, complete with baby, from the beam on the front porch of the smallest cabin where the McLeans crowded in. Her bare feet slapped the wooden deck, curling into little balls as the jolly jumper snatched her up. Janie McLeanie. The other three McLean kids were boys. Janie was dressed in pink. Her diapers had pink polka dots on them.

All the families had arrived by now. There were no girls Maffy's age but the two Lindell girls in the biggest cabin were close. Paige was one year older and Carol one and a half years younger. The Lindells took their time coming down to the beach. Each August meant deciding all over again whether they would play or whether it was just too juvenile. Once more they figured they could hold off their maturation till September.

"Two teams," her father said. Owen's team had Jim and Lawrence until her father split them up and made Jim the other team captain. Maffy went with Jim, and Henry followed her like she knew he would. The Lindell sisters went with Owen and Lawrence like she knew they would. It was three against four but the Lindells would be more trouble than help, mincing along in white shorts that would stay white.

"Captains, look alive! Muster your troops."

"I don't like mustard." Henry's voice was small and concerned.

Her father laughed. Henry got that crease between his eyes.

"I want a dry piece of seaweed that will have to pass the moisture content test, an oyster shell, an eagle feather, a pine cone, a piece of arbutus bark, and a . . . a snakeskin."

"Hugh!" her mother shrieked. She was deathly afraid of snakes. She always made Owen walk in front through tall grass. Maffy had caught one once and waved it in her mother's face. Stop screaming or I'll give you something to scream about.

By the time the teams burst back onto the beach with everything but the snakeskin, her father and Mr. Johns were having a drink, the toll of family vacations and all. Her father had forgotten the moisture content test. Without the burden of the Lindells, Jim's team had come in first. There was no prize.

"That's not fair," Maffy said.

"Life isn't fair." Her father paused. "Did you have fun, Nuffer?"

She looked at him. The skin around his eyes crinkled like crepe paper when he smiled. His eyes were very blue. One front tooth crossed over the other. Like hers.

Maffy got to sleep in the top bunk for the first half of their stay. Every year Owen said he didn't want the top bunk but changed his mind when they started unpacking in the small room with the woody smell. The first ten days were the best, after that, each day was a day closer to going home.

She and Owen could keep each other's secrets. He wouldn't let on to someone like Paige that Maffy had a Princess Anne paper doll and her full wardrobe tucked into her secret hiding place on the top bunk between the mattress and the cedar wall, just like she'd never tell that the books under his covers were *West Coast Flora and Fauna* and *The Night Sky*.

She climbed up to the privacy of her bunk. The cabin was so small she could hear everyone breathing. Her father and mother were talking softly on the porch. She smelled the musty wooden ladder hanging at the head of her bunk. She could get up and down it almost as fast as Owen could get into the bottom bunk. It was too dark to see the knot holes in the wood above her face but she could see each one in her mind. Her blanket was soft, washed a thousand times. Last night some other kid had slept under it. But it was her mother who had started it all. From the top bunk she could see the water. The moon left a ribbon of light across the cove.

"The lights begin to twinkle from the rocks," Her father's voice, reverent in the darkness.

"The long day wanes; the slow moon climbs . . ." Her mother's voice. Proud. Full of knowing.

"The deep moans round with many voices. Come, my friends . . ."
"Tis not too late to seek a newer world . . ."
"Push off, and sitting well in order smite . . ."
"The sounding furrows; for my purpose holds . . ."
"To sail beyond the sunset, and the baths . . ."
"Of all the western stars, until I die . . ."

They see-sawed through the poem. Her mother had the last line. Only it wasn't the last, there was more. Her father could recite it all but he knew where they would stop tonight. *Ulysses* was his favorite poem and he knew when to stop.

*

Her father shoved the pitchfork into the sand of the second cove and heaved up a muddy mound. Water rushed to fill the hole. Maffy plunged in and felt for clams. The water sucked back down the tiny tunnels that led to more clams. She dug with her fingers, and forced another clam out of the muck.

"That's good, Nuffer. Four buckets should do it. We'll fill them with fresh water and the clams will squirt out the sand and grit in their innards."

The clams they'd dug yesterday were simmering on the gas stove with onions, bacon, potatoes, and clam juice—the Saturday night campfire feast. At the last, her father would add three quarts of milk and four quarts of cream. The cabin smelled of the sweet saltiness of clams.

The campfire was big enough to have chowder warming at one end and pots of clams boiling at the other. In between were saucepans with butter and lemon. The long picnic table was filling up with baskets. Mrs. McLean let her kids roast wieners over the fire. Hot dogs were where Maffy's mother drew the line.

"Well, men," her father said to the three little McLean boys, "your first roner wiest of the summer."

Janie was tied to the leg of the table, waving her bottle in her small hand. Spurts of grape Freshie popped out the rubber nipple and landed on her dirty face. The other hand held a raw wiener.

Mrs. Lindell was presenting her casserole, folding back layers of dishcloths like it was a Christmas present.

"Come girls, my famous tuna casserole is being unveiled," Owen trilled in his best falsetto. "With cashew nuts and parsley garnish."

They watched from a safe distance as the Lindells sat down in front of place mats neatly positioned on the long picnic table.

Her first clam of the year. Most kids didn't like them. They were right up there on Maffy's list of Twin Coves' Best. After she'd eaten eight clams, dipped in lemon and butter, she and Owen crowded around the big pot of chowder, eager for the first taste. They'd peeled the potatoes and cried through three onions each.

After the chowder was gone and the moon had risen round and orange, like a Chinese lantern, her father got his guitar, settled on a log and started to strum. It was something that her father's hands could build a house and a boat, and still find one string out of six without looking. He knew every song asked for. *The Quarter Master's Store*, could go on as long as anyone could think up a verse that rhymed with a kid's name.

"*There was Myfanwy, Myfanwy, doing the LAUNDREEEE, In the store, in the store.*" Paige was feeling her oats tonight.

The moon was climbing higher, growing paler, and her father's voice was soft as thistledown. "*Down in the valley, valley so low, Hang your head over, let the wind blow.*" He sung the sad songs best. He sung them alone. No one would risk drowning him out. "*If you don't love me, love whom you please, But throw your arms round me, give my heart ease.*"

A few of the mothers were wiping their eyes. Maybe Mr. Johns too. He was soft, like Henry. The McLeans were packing up. It had been Janie's first campfire.

> "*The keen stars were twinkling,*
> *And the fair moon was rising among them,*
> *Dear Jane!*
> *The guitar was tinkling,*
> *But the notes were not sweet till you sung them*
> *Again.*"

"Bravo, Hugh." Mrs. McLean sounded awed. "A poet and a scholar." Mr. Johns said.

"Shelley," her mother said.

"Can we go swimming, please, please?" the Johns boys pestered. "C'mon Ma." They were good at getting their way and the other parents had to go along. All the kids sped up to their cabins and threw on their bathing suits. Maffy grabbed the blue picnic blanket. The other kids didn't get cold like she did; lips blue, teeth clattering like something from a joke shop. Her mother said that maybe she'd gain weight this summer. "Anything is possible."

The water was blue velvet. She swam down the golden path of the moon and did a duck dive under the raft to see the phosphorescence. Down there the moonlight didn't outshine it and her arms waved before her like sparklers on Halloween. Pinpoints of light twinkled in the wreaths of mussels growing thickly under the raft. Like fireflies. The other kids wouldn't go under the raft, not even in the day. It was like entering the Milky Way, dark and starry. At night the sea could go on forever like galaxies in heaven.

She could hold her breath a long time. When she came up, Jim, Lawrence and Henry were already on shore and Owen was calling for her quietly so her mother wouldn't know she'd gone under the raft. They swam in together and hobbled on numb feet to the fire. The Lindell girls had their suits on but hadn't gone swimming. Parading around in a dry bathing suit was what Paige would do.

Lorraine Johns was laughing with her father, accidentally bumping into him a lot, slopping her drink and quoting poetry. Ogden Nash won't do it, Mrs. Johns. She went over to him, wrapped in the picnic blanket. She leaned against his warm legs. His arm went around her and he walked her toward the fire built up to warm them.

"Hugh, come on, it's after ten. Or would you rather stay with Lorraine? She's easily impressed."

Maffy felt her father's legs stiffen and turn. Felt him stagger as he lost his balance. His arm let go of her and rum splashed, the smell strong and sickening. He lurched backward and she lurched forward, into the fire, blue picnic blanket trapping her feet. She put out her arms to stop herself.

"Oww oww owwww!" Pain shot through her left hand.

Someone was slapping at her head.

"Be careful, Hugh! You're drunk."

Her mother's feet were coming toward her. Cold water slopped on her head. Hands came down to pick her up in the blue picnic blanket that stank of smoldering wool and clams.

"Get it off her, bring a blanket from the McLean's."

"It's her hand, she's says it's her hand."

"Hold her head up, let me have her."

She saw the stars zigzagging above her and heard Henry's scared whisper, "Is she dead?" Then he was crying, big howling sounds.

"It's okay honey, you're okay, don't cry," Mrs. Johns said in her ear.

It's Henry who's crying, she wanted to say, but couldn't get her breath. The stars stopped whirling wildly and she saw the knot holes in the ceiling above the old brown chesterfield in their cabin. She knew all the knot holes, not just the ones above the top bunk. She had counted them in groups of four. There were no more voices now, just her mother's heavy breath as she tried to tear Maffy's bathing suit off her.

"I'm okay, I'm all right, I'll get my pajamas on."

Her mother sat back, exhausted and unable to reach Maffy anyway, with her stomach in the way.

Minutes later she lay in the top bunk, hand hot and throbbing. Her mother's hand was cool and gentle on her forehead. After a few minutes, she pretended to be asleep. Her mother stopped stroking her head and Maffy was alone. Where was Owen? It would have felt better to have him below her, kicking the mattress when he thought she'd fallen asleep. Her parents were in their bedroom, separated from Owen's and hers by a striped curtain.

"You've gone too far, staggering around with Lorraine. Damn you, Hugh! I should have married Ed Wilson."

"Why didn't you, Eleanor, why didn't you marry the lovesick piano teacher? He wouldn't have lasted a year with a cold creature like—"

"You're a dreamer. And Myfanwy's just like you. In a daze, talking to fairies. It's a miracle she wasn't badly burned!"

"For pity's sake, woman, leave it alone."

"Really, Hugh—Lorraine?" Her mother's voice had that edge, like she was going to really blow, any minute now. "How much humiliation do you expect me to take?"

She managed the ladder, left hand hugging her chest, right hand gripping the rungs. Her mother's voice was rising, her father's low and scary. She unlatched the back door without being heard. The fox in her stomach gnawed. She held on to the fir tree behind the cabin and threw up.

Chapter Eight

His comb was redder than the fyn coral,
And batailed, as it were a castel-wal

Geoffrey Chaucer

Winton Miles pulled on the jib and the wind caught the sail. They were leaving for the island in a week and this year he'd sail there, up the coast of Vancouver Island, through the tricky waters of the Strait of Juan de Fuca. Through the even trickier Dodd Narrows to Gabriola Island. He'd have to navigate that at high tide. A tide chart. He'd need to check it. Lily would take Janna in the Cadillac. He missed the roar of the Chris Craft, more satisfying than this impotent flapping of sails. Sailboats were for fools like Hugh Morgan.

Time to come about. He pushed the tiller hard to the left, ducking as the boom swung over his head, and pulled hard on the main sheet. He was confident sailing solo and settled back as the boat glided towards the Oak Bay Marina. Lily was not happy about the idea of sailing. She had no argument with him sailing, but she didn't want Janna on board. Lily herself wouldn't step foot on it, giving them something tangible to fight over. Why did he suddenly want to sail, she'd asked? Janna could learn at the Yacht Club if it was so important that a girl know how to sail. Where was his common sense?

The mainsail was luffing. He pulled the tiller toward him, the bow moved cleanly to starboard and off she shot. Lily would thwart him if she could. Bring him down. There will be no divorce, he'd told her. She'd just looked at him and lowered her eyes, long, pale lashes half moons on pale cheeks. Pallid thinking woman endlessly musing in her greenhouse. Thinking women were the worst kind. Like Eleanor. Thought she was smart but what did she have to show for it? Winton needed a vivacious, supportive woman. One who appreciated the cut of his jib. A grateful, incurious woman. Did Lily think she could cut and run? Yes he'd used her money, the land had belonged to her family, but had any of them seen what land meant?

The wind whistled through his hair. He pulled hard on the mainsheet, muscles aching, feet propped on the centerboard, lean body arching over the gunnel. He was running before the wind now. Jibing. "A maneuver best avoided by the beginner," the sailing manual said, but he wasn't about to start playing by the rules. The wind was across the stern. The main was sheeted, allowing the boom to swing under control to the opposite side. He'd memorized this part.

"A properly executed jibe in a moderate wind can be entirely safe, but an unintentional jibe may injure someone or damage the rigging and in heavy weather, may dismast her." The wind could pick up in a minute in these waters, Hugh had warned him. There was a fool. No guts, no nerve. Just like Alistair.

Winton pushed savagely on the tiller and water rushed over the gunnels. The wind was ripping at the sails and he was taking on water over the bow. He grabbed the mainsheet as the boom swung, missing his head by a hair. He got hold of the tiller and eased her off the wind, freed the sheets, her sails slatting in the wind's eye, giving his heart time to slow down, giving him time to fight off the panic. Just a fleeting moment of panic. It happened to the best of them, men with the courage to risk.

As suddenly as it had picked up, the blow eased. Winton pulled back slowly on the tiller, bringing her to starboard to pick up the wind again, and headed back to the marina. Back on course. His life was on course. He knew what he wanted, knew what he deserved. People bring on their own fate, create their own ends. The churning in his stomach eased, a sense of well being returned. Tested by a storm, he would always win.

Chapter Nine

·◈·

That thou, light-winged Dryad of the trees,
In some melodious plot
Of beechen green, and shadows numberless,
Singest of summer in full throated ease.

John Keats

The Phalaenopsis orchid was bare now, the last graceful blooms wilted. Next to flower would be the violet orchids with their small, delicate heads. Lily brushed the hair off her forehead. The height of the summer heat was upon them making her greenhouse even hotter. Jean Baker would come and water the plants while they were on the island so the orchids would survive. Jean lived just a few houses away and loved gardening as much as Lily did.

There was a lot to do today to get organized for their vacation. Janna would help, so eager to get to Twin Coves to see Myfanwy. Poor child, with her burned hand, her hair chopped off where the fire had singed it. Eleanor had phoned about the fire.

Myfanwy had spent a good deal of time with Lily in the greenhouse this summer, learning the names of the plants, eager to know what they needed to flourish. She was like that with people too. Janna herself was beginning to bloom like a glorious orchid. Myfanwy hadn't had her growth spurt yet, but she would.

Her parents were tall. The two girls were so close, best friends. How would they cope with separation when the time came?

Lily left the door to the greenhouse open to let in the August air. She had to get going. What was the best plan for today? Find a large rock and roll it up Lansdowne hill? She walked across the concrete path and went in the back door. The small utility room was perfectly organized. Big wicker laundry basket ready for her humus streaked shirt. Drying rack ready for her boots. Small mirror mounted above the sink, so while washing her hands she could check her face, ensure her hair was still trapped in its black velvet ribbon. She swirled the hot water around the sink, making sure to get the ring of grime. Winton liked a tight ship and a smart looking ship's company.

Winton—swirling around in his own grimy water. His development had been given clearance, all his ducks were lined up. All he needed before the city council met in September was Lily's signature. The land he was developing was in her name. The lawyer had insisted. It was her money that paid for it.

He had time on his hands right now, so he'd bought a sail boat. With his thirty-foot gin palace in dry dock for months while the hull was refinished, he was ready for a change. He was sailing the new boat to the island. The arrogance of him. He would sail it into Twin Coves to show it off to Hugh, who'd laboured on his own boat for two years now, and was only marginally closer to launching it. He'd run out of money more than likely. The fittings were what ate up it up.

The kitchen was warm. The light pine of the cabinets glowed as the sun hit them. The sweep of pale yellow arborite flowed effortlessly around corners, from sink to range to fridge. With the kettle on to boil, she took out two cups and saucers, white bone china with yellow cottage roses climbing up the sides of the cups, spilling over the edges of the saucers. A fine edging of gold made an effort to contain them. She padded to the bottom of the stairs and called to Janna.

"Darling, come and have a cup of tea, then we'll get going on the packing."

They'd easily get the packing done—they were only going for a week. It was the way Winton liked the house left that was the effort. Not a newspaper lying around. Not a towel moldering on the bathroom floor. Did he think of their perfect home awaiting them, as he conducted their holiday at the island resort? Lily loved Twin Coves, the mildewed cottages, the rank smell of outhouses, the beauty of disrepair, but Winton wouldn't hear of it. Impossible to imagine Winton's firm white behind filling the outhouse hole, perchance to encounter the dreaded black widow spider of west coast outhouse fame lurking just under the opening. The early outhouses, those pioneering prototypes, had had a round hole. Now they were flared out at the rear to comfortably accommodate the most constipated of habitues. No, they couldn't go there. They went to that stuffy resort. And only for a week.

"Come on, Janny. Your tea is getting cold."

This year Winton had suggested something totally out of character. He wanted to take Janna camping on the Olympic Peninsula. He wanted to take her during the midst of their family vacation at the resort.

"You want to drag Janna all the way down there, on her vacation?" She had tried to keep her tone civil.

"I'll charter a plane."

"Be serious, Winton."

"I am serious. Never more so. The beaches are vast on the west coast and the rainforest is spectacular."

And so it was decided. Lily wasn't invited. Was he that desperate to get away from her? Hugh was Lily's salvation, agreeing to go too, much as he must loathe Winton. And Winton had to cooperate. Janna wouldn't go without Myfanwy and Owen. The plane would pick them up at the resort and fly them south of Seattle where they would pick up a rental car. It was unbelievable what Winton would do, what he was willing spend, when he smelled even a whiff of resistance from her. Once in the rainforest they would camp. Another reason to ask Hugh to go along. He had all the camping equipment. Hugh and Eleanor camped in the Gulf Islands off Nanaimo, or they used to. Eleanor had loved it once—the two of them off in the wilds.

She turned and saw her daughter settling into the yellow vinyl of the breakfast nook, her hair an aureole of orange around her flushed face. Lily imagined that hair under her blue Girl Guides hat. The Guides were the reason for the overnight trip. Janna wanted her camping badge and Winton was going to see that it happened. Myfanwy would get hers too, off in the wilds of the Olympic Peninsula. Lily shook her head. It was odd, this interest in Janna. Usually he was too busy to notice her. But there was no arguing with him.

As she watched her daughter sip her tea, Lily felt the warning twinge of pain in her neck and the first stab behind her eyes. There was no way to ward off a migraine when the sun was blazing.

"It's stress, Mrs. Miles, all in your head," Dr. Gregson had told her. He was a large fan of his overworked witticisms. "What have you got to worry about, eh?"

She reached for an ice pack, placed it on her left temple, and wrapped her headache band around it. She located her sunglasses, and wedged them on under the tight band, which would hopefully cut off all feeling past her nose. She poured Janna's favourite cereal, allowed only on weekends, into two bowls, added milk and turned back to the breakfast nook.

"Mummy, you look like Lucy when she's trying to fool Ricky." Janna slid out of the nook and found her new sunglasses bought for the holiday. They stared at each other through blackened lenses, laughter propelling small missiles of Frostie-O's.

"Maffy's family eats Shreddies for breakfast. Her father calls them Chokies." Janna's laugh had a note of hysteria.

Out of nowhere they were crying. Things not spoken of were not unknown. What can I tell her? Lily wondered. Nothing right now, but soon. She hummed a few notes of their tune. Janna wiped her finder under her nose and launched in.

"Rain to grow the flowers for her first bouquet." Her child's voice held a breathy sweetness, and Lily's, when she joined in, was aching.

"But April Love can slip right through your fingers, so if she's the one, don't let her run away."

"Okay, April Love, don't let this day slip away," Lily said. They had each other, they'd survive. "Go get dressed and make sure your clothes are all in the suitcase. Everything I laid out. I'll clean up this place."

The place was already clean. It was in a constant state of order due to Winton's bullying. Not the kind of bullying you could put your finger on mind you. His was the bullying of the pained voice, laced with logic. Always calm, patience personified, volume rising only slightly when expressing the poignant confusion of the wounded. Am I expecting so much? Is it too much to ask? Poor soul, burdened with an emotional woman, bearing the weight of the world while she grew orchids. Winton liked the role of hero though. Heroes soldiered on taking comfort where they found it, as soldiers were entitled to do.

She snapped her dust cloth at the pictures lined up on the grand piano in the large living room. The living and dining rooms flanked the spacious entrance hall. The antique dining room suite battled for tastelessness with a blue brocade chesterfield and matching chairs. Underneath was thick blue carpet. All of it Winton's taste.

She went upstairs to their bedroom. Here things weren't quite as perfect, since Winton had lost steam when it came to their room. He'd stopped his frantic spending some months ago and they still slept in the old double bed with its square wooden headboard that had once belonged to her parents. Still housed their clothes in the old bureau with the square mirror that was losing its silver backing. She loved this furniture and would have felt at home in this room if she hadn't shared it with Winton. She'd chosen yellow chintz for curtains and had a bedspread made to match. Eleanor had put her onto chintz. Eleanor could make any room interesting, combining antiques with rattan, setting furniture at odd angles, painting a piano green. Although the prosaic likes of Daphne scorned her, Eleanor's ideas always worked. There was no evidence that Daphne had, as yet, experienced an original idea. Her home looked like a scaled down *Gone with the Wind* set, lace doilies on pink silk davenports.

They just managed to make the ferry. The water was choppy and Lily didn't get out of the car. She rolled the window down and watched Janna standing by the rail of the car deck, as the ferry left its berth and headed for Gabriola Island. They'd got everything done by nine and then gone downtown to find something for Myfanwy. Janna had chosen a stuffed dog, a small black spaniel. It was made in England and was very lifelike. The fur wasn't the cheap, fluffy fur of the usual stuffed animal. Its nap was flat, its small head sleek, the ears long and silky. Its eyes were deep chocolate glass, looking for all the world like they could keep you in their sights. The dog was positioned in a patient sit. Janna chose it instantly and Lily hadn't thought for a moment to complain about the price.

Janna turned to wave, wind gusting bright hair across her face. Her laugh was surprisingly loud out of her delicate mouth. Her excitement was growing. She couldn't wait for Myfanwy to see the dog, couldn't wait to camp in the rain forest, her ten year old self bedding down under trees hundreds of years old. Lily had never escaped into the world Janna and Myfanwy inhabited. All her life she'd allowed herself to be channeled into appropriate roles. Beautiful women married well, were gracious and benign, devoted and dutiful. A game of bridge, the garden club, the art gallery. Hallmarks of her role. Janna and Myfanwy spent their time imagining they were someone else. Having fun.

Janna opened the car door.

"We're almost there! When can I give Maffy her dog?"

"We'll go straight there, darling, straight to Twin Coves. I told Eleanor we'd spend the afternoon with them. Winton won't arrive in the boat until dinner."

"Why is he sailing now, Mummy?"

"I don't know, Janny. Maybe he wants to show Hugh how it's done." Lily covered her sharpness with quick laughter. "Let's stop at the farmers' market and pick up some corn. With all this sun it'll be sweet by now."

"Dad said that after our trip to the rainforest, he wants me to learn to sail."

"Maybe Myfanwy and her dad could go along for the lessons. After all, Hugh's the expert sailor." With Winton's pride, she'd have to go gently. He was so scornful of men like Hugh. Truth was, he was threatened by them and anxious to outdo them. Hugh was miles ahead of Winton, like Alistair was. Alistair. Her face flushed with excitement.

The ferry docked on the northern end of the island. The air smelled of sea and earth all at once, as they wove south on the perimeter road. Both the resort and Twin Coves were on the sunny western side. Now the road veered inland and they lost the sea to farms with ancient apple orchards, bent trees covered in lichen, still bearing fruit. They stopped to buy two dozen ears of corn, green beans and a swath of white and pink snapdragons. Pink wasn't Eleanor's colour, but who could resist them? Eleanor would add salal and a touch of mustard yellow tansy, transforming the sweetness of snaps into something wild, throwing colours at each other with confidence. Lily hesitated, then added a bunch of burnt orange gloriosa daisies massed with blue delphiniums.

Winding down Larkspur Lane was a religious experience. Leafy maples formed a green cathedral. Their branches arched above like the filigree of stained glass, filtering dappled sunlight onto rusty arbutus boughs—pews—curving low to the earth. Douglas firs soughed in the choir loft. And there, waiting on the side of the road, was the acolyte, a look of listening in watchful eyes. Bare brown arms wrapped around a thin waist, bandaged left paw rested in the crook of the right elbow. Slender legs reached long below voluminous green shorts. Dirty bare feet rocked in the dirt. Now there was recognition and a widening smile turned her forlorn look mischievous. Lily's throat loosened. She stopped the car and Janna leapt out.

"Maffy, what happened to your hair?"

Even under her remarkable headgear, the damage to Myfanwy's hair was unavoidable. Janna knew about the fire of course. Lily had told her, but in that first moment of seeing, knowledge was forgotten.

"I mean it's cute," Janna said quickly. "I like it." She turned to her mother. "Can I cut my hair too?"

Lily's throat was working again. She'd brought her smallest pruning scissors.

"Fawn, sweetheart," she called to Myfanwy. "What a wonderful Indian you are! We have a surprise for you."

"Maffy and I will run the rest of the way, Mummy. We'll give Maffy her surprise when we get to the cabin."

Lily watched them go, taking in the wonder of Myfanwy's costume. She was an Indian, wearing no clothes but those shorts that Eleanor made by the dozen, with legs like shapeless tubes. Janna had wanted to buy a pair of real shorts for Myfanwy, store bought shorts that fit her. Of course they couldn't buy her a pair of shorts. How would Eleanor react to that? How would any mother hunched over a sewing machine react? But those homemade shorts were the right colour—the green of salal.

Myfanwy had created a long chain of salal leaves by poking small twigs through the leathery leaves to hold them together. She must have sharpened each twig with her burned hand. The salal chain wrapped around her forehead and trailed down her back, a perfect Indian headdress. Its glory was the eagle feather poking out of the back. They should have found her a pair of moccasins, Lily thought. Myfanwy had wanted a pair ever since last summer when she'd first become an Indian.

She drove reverently down the aisle of fir needles and yellow arbutus leaves. The afternoon stretched before her with hours to go before Winton arrived.

Eleanor poured gin and lime juice and Lily leaned back in the blue deck chair on the grassy knoll overlooking the beach. The canvas was at its most comfortable—that giving moment before it rotted away completely. At her feet bits of orange fluff ruffled in the breeze. Janna's hair. They'd saved the long hanks and just the fine wisps waved here and there. They'd made a party of it. A day at the beauty parlour. Paige Lindell had sauntered by looking resentful. Paige had tried Myfanwy sorely according to Eleanor, now she wanted in on the fun. They had allowed Henry to watch.

Lily closed her eyes and felt Myfanwy's head under her hands again. The fine hair had been easy to cut into a smooth cap that lay snuggly against her well-shaped head. A fawn, dotted with freckles, eyes even larger now.

"She's doing very well," Lily remarked, as Eleanor handed her a glass. The bite of gin was just what the doctor ordered.

"Her hand is badly blistered but thank God her face was spared. Frank Lindell had a bucket on her so fast the fire only got her hair. Mercifully, the clam pots were right there. He threw one, clamshells and all. Hugh was no help. He caused it, drinking of course. And Myfanwy would be traipsing around with a picnic blanket wrapped around her, hanging onto Hugh. It's a miracle it wasn't worse. If we could afford a holiday in a decent place, like your resort . . ."

Eleanor trailed off into heavy silence. When she got like this it was everyone's fault.

"You've been through hell. When your child is hurt, it's sheer hell."

"It's not just that. It . . . I don't know, Lily, I don't know anymore."

"Tell me. Is he drinking that much? I mean, I know he can be difficult, but he's working hard, isn't he?"

"Oh yes, he's got his work. The Kerrs bought that challenging lot on Rutledge Street. They wouldn't sacrifice a single tree. After the initial sparring, Hugh got them to take out three of the oaks. Each window, and you can imagine how many windows, looks out onto a single tree. The house is like a gallery with the art on the outside."

"Hugh is very talented."

"He gets to use his talent. He's got that outlet. He drinks on weekends, to unwind, after a fulfilling week of work. Then he's got the boat . . . and the kids of course. They adore him."

"They love you too, and so does Hugh—I'm sorry, I understand, I do—but at least he's human, Ellie, he's got heart and humour. Winton's heart is pumping ice water. He's not right, somehow. I can't . . . I can't explain it."

Eleanor looked concerned. "What do you mean?" Her voice was sharp.

Lily took a deep breath. "I have two dreams at night, Ellie. One or the other almost every night. In the first dream I am happy. I am loved by someone. We live in a simple house, a log cabin, only it's on water, like a house boat, you know what dreams are like. I lie in this man's arms and listen to the soft slap of water. I don't remember much, only the feeling of contentment. Not wildly happy, just at peace. I wake up and realize what it is like to know peace in a marriage. I don't ever remember knowing that. Waking up is the worst moment. Waking up and letting go of the relief of being loved." Lily stopped. Eleanor sat like a stone.

"In the second dream," she went on after a minute, "I am dying. I'm sick, which is the cruelest way to die, because you know it's coming. I always thought that if I knew I was dying, I'd just want to go, right then. But that's not what happens. I want to live even while I'm dying. I've got three months, and I want them. I want my freedom. I want to live the truth. But I get closer and closer to death, and the hopelessness overtakes me. The loss is stunning, because of the time I've wasted, maintaining duties, maintaining the lie I've lived. I know in my dream that I will die the lie."

The air was hushed, and for once, so was Eleanor. But not for long.

"The first dream, Lily, who was the man, do you know him?" Eleanor, as usual, was missing feelings, wanting details.

"Yes, Ellie, I do. You know who he is." Why couldn't she even whisper his name? To say it out loud terrified her.

"Have you seen him since Seattle—the dance? Does Winton know?"

"No, Winton is too involved in his development. It goes ahead next month. He thinks I've settled back into our stifling routine"

"And you haven't?"

Lily heard the warning in Eleanor's voice. Even a smart woman like Eleanor couldn't understand what it was like to have everything and know it would never be enough.

"What do you want, Lily, to leave Winton so you can be some other man's wife? You'll still be a wife."

"Who turned us into mere wives? Our husbands? Our children?"

"Our mothers? Smothering dreams, ferreting out failure?"

Lily chuckled. "Father, uncle, teacher, preacher."

"Who can we exclude?"

"Your English prof. He saw your ability as a writer."

"Operative pronoun, "he". He saw me as Elizabeth Barrett to his Browning. I was vulnerable, insecure, and he, the savior. His wife was at home with four kids. The worst of it was I never knew if I was really good or if he was just buttering me up."

"He'd have been drawn to your brain!"

"No, well maybe—thanks Lily—but there was more than a hint of something else. I won't be vulnerable again."

"The old goat. You're good, Ellie. We both know it. I've read your poetry."

"I'm not so sure. Besides, it's past time, isn't it? And what about you? With your depth and compassion, you could have been—well, you could have been anything you wanted to be." Eleanor shook her head. "Winton snatched you out of college before you could finish."

"Thank you Eleanor, for understanding what it was like. I hated to leave my studies. There was so much about abnormal psychology I wanted to know. We were bright young things then, with ideas, plans . . . like them." She nodded to Myfanwy and Janna, racing up the hill. "I want more for our daughters. Myfanwy is just like you. Eyes the green of spring wheat. She's going to be striking."

"She'll need braces. We'll deal with that in the fall. Owen's our beauty." She shifted her weight in the chair. "I used to try to curl her hair, dress it up a bit."

The girls were almost upon them, laughing their way to the cabin to get their bathing suits on. The tide was ready.

Eleanor sighed. "She's a good child, excited about the baby."

"I see you in her, Eleanor. It's what I love most about her."

The girls ran by, lost in their own world. The silence lengthened. Eleanor stretched out her long, once beautiful legs, veins straining against heavy elastic stockings. In this heat. Hugh joked he was a leg man, but Eleanor's would never be the same. Lily reached impulsively for Eleanor's hand.

"I've brought us a box of Roger's, Eleanor. We'll make pigs of ourselves, never mind Winton."

Eleanor's laugh rose beneficently. "Well then, *God's in His heaven—All's right with the world.*"

Did she mean it, or was it a dig? As if a box of chocolates could make everything right. Enigmatic Eleanor.

Chapter Ten

—⋅⟨ɜ⋅ɜ⟩⋅—

Bards of Passion and of Mirth,
Ye have left your souls on earth!

John Keats

It was going to be hard to get the black dog in. She stared at
the contents of the small duffle bag lying on the bottom bunk.
Owen had finished his packing, managing to get in four of his
books—one on the stars, one on flora and fauna, which was
absolutely necessary in the Olympic Peninsula rain forest, and
two Maffy didn't recognize.

She could leave out her sweater. It'd been boiling all week.
Could she leave out *Trixie Beldon and the Mystery of the Barking Dog?*
She stuffed her sweater under her mattress. Her mother would
never know she hadn't packed it. She was going to spend all
that day and the night at the resort with Janna. Her father and
Owen would come over first thing tomorrow morning and their
adventure would begin. The problem was Henry. He'd started
crying when she told him.

It was nine o'clock, time to go. Maffy ran down to the Johns'
cabin to say goodbye.

"I'll see you in two days," she told Henry. "Not tomorrow but
the next day."

"That's more like three days."

"Here, Henry, my eagle feather. You can have it."

"For keeps?"

"Uh-huh."

"Myfanwy, get a wiggle on," her father sang out from their cabin.

"I've got to get my Trixie Beldon book," she called as she ran back to the cabin.

"Ask not for whom the dog barks. You won't have time to read."

Her father drove her down the island to the resort where the Miles stayed. Tomorrow morning he and Owen would be back and they would all board the sea plane for South Seattle harbour where Mr. Miles had a rented car waiting for the trip to the Olympic Peninsula. The flipper in her chest was pounding. Would it be more beautiful to fly over the water than to swim in it?

Janna was still asleep when they got to the resort. Mrs. Miles figured Janna needed to store up sun and sleep for the long winter ahead, like a squirrel with nuts.

They went to the dining room for tea.

"Hugh, have a bite of breakfast. Please." Maffy had never seen her father eat a breakfast he hadn't made. Mrs. Miles put a cinnamon roll in front of her. "Janna is very excited. Thank you for arranging all your camping equipment. Thank you for everything, Hugh. Winton will be here for breakfast soon. He's down at the boat dock making sure his sailboat hasn't depreciated overnight."

"We'll get our camping badges, then we'll have five each. Mrs. von Bauerenhoff said that when everyone has their badge and can troop the colours, we'll go camping at Mount Douglas Park. She knows the trails and the best hiking songs."

"Take your daddy along and you could earn your poetry badges."

Maffy giggled. "There is no poetry badge."

Mrs. Miles pursed her lips. "Well, why not? It can't all be a Teutonic frenzy of pitching tents and digging latrines, goose-stepping round the campfire. The Valkyries ride again!"

"Velkom to Valhalla, Wagnerian Vunderland," her father said.

"Wagner's music is better than it sounds."

"And Tchaikovsky's isn't as good as it sounds . . . isn't that the way it goes?"

"Seriously, why can't the baroness in jack boots gentle her troops? A respite from maneuvers. Why not a poetry reading?"

"Why not indeed? Perhaps that's Valhalla . . . *Souls of poets, dead and gone, What Elysium have ye known.*"

"Keats! My favourite. Who's yours?"

"Tennyson—lion of literature. *Ulysses* was his hour."

"What is it about that poem?"

"Its challenge. Moving ahead in the face of defeat. The regrets of old age loom, when you haven't given life your best. Better to die in your prime than to live on without pride."

"I could tell you about regrets—the regrets of youth. Of mistaking one twin for the other."

"For pity's sake, Lily, what do you mean?"

Mrs. Miles shook her head. "Nothing. Tell me more about Tennyson."

"What if we grow old and idle, without pride, having failed at life?"

"Failed? But Hugh, you're not old . . . or idle. Success will come, it already has."

"Has it, Lily?"

"You and Eleanor have more in common than you think. You should talk to her. Really, you're two of the brightest lights, and listen to you!"

"She's the one not interested in talking anymore. Criticizing, yes, talking, no."

"She's pregnant, exhausted."

"I know, Lily. It's late for children, but it was what she wanted. And she is strong."

"She's a rock. I'd be lost without her. We all would."

"You're right." He paused and looked at Maffy. "How about finding out what's keeping Janna. That sleepyhead ought to be on deck by now."

She took the cinnamon roll in her right hand and headed for the Miles' cabin. Each cabin in the resort had two bedrooms, a bathroom and a sitting room, but no kitchen.

"Janna, are you awake?"

"Uh-huh."

Janna's hair was the color of a toasted oat cake, according to her father. Now that it was short, it seemed lighter, almost golden where it curled around her face. "You're like an acorn," her father had said of her blunt brown hair. "A freckled acorn with a perfect cap." She'd rather be an acorn than an oat cake.

"Get up, come on, if your mother comes back she'll make you eat breakfast and everything. We won't get our five swims in."

"Okay, okay."

"Put on your bathing suit. I wore mine under my clothes." It was tradition to swim five times a day. The weather didn't matter.

They dove in. The water was at its coldest and Janna screamed, really awake now. The beach had the same white shells as Twin Coves did, but it was much bigger. Room for the boat dock and the water slide at the end of the dock. Just as the fun was beginning, Mr. Miles came down the path.

"You girls shouldn't be swimming this soon after breakfast."

"I haven't had breakfast, Daddy."

"Well, why not? What are you doing, swimming before breakfast?"

Lots of people do. Why did Janna always tell the truth?

"Come on then, you can't go to the dining room like that. Get up to the unit, get dressed and get a comb through that hair. Whose idea was it go swimming?"

He knew, of course.

He was walking quickly up the beach path, which was being raked by a teenaged boy. Mr. Miles stopped.

"You, young man, what's your name?"

"Chuck, sir."

"Well now, Chuck. Do you have a last name?"

"Chuck Walker."

"Well, Chuck, let's walk'er over to my unit. There's some raking that's been overlooked. The arbutus leaves on the rock slope out behind. They pose a hazard. They are very slippery underfoot. If Mrs. Miles slides on those rocks, she could be badly hurt."

They'd reached the Miles' unit. Janna ducked in the back door and into her room.

"See here, Chuck," Mr. Miles said, waving his arm toward the back of the cabin, "This needs to be raked first thing every morning. Janna, hurry it up in there. I'm going to the dining room. Come as soon as you're ready."

Maffy stole a look at Chuck who was raking the rocky shelf. There were spots where thick moss clung. He looked up and saw Maffy watching him. His face was red.

"He's not my father," she blurted out.

He could probably tell. The waitress in the dining room seemed to know she didn't belong there.

"You're lucky, kid." When he smiled, Chuck Walker's face changed completely. "Think it's safe now?"

The rocks were barren, every shred of their mossy carpet gone.

It was worse at dinner when Mr. Miles' powers of observation were on red alert. He was like a robot, doing three things at once—rising out of his chair to shake hands with someone passing by, waving to another man across the room, and all the while, watching her eating habits, clumsy now, thanks to her burned hand. The man could do it all.

"Aren't you hungry, Fawn?"

"I've eaten quite a lot, Mrs. Miles."

"How about some peaches for dessert?"

"You can shovel those in with a spoon," Mr. Miles said, waving his wineglass at the barman.

"I'm stuffed, may we be excused?" Janna asked politely.

"Don't say 'stuffed'. Say you are finished." He was shaking someone's hand with both of his, one to grasp, one to slap over the top, vice like.

*

She was waiting when the Chev rounded the corner at six-thirty the next morning. Her father caught her under her arms and hoisted her above his head.

"Well, Nuffer, had enough?"

She grinned, the sun in her eyes. It was over an hour since she'd watched it come up. Owen had made her a peanut butter and marmalade sandwich. They dragged the sleeping bags, the cooler and all the other stuff down to the beach, ready to load onto the plane. It would skate in on two big pontoons, Mr. Miles said. Mrs. Miles came out of the cabin, tying a blue ribbon around her ponytail. She was wearing light blue pedal pushers and a white sleeveless blouse. *Sugar in the morning.*

"Janna's on her way. You've got a beautiful hot day ahead of you."

A tiny speck in the sky turned into the plane that landed smooth as an eagle. They waded out and climbed on its pontoons and into the little cabin. Before she could get really scared they were off. It was so beautiful she forgot all about her sandwich, and couldn't have eaten it anyway, she figured, the excitement in her stomach and all.

Four hours later they caught their first glimpse of huge waves crashing on a long sandy beach. She was sitting in the middle of the back seat of the rented car that smelled like lemons. Owen was telling them why the west coast of the Olympic Peninsula, wild and exposed to the ocean, was different than the east coast. Trees hundreds of years old weren't as big right next to the open ocean, Owen said. They were stunted and bent back over the land. They fought off winds blowing all the way from Japan.

At eleven-thirty they arrived at the beach at Kalalocks, named by the Indians, her father said. Huge logs lay all over, scattered like a giant's pick-up sticks. And across the street from the beach and down a small winding road was the campground in the rainforest where they would camp tonight.

"We'll have lunch on the beach, then set up camp later," Mr. Miles said.

She didn't care about food. It was the thundering ocean that mattered. Scattering clothes on the sand as she went, she tore into the waves, Owen and Janna right behind her. The cold made her legs ache and the rushing water sucked the sand from under her feet. Waves crashed at their bodies. Owen flung out his chest for the sea to bash against. Janna was screaming, but you could tell she liked it. Out deeper, where the waves weren't white on top, just rolling walls of water, there was more kelp than she'd ever seen—miles of it waving slowly up and down. Even further out, a huge rock jutted up, black and craggy. It was crowded with seals, throwing their heads back, barking like dogs. They held hands and lined up against the foamy waves. Owen began to bark, too, and then they were all barking wildly with the seals.

Her whole body was numb. She stumbled back to the beach and threw herself on hot sand that steamed like toast on a cold morning. She listened to the roar of the ocean and faint noises from Janna and Owen. She felt a tiny prick on the back of her neck. Sand bugs were jumping around her body. She got up and began to walk, pretending not to hear Mr. Miles yelling at them.

"Hurry it up, lunch is ready! We haven't got all day."

Yes they did. She'd seen something shiny. It was a green glass ball, big as Janna's beach ball, in a net of rope. It was heavy. She carried it back to her father.

"That's a Japanese fishing float, used to keep nets aloft. It's traveled all the way from the Orient, rolling like kelp on the long ride. A real find."

She would put it where Venus would have gone.

The rain forest was silent and spongy underfoot from one hundred and ninety inches of rain a year. Maple trees were coated in bright green moss. Ferns sprouted out of their trunks like hairs on a mole. The fir trees were so tall their blue-green branches brushed against heaven. Five sets of arms couldn't go round them. The giant cedar trees had been used by Indians to carve canoes because they were rich with sap, and didn't rot. How did a father like Mr. Miles know things like that? Janna danced around him until he put her on his shoulders. She reached up, trying to get closer to heaven herself. They found a clump of mushrooms feeding on the decaying wood of a fallen tree. Mr. Miles picked one and explained the crowded gills on the underside that gave off spores.

Hobo stew was the critical moment of their camping badge. The hamburger in the cooler was still cold. Janna scraped the carrots while Maffy washed the new potatoes. Mrs. Miles had put in green beans too. She loved them enough to eat them raw, like other people ate potato chips. They would cook theirs in the stew. Owen showed up with tiny ferns called fiddleheads. They lit a fire using only one match, feeding it with twigs, till it got into the swing of things. Mr. Miles objected to the bark they'd collected on the beach.

"It's damp and burns with too much smoke. Look sharp, Owen, find some dry wood that will burn white smoke."

"What are we doing, Winton, choosing a Pope?"

The hobo stew passed muster. Dessert was roasted marshmallows. Maffy ate four and Owen ate half a bag. Janna tried sneaking them when her father wasn't looking.

The dark came earlier each night but Owen was prepared, his flashlight throwing spooky shadows. He wasn't about to be caught with no way to read, not even for one night. He brought out the books, the ones she didn't recognize. The first was *Man-eaters of Kumaon*. He made them beg—"Tell us a story, please, Owen"—but he was dying to start in. His voice was calm. He let the words tell the story.

"A small village in India was terrorized by a man-eater. Two people from the neighbouring village had been killed. The people wouldn't leave their huts, not to find food, not for anything. The village smelled terribly of humans too afraid to enter the jungle. The tiger was drawn to the smell of these people living in his jungle.

"One brave girl ventured out. She was fast and thought she could out run the tiger. Her little brother was too young to go any longer without food. The grass in the jungle was tall and she quickly disappeared. The villagers waited for her return. Then they heard the screaming. They ran to the edge of their village. Suddenly, the tiger appeared, not thirty feet away."

Maffy and Janna moved closer together.

"He was huge, the largest of all the cats. His head was the size of a wash tub, paws the size of dinner plates. His shoulders rippled under his orange and black striped coat. His thick rope tail swung behind him. The villagers saw in horror that he had the lifeless body of the young girl in his jaws. The tiger turned to stare at the villagers, then slid back into the jungle.

"An Englishman, a Sahib, living in a big palace in India, went out and shot the tiger, who wasn't a he but a she. A tigress who'd just given birth. She had a lop-sided jaw. Her canines were broken down to the gums on the right side. She'd been shot once before, but the bullet hadn't killed her. It had taken her biting teeth so she couldn't hunt. The Englishman shot her dead and discovered she had broken teeth and cubs to feed. He was a hero. The cubs ended their lives in a zoo."

The fire was crackling loudly. Mr. Miles had piled on dry wood.

"They'll be gone at this rate," Owen said. "Extinct."

"Bleeding heart nonsense. They'll never be extinct. The Englishman got himself a tiger skin rug." Mr. Miles' contribution to the campfire.

"A sad story," her father said. "An important one." Owen's smile lit on him.

They lay on their backs around the campfire. It was very dark now, the sky ran on forever. Maffy shivered without her sweater. "Look at all the stars. Tell us about them, Owen."

"Okay, find me the Big Dipper. Ursa Major. That's the easiest. Follow my arm. See it? And off the end of the dipper part, not the handle, but the cup, is the Pole Star. See that very bright one in the north?"

"Yes, there it is!" Janna sounded shocked. She didn't know stars made patterns. Her class hadn't even learned the solar system last year. There were one hundred thousand million stars in their galaxy alone. Give or take.

"Okay, now find Orion. First find three bright stars—Orion's belt—all in a row. Orion has a retinue of very bright stars. Now look away off to the right." He pointed with his hand.

"That's the Pleiades," their father joined in. "The Seven Sisters. The sailors used that cluster of seven stars to navigate by."

"That's what we're going to call our boat," Maffy said. "The Pleiades. A pleasing name!"

"Well, Morgan, you'd better speed it up. I've heard stars burn out. Better finish your boat before there's only six sisters." Mr. Miles' voice was loud in the dark.

"Anything's possible, Winton." Her father's voice was quiet. "Let's see if we can spot Gemini. Owen?"

"Yup, there it is, Dad. Go back to Orion's belt and look left this time. You got it? The Pleiades is to the right, Gemini to the left. Those two bright stars. The Twins."

"Gemini is interesting," her father said. He'd taught Owen everything he knew. "Stars wax and wane and sometimes they do burn out. Castor used to be brighter than Pollux, but is half a magnitude fainter now. Stars that were once bright can fade away. Castor and Pollux. The Dueling Twins. Who will outshine whom?"

Mr. Miles stood up. "It's time for bed. Get into the tent, Janna."

He hadn't noticed she was already asleep. She'd crawled into her sleeping bag about the time of the Pleiades. Mr. Miles had bought a tent especially for this overnight, just big enough for Janna and himself. The Morgans would sleep under the stars, and when they lined up their bags on either side of Janna and covered them all with a tarp, Mr. Miles went into his tent alone. Once in a while he knew when to quit. When everyone was quiet she shook Owen, sleeping next to her. She and Janna were in the middle, her father on the other side of Janna.

"The other book, Owen. What's the other book?"

"It's about cougars. The cougars of Vancouver Island. I'm the first to borrow it."

"Have you read it? Tell me about them."

"There are more cougar attacks on Vancouver Island than anywhere else in the world. They get hungry, thirsty too. They steal in from the wilderness, but only when they're desperate. Cubs to feed." His voice was sleepy, he was drifting off again. "It would have scared Janna. Go to sleep."

"What's a magnitude, Owen?" She would hold on to this night as long as she could.

"Tell you in the morning, Maffo."

But in the morning, magnitudes were forgotten. They woke to the sound of Mr. Miles' voice.

"Guten Morgen. Get a move on." He reached into the trunk of the car to make room for his tent, and missed Maffy's father's quick salute. Janna didn't. She looked confused, like she wanted to laugh, to be part of the joke, but not really feeling part of anything. Maffy's father reached for her. Reached for Maffy too, holding them under his arms like sacks of cement.

"Right-oh, Miss Oat Cake, tally-ho, Nuffer. We're off. Owen lad, step lively. *There's miles to go before we sleep.*"

They crowded into the rented car. Mr. Miles wasn't used to riding in a Chev. He had a new Cadillac that Mrs. Miles had been allowed to drive to the resort instead of her old Nash Metropolitan. It was the first one like it on the road. The 1959 Caddie, and it was still 1958. "A land yacht," her father had said, the night Mr. Miles had driven it home, "Abounding in every excess. A colossal grill, double headlights. Best of all, wait for it folks, the famous tail fins. It's all here in Cadillac's luxury flagship. Be sure to order it in red."

Mr. Miles had.

But even though Janna's father didn't like driving in a crummy car it was better than having three kids messing up the back seat of a Cadillac. He'd have had to pay extra if they wrecked a really nice car. This way, they could bring home shells. They'd found sand dollars and mussel shells the size of pears. A salty, living smell oozed from the back seat, but it didn't matter in a Bel Air.

Chapter Eleven

———◈◈◈———

"Break, break, break,
On thy cold grey stones, O Sea!
And I would that my tongue could utter
The thoughts that arise in me.

Alfred, Lord Tennyson

"Permission granted to come aboard. Come on, Lily, you'll love it." His voice was wheedling. He was determined they go sailing. "The water is calm, just a hint of wind. We've a good reach, let go the mooring line and come amidships."

He stole the yachtsman's language with the same aggression he did everything else. The sun was playing on his face and she saw him once again in the freckled sunlight flickering through the cherry trees of the university campus. His smile broadened. He grabbed her arm and pulled.

"That's it! Come aboard."

He spoke heartily now, all confidence and unrelenting charm. He looked twenty-five again. Fit and tanned. How can you resist me his eyes asked? Yes, he was confident, even after their fight last night over the signing of the papers for the development. Hadn't he made enough money? Going sailing would appease him, hold him off till the holiday was over and she could get back to Victoria and figure a way out.

She settled in the stern, Winton shouting more nauticisms.

"Casting off the bowline, make ready to lower the centerboard. We're underway."

Was it all a joke on Hugh, who was a true yachtsman, or did Winton believe the nautical language made him a romantic figure? She clung to the sides.

"White knuckles on the gunnels!" He was euphoric now that they were actually underway.

"Not too far out, Winton. Turn around now. Please!"

"Come about when we've only just started this little trip?" He leaned toward her, his eyes slits in his ruddy face. Where was her life jacket? Why hadn't he made her put it on? What kind of a yachtsman was he? She edged away from him, eyes darting around for the jackets. There they were, up front, under the seat in the bow. She moved toward them and felt his grip on her arm.

"No, Lily, sit still. It is very dangerous to move about when we're underway."

"Winton, I want to go back. I shouldn't have agreed to this. I'm sorry, I'm frightened." Her breath was ragged. "We need to pick up Janna at Twin Coves. I told Eleanor—"

"No, Lily. We'll be fine. The breeze is freshening—the last sail of the holiday."

They were nearing Dodd Narrows, the most dangerous caldron of water in all the Gulf Islands. Not even Winton would go near the swirling currents that separated Mudge and Vancouver Islands. She sat frozen in her place, the rib of the sailboat digging into her lower back. Eleanor lived with that deep ache every day. She also lived with Hugh's brilliant, brooding mind, so like Alistair's. What would Lily discover about Alistair when finally given the chance? Poor Eleanor, angry and strident, coping with her own moods as well as Hugh's. It was convenient to blame an angry wife, but only Eleanor knew what went on behind the scenes. She and the kids. Lily saw Myfanwy's face again as she stood by the road, pensive and alert. Owen's face, defiant yet resigned. Resignation took the greatest toll. What would Eleanor do if she were out here, wind in her face, fear in every atom of her body? Eleanor would never have agreed to this sail in the first place. She would never allow herself to be bullied. Now he was getting ready to change directions. This involved a lot of scrambling for ropes, and the whole boat would reverse itself, like a mirror image. The boom was swinging toward her.

"Prepare to come about!"

Winton sounded excited now that he was proving himself a great sailor and her a coward. Maybe now they could go back.

"Coming about!" he shouted over the rising wind.

She crouched as the boom swung over her head and then slid over to the other side.

"You're frightened, aren't you? Afraid of becoming a water lily?"

His auburn hair gleamed in the sun and his teeth sparkled. You'll wonder where the yellow went when you brush your teeth with Pepsodent. You'll wonder where your fellow went when you wash his feet with wet cement. The mafia used cement shoes to drown people. She looked at her bare feet. Janna and Myfanwy's feet got so blackened in summer, they were impervious to cleaning. Janna, gentle and vulnerable. She looked up. Dodd Narrows lay ahead.

"Winton, no! We must go back, please, please. I . . . I'll sign for your development, you always knew I would. For God's sake, Winton, please!"

"You've already signed."

"What? What do you mean? We'll see the lawyers when we get back, right away, and I'll sign."

"You've already signed, my darling. I don't care about your precious signature—so neat, so even, so totally without anomaly."

The wind whipped tears out of her eyes. "Well, good then, that's settled. Your development will be a huge success. No one is as good at business as you are."

"That's right, Lily, and I won't be thwarted."

"Fine, good, I'll support you, whatever you want, whatever freedom you want." He wanted to terrify her, to remind her that no matter what, he'd win. What a fool she'd been to agree to this. She'd underestimated him. This would keep her in line for a long time. So be it. The boom shuddered and the sails snapped in wind that came from every direction. Winton let out the main sheet and the boom swung wide at right angles to the hull.

"We're running before the wind, Lily. Jibing. Watch it, the boom can swing wildly. If the wind shifts, she's a free agent."

His voice was grim now. Had he lost control? He would never jeopardize his own life. She turned and looked into his face, so like his brother's yet lacking humanity. He returned her look steadily. Was it fear in his eyes, not of the sea but of losing his pride? Was jealousy driving his ruthlessness? He pushed hard on the tiller and looked beyond her, over her head. She turned and saw. The boom, bearing down on her. A bolt of pain shot through her shoulder and she plunged over the side. Water flooded her mouth. She floundered wildly and struggled to scream. There was no sound, just a gasping choke as another wave hit her. Her shoulder burned, her arm flopped uselessly. Winton's face was growing smaller, no sun on his teeth. He flung an orange life jacket overboard. She kicked frantically toward it, paddling with her good arm.

It was no good. She would never reach it. She wasn't intended to. The whirlpools were winning, pulling her down. She swallowed more water. Her shoulder no longer hurt. She felt nothing but numbing cold. Kick! Keep moving!

A wave, a huge one this time, engulfed her. She struggled for the surface. One last look at Winton's frozen face as the water fought to claim her. One last thought. Janna.

Chapter Twelve

———— ·❧❧· ————

Break, break, break,
At the foot of thy crags, O Sea!
But the tender grace of a day that is dead
Will never come back to me."

Alfred, Lord Tennyson

Her feet hung over the bed like sausages. Would they hold her? Eleanor felt cold, like an icy tide was washing over her. There would be no Indian summer this year. This year so much had been taken away and nothing would be given back. She made her way to the bathroom to get ready.

The nightmare from which she thought she'd never waken was easing. This dull ache was worse. The nightmare had focused her, made her react. Now there was only hopelessness. She'd have to face everyone else's grief when she knew hers was different. She couldn't explain that Lily had evened her out, made her human. The loss of a friend could be worse than the loss of a husband. She'd needed Lily to survive a husband. Lily's unhappiness had helped her deal with her own, and only Lily had understood that narrowness of Eleanor's spirit. Lily had held back the wormwood smothering Eleanor's heart and now she would give anything for Lily to have known the happiness she had been so close to.

The funeral was at two o'clock in Oak Bay United Church. There were no grieving parents. Lily had been orphaned by a car accident when she was barely out of childhood. No one to run to. Eleanor gave in to the question she'd been beating back for seven days. Seven days since Lily had drowned. Why had she gone out in that boat?

"It happened so quickly," Winton had said. "I couldn't come about fast enough. I made her wear her life jacket, but she hadn't tied it tight enough, you know how Lily was. Oh God, the life jacket—all that's left."

What did we know about how Lily was, Winton? What did you know? What did you care about who she was? Whatever happened on that sailboat, you'll spend the rest of your life justifying it.

Winton's mother had brought up navy blue poplin for Janna, smocked with the softest green. Only in Seattle. The navy silk hair ribbon was designed to tie up Janna's long hair. Obviously Winton hadn't told his mother those red tresses were gone—and no Lily for the old girl to harrumph at.

Janna would be in line for everything now. She looked small and white, summer sun bleached out of her, ribbon around her head, like something on a bald baby to proclaim its sex. She moved like a robot, pulled along between Isabelle and Winton. The grieving family. The devastated widower. He'd careened into Twin Coves seven days ago with the news, Cadillac barely missing the big arbutus. Steady on, Winton, don't sacrifice the car.

Seeing the Miles on display today made her face burn and her heart thunder. Seeing them without Lily. How would Janna ever cope? Winton's face was carefully composed; Isabelle's like a stone carving from Easter Island. What was she thinking? She knew Winton better than anyone. Lily had seen through them both and Isabelle knew it. And where was Alistair?

She dug her fingernails into her palms and focused on the music. Bach, of course. Couldn't they have remembered the Chopin she loved? Lovely Lily. Her beautiful fingers had nurtured all the feeling out of the Etude in E flat. Though even Lily's hands couldn't master the piano concerto—they'd been so small—it had haunted her house on the hifi. And her romantic poets. Eleanor felt a pang, remembering her own disdain of Keats and his *Ode to a Nightingale*. *My heart does ache*, she thought, and if only a *drowsy numbness would pain my senses,* little nightingale. Keats had understood death as it stared him down. Romantic young beauty—gone—and now Lily.

She glanced down at Myfanwy.

"It's all right, dear. Do try to stop crying." Would she feel like this if I died, Eleanor wondered? Draw a veil. Don't think about it.

She turned and saw the Greens coming down the aisle. Daphne looked perfect in her artificial way. That hair colour was not one found in nature. Today she wore the same black dress as Lloyd's service but no broad brimmed veiled hat. Instead she'd opted for one vivid peacock feather bisecting her lacquered blonde head and sweeping under her pointed chin. Daphne turned at that moment and met Eleanor's eye.

"She looks predatory," Eleanor whispered to Hugh. "Like a cat on a hunt."

"*Tiger tiger, burning bright, in the forests of the night.*"

She moved closer to him. "*What immortal hand or eye, could frame thy fearful symmetry?*"

Her grey maternity dress was hot. I look like a whale, she thought, among these women in their smart clothes. She could feel Myfanwy's eyes on her. She took her daughter's small, bony hand. The rough spot on her palm was all that was left of the burn. She felt a scab on the little forefinger. A barnacle cut?

The minister started in.

"Lily Elizabeth Miles was a woman for whom the word 'love' was a verb. She loved with every fiber of her being and all of us present today are the better for having felt that love. And now we must let go of that loving presence, but not the spirit, for the spirit of Lily lives on in each of us who have felt the touch of her love in our lives. Lily lives on in her beloved husband, Winton, in her cherished daughter, Janna Elizabeth, in her devoted mother-in-law, Isabelle, and in her many friends gathered here today to bid her good bye. But death is only au revoir, not good bye, for we trust in God's will. As Paul tells us in his epistle to the Romans, chapter eight, verse twenty-eight, *And we know that all things work together for good, to those who love God.*"

What could loving God do to still this pain? She began to rock, slowly, imperceptibly, Myfanwy's hand tight in her own.

"We will see our Lily again, for as the poet Kahlil Gibran tells us, *Life and death are one, even as the river and the sea are one.* Lily has gone to the sea, while we flounder in the shallows still, and have yet to know what she now knows. Have yet to go where she has gone."

Eleanor glanced at Hugh. He would be writhing over this holy man quoting Gibran, but Lily would have loved this poet, if she'd known of him. Perhaps she had. Just one of the things she would never know about Lily. Never discover how she would grow old or with whom, how she would love her grandchildren, how she would remain constant to a cynical friend. She would have. She would have gone on tempering Eleanor no matter what. Tempering the world with her slim beauty, her graciousness, her ridiculous capri pants, her sleeveless blouses—Audrey Hepburn, with hair like Botticelli's Venus.

Now a hymn. *Guide Me O Thou Great Jehovah.* At least they would usher Lily out with something decent, something you could hang your faith on. Winton couldn't know this hymn was bedrock to the Welsh. Would never have allowed it if he had. When the comfort of the hymn was over, the Bible readings continued. George Baker was revealing the number of rooms in God's house. Winton apparently had called on his business acquaintances to speak. He had no friends and Lily's were dangerous. Another hymn. *Amazing Grace.* Amazing what people chose when there was so much to choose from.

At last it was over and the minister was warming up for his final blessing. Now what? Great Jehovah, Hugh was getting up, was striding to the pulpit. Winton couldn't possibly have asked for testimonials. What had gotten into Hugh? He looked incredible. Gold hair, bright as dawn, breaking over his forehead in that way it had, blue eyes firing like pistols. His slightly Roman nose gave him an ascetic look, and that mouth . . . that was where his strong features softened. Why had a man like this married her? He was tall in the pulpit, his six feet overshadowing the anemic minister who wisely stepped aside.

"Lily is gone," Hugh began, "and where or why we don't know. Christian promises do little to mitigate such loss. Will we see her again? No. Will we remember her? Yes, in a thousand ways. I will remember her blythe spirit, her gentle warmth, her clever wit. I will remember her love of poetry. Lily, *Thou light-winged Dryad of the trees*, are you singing of summer, *In full throated ease?*"

This was why she had married him. He was quoting Keats though he felt the same as she did about this poet. But Keats had been Lily's favourite. And who better to describe the gossamer than Keats?

"Are you now the *Murmurous haunt of flies on summer eves*, Lily? Our soft and loving Lily, you were also strong and courageous. I'll remember you better in the words of Tennyson—you, who died in your prime, with pride in your heart for who you were. A few lines from *Ulysses*, I beg your patience. The last words I shared with Lily.

> *It may be that the gulfs will wash us down;*
> *It may be that we shall touch the Happy Isles,*
> *And see the great Achilles, whom we knew.*
> *Though much is taken, much abides; and though*
> *We are not now that strength which in old days*
> *Moved earth and heaven, that which we are, we are—*
> *One equal temper of heroic hearts,*
> *Made weak by time and fate, but strong in will*
> *To strive, to seek, to find, and not to yield.*

"Good-bye, Lily. May your heroic heart touch the Happy Isles, and may you see the great Achilles face to face."

The church was silent. The congregation was his. No one could bear it to be over, when they would have nothing but their loss. Eleanor's left palm was burning from the pressure of her fingernails. She'd bitten them jagged for this occasion. Her right hand clutched Myfanwy's scarred little hand. Hugh's face was remote as a stone. What went on behind those streaming eyes? Eleanor looked around at stricken faces, staring at him. He relented, his smile brightening the dark day. Then he was singing. The purity of his Welsh tenor made Eleanor's skin prickle.

> *"Eternal Father strong to save, Whose arm has bound the restless wave,"*

The sailors' hymn—as close as he could come to believing. Slowly they joined him. Some sang, most could only hum. Their final good-bye to Lily.

> *"Who bade the mighty ocean deep, Its own appointed limits keep:*
> *Oh hear us when we cry to thee, For those in peril on the sea."*

Chapter Thirteen

———◈◆◈———

Our birth is but a sleep and a forgetting:
The Soul that rises with us, our life's star,
Hath had elsewhere it setting
And cometh from afar.

William Wordsworth

For the second year in a row she and Janna weren't in the same class. Just as well. Mr. Bell would only break Janna, now that she was made of glass.

For a long time after Mrs. Miles died, her parents hadn't fought. Almost two weeks. Tonight they were in the living room with the hifi full blast. Her mother said Showpan was Mrs. Miles' favourite composer and they were going to listen, whether or not anyone liked it. Maffy did like it. She liked it at night when she was going to sleep. She imagined Mrs. Miles playing it on her grand piano. The music was perfect for Mrs. Miles' hair to wave to. Her hair was butterscotch now, waving in the water like streams of kelp. The night was dark and Mrs. Miles was gliding smoothly through the phosphorescence, through the Milky Way, under the raft at Twin Coves. Her fingers fluttered like sea anemones. Phosphorescence glittered in her eyelashes. She was drifting now, rolling onto her back like a seal. Maffy tried to roll too, the top half of her body turning, bottom half following like liquid from a fountain. *Rocked in the mysteries of the deep. Oh Lord lay me down to sleep.* Mrs. Miles's voice was different now. It was softer and it didn't drown out Maffy's voice like most adults. Now it was so soft she couldn't hear it anymore. She stopped singing herself in case she was drowning out Mrs. Miles, but there was no sound.

Maffy opened her eyes. She couldn't see anything—no phosphorescence, no Milky Way. She heard the hifi playing her father's sea shanties, his favourite record after the bagpipe band. It wasn't Mrs. Miles singing, it was only a record. The pillow was wet under her cheek. No one expected Maffy to be this upset because Mrs. Miles had died. She still had a mother.

*

It was two days till Halloween. Christmas and birthdays got complicated sooner or later but Halloween was just the two of them, Maffy and Janna on their own, with no parents fighting or bossing them around. Except for those times when Mrs. Miles had made their costumes, parents had nothing to do with Halloween. This year they were making their own. Maffy had got the idea from seeing a rubber mask in the joke store on Government Street.

Last year they had been pumpkins. Mrs. Miles had seen the costumes in the *Ladies Home Journal.* She'd worked for weeks, using chicken wire to make round frames with holes for their heads, holes for their arms, and room at the bottom for their legs to stick out. Janna and Maffy had helped her cover the frames in orange crepe paper, wrapping it round and round the chicken wire. Mrs. Miles had bought pink ballet tights and dyed them dark green. Maffy's mother had knitted the two orange hats with dark green pompoms. It was hard to walk. Their arms stuck out like sticks on a snowman and they kept bumping into each other, but Mrs. Miles was pretty happy with the whole thing, and they told her they were the best costumes she'd ever made. In her orange cage, Janna glowed like a candle was lighting her up from inside. That was last year. Now Janna never glowed. Now she was bluish white.

The problem with pumpkins was they couldn't be anyone. What would one pumpkin say to another pumpkin?

"How's everything in the patch?"

"Pretty good."

"We had a cold night didn't we?"

"Almost cold enough for frost."

If they'd gone out as big trees, they could have had a meaningful conversation.

"How's everything in the rainforest?"

"We've seen changes. That wind twenty-seven years ago took down my mother and my brother was chopped down. He's now a canoe. The woodpeckers are keeping me up and the squirrels are driving me nuts. I'm hoping next century will be better."

The masks from Eaton's were just ugly old women with warts and grey scraggly hair but they were scarier somehow than the monster masks. She and Janna could just put on their mothers' coats and she'd wrap those dead foxes around her neck.

On Halloween night Maffy hadn't figured on the foxes being scary. Her grandmother had worn the dead animals around her neck with the feet and tails hanging down. When Maffy put them on she got that creepy feeling she liked having on Halloween. Janna wore her mother's short fur jacket and Maffy wore her mother's brown wool jacket. They looked like the awful old women you saw waiting in line at the meat locker where all the mothers kept their frozen beef. Little old women waiting their turn to go in that huge frozen vault. Whenever she had to go in she wouldn't let go of her mother's coat even when her mother tried to shake her off. What if one of those awful old women locked her in? Freezing to death among slabs of dead meat. Yes, old women could really be someone.

Janna was quiet. Maybe this wasn't such a great idea after all, wearing their mothers' clothes.

"I say, Edith," Maffy said, "that Mrs. Green gives out shabby candy. With all her money she could do better. Probably her fat daughter ate all the good stuff before we even got there."

"Yes, and Mabel, did you notice her hair?"

"Like a spider's nest. There are black widow spiders living in that big blob of back combed hair."

"They say she poisoned her husband."

"If she can do it so can we."

"We could start by putting salt in their tea instead of sugar."

That was the worst Janna could think of. Maffy had been planning something much better. "We could dig clams from a cove with red tide!"

"But we'd get caught. We could never do it. Even if we really wanted to."

"It's okay, Edith, we can do anything we want and not get caught."

"Yeah, we could put rat bait in their tea!"

After awhile they trailed off into silence. Janna seemed afraid to keep it up and Maffy could feel that old shivery thing coming on. They climbed up the two pillars guarding the entrance to one of the grander homes on Beach Drive and left their masks on the top. Someone in the stately Uplands would wake up to a surprise. They went home early.

At her house Maffy opened the back door and heard the music creeping down the hall.

"It's *Danse Macabre*," her mother said. "By Saint-Saens. The spookiest music written by a half decent composer. Except maybe that prelude by Rachmaninov. C sharp minor. With all the stops pulled."

Her mother loved to show her stuff. Too bad there weren't more people to show it too. She had to agree with her mother. It was spooky. Here it was Halloween, almost wrecked by little old ladies with minds of their own, and her mother had saved it.

She burrowed into her Heidi bed and wondered what Janna was doing, alone in that house with her father. He'd forgotten it was Halloween and had turned the porch light off so no one would knock.

*

That fall, her mother was the heroine of the school. She'd raised more money than anyone else for the annual school bazaar. She had donated a doll with real hair and had been selling raffle tickets for weeks now. The winning ticket would be drawn in two weeks, at the bazaar. The baby wasn't due for another week after that, which meant her mother would be there and she'd draw the ticket.

"Myfanwy Morgan's mother donated the doll and made all its outfits," Mr. Bell pealed to the class. It wasn't necessary to add

"Morgan" since there couldn't possibly be another poor kid named Myfanwy.

The six outfits her mother had made were pinned up on a large piece of cardboard covered in dark green felt. The doll sat in front of this display which was put in the most important part of the auditorium where everyone would see it when they first came in. Even people who didn't like dolls, including all the girls in grade six because they maintained they were way too old for dolls, were hanging around the booth. Some probably thought just looking at huge Mrs. Morgan was worth the price of a ticket. No one else's mother was pregnant.

Her mother sat at the booth in the auditorium, scrawling out raffle tickets as fast as she could in her terrible writing that no one could read. The same hands had sewed perfect seams on a tiny blue gingham skirt. Maffy remembered the steady clicking of the knitting needles as the little turquoise outfit had taken shape. Her mother was more relaxed when she knit. The sewing machine sitting permanently on the dining room table took more out of her but those little skirts and jackets never revealed what went into making them. Her mother liked to sew, it seemed, and had pretty much stopped talking about teaching at a university. Maffy had watched all the outfits take shape for the doll with shining brunette hair. No one knew how much she still loved dolls. There was safety in her mother doing this for charity.

She bought twenty-six tickets. They were five for a dollar or twenty-five cents each. She spent all her allowance on candy but the money she'd earned weeding her mother's prize asparagus bed last summer had gone toward the doll. A lot of tickets had sold but she stood a good chance. It seemed right that she should have this doll. She had a kind of golden feeling about it all, like the right thing was going to happen. Her friends and even Owen's friends had bought tickets but no one had as many as she did. Her mother's friends had bought tickets but surely if they won, wouldn't they give the doll back? Give it to her? Denise and her mother had come tonight and even horrible Mrs. Green had bought a dollar's worth. Big spender. Denise had gone on about the doll, choosing her moment, when she knew Maffy would overhear.

"Dolls are infantile but Mother bought tickets anyway. Poor Mrs. Morgan and her latest project. You just couldn't not buy tickets or she'd have another breakdown."

Another? She loathed Denise Green.

Janna wandered over looking mournful. "When's the draw for Audrey?" she asked.

Janna had already named her. If Janna won Maffy decided it would be as good as winning herself.

"Not for a while. People are still buying tickets," Maffy said, importantly.

"Let's go to the hot dog booth."

"How much?"

"Twenty-five cents. I'll get you one."

Maffy had used her last quarter on a ticket. Janna always had lots of money now. Her father didn't know what she needed so he gave her money. They roamed around the big auditorium. It was easy eating on the hoof like this. No one noticed them, apart from the way everyone was always noticing Janna.

The principal was ready to announce the draw. PrinciPAL. That was how they'd been taught to remember the spelling. The principal was your pal. Would he be? There was a lot of pushing and shoving around her mother's booth. After fumbling around for his glasses, the principal rolled up his sleeve and reached into the glass bingo ball they'd borrowed from the Catholics. For ages he stirred hundreds of red paper stubs around in the big see-through container. People were calling out for him to keep on stirring so they could keep on hoping.

"Get on with it, man. Those who can, do, those who can't, teach," her father said. They were both pretty tense. He'd bought a lot of tickets too, all in her name. She reached for his hand. Finally the principal stopped stirring and turned his beaming face upon her mother.

"Come forward, Eleanor." They were on first namers. "Come up here on this stage and draw the winning ticket. But before you do, let's have a warm round of applause for Mrs. Morgan, who created this beeeoootiful raffle in aid of Willows Elementary School."

Maffy's cheeks were hot. Her ears were on fire. She was proud but worried too, worried someone would make a crack about her mother's size, worried she wouldn't win the doll. Her mother walked her weird walk, like she had a watermelon between her thighs. Older sisters got pregnant. Unwed mothers. There was a thrilling shame to it. This wasn't thrilling. Was it shame? But no one said a thing, not even under their breath, if the smiling faces weren't lying. Her mother looked tired but bright eyed. This was her moment. She rolled up the sleeve of her maternity top. Reaching her arm into the glass ball made her top ride up and the bottom of her huge stomach showed. No one breathed. She pulled her arm back out with the single red ticket stub pressed between her thumb and forefinger. She handed it delicately to the principal. He brought it to his face, hesitated, squinted a bit in spite of his glasses, and hesitated some more. Finally he looked up.

"The winner of the beeeoootiful fifteen inch doll and her entire new wardrobe is . . . Dancing Queen!"

Dancing Queen? Who on earth was Dancing Queen? The crowd was silent. They'll have to draw again, Maffy thought. I can still win. I can still . . .

Her mother laughed. "I'll read it!" She took the ticket from the principal and squinted at her writing, making a big deal of how bad it was. Then her smile faded. The ticket fluttered to the floor. She looked up. Her face was kind of crinkling. "It's Daphne Green," she whispered.

*

Her mother's cry didn't startle her at first. She was used to it. The high pitched shriek could have been a stubbed toe, a burned finger, snarled hair caught in a comb. If it was true like she'd read, that women could stand nine times as much pain as men, where did her mother fit? Another cry, more like a squawk, and Maffy heard her name being gasped. She left her bedroom and headed for the den and her mother's voice. A louder cry sounded and she broke into a run. At the door to the den she stopped. Her mother was bent over, one hand clinging to the back of a kitchen chair, the other gripping her swollen stomach as if she could hold in what was coming out. Water trickled down the inside of her left leg. Her mother straightened slightly and looked up. No words were needed. The baby was coming. She felt something sour rise in her throat and she wanted to run but the look of pain in her mother's eyes stopped her. The water gushed now, down both legs.

Taking her mother's weight on her right arm, Maffy half guided half pushed her toward the couch. It took ages to cross those seven feet, as if they were in the slow motion part of a movie when everything crawled along so you didn't miss a thing. Her mother was gasping and bending and finally falling unevenly onto the couch. Maffy began to cry and for once her mother didn't get mad. She was crying too and her hands were shaking.

It was ten years since her mother had had a baby. She'd had been there for that one too. She made her mother even herself out on the couch, grabbing pillows and pushing them behind her head, bossing her to lie back and let go of her stomach. Her mother obeyed. As she eased herself back, her legs began to bend and open. They were fat and puffy. The skin on her ankles looked tight.

"What's the doctor's number?" Maffy shouted. "The number!"

"Call Nadine Smyth next door. Tell her to come! She's a nurse. I won't make it to the hospital, even if an ambulance . . . aaaiiigh!"

Maffy started dialing, fingers shaking, like her mother's. Why did the Smyths' number have three nines in it? It took forever. No answer and her mother screamed for her to come.

"There's no time, the baby's coming! I can feel it—aaaiiigh."

Her mother scrabbled at her housedress, pulling it over her knees. She wasn't wearing underpants. They wouldn't fit anymore. Her swollen skin was very close. Maffy tried to run but her mother was quicker, fingers digging into Maffy's wrist.

"Don't leave me. I need you. Please!"

"What can I do? I need to call the doctor. Let me call the doctor!"

Another cry and then her mother began to groan.

"This is all Hugh's fault. I never wanted this baby. Oh God, it's going to kill me. Aggghhhh. Help me, Myfanwy, do something!"

"I don't know what to do! How can you say you never wan—"

"Shut up!" Her mother was panting now, no breath left for yelling. Maffy's gaze left her face and crept down the long, heaving body. Between the mountains of her mother's legs, down in the dark valley, a ball was growing bigger, then smaller. Bigger then smaller. Then bigger and bigger, pushing between her mother's thighs. Maffy kneeled down, concentrating now.

"It's coming, I can feel it," her mother groaned. "Aaahhh, it won't . . . it won't live, coming like this."

A tiny head pushed into Maffy's waiting palm. "Here's its head!" Faster than she could breathe the even tinier body slithered into her other palm. "And now it's . . . HIS body. It's a boy! A boy, Mum!"

"It won't live, coming this way."

Maffy held the tiny wet body. A purple rope was wound around his neck. She laid him on the couch, between her mother's legs. She tried to loosen the rope, but it was tight and slippery. She gripped it hard as she could, scared she'd hurt his slithery neck. She pulled. Her breath burst out of her as the purple rope snaked away. She reached for the green afghan Grandmaf had crocheted and tried to wrap it round him.

Her mother's voice was calm now. "Call the doctor, Maffy. The number's by the phone. Call Dr. Gregson, then your father. There's a good girl."

She put the baby on her mother's body, with the afghan over him. Her mother reached down, steadying him, wiping the white film off his tiny blue face. Her hair was soaked and her eyes were crying, but her mouth was smiling, just a bit.

Chapter Fourteen

·⧫·

Then in the dawn with the coming of daybreak
The war-might of Grendel was widely known.

Beowulf

Seven days until Christmas. Eleanor was awake but if she kept her eyes closed she could hold off the day just a few moments longer. The annual Christmas visit. They would be here by noon. She wouldn't know until her mother stepped through the front door how the day would go. Her mother didn't even have to speak. She would of course, but in those first ten seconds of silence while she assessed the state of things, evaluated the level of disapproval the situation owed her and made her decision as to what tone she would put on the day; well, it was those ten seconds that set the tone. Her mother might be cheerful, then again, she might not be. Eleanor opened her eyes and stared out the window. It was raining. That wouldn't help. Her mother expected so much.

Today her mother and sisters would meet Ross. Would they continue to disapprove? Could they, after they saw him? They'd been very disapproving when she'd broken the news. But they had provided a pram. Perhaps it was just a moment of sentimental snobbery. A pram in Victoria . . . on the streets of the Uplands. It was not an opportunity to miss. Whatever the case, it was a very grand pram. Would seeing him move them as it had everyone else? He'd been very frail but was gaining strength. And he was heartbreakingly beautiful. She could not afford to have her heart broken.

Neither of her sisters had children which qualified them for expert status. It was only after you had children that you never again were sure of anything. You couldn't know your children with any certainty. Could a mother survive knowing who her children really were? And would Eleanor herself ever really know her own mother? Old Grendel would be here in four hours. No, she would never know who her mother had been before she'd donned the cloak of motherhood. Owen and Myfanwy—and now Ross—would never know her. Would they want to? Could her inconsistencies and inadequacies be seen through any lens other than motherhood? The cloak of motherhood defined you and if it didn't you'd wear your guilt like a shroud.

She got up and went to the kitchen. Her kitchen, but only until noon, when her sisters would take the helm. "Your dressing is too spicy, Eleanor. We have to consider Mother's stomach." She put everything they'd need on the counters, but knew they'd be into cupboards all the same. She had washed the outside of the peanut butter jar and scrubbed the inside of the cupboard where a particularly stubborn stalactite of jam still glistened.

Eleanor went out to the carport to get the potatoes from the cold box. Hugh was tinkering on the boat when everything else needed doing. She heard a rustling inside the large wooden box Hugh had made to house their vegetables. She lifted up the lid.

"My God! There's a racoon the size of a malamute in here!"

"Steady on, old girl," Hugh said. He bounded over with the agility of someone much younger. "They really don't like potatoes. Perhaps he's just keeping warm in here." He waved his arms and the raccoon leapt out and scuttled away. "How many?" His smile was sweet. He alone knew what these Christmas visits took out of her.

She leaned into him and his arm closed around her. "There's seven of us, so I suppose seven."

She'd barely cleaned up from breakfast when she heard her mother's voice.

"Eleanor? We're here."

The words hung like icicles in the cold house. She was two hours early.

"Eleanor?"

"Hello, Mother. The early ferry? Happy Christmas."

"You're not dressed?"

"Alice, Bea, welcome to Bedlam."

"You look exhausted," Bea said. "Open your present now, we've found you something pretty, something decent."

The housecoat they'd bought was old rose. Size fourteen. Taking no chances. The same old rose colour of her mother's suit. The colour went perfectly with her mother's grey eyes and soft blue curls. Her mother held out her soft pink cheek for a peck. Eleanor's arms hung useless at her sides.

"We'd like to eat at four, Eleanor. You girls will need to get that bird in the oven soon. We'll get the seven o'clock ferry back to Vancouver. These trips are tiring."

"Next year we'll come to you, we'd love to, it would be a chan—"

"Oh no, dear. I don't think so. We're not equipped for children. I'll have my cup of tea now. We brought our own, Murchies English Blend."

Alice rustled in her black patent bag, the size of a suitcase, and brought out a small tin and a foil wrapped parcel.

"Some short bread, too, for mother's tea."

Three small envelopes were placed on the coffee table. No names. No need. They'd all be the same. *Merry Xmas, from Grandmother.* Tawny two-dollar bills tucked into Christmas cards shaped like wallets.

"Where's the child?"

"Myfanwy is rocking him. We moved the rocker into her room for the time being—such a little mother. She's thrilled with Ross, We, we all are." Her tone was confident yet even now she couldn't completely harness the plea. Please love him. Love me. "He drops back to sleep about this time. I'll call Myfanwy, she'll bring him."

"Let him sleep. For now, a cup of tea."

*

Two days till Christmas. Eleanor was able to squeeze into the green silk, but would the shoes dyed to match fit? Tonight was the smorgasbord at the Empress Hotel. Donna Green was coming over to stay with Ross. She wanted to earn money for university, so she maintained. But Daphne and Denise were going to the smorgasbord. Daphne was coping well with grief.

"What a mercy Winton is here to help," she'd told Eleanor a few days before. "Such a terrible time for us both. He set up the Christmas tree for me. I'm doing it for my girls."

My girls, my foot. My fat foot. They were definitely never going to be slim again. Everything was different now and her feet were the least of it. She rummaged around in the jumble in the closet. There had to be a pair of shoes she could weasel into. If Daphne could go to the smorgasbord so could she. She hadn't been up to much since the birth, but tonight she would go. Christmas at the Empress was tradition. They'd been going since Myfanwy was three. She'd worn a white dress with green smocking with bloomers to match. Hugh had carried her in his arms and she'd wrapped her arms around his neck proudly. Everyone remarked on her eyes. It wasn't just the size of them—like saucers—it was something more. How did a child look wistful and knowing at the same time?

Yes, she had to go to the Empress. It was like an article of faith that they all attend. It was tradition. Hugh would remind everyone at the party that the dowager Empress Hotel was enthroned on a swamp once sodden with trash, her foundation floating aloft a mudflat on a thirty foot deep concrete slab. He could get away with murder with his smile and his wit. He loved to take the mickey out of a bastion like the Empress. Tonight he would look up at the elegant carved ceiling of the Empress dining room and snort. It was molded plastic painted to look like wood.

Eleanor turned from her closet as Myfanwy came into the bedroom.

"Rossie is crying, Mum."

She'd taken over the baby since the day he'd come home from the hospital. He'd spent three and a half weeks there, just to make sure, Dr. Gregson had said. Sure of what? she'd asked. "He's fine, he's going to be fine, Eleanor." She hadn't slept much those three and a half weeks and her strength hadn't returned. But she would not miss tonight, not after she had somehow managed to supervise the decorations again. She would not give up.

"Babies cry." She sighed. "All right, I'm coming. I just want one night out. The whole Christmas season isn't going to pass me by."

"I'll stay home with him tonight. Let me look after him."

"You're too young. We're going as a family. You love the buffet, Myfanwy. Janna will be there, and what would she do without you? You can see the suite Princess Margaret stayed in last summer. The first royal to stay overnight in the Empress."

Eleanor stared gloomily at the dyed green shoes. It would have to be the navy crepe and navy pumps. Myfanwy was gone.

There was no sound of the baby. She crawled into bed and pulled out her knitting. She was almost finished, could get it finished if Myfanwy walked him until five o'clock. He shouldn't be hungry until then. If he cried, he'd just have to cry it out. She could not allow herself to feel the instinctive pull she'd felt toward Owen. Did children know when their mother was drawn to one more than the others? She'd always known with her mother. But then her mother had given her so many clues. And when clues weren't enough, Alice had been there to drive the point home. Bea had been touched by Ross, holding him after they'd choked their way through the turkey, bunged into the oven at ten in the morning and dry as a biscuit. Her mother and Alice hadn't been touched. Where had they stowed their hearts?

She heard the small, precise knock on the bedroom door, and shoved the knitting under the covers.

"Now what?" she snapped.

"He may be teething. I won't leave him with a Green. I'll stay home with him."

"Oh, Owen, I thought you were Myfanwy. She's been at me all day about Ross."

"Mum, he's teething."

"No he's not, he's too young. He's just fretful, and you're not staying home."

"We can't leave him with Donna. She's scared of everything."

"You're coming. Donna is fifteen years old and she's spent hours with Ross in training for this very night. Owen, please—think of your new jacket."

"I don't want to wear it. Maff should have got something new too. That angora sweater she's been drooling over with the rabbit fur pompoms."

"But she hasn't grown, Owen, not like you."

Owen shifted Ross to his left arm. The light from the hall framed their heads in the doorway. Ross's hair was so white it was silver, like a tiny old man, with a corolla of down. Owen's hair was the golden blaze of his father, but as a baby he'd been just like Ross. Owen cradled Ross's head in his right hand, steadying it. The man Owen would be was standing in front of her. There would be none of Hugh's capricious charm; his warmth chilled by sudden squalls that could blow in at any moment. Owen was measured, contained, looking on the world with eyes like worlds themselves.

"Please Owen."

He held her gaze, reading the plea in her voice. She turned her face back to her pillow.

The Empress was crowded and hot. They checked their coats at reception.

"Try to be friendly, Hugh, it's only for a few hours. You spend hours on that boat. This is my first chance for a night out and I'd like to enjoy it."

"I've never aspired to the social heights you do, Eleanor. I'm no match for this roomful of beautiful people. You have to be born to this sophistry and pretence. Isn't that what these people believe? You can't learn it, you're born to it."

"Can't we just have an evening out? These people all know how to have fun."

His face was impossible to read, impossible to know whether he'd warm up. Last year he'd had too much to drink and fallen through the plate glass door that led to the Empress Hotel's Palm Court Conservatory. Now it was cordoned off, mute reminder of seventeen stitches for him, weeks of humiliation for her.

"Are we fun people, Eleanor? Is there any point to this socializing? The same people, the same conversations. The same observations about the human condition. It's unnecessary to observe again. Still, people do."

"For God's sake, Hugh, say it a little louder. There may be one person here you've failed to insult."

"Men tricked up in monkey suits for the Empress Buffet. Look, there's George Baker in a tuxedo the size of Texas."

"Perfect, that's everyone." She followed Hugh's gaze to George, the biggest land developer of them all. His bulk was anchored by unnaturally small feet shod in patent-leather shoes. His face was red. Men like that made money with nothing more than native cunning and ruthlessness. Hugh was right. Life wasn't fair. This event highlighted all the ways he was different. Tonight there was only one way to measure success.

George was mid-way through some self-absorbed story, gesticulating wildly, sloshing eggnog in the face of—was it Winton with yellow goo dripping down his handsome face, dribbling down the front of his impeccable suit? She caught Hugh's eye. His own drink was dangerously close to spewing from his twitching mouth. And here came Jean Baker, enjoying the sight of her husband's faux pas as much as they were.

"A direct hit, I'd say. That's an attractive dress, Eleanor."

"I look like a nun."

"Well, yes, there is a clerical tone. The decorations came off. Where did you find dwarf pine? And white poinsettias. Less blood thirsty than the red. There are enough carnivores in this crowd. Is that Daphne over there, mopping up Winton?"

"I do believe you're right, Jean. Let's go help. Her sartorial statement tonight is remarkable."

Clouds of black chiffon blew around Daphne Green's backside.

"Dare we get that close to the tornado?"

"A chance I'm willing to take, I don't want to miss this—Daphne and Winton clinging to each other like two refugees on a one-man raft."

Daphne was laughing loudly, hoping to prove there was more fun where she was and you weren't. Her heart shaped face come to a point at her chin. She had large, well-shaped eyes. Eleanor had to give her that, but it rankled. They were deep brown, hypnotic perhaps, but with none of the depths of Lily's fathomless oceans, which had been every blue imaginable, and settled most often on the beryl of the Mediterranean Sea. Nor did Daphne have any of Lily's refinement. Daphne's skill lay in making Winton feel like he was the only man on earth. He couldn't risk another Lily. And when Daphne turned her eyes on him, Winton was blinded. Word was many were the men who'd been blinded.

Jean and Eleanor weren't the only ones taking them in but the happy couple was impervious to talk. Eleanor knew that in their minds their orchestrated grief legitimized everything. Like those parents in far off tragic countries—the ones in National Geographic—who would mutilate their children then troop their losses, set them out on the street to beg for pity money. Could anyone be that desperate? Was Daphne? Of course there would always be fools like Nancy Tippet, going on about how wonderful it was that Winton and Daphne had found each other, suggesting some miraculous discovery like insulin. They didn't need to wait a dignified year. They were entitled to a little happiness after what they'd been through. They were reconstructing a family for their girls. Janna would only ever be Lily's girl.

Jean thawed Hugh out in no time and the evening took on a festive tone. In came the boar's head, accompanied by asthmatic pipers. In came the jesters singing "*Here we come a wassailing, among the leaves so green.*" In came the flaming figgy pudding, the size of an igloo, hoisted on the shoulders of more jesters, looking irritable in striped leggings and hydra hats. The one on the left stumbled and the pudding listed and seemed ready to slide right off its litter. Sprigs of holly fell from the ornate platter.

Myfanwy had kidnapped Janna from her table and they were scurrying behind the jesters, like court dogs looking for scraps. Eleanor guessed that they were far away from the Dickensian Christmas these privileged Victorian families were enjoying. They were with Fagan on the streets. Maybe Myfanwy should have had something new to wear. With her freckled skin and brown hair, what colour would be best? She was such a contrast to Janna. Even draped in sadness, Janna shone this Christmas in a deep green velvet dress with a dropped waist and puffed sleeves. Myfanwy's blue jersey was still a good fit. She would look pretty in green, of course, but not the drama of Janna's green—something soft—the gentle apple green of spring. The little face turned toward her. Eleanor reached out her hand and Myfanwy grasped it.

"Settle down, Myfanwy. We're about to eat."

The buffet was irresponsibly lavish. Hugh, as usual, had a point. She looked over at him, his movie star looks achieving an appropriate remoteness.

The jesters disappeared and in traipsed the Little Players in Search of the Nativity under the careful direction of Violet Hicks.

"How long till they come upon the manger?" Jean whispered.

"Ten minutes, tops . . . too long," Eleanor said. She sat back in her padded velvet chair, ready for the obligatory troupe of children acting out the ages old story. As pageants went—and she was an expert entitled to opinion—this was a low point for the Baby Jesus. The shepherds were punching each other, subtly but effectively, and Joseph was picking his nose. A woman at the next table—Joseph's mother?—crawled toward him with a handkerchief.

"These kids need a deeper gene pool," Jean said, sotto voce.

After the Christmas pageant, in marched the cathedral choir. They sang like angels but word was behind the scenes there was infighting in this Magnificat. Lily, who should have been singing, had told stories of the egos that jockeyed for pride of place in the cathedral choir. Only a few were good enough for the Empress Buffet. They were an accomplished lot but the biggest ego of all belonged to their director, Ginger Rogers. Had she orchestrated that name like the she did everything? If Daphne was the tornado, here came the hurricane. Ginger's home perm was taking a while to calm down. Her grey hair bloused about her large head like a swarm of bees and her tent-like black sequined dress was further garnished with a corsage of red poinsettias, so tiny they must be artificial. A woman with an imperative need to be noticed.

"Gingervitis is in top form, but when she turns her back on you, it's her-assment, pure and simple," Hugh deadpanned.

A sad looking girl, Ginger's daughter by the looks of her hair, stood by turning sheets of music.

This small contingent of the Cathedral choir, the first stringers who could sing the Palestrina Motet a capella, performed twice a year, on Victoria Day in the outdoor bandstand in Beacon Hill Park, and Christmas, at the haughty Empress Buffet.

Chapter Fifteen

Into the street the Piper stept,
Smiling first a little smile,
As if he knew what magic slept
In his quiet pipe the while.

Robert Browning

You could tell it was close to Christmas. Her father was at it again. She opened the bedroom door, went in, and closed it behind her. She sat on their bed and waited for him. The bed had a padded headboard covered in the same chintz as the curtains and the little rattan chair in the corner. The chintz had mauve flowers with green leaves on a white background. It went with the cream-coloured furniture and the light green carpet. It was the only real carpet in the house. A tall boy stood against the wall and her father left his change sitting on top of it. Sometimes she would help herself. He'd have given her money but this way he didn't know many horseshoe suckers she could go through in a week. She waited on the bed. He was in the closet putting on the kilt.

"Can you do this up, Nuffer?"

He gestured to the purse that hung neatly in the centre of his kilt, the kilt that snapped back and forth when his slow march got its rhythm. He always put it on to play the bagpipes. He was practicing to pipe in 1959 at the New Years party. The pipes needed warming up first. It took a while of whining and screeching, like slamming the door on the cat's tail but eventually the pipes reached their perfect warmth under her father's left arm. He could play any instrument but the bagpipes took more doing than the mouth organ and the guitar all at once. She liked the wild whine of them, but there was sweetness too.

The best part about Christmas, about winter nights closing in, was that he was inside playing the pipes. It was too dark and too cold to be outside on the boat. The fights didn't happen as much when he wasn't out "messing about in boats".

The deodorant bottles had caused the last fight. The running lights on the boat were two Old Spice deodorant bottles with the twisted glass that her father thought was perfect, fitted over the green light bulb on the right and the red light bulb on the left. Starboard and port. Her mother thought they were primitive. It didn't matter that he'd saved money.

Her father had gone from *Scotland the Brave* to *One Hundred Pipers*. He explained the music, so she could imagine it. One hundred pipers, an' a', an' a', coming through the braes, tassles streaming, white spats gleaming, kilts swinging through the Scottish mist. Goose bumps sped up her arms. The pipes demanded loyalty her father said, an unbroken hymn to Scotland. He wasn't like the pipers at the Empress. There would be no Christmas carols squeezed out of this tartan bag.

*

This would be the last year for angel hair. Next year Rossie would be able to reach up and paw it. She was sure Rossie would be walking next year just like she was sure any day he'd recognize her face. She'd know his anywhere. He looked like Owen and her father, but whose eyes would he have? Would they turn turquoise like Owen's or deepen to the blue of her father's eyes? She prayed they wouldn't turn green. He needed to be beautiful.

They had the tree up and Owen was working on the lights, testing each in turn. One was burned out so they were all out. Like this family.

"It'll be the last one," Owen muttered. "It's always the last one."

"You could start with the last one."

"Then it would be the first one, Maffo. And if I went back and forth from end to end, working my way to the middle then it would be the middle bulb."

Suddenly the lights came on and with them, Christmas. It was the lights that made it feel like Christmas inside the house. Outside it was the deep red mulberries that grew all over Uplands Park. It was the snowberries, fat and creamy. It was the grey, wrangling trunks of the oak trees with their branches spooky against the December sky. Winter in the park had its pluses. No one was ever out walking on the short, dark days. The people went in and the trees came out. Without their thick, olive-coloured leaves, the oak trees took shape, each one unique. Some were twisted and bent, growing in the path of Victoria's winds. Others, more protected ones, were almost regular, like an elm.

She opened the box of decorations and pulled off the tissue paper wrapped around each one. The balls were red and green and blue and silver and one old fashioned pink one left over from her grandmother's tree. Her grandmother didn't put up a tree anymore. Too much bother she'd decided. Each December at school Maffy made a decoration that ended up on the tree. Did teachers really think parents wanted their Christmas trees messed up with a paper mache ball or a Christmas tree made out of green pipe cleaners?

The tree needed help. She took the tinsel and carefully attached one strand at a time so each bit shimmered. It helped fill in the bald spots. Pretty soon, they wouldn't be able to watch TV through it. The biggest problem with their tree was always the cat. They didn't hang balls on the lower third of the tree but that didn't stop her. Even though she was old, Whittler still loved leaping at a Christmas tree. It didn't get much more pathetic than walking into the living room and seeing the tree flat on its face. By the time her father got around to guy wiring it . . . well, then Whittler would use the pail of sand it stood in for a litter box. The cat was getting away with murder while the rest of them could barely breathe.

Maffy studied the tree for the best possible positioning of lights. Two red ones in a row threw things off. One string of lights had glass tubes filled with coloured water. When the lights got hot the water bubbled. When she was satisfied that each light was right and the most had been made of their tree, she swirled angel hair carefully around each bulb.

The day before Christmas it snowed. She knew it wouldn't stick but even so it was pretty amazing to see fat flakes coming down on Christmas Eve. Her father had come home early from work and was outside covering the boat with a tarp. A hundred hallelujahs were soaring from the hifi. The kitchen smelled fruity and ripe from the chopped apples and soaking raisins. She'd helped her mother and in the warmth of that steamy room had been told she'd get credit for the turkey stuffing this year. Her mother had been smiling since the Empress Buffet and had been hinting around to Maffy that there was a pretty good present for her this year.

The doorbell rang.

"Happy Christmas!" her father sang out.

"Now what?" her mother said.

"You've got a heavy load, there. Sloppy weather too. You've miles to go before you sleep . . . How about a little snort to bring in the blessed season." Her father was talking to the postman.

"Well, I won't say no. The best of the season to you." The postman's voice grew louder and her father beamed into the kitchen to get the glasses.

"For God's sake, Hugh."

Her father looked hard at her mother. "Where's your humanity, Eleanor? The man's carrying fifty pounds of mail and a disproportionate amount is for us."

"Really?" Her mother was pleased now. Every Christmas Eve they opened all their Christmas cards at once. They got a lot. Maybe because they sent a lot and theirs were homemade. Homemade didn't mean a picture of themselves, like the Greens' card. Mrs. Green in the middle on a pink velvet chair with Donna and Denise at her feet, Christmas tree on her left, fire blazing on her right. A Burl Ives moment. Mr. Green had been there too, of course but who could remember where? He was the kind of person you only thought about now that he was gone.

Last year their card had been a Christmas tree that her father had sketched on deep green paper. He'd drawn each tree in India Ink, swooping branches flowing down the paper. Then he'd cut out the trees, scissors moving like a magic wand, giving each tree a different shape. Then he drew in four circles, like Christmas balls hanging on the trees. He'd had fifty copies made of a picture of the four of them and it was Owen's job to cut out their faces fifty times and Maffy's job to glue them onto the four circles on each tree so they looked like ornaments, faces staring roundly from green boughs. Her mother had dotted the trees with daps of glue and then sprinkled silver glitter onto them, which looked like phosphorescence in a deep green sea.

This year they hadn't sent cards. Had the Greens? What kind of a happy family portrait would you get when the father was felled by a tragic heart attack?

Her father and the postman were sitting by the fire in the living room. Her father always had so much to say when it wasn't to one of the Uplanders.

"Any excuse for a drink," her mother said, filling the room with exasperation. The doorbell rang again.

"Hello, Nessie! Come in, and Happy Christmas. Again! Have a Christmas drink with us. This is the good postman."

Her father's secretary was standing in the door with a small plastic bag. Her thick ankles were hidden by plastic galoshes.

"No, no, I won't come in," she said. "I just stopped by, a few little things. I forgot to give them to you at work . . ."

"Well, well. It's Agnes. How sweet of you to come by at dinner on Christmas Eve. Presents? How kind." Her mother had suddenly appeared, and stood with her arms folded over her chest as her father's secretary handed three parcels to him.

"Just little things for the children."

Miss McIntyre headed out but the postman seemed pretty comfortable, like it would be a really long time before he slept.

After the postman had sloshed out into the snow and after dinner was over, it was time for the annual Christmas Eve Cultural Extravaganza. Her mother's words. First Maffy played *Oh Christmas Tree* on the piano her mother had painted green.

"A green piano? Dear me, Eleanor. Well, it doesn't matter what I think, as long as you like it. You're the one living with it." Her grandmother's words.

Then Owen played *Oh Come All Ye Faithful* with her father singing along in Latin. He'd learned Latin because he'd wanted to be a doctor. After Owen, her father read poetry. When all the other families in the Uplands were snugged in reading *The Night Before Christmas* or St. Luke from the Bible like the Smyths next door did, her father was reading *The Pied Piper of Hamelin.*

"*RATS!*" he exclaimed, and the story of the piper, who everyone took for granted, unfolded. "*They fought the dogs and killed the cats, And bit the babies in their cradles.*"

Poetry always made him cry. Her mother said it was the Welsh in him and thank God it was Browning, not Dylan Thomas. Maffy was used to it now but it still felt a little shivery to see a grownup man cry. His voice became soft and quiet, and they had to listen carefully. She knew the words by heart but strained to hear her father saying them in his sad, singing voice. "*And ere he blew three notes, Such sweet soft notes as yet musicians cunning, Never gave the enraptured air.*"

The stockings had been hung by the chimney with care but what would Saint Nick think if he were there? She knew there was no Saint Nicholas. But weren't kids supposed to be allowed to imagine it? Image the old elf's jolly smile, not snarling faces, fighting on Christmas Eve. Her mother's voice rose again. Why were they fighting before Christmas had even started? The fox leapt in her stomach.

"I knew immediately!"

"What you know, Eleanor, is very little."

"Don't you belittle me. You, bringing in the mailman, on our Christmas Eve, and then her. I knew immediately."

"For the love of pity, Eleanor, take the needle off the record. There's nothing to know!"

"You had lunch with her, didn't you? A long liquid lunch while I'm here with all this on the day before Christmas."

"She's my secretary. That's what people who work together do at Christmas. And we do work. Sometimes six days a week, from eight in the morning till six at night. We've got some good projects, the Thompsons' addition for one, and by the way, Eleanor, after that pathetic bit of Christmas, Agnes went back to an empty apartment on Quadra St. She'll spend Christmas with her brother's family. A brother with the sensitivity of a Hun."

"She'll spend Christmas serenely on the sidelines."

"You're a hard bit of work, Eleanor."

"Don't you give me that look! Don't you dare. What I'd give to sit on the sidelines, even once! The work of Christmas, the cooking alone, feeding Ross takes forever and then he's hungry again in an hour."

"How can you be jealous of Agnes?"

"Jealous? You think I'm jealous of that little snippet?" Her mother's voice was heading into a crescendo. "I'd just like to have lunch out the day before Christmas, that's all."

Head jammed under her pillow, Maffy began humming. She couldn't hear the words, but knew her father was having his say now. He wasn't calm anymore. He was yelling. She hummed louder, no tune—just a noise inside her head that turned white and high pitched and let no other sound in. After awhile her head was sweaty and hot. She lifted the pillow.

"It's not right! I know where the money's going, it's pouring down your throat, Hugh, and now hers—"

"You spiteful—"

Head back under the pillow. It was hard to hum with the rock in her throat and the fox in her stomach. If she rocked back and forth on her stomach her pillow moved so she turned on her back, wrapped the pillow around her ears and locked it with her elbows.

The house was cold and empty. There was no sound as she wandered through it. She had to go, but the bathroom door was closed, a light coming from the crack under the door. She had to go, but who was in there? Could she go outside? It was dark and cold in the house and it would be even colder outside. A low rumbling started from behind the bathroom door. A rumbling, growling sound. Slowly, she opened the door. Something was in the tub, its broad back to her, pasty white flesh covered in long black hair. Something was sitting in the bathtub with the hair of an animal and the shape of a human. She tried to run but her legs wouldn't move. Slowly, slowly the thing turned its head. A long snout in a hairy face. A wolf's snout under sharp green eyes. Her mother's eyes. She slammed the bathroom door. She needed to get outside but her legs wouldn't move. She couldn't get her breath, couldn't make a sound. She heard water sloshing in the bathtub, the sucking noise of someone climbing out. More air, she needed more air. She flung the pillow to the floor, dragging her breath in through her nose.

Crying was scary because what if you couldn't stop? She lay in the dark thinking about this. Going back to sleep wasn't tempting and besides, it was nearly four when the house was hers. She slipped out of bed and stumbled over her pillow. The floor was cold but she didn't look for her slippers. Better not to put on the light. It was Christmas Day. If she turned right out her door and went past her parents' room that would be her fastest route to the Christmas tree. The presents would be laid out, not wrapped, as if Santa had just pulled them out of his sack, looked them over and made his decision right then and there. What would Maffy like this year? It'd been years since she'd believed in Santa, but her parents still laid things out like he'd just popped down the chimney. Turning right would also take her to the bathroom on the other side of the hall. She had to go.

She turned left, slipping along the icy floor, past Owen's and Rossie's rooms, down the hall to the back door. She went outside and squatted in her mother's prized asparagus patch. Watch out for yellow snow. Then she headed back on numb feet, through the back door, through the kitchen, not stopping to open the fridge, though the spicy smell of stuffing would be worth it. Through the den, then a right turn into the dining room, and finally, into the living room. It was too dark to see the tree and the presents under it. She crept toward the corner where the tree stood and groped for the cord, and then the outlet. With her back to the tree, she plugged it in. She didn't turn around. The lights of the tree lit up the space around her and she sat for a while in the dim glow. The room had a holy feeling. It was Christmas morning. She might be the first person in all of Victoria who was greeting the day. Jesus' birthday after all. No one ever wished Him Happy Birthday, but that was what it was all about. The day could still be a good one. It was Christmas, after all. After a while she felt a little holy herself and decided that everyone else in the house could wake up with the same feeling. It could happen. Please God.

Should she pull the plug and sneak back to bed? Owen would be up soon. He allowed as how he didn't get excited anymore but he'd be up early, racing to the tree, as unexcited as could be.

Should she turn around now and look at her presents? No, she should wait for Owen, stretch out the suspense. She should pull the plug and go back to bed.

Slowly, slowly, she turned her head. Under the Christmas tree lay a doll, dressed in turquoise. A turquoise toque lay beside its shining brunette hair. It must have fallen off. Maffy picked up the tiny hat and lifted it to her eyes. They were watering but she could see, even in this faint light, that it was a different toque than the one on the doll at the school bazaar. It had a few rows of deeper turquoise to finish it off. Her mother had run out of wool. She'd finished it with the new wool Mrs. Baker had bought for her. Her mother had done it all over again. This time for her. Maffy put the hat carefully on the gleaming head. There were two other outfits, laid out, like her mother had laid out clothes for her when she had been in grade one. A blue gingham skirt and pop top, and a dress. A dress like hers, with daisies on it. She picked up the doll and held it against her thumping chest.

Owen had explained the Theory of Relativity. This was how she needed to understand it, Owen said. When you expected something to be really bad and it turned out to be okay, then it really felt better than okay. It felt good. It worked the other way too. It all had to do with how things were connected to each other in the mind. That was the Theory of Relativity. Said Owen.

Christmas Day felt good. Her father gave her mother the last in a series of Royal Dalton figurines. There were twelve in all—children representing the months of the year. Their faces were so real they looked like they could speak. Her father had started giving figurines to her mother the Christmas after Owen was born. December's child was a girl in a red coat with a white fur muff and collar. She was throwing a snowball. Her dark curly hair flew around her face and you could hear her laughing a loud, happy laugh, and calling, "Watch out!" All twelve children were now in the china cabinet in the living room. It was like their own museum. Maffy was never allowed to touch them but she loved looking at their perfect, unconfused faces.

Grandmaf had sewn a marble bag for Owen. She'd filled it with jacks and cat's eye marbles. Big turquoise ones. She'd embroidered the outside with stars and a comet tail. Funny how Owen could be so smart about relatives and stars and still get wound up over a bag of marbles. Maffy had given Owen a picture of a tiger with two well-fed cubs. Grandmaf had made Maffy another outfit for her doll, which she'd already decided to call Audrey. It was a skating skirt and little bolero top. She'd even found a pair of doll skates. She'd slipped Maffy another gift too, when no one was looking. A gift that wasn't wrapped and wouldn't count as favouritism. It was a book. She'd never seen one like it before. It had a white horse with a curly horn on its hard cover and its pages were blank.

"An empty book, Grandmaf?"

"Yes, Maffy. Just imagine!"

Almost as good as the doll was the gift from Miss McIntyre. Her gifts hadn't been under the tree on Christmas morning. They had just showed up on Maffy's and Owen's beds when lunch was over and they was told to lie down and rest until three. Maffy's gift was a rocket radio. How was it possible that she could attach the clipper to her bedsprings and hear music? The red and grey box with the picture of a rocket taking off said, "no tubes, no batteries, no transistors, no electricity". It was tuned with the "space probe" on the rocket's nose. Miss McIntyre had written a tiny card tucked inside the box. "I know you love music". She put the earphone in her left ear. A chummy voice was dreaming of a white Christmas. How did Miss McIntyre know? Her father must talk about her. Maffy felt something jumping inside her, something full and good.

Her stuffing was okay and the snow stuck after all. Late that night, when the moon came out, she put on her new white mittens from Aunt Alice, and wrapped the white wool scarf from Aunt Bea around her neck. Owen was wrapped up too and they snuck outside, flitting like bats flying blind from a barn, hurling snowballs and spinning till they fell backwards in the snow. It wasn't much of a moon. Not enough to see faces by. In the shelter of darkness, in the warmth of the snow, Maffy imagined her own face beautiful, wreathed in white fur, laughing a loud, happy laugh.

Chapter Sixteen

·⟨·⟩·

To see a world in a grain of sand
And a Heaven in a wild flower.

William Blake

1959

April brought Janna's birthday but no hint of wild flowers. Would the earth ever warm up? Janna's grandmother was coming for the birthday. The birthday that Maffy wasn't invited to. It didn't seem possible that so much could be so different now. The birthday was a dinner party at the Union Club and then a symphony at the Royal Theatre. She had looked up "union" in her red dictionary. "The act of bringing together, an alliance of persons." More and more things made less and less sense. Janna had gotten so excited about her party she'd started to cry. Nobody had better start singing *April Love.*

April had so much potential. Last year on Janna's tenth birthday, she'd had an Easter egg hunt. When Mrs. Miles planned something, you wanted to do it even if it was juvenile.

Dawn was coming and she could make out the trees in the park. The oaks were tufty now, with branches of bushy green. It was harder to see their personalities but those tufts held nooks where birds could nest. She remembered Mrs. Miles coaxing her and Janna. "One more nest, darlings!" They'd found it in the crook of the oak tree way off in the corner with the branch that arched so low to the ground it was like a swing begging you to sit on it. There were oak trees all over the Mileses' back yard but that one had the most personality. Mrs. Miles had known to hide the best nest there. It was a real bird's nest, all soft inside, with downy feathers stuck in the straw and mud. Mrs. Miles had known not to wreck it with a bunch of pink and purple eggs, either. She'd put two perfect chicks in it. Maffy would keep her tiny yellow chick forever. It was the size of a fifty-cent piece and had real feathers. Seattle, her mother had said. This time last year she hadn't thought she'd be worried about Janna, whose life had been pretty much perfect. Today was Saturday and they were starting their spring routine. Soon as it was a reasonable hour, she'd go get her and they'd spend the whole day off on their bikes. But this year Janna was sad, and going off with her meant leaving Rossie.

Still, it was important to get Janna out of her house. Even worse than having her grandmother there was having Mrs.Green there, cooking casseroles in Mrs. Miles's kitchen, lording it over Janna any way she could. Ever since the day Mr. Green had died, Maffy could feel how much Mrs. Green loathed her. Everyone else had been staring at poor old Mr. Green lying there like a sausage, but Maffy had been watching Mrs. Green and Mrs. Green knew it. There'd been something wrong about her mouth. Something too firm and dry.

Yes, things were getting worse and worse with Mrs. Green and her daughters around. Donna was okay but it was unimaginable that Denise would be at Janna's eleventh birthday party and not her. The thing was, Maffy was glad not to be going. But she couldn't let Janna know that. Quelle Belle Mess. She had to hope that Mr. Miles wouldn't be stupid enough to let Mrs. Green hang around for long.

It was just the shock, everyone said. "They've been through so much." It was pretty shocking how the world could change and how nothing could be counted on. How Denise Green could end up at Janna's birthday party.

She headed out on her bike towards Janna's. Rossie had been crying when she left, not the usual hollering of babies, but real tears. She'd changed his pants. His stomach button stuck out like a tiny white mushroom. She'd pushed it in and he'd stopped crying. She'd let it out and he'd started crying. In and out. Stop and start. It hurt him. She was certain. Then they were both hollering. Her father had come in.

"Rossie must hurt, Dad." She pushed in his stomach button again. He stopped crying.

"It's all right, Nuffer. He's just distracted when you do that. Distracted from his hunger." Her father had swung Rossie into the air, catching her eye as he did. Other babies were rolling around, even sitting up at five months. She'd read it in *Better Homes and Gardens Baby Book*. She and her father both knew Rossie was no *Better Homes and Gardens* baby.

Maffy reached the entrance to Janna's house and walked her bike down the driveway bordered by the stately garden. Mr. Miles didn't like them riding in case they stood on the brakes and left marks on his assfault. They could spin out on the gravel all they wanted at Maffy's. She could hear him swearing as she neared the huge house. His golf clubs lay next to his Cadillac. She turned the corner to the back door where Janna would appear, and there he was, up a ladder that was propped against the house. Was he cleaning the eaves? There were no leaves up there now. It was spring. What was he looking at under the roof? His face was red, like it had been boiled. Closer now, she could see he had a garden trowel in his thick right hand and was holding onto the garage roof with the other.

Janna came out the backdoor looking pale. There'd be no one to make sure she got her dose of sun this summer. They looked at each other but neither said a word. What was Mr. Miles digging at under the eaves? Then they heard it. The faintest cheeping coming from under the roof. A small bird swooped frantically over Mr. Miles's head, not making a sound, just wheeling and diving. He jabbed the trowel at the cheeping noise, so soft they must have just learned how to make it. Cheeup, cheeup. It was the smallest sound she'd ever heard, like Janna's breathing in the night. Suddenly, there was an even smaller sound. A tiny plop, a tiny head hitting the cement walk that ran the length of the back of the house. The baby bird had no feathers. Its body was see through and the soft purple veins weren't pumping anymore. Its mother was screaming now. Mr. Miles lunged at her and her nest, hoping to kill two birds with one slash. The cheeping was barely there now. The trowel clattered to the cement and Mr. Miles climbed down the ladder, the bird's nest in his right hand. Janna had gotten her bike and was pedaling fast as she could down the driveway. Maffy walked her bike, afraid Mr. Miles would start in about tire marks. He always could do two things at once. Now there was no cheeping at all. She looked back once, and saw Mr. Miles closing the lid on the garbage can. The mother bird was gone.

Janna was waiting for her at the corner. They started off again but Janna's feet couldn't seem to connect with the pedals so they walked their bikes. They walked down new streets Janna's father's development had caused. Finally it was spring. Birds' nests and new houses were going up. They wound down a street so new there was only one house on it, still under construction, with its gravelly backyard gouging into Uplands Park.

"We haven't been to this side of the park in ages," Maffy said. "When did this happen? This new house right where that old oak was."

"The one with the hollowed out trunk."

The new house was taking shape. Its piles of raw pink lumber smelled sickly sweet, nothing like wood was supposed to smell. A sheet of beige arborite was leaning up against the newly finished garage wall. Maffy and Janna circled the house. They saw white fawn lilies and purple shooting stars finally blooming around the workmen's outhouse. There must be a lot of them under the outhouse. She hadn't seen a chocolate lily yet. They were the rarest of all the wild flowers in Uplands Park. The rarest and the most beautiful.

The house had double front doors with big "picture" windows on each side. Staring through these, they could see the staircase to the left, leading up to what would be bedrooms. Next to it was a hall, down which they could see the outline of a kitchen counter, where the beige arborite would go. The kitchen had the same lay out as the Miles' kitchen. They circled back to the arborite leaning against the wall. It was Saturday. There'd be no workmen today. Janna touched the arborite with her foot. It shimmied slightly under her weight. It had spring in it, like a safety net for trapeze acts. Then she backed off. Maffy placed her own foot tentatively onto the gleaming slab. When it held, she added the other foot, and slowly, very slowly, began to bounce.

The new house was surrounded by oak trees. Perfect privacy. No one would invade this calm backyard. Janna got on the arborite and they both began to rock. Gently, then not so gently. A violent cracking noise ended their circus act and they fell, knit together on top of the two jagged pieces of arborite. They managed to mash a few more shooting stars that up till then had survived the destruction going on around them. They should run. The sound of the arborite breaking vibrated in Maffy's head like a gunshot. They should run, get out of there fast.

They went back to the front of the house. No cars came down the street. Next year there'd be a whole parade of houses on this street, and no oaks. She walked up to the big double doors again. They weren't locked. Janna didn't argue like she usually would. They went in. The workmen had left tools around. Maffy picked up a hammer with a rounded end. It was small, almost dainty. She gave it to Janna and picked out a larger hammer for herself, one end of its head big and flat, the other end pronged for prying out nails. It was too heavy for one hand. She hefted it like a baseball bat.

They slunk through the house. It was almost finished. Why hadn't it been locked up? The kitchen counters were plywood, waiting for the arborite. Maffy tapped the fridge lightly with her hammer. Small dents appeared on its gleaming white door.

They went into the bathroom. It took more than a tap for the mirror.

"Give it a good one, Janna. You've already had your bad luck. Go ahead, break the mirror."

Janna lashed out with her right arm and the mirror shattered with a terrible sound. They leapt back from the splintering glass. The toilet was tough, but they managed to crack the aqua blue seat.

By the time they reached the living room they couldn't seem to stop, leaving a mosaic of round holes on smooth beige walls.

Janna was panting, her face like a stop light. Her right hand was bleeding and her eyes were huge and wild. Maffy was finding it hard to get her breath and her bangs were wet and plastered to her forehead. She had that feeling down inside like she might wet her pants.

"C'mon Janna, we better get out of here."

They ran out the front door of the new house and into the park. She heard Janna behind her breathing hard and then the terrible yowling began. She swung around to see Janna on her knees, arms wrapped around her stomach. Her new pink pedal pushers were getting dirty. Her head was tucked into her chest and the yowls tore out of her, fierce and desperate, like an animal in a trap. Then, even worse, came a pathetic, weak mewing. She dropped down beside Janna and saw the chocolate lily growing right by the path. The first one this spring. Its delicate brown fronds were lightly speckled like they had freckles. They had been Mrs. Miles' favourite. Janna was rocking now, and wailing again, like she'd never be able to stop. She knelt behind Janna, with her knees on either side of hers. She wrapped her arms around that hot, heaving body, rocking back and forth with it. It was hard because Janna was taller but she managed to hold on. After a long time the rocking stilled and the noise stopped. Now there were just giant shudders coming from Janna. She started to speak, her voice crying into her words.

"The mother bird trusted her! That's the wor—the worst of it. She trusted Mummy to protect her. She built her nest there every year, she—aaawww." Janna was crying again. More time went by. Maffy didn't let go.

"It was warm there, next to Mummy's greenhouse. That's why the bird nested so early, she said. Most birds don't have babies in April. She said they were my bir—my birthday present. She'd never let my fa—never let him near the nest."

Janna finally got stiff, down on her knees like that, and they both rolled onto the thick moss. The chocolate lily was safe. They managed to roll the other way. The sky was pillowed with white clouds and the sun tightened the salt on their faces.

Later, they crept back to the new house and got their bikes. They were a long way from home but they didn't ride. They just walked slowly back to Maffy's. For once, Janna wanted to come in. Maybe she needed to test herself on an adult before she went home.

They went in the back door, Janna going first, and letting out a little yelp when she forgot how not to get her fingers pinched by the door handle. But she didn't cry. They went into the kitchen and looked at Rossie, who was hanging in his Jolly Jumper from the middle beam in the family room. Why didn't he kick off with his feet like Janie McLeanie? This jumper wasn't so jolly. But he could hold his head up. He could keep it from lolling around now. His eyes focused on Maffy and his mouth curled into a smile. As usual, she tried to stay tough for five seconds, tried to keep back and stay tough. Something about Rossie scared her. It was same with Janna now.

"Myfanwy, get busy and peel the potatoes. Where have you been?" Her mother strode into the kitchen, taking them all by surprise.

Rossie's lips, quick to smile, now quivered. But Janna didn't seem anxious to leave. When her mother saw Janna, the mad look left her face.

"Oh . . . Janna. Hello, dear. We're so, uh, we're so pleased for you all. Oh, perhaps I shouldn't say . . ." Her mother's face was a rare thing at that moment. She looked confused. Something was up.

"Well, dear . . ." That word again. "Your father just called, wondering if you were here. He has . . . some news for you. Run along now, your grandmother from Seattle has arrived."

Janna only had one grandmother. Of course she knew she was from Seattle. Horrible Grandmother Isabelle.

"Your father has a special gift for your birthday tomorrow, Janna, but he, he's going to tell you today dear, so off you run, but we're here—right here—come back after dinner. It's Saturday, we watch Lawrence Welk. With popcorn." Her mother finally stopped babbling and looked helplessly at Maffy. She didn't seem to care about the potatoes anymore.

She hadn't seen Janna that night for Lawrence Welk. Had her mother really thought Janna would be able to get away from Grandmother Isabelle the very night she arrived? Besides, what good would Lawrence Welk do? Doll-faced girls in identical dresses, lipsticked mouths singing *Tennessee Waltz*. Sad songs with grinning teeth, hair swinging into matching flips. The only difference in them was their height, but their dresses all ended the same distance from the floor. Lawrence had it figured out, swooning over his accordion until it was time to dance. Then Myron Floren took over and old ladies from the audience—the geritol set—lined up for the thrill of waltzing with the Welker for seven seconds. There was no grass growing under his patent-leather shoes. *Good night, sleep tight, and pleasant dreams to yoooou, Here's a hope and a prayer, that every dream come truuuue.* Her parents loved it. She sort of loved it too.

What if her dreams came true? She crept to Owen's door and knocked.

"What is it?"

She didn't tell him about the house. Not even he could be trusted with that. But he could be trusted with birds.

"Doesn't anyone realize, doesn't that sadistic fool realize the energy that goes into raising baby birds? Building a nest? The amount of food a mother bird needs herself so she can find energy to feed her young? Every wing flap—does anyone know what that takes? The energy of the whole universe is represented in that mother's tinily beating heart. That forlorn heart beating dejectedly, somewhere tonight."

It helped knowing Owen was in the universe.

She didn't see Janna on Sunday or on the bus on the way to school Monday morning. When she got off the bus with Owen, she noticed the police car in front of the main entrance to the school.

It was nearly ten-thirty when the policeman came into her class. He was fat and dark with the jowls of a bulldog. His stomach hung over his thick black belt, which had a gun in a leather holster attached to it. He was going around to all the classes, he said, to talk about vandalism in the Uplands.

"—useless, senseless destruction of a beautiful new home on Uplands Park. A lot of you lucky children live in the Uplands, don't you? I wonder if you know how lucky you are, and yet someone, maybe one of you, has seen fit to wantonly vandalize someone's dream house. If any one of you knows anything about this, or saw any—"

It was hard to hear over the roaring in her ears. She'd been planning on getting to the toilet fast at recess but now it felt like grade one again and she'd be going right there in her seat. The fox was tearing around down there, frantic to get out. Had the policemen been to Janna's class yet? Was she even at school today? Would she tell? Maybe she already had and this dog-faced lawman already knew they'd done it. Was he looking at her? Janna couldn't lie nearly as well as Maffy could. Did that mean Janna couldn't not tell the truth? They weren't the same thing, lying and avoiding telling the truth. Or were they? Where would Janna draw her line?

Finally it was recess and she found Janna in the girls' room. The skin under her eyes was purple. Her eyes were red. She wasn't as pretty today. Neither said a word. Slowly, almost invisibly, Janna shook her head. Then she was gone.

Chapter Seventeen

Look like the innocent flower,
But be the serpent under't.

William Shakespeare

The usual signs were there. Clean floors, cookies cooling on the marble, laundry neatly folded. "She's family," Hugh said. "How can you feel beholden to family?" His mother was warm. She hugged the children, easy as breathing.

There was no need to get out of bed yet. Hugh had picked his mother up early on this auspicious Saturday. She would care for the baby all day. Hugh hoped that would get them through it. Too bad it was going to be sunny. Eleanor stretched. The knife inched up her lower back. She was no good in the morning. She curled up on her side. Just a little more sleep.

The house was still dark which was odd. Here it was, the first day of summer. Her birthday. She always woke up early on her birthday and it should have been light out. She moved quietly down the stairs, careful to walk on the outside edges of each stair. The middle part, especially on the fourth stair down, creaked. Quietly she went, down to the huge kitchen where the Chinese house boy was lighting the stove. It was so cold for June. Out to the back veranda, big enough to house the freestanding garden swing she wasn't allowed on. "Grownups only. Your shoes are dirty." Her birthday present would be on the back veranda. But there was nothing there. Where was the tricycle?

"You're not having a birthday this year. Birthdays mean a person is growing up. You're still the useless child you were last year. Useless, and so much more work for me. Jesus, Mary and Joseph, so much work."

Two claws clutched her shoulders, rattling her back and forth. She tried to break away.

"It's no use going to your precious mamma. She didn't want you five years ago. She doesn't want you now."

If she could just get free of those claws and find her mother but Alice's grip was strong. Stronger and meaner every birthday. The rattling was shaking her brains around in her head. Alice told her she'd rattle all her brains away if she didn't grow up and become useful but nothing she did counted for useful.

"Eleanor, wake up. Wake up! Myfanwy's made you breakfast in bed."

She opened her eyes and saw Hugh's blue ones staring down at her.

"Please. I'm awake, stop shaking me."

"Eleanor, Myfanwy has made your birthday breakfast." His tone held a warning.

Why had she allowed herself to fall back to sleep? Why did Hugh always have it in him to be the good parent? She turned toward the door to where the girl stood, tray balanced carefully. There was a yellow rose, still a bud, in a drinking glass, a cup of tea and two pieces of raisin toast. Just what she wanted. Eleanor met her daughter's eyes and saw the question in them. Will you be a good and grateful mother? Will you get up and make yourself useful? Myfanwy had always made herself useful, and she'd had a trike on her fifth birthday. Her smile was tentative, anxious to please. It was her eyes that Eleanor avoided. They didn't miss a thing.

"Thank you, Myfanwy. How nice." The grip on her shoulder eased. "Where's Owen?"

"He's out with Bosun. Running."

Running. That was what Owen did now. He ran along the beach with the dog racing ahead and doubling back to make sure Owen was following. She'd seen them. One rain battered day she'd been driving by Willows Beach in the shuddering Hillman. Owen had sped by, plowing through the sand, where the waves hit, running shoes clutched in his hands. He hadn't noticed the unmistakable olive car, or his mother slumped behind the wheel. The look on his face wasn't watchful like Myfanwy's. His eyes were seeing a world within. He hadn't seen her that day. And he wasn't here now on her birthday morning. But Myfanwy was, Hugh was silently saying.

"He'll be back soon," Myfanwy said. "He's got something special for you. He's gonna surprise you."

"Going to. Going to surprise me." She enunciated each word deliberately, then bit into the raisin toast. Hugh had retreated. "Are your white shoes clean? What about socks? Your dress is ironed and in your cupboard but don't put it on too early and heighten your chances of getting it dirty."

"I've got a present for you too."

"Lovely . . . that's lovely dear, but shall we wait until Owen is here? Perhaps tonight? For now, I'll just have my tea in peace."

Eleanor sat up against the padded chintz headboard. That dream again. That birthday, thirty-five years ago. Her father had just died. There had been presents. That part of the dream wasn't true. The rest was. Her mother had languished for years after her father's death, rising like a phoenix after Eleanor no longer needed her. Meanwhile, it was Alice at the helm. Bitter, resentful Alice. Yes, there'd been presents, but no trike. There was a rag doll and a new sweater. Alice had seen to it. A trike would have meant she could play with the little girl across the street, zooming up and down the wide sidewalks of Vancouver's west side.

Eleanor had been sent home from school once too often because her clothes were dirty. How could you send a child home from school for having a dirty dress? A six year old child. No one thought to ask, Why hasn't your daughter got clean clothes? So she'd failed grade one. It was hard to concentrate with a teacher who saw your dirty clothes and saw your vulnerability. "Unacceptable" her teacher had said.

Alice hadn't failed. She'd left the convent at fifteen, when Eleanor was born. She'd left to help raise her. So went the myth of Alice the Martyr. Swatting Eleanor with her big-knuckled hand. "It hurts me more than it hurts you!" What a saint. Years later, Bea had revealed the truth. Alice had been asked to leave. Told to go home. They hadn't used the word "fail," but there was nothing more her teachers could do. Like being told to leave the hospital when all hope is gone. The family was unbalanced that way—very bright or very stupid. Convents could tactfully send people home. Public schools failed you. Eleanor had been sent to a public school. By the time she came along, the family was investing in mink, not education. Eleanor had failed, gone home, and learned to wash and iron, so she could go back to school. She'd learned not to get her clothes dirty. It was easy without a trike. Alice had bought herself a mink coat for her twentieth birthday. Their father had just died and she was in charge.

Her father's hands had been long and blue-veined with thin tapered fingers. Before the cancer, those hands had been warm on her plain brown head. She'd trailed him everywhere reaching for his hand.

Eleanor could hear the baby howling somewhere beyond the sarcophagus of her room. Hugh was right. She needed his mother, today of all days. Daphne Green's wedding day.

She got out of bed. It was only a year since poor Lloyd had been laid to rest and barely ten months since the loss of Lily. Winton might have waited a decent interval but Daphne pushed.

Myfanwy stood in the doorway.

"Janna's on the phone. She's asking for you, Mum. She must be desperate."

It was so obviously the truth, Eleanor didn't waste time taking offence. "That poor child." A rose bower had been constructed where Lily's green house had stood. A swimming pool, where four oaks had once endured. "I'll go talk to her. Run me a tub, there's a good girl."

At two o'clock they traipsed down to the Miles house where cars clogged the road and fought for parking. Winton had instructed the Morgans to leave their car at home, though Eleanor was in high heels that would never again fit properly. Would those instructions have come if they'd owned a new car instead of the Chev? What about parking the ancient green Hillman squarely in front of the bridal venue? As it was, Winton's and Daphne's dueling Cadillacs shone in the driveway. It hadn't taken Daphne long to trade in the once special Plymouth Fury. Odd they weren't in the garage, but then, maybe not.

In the months since the wedding had been announced, Daphne had taken over Lily's home, working her magic in each room. A fresh look, she liked to say. The major renovations would come later. It was the grounds that had really felt the sweep of this frenetic new broom. They had been Lily's domain, they threatened Daphne most. There was the infamous arch of roses, pink, of course, under which Daphne would marry her prince. If he remembered another wedding day when he'd awaited an exquisite bride, Winton gave nothing away. He scythed through the crowd, crushing hands and clasping shoulders, dodging tubs of hydrangea, pink of course, ducking under hanging baskets dripping in Babylonian splendor, kicking at Daphne's toy poodle, decked in two pink bows for the occasion.

They settled themselves on delicate white chairs lined up in Lily's backyard. At the end of each row was a nosegay of more pink roses with white tulle bows. Down the middle of the two banks of chairs, a white runner lay on the perfect green grass.

Music poured through the open French doors that led into the den. They'd rolled Lily's grand piano to where it could be heard. Eleanor caught a glimpse of an ample woman in pink punishing the instrument with Dean Martin songs. *When the moon hits your eye like a big pizza pie, that's amore.* Maybe later she would sing.

The Bakers sat four rows up. They'd postponed their trip to Banff for this event. George wouldn't offend Winton and Jean wouldn't dream of passing up the weeks of mileage this wedding would provide.

A genial minister was positioned in front of the rose bower. The pianist charged into *The Prince of Denmark March,* bringing Winton down the white carpet. Prince, my foot. He was Chaucer's rooster, vain and strutting. Chaunticleer—the most beautiful rooster of them all, strutting through this unhappy horde pilgrimming in hell. Once under the rose bower he grasped the minister's hand and wrung it athletically. Then came the girls, clad alike in pink. Donna looked scared, Denise smug, chest like a four master under full sail. Janna moved toward their father like she was walking the plank.

Yes, he was their father. "They are all Winton's girls now," Daphne had preened, calling with last minute instructions about parking rights. It was this announcement that had prompted Janna's phone call this morning. She didn't care about Winton being father to Donna and Denise, but she couldn't call that woman "Mother" on demand. Daphne had stepped over the line. Eleanor's advice had been simple. "If you never address her, dear, the problem is dealt with."

The dresses were chiffon and who would put pink on a girl of Janna's colouring? It was just the beginning of the new Miles collective. They were carrying baskets of pink rose petals. Janna was dumping fistfuls at a time on the white carpet. The girls assembled woodenly around the rose bower and the pianist paused. Would she play, *Here Comes the Bride?* No, she wouldn't. The pianist had obviously made the selections—Daphne knew little about music—and just as obviously had a sense of humour under her pink satin awning. Eleanor smiled at the muscular rendition of *Arrival of the Queen of Sheba.*

Acres of white chiffon had been called up for active duty for Daphne's wedding gown. It fell from the waist in cascading tiers. The bodice contented itself with the drape of a Grecian neckline. A wise choice considering the paucity it covered. Mercifully, Daphne had drawn the line at a veil. A tiny puffball danced in joy at her feet. Daphne loved that little thing. Dogs were loyal creatures.

The service was over and Daphne swept down the aisle with her prince. Her smile said I'm Mrs. Winton Miles and this is my home now. How long, Eleanor wondered, before Winton would yearn to shake off that grasping arm? She would always be hanging on. Still, she looked good, younger than her thirty-nine years. But then, she had the time to perfect that face.

Hugh had her elbow in his firm grip. She was being shoved toward the ebullient bride.

"*The loud laugh that speaks the vacant mind,*" he murmured. "It's time to greet the darling couple. Just smile, they'll do the talking."

"Eleanor, how *are* you . . . the baby . . . and today's your birthday. Forty! How *are* you all managing?"

"We're entering the Seventh Rapture, Daphne."

"Morgan, my man, let's do that Olympic Peninsula again soon. Good to see you, get yourself a drink."

Thus dismissed, the Morgans headed for the sidelines. A tall, gaunt man crossed Eleanor's path.

"Oh hello, Howard, ah Harold, yes it's Harold isn't it?"

"Henry."

"Of course," she said. "It's been years. Was it you or your brother who died?"

Hugh was like a border collie corralling her to the drinks tent. "Tap it lightly. Try to show a modicum of interest."

"I relate better to the dead. If Eleanor of Aquitaine were here, I'd be interested."

"That's irrational, old girl, even for you, and if Eleanor of Aquitaine were here, she'd beg Henry to lock her up again."

She looked around balefully and noticed something new to focus her annoyance on—the way Daphne appropriated other peoples' children as if they had a role to play in her life. It was Owen she was interested in now, as he made his way through the receiving line. But the Morgans were of one mind, and Owen, a model of detached politeness, avoided Daphne's embrace, nodded to Donna and Denise and went straight to Janna. He was careful to keep Myfanwy in tow, as he led Janna away. The three of them disappeared through the French doors. Minutes later they were back, Janna now dressed in one of her beautiful Seattle dresses. Crisp white cotton. The little minx was wearing white at a wedding. Obviously Isabelle Miles was keeping up Lily's tradition of outfitting Janna. Would she be providing dresses for three now? Not likely.

Jean Baker appeared, cigarette smoke funneling through flared nostrils.

"You'd think she'd have the sense to be embarrassed by a display like this, but no, her confidence accentuates her stupidity. Want a puff, Eleanor?"

"I'd better not. I'd be up to a pack a day in no time."

"Oh no," Jean moaned, as Nancy Tippet hove into sight.

"Hello, hello! Isn't this a glorious event? A sunny day and what a wonderful ceremony. They're such special people, perfect for each other, and of course, it's perfect for the girls. Three sisters. I couldn't be happier for them." Economy in communications had never been her strong suit.

"Yes, Daphne's got herself a cushy little wicket," Jean said, crushing her cigarette in a nest of rose petals.

Nancy frothed on. "It just makes me sure there is someone upstairs, looking out for us all."

"As far as I can tell there's a croupier upstairs and he's loaded the dice," Eleanor said. "Who looked out for Lily and Lloyd?"

Nancy looked confused. Croupier?

They advanced through the grounds towards the tables spread with cloths of remotest pink. Pale roses drooped from silver vases and white serviettes displayed the bridal couple's names in silver print. The food was lavish. Where were the children? They'd better take advantage because she wouldn't be cooking tonight. Not in this heat. Not on her birthday. She saw the girls in the corner of the grounds by Lily's favourite oak tree. They were talking to a tall man. She couldn't see his face. His back was turned, but he was holding their hands joking with them by the looks of things. They were running this way now.

"For heaven's sake, Myfanwy, slow down. It's a wedding, not a track meet. Who is that man?"

But her daughter was off to the dessert table, Janna right behind her. Atop more pink tablecloths, silver trays offered petite fours, piped with white icing—a W and a D entwined in carnal glory. Silver bowls held plump strawberries. Ladyfingers nestled between chocolate mounds topped with cherries, sweating in the heat like nipples in a tribal fertility dance. It was these that Myfanwy was beading on. In the centre of it all rose the wedding cake, a five-tiered extravaganza, poised and ready.

Jean, her mouth full, was gawking over her shoulder into the far corner of the backyard. "Good God, Eleanor. Why didn't you tell me about Winton's brother?"

"What? You mean he's here?" She'd never met Alistair. He hadn't come to Lily's funeral. There'd been explanations of illness. "How do you know it's him?"

"Look at him!"

Jean pushed her towards Lily's favourite oak with its twisted branch sweeping the ground. Sunlight filtered through leaves and there was Winton propped up against the grey trunk. Why had he changed his clothes? Why wasn't he holding forth amidst a captive audience? He watched her approach, and stepped forward to take her hand.

"Hello, Eleanor, I'm Alistair."

"Lily never told me. You're . . . you're twins!"

His hand was rough and warm.

"Identical," this other Winton replied, with a self-effacing laugh. "Identical except Winton's better looking, younger looking."

It was true. At close range there were years between them.

"I never knew Winton had a twin. That Alistair—that you were his twin. How did you know me?"

"Lily told me. I'd know you anywhere. And your daughter, she's just like you. Janna follows her everywhere. It wasn't hard, Eleanor."

"How can you stand this nightmare?"

"I needed to see Janna, especially during this nightmare." A slight smile. His teeth were crooked. Had Winton's been capped? Strange how imperfections made men attractive.

"Why didn't Lily tell me you were twins? Why weren't you at her funeral?" What was wrong with her? Why was she firing at this man?

"Lily didn't see us as twins. She only saw the differences. As for the funeral . . ." His eyes closed, his voice gave up.

The shock was wearing off. They stood in the arm of the oak tree and Alistair allowed her to stare. He did look older and infinitely more attractive. His auburn hair was greying and his navy blue eyes were lined and weather worn from years of ranching on the island. His smile had warmth. His face invited you in. Lily could never have explained how different identical twins could be. Lily had loved this man that she'd met on her wedding day. Looking up at the same face, the same eyes—those eyes—and realizing, too late. It would have been better if Lily had never seen into the depths of Alistair's eyes.

"You loved her, didn't you."

"I love her." He squinted as a slight wind ruffled the oak leaves and sunlight fell on his face. He was telling the truth. It was a relief to know Lily had had that.

"Lily adored you. When she allowed herself to think of you, I could always tell. Her eyes glowed, her mouth softened. There was a certain look she got and I knew she was with you."

"Thank you, Eleanor. Lily loved you too. Deeply. Do you know much she looked up to you? How much she admired your strength?"

Eleanor could feel that strength failing her now. "The loss has been unbearable at times. And you. How you must have suffered. I'm so sorry, Alistair. Lily's death just about killed me. What it was like for you . . . and Janna, I cannot imagine."

"Lily was my life. And now Janna is. I've tried to make it easier for her. May I phone you, Eleanor? From time to time. I need to know she's all right."

"Of course. Anytime. It would be a relief to talk. I'll give you the number."

"I know the number."

Someone was clinking a spoon against a glass. The darling couple was about to kiss.

"That tears it!"

Alistair smiled. "They're about to tuck into that Taj Mahal of a cake. This marriage will be its own reward."

Myfanwy and Janna materialized out of thin air. Alistair reached easily for Janna's hand and Eleanor felt relief for the child. Her uncle was here for her alone on this ghastly day. He reached out his other hand to Myfanwy. She took it and leaned against this man she'd just met, like he was Hugh.

It was too much—the heat, the drone of Winton's self-congratulatory speech, the look on Daphne's face. She gazed up at Winton with round rabbit eyes, hanging onto her man. Be careful what you wish for Daphne. Where was Hugh? Why wasn't he there for her to lean on?

"We're leaving, Myfanwy. I'm not feeling well and there's the baby. I need to get home to him.

Chapter Eighteen

Go, Little girl with the poor coarse hand!
I have my lesson, shall understand.

Robert Browning

The small, hot hands felt alien in his two callused ones. One lay softly in his palm like a wounded dove, the other was alive and tense, a different little animal altogether. The warm bodies closed in, making his suit even hotter. They were like the puppies in the barn, nursing off the ewe when she'd let them. Then the small hands were gone, flitting off to dance through the oak trees to the buffet tables, confident he'd be there when they came back.

He wasn't eager to mingle. His gaze settled on the new swimming pool. The oak grove had been desecrated with a concrete hole filled with violent turquoise water. Lilies floated everywhere. Lilies! It was incomprehensible. Winton—reminding the world of so many things with that one obscene image. But the world he now lived in didn't know. He'd created a new life, and of course, there'd never been any proof.

He had tried to imagine Winton's new wife and Janna's new stepsisters. Would there be any comfort for Janna from any of them? Was it better for her to live alone with Winton or live as a part of this ill begotten new family?

Alistair's greatest concern had been facing his brother. For such a long time he'd been afraid of Winton, afraid of being his twin. Where did one leave off and the other begin? And now here he was, standing in beauty of this oak grove, witnessing events he could not have imagined. The meeting had been calm. Winton had remained aloof but Alistair could see his driven nature had intensified over the years. Pity welled up when he wanted to hold onto fury. For so long he'd wanted to kill Winton, but now, in this place, seeing his brother's manic effort to pretend that this would be all right, he felt pity.

He turned his gaze to Daphne. "My brother-in-law," she'd gushed. She was vivacious and remained firmly at Winton's side. This was what he needed. Someone he could control and eventually ignore. But this woman would never be ignored. Her presence would grind like sand in an oyster. Winton was attracted to needy women. Lily had been needy once, but then she'd become strong. This one would become too needy with no pearl in the offing. More like a honeysuckle vine, cloying and sweet, clinging for life.

Had Lily been right? Had Winton suspected? And if he had, what had it been like for him, with all his pride? Was this new wife how he distracted himself from facing the truth about his first wife and his own brother?

Winton was vengeful but he'd been vulnerable once. From the time they were four, their father had seen into Winton's soul. Had he exposed Winton's weakness, or created it? Had Winton chosen to fulfill his father's fears? Or had that dark core always been there, suppurating quietly, then not so quietly, all these years? What toll had being a twin taken on Winton? A lifetime spent searching for ways to be unique.

Alistair turned his gaze to the "sisters". The tale was never more clearly told than through the offspring. Janna, as iridescent as her mother had been, was always there to remind Winton. And the other two—he turned away and leaned into the strength of the oak tree.

The afternoon heat intensified. It would have been cooler when Lily had lived here. More shade from oak trees now gone. How had she endured this kind of life? He longed to be gone but there was Janna. He straightened up, reluctant to leave the rough warmth of the bark. There she was, poking at the cake, so easy to spot. Her brilliant hair clouded around her head. A golden boy was making her laugh and the elfin child who'd so recently held his hand was now holding Janna's. Owen and Myfanwy. They were as Lily had described them. He shifted his gaze, sensing movement on his left. A distinctive looking woman was bearing down on him. Eleanor Morgan. The elfin girl grown up and grown angry. Her face wore a look of shock. He forgot, so rarely did he move in Winton's world, the effect his presence had on those who didn't know. And most didn't. Winton had always avoided any mention of his brother and for different reasons, so had Lily.

Eleanor was standing in front of him. Beneath her shock was a look of fatigue. In spite of this, her face had drama. Her nose was prominent and her cheekbones formed ridges along her angular face. Her green eyes were intelligent, with a deep groove between them, from frowning by the looks of things. Her brown hair was the only soft thing about her, yet without the tension, her mouth would be full and animated with the perfect teeth her son had inherited. He reached out his hand.

"Hello Eleanor. I'm Alistair."

Long after the Morgans' exit, he could see Eleanor's eyes. Lily had tried to explain Eleanor. He'd wanted to understand these people she'd been closest to. He could see the decency she'd been drawn to. The wit in Eleanor he hadn't seen, but it was there. A wit that would need a goat. Hugh would be hard pressed to hold his own. A man who looked like he did usually could, but Eleanor was different. Their prize was Owen. He looked like his father but the character building on that face would be hers. And Myfanwy, holding Janna's hand. She had her mother's firm, lineal look, the same cheekbones. Only her mouth was Hugh's.

He could feel the softness of those two small hands. From the life in Myfanwy's, Janna would find strength.

Chapter Nineteen

———— ·❧·❧· ————

Does the road wind up hill all the way?
Yes, to the very end.

Christina Rossetti

It was the final day of school and everything had changed. This time last year she and Janna had watched Mr. Green die and thought it was the worst that could happen. Janna's father and the New Mrs. Miles weren't back from their honeymoon yet but it was only a matter of time.

She patted Rossie's back. Her father said no one could burp him like she could. When he learned to crawl, the burps would come on their own. She walked him up and down the living room, pacing out the squares of straw matting as she went, first by one's, taking baby steps, then by two's, then by three's, taking giant steps.

First Rossie would have to learn to sit up. He'd have to balance on his seat before he could shift his weight to his knees and hands. She'd tried to get him to sit every day for two months. The book said babies could sit by six months. Rossie was eight months. Up and down she went, smelling his baby smell. Finally he burped and his small body settled. She leaned him back in her arms so she could see his face, lips like roses in clover, hair like dandelion fluff dancing around blue bell eyes. When he saw her face he smiled. She smiled back but her chest tightened. Why did everybody tell her not to worry? If she worried about Janna and Owen and her parents' fighting, why wouldn't she worry about Rossie? The question was why weren't they worried? Mrs. Miles, the Real Mrs. Miles, would have listened.

She shifted Rossie to her left shoulder and kept walking. The last time she'd seen Mrs. Miles, she was waving good-bye as they left for the Olympic Peninsula, and the time before that, she'd cut Maffy's hair. She could still feel those soft hands gentle on her head. The Real Mrs. Miles had taught her how to transplant an arbutus tree, telling her they were fragile, like children. The most fragile things could grow strong she'd said, if they learned to grow around things, like the arbutus. It gave them their special beauty. She'd pressed her hands over Maffy's when they patted in the earth and moss.

She'd lost track of the squares. She knelt in front of the couch and sat Rossie down on the middle cushion. She held him under his fat arms and slowly, slowly, took her hands away. Over he rolled. It didn't hurt. He liked it. It was his favourite game.

"Please, Rossie, learn to sit."

His mouth turned in, like it was being sucked down his throat. He didn't like it when she cried. He'd cry too. She held him to her tight chest. *Mr. Sandman, bring me a dream, make him the cutest that I've ever seen.*

Tomorrow. She'd think about tomorrow, the first day of summer vacation. She and Janna had plans. Thinking about that meant not counting the squares of straw matting all over again. They would start with the ceremonial burning of the flower girl's dress, an idea inspired by Maffy's father. At the end of every year at Twin Coves, her father would burn his shorts. Everyone gathered for this event like they did for the clam chowder and the campfire songs. Every year he took a pair of cut-offs to Twin Coves. They started out in life as jeans that he worked in all winter until the knees were gone. When summer came he cut them short and wore them every day, no matter what the weather, to remind everyone that it was summer. A white T-shirt and cut-off shorts, with a thin piece of rope to hold them up, was his Twin Coves uniform. If it got really cold he'd wear his old Indian sweater. By the time three weeks were up, the shorts needed to be burned, he said, because the ringer washer could only cope with so much. Her mother harrumpted herself into that coping category too. The burning of the shorts was a sad moment. There'd be no one gathered for the ceremonial burning of the flower girl's dress. And it wouldn't be sad.

Rossie was heavy. She'd sung him to sleep but she kept walking up and down, his fuzz of hair tickling her chin.

Grandmaf was coming through the door. Her father had picked her up to baby sit while her parents were at the Bakers' annual beginning of summer party. Grandmaf wasn't that tall but her arms were long enough to go around both Maffy and Rossie.

Once her parents had left, her father looking like Prince Philip, she and Grandmaf read to Rossie. They started with fairy tales so Rossie would have the basics, only Grandmaf changed the endings so Little Red didn't wait for the woodsman to save her. Turned out she could be pretty tough with an axe herself, and Goldilocks didn't run. She and Baby Bear became good friends. When Owen came in with his new space magazine, they went to Jupiter to count moons. Scientists had found another one orbiting around the granddaddy of the solar system and Owen was going into orbit himself.

When Rossie fell asleep, Grandmaf didn't put him in his crib right away, and the four of them sat on the couch while she told them stories of the days before Galileo, when people believed the sun revolved around the earth. Bosun lay on Maffy's feet. She took off her socks, rolled them into a ball and gave them to him. He loved to chew on socks.

She awoke at three o'clock, an hour earlier than usual. Only a few more hours and she could sneak off to get Janna. She was much easier to wake now. She wasn't sleeping as well now that she was waking up to the Wicked Stepmother and two stepsisters. Which was worse—coming home from school and finding them there, or waking up to it? At least in summer Janna could clear out before any of them woke up. Janna could get around people quite easily in that big house. Funny how the house hadn't seemed so big and important when The Real Mrs. Miles had lived there. It had smelled of flowers. The vinyl under her bare legs in the breakfast nook had been warm, the den, with its stash of comics, had been messy. The house had been smaller, friendlier then. Now you weren't allowed to leave comics lying around and the greenhouse was gone, the orchids thrown out. Her mother had had a bird over that. She didn't like orchids—Maffy was keeping score and there were more things she didn't like than did—but her mother would have found them decent homes.

She got up. She needed to get Janna out of the house early if they were going to smuggle out the flower girl's dress. She filled a bowl with chokies. Too early for the raspberry patch, maybe next week, if it stayed sunny. She poured the last of the milk on her cereal and thought about putting the empty bottle in the carrier for the milkman. She put it back in the fridge instead. She wouldn't be around to hear her mother sigh. She had the first day of summer ahead of her. She ate standing over the sink, ran water into the bowl and put it back in the cupboard, wet. She wouldn't be there when her mother woke up and reached for it.

She grabbed her lunch kit that Grandmaf had packed last night and headed for the carport. She packed it in the saddlebag behind the seat. The kickstand was stuck. She was stabbing at it with the heel of her running shoe when she heard the gravel crunch behind her. It was five o'clock. Who could be up? She turned to see her father stepping off the last rung of the ladder that was propped against the boat which sat high in its scaffolding in the driveway. He didn't look like Prince Philip this morning. His hair was matted on his forehead and he'd slept in his clothes. He stumbled toward her, carrying a bottle, with very little in it. He looked up and managed a smile, like he always did.

"H'lo, Nuffer, setting sail for the day? Cast off, Little One, I'll batten down the home hatches." His mouth smiled again but suddenly he tripped. He went down, tucking the bottle under one arm, reaching out with the other. One arm wasn't enough. Why hadn't he just dropped the stupid bottle? Why had he let himself fall on his face in the gravel? She heard her bike crash behind her. The kickstand had unstuck.

"Daddy, get up." She kept her voice low. No one could wake up and see this.

He lifted his head, still smiling, always smiling at her. There was blood on his left cheek but it didn't look too bad. It was his left hand that was really bleeding. Would this hurt as much as her burn had? Would it leave a scar?

"S'all right, Nuffer, you head off. You're rigged and ready." He didn't seem to wonder where she was going so early, just knew she needed to go. His blue eyes looked confused, like he didn't know for sure where he was or why he was bleeding on his best grey slacks. But his mouth was still smiling, even with blood trickling down it. "Go on, the wind is good."

He was standing now, steadier, like the fall had woken him up. If she left, would he wake up Owen? Rossie slept soundly but Owen didn't. If she left would her father feel as sad as he looked? He walked slowly toward the carport. Maybe he'd lie down in the car for a while but he was bleeding. She followed him to the back door which wasn't locked. She'd left it unlocked when she'd left a few minutes ago. Good. The back sink was empty. Good. It must have hurt a lot when he held his hand under the tap but he didn't make a sound. She found an old brown towel under the sink that wouldn't show the blood. She hid the bottle under the sink, with all the other ragged old towels, grateful there were cupboards like this that could hide things for ages. The ironing cupboard in the kitchen had clothes that might never see daylight again, all jumbled together in one big ball. The Gordian knot, her father called it. The pencil drawer by the phone in Janna's house actually had pencils in it, all the same length, all sharpened, and all headed in the same direction. The bleeding had stopped and she wet another rag for his face.

They went into the kitchen where he settled in at the table. She put the kettle on and got out her father's mug. The morning called for two tablespoons of tea in the bottom of the old brown teapot. She decided to take the empty milk bottle out of the fridge after all. The milkman wouldn't be there till Monday but there was still one full quart. She opened it and poured a large amount into the mug. The kettle was screaming. She poured the water and left the tea to steep under Grandmaf's knitted tea cozy. Her father's head was down and he was stuffing the wet rag into his eyes.

"Daddy?"

He made a muffled sound. She poured his tea and added extra sugar.

"Here's your tea. It's milky and sweet, the way you like it."

He raised his head. His eyes were watery blue like the ocean when the north easterly blew. Little waves were running down his cheeks. The salt would sting. Was this how Ross felt when she cried? If she went to the Milky Way would he come with her? If she dove in through the seaweed, under the raft, would he follow?

"Myfanwy, Little One. It's the first day of your summer holiday. Go and play while you can. Just give Brown Betty a fair wind, then off you go."

She pushed the teapot in his direction. If only he wouldn't smile like that.

She got her bike upright and took the lunch out of the saddlebag. She stuffed the brown towel in instead. She would burn it with the pink dress. Bosun had slipped out the back door with her this time. He didn't like anyone going off without him but they always did. She felt the little fox and knew she wasn't hungry anymore. The sandwich made Bosun feel better. He licked her face, his slobbery tongue dragging all the way from her chin to her right ear. She didn't look at his brown eyes. Pedaling down the gravel driveway, she heard him running alongside, panting with excitement, but at the end he stopped. He knew not to go farther. Without looking back, she knew he was under the oak tree at the end of the driveway, lying in wait to welcome her back.

Chapter Twenty

—⟨⟩⟨⟩—

Ring out the old, ring in the new.
Ring happy bells, across the snow:
The year is going, let him go;
Ring out the false, ring in the true.

Alfred, Lord Tennyson

1961

"For God's sake! The dog has eaten the shrimp dip. We're not the Royal Family, where the corgi's eat shrimp!"

"The old girl's in top form," her father whispered. "High dudgeon is her finest hour."

The front door banged. Bosun was banished.

She and her father were hunkered down in the relative safety of the living room doing the final organizing of the party games. The Morgans' New Year's Eve party was an established inevitability and the pressure was on to outdo last year's. The odds were good. No one was expected to stay sober and no one was more entertaining than her father. A drinking man he called himself. On New Years, they were all drinking men and the odd drinking woman. Her mother didn't mind Mrs. Baker getting soused.

Along with Charades her father had come up with a word game cued by props. He set a whole-wheat roll, the only kind her mother would buy, on the coffee table beside two glasses of punch. The genius who guessed "roll with the punches," got a 1962 calendar of Victoria courtesy of The Great White Developer whose picture just happened to be on it. Her father had nine other phrases lined up so theoretically each couple could go home with a calendar whether they wanted to look at Mr. Miles' face every day for the next three hundred and sixty-five or not. But of course, not every couple would win one. You had to be smart and quick. There were few who could compete with Mrs. Baker. Come the end of the night, she'd be begging people to take those calendars off her hands. "You can live without friends but not without neighbours," her father always said, and when Mr. Miles offered ten calendars you took them.

Neighbourhoods included people you couldn't stand but no one was left out on New Years Eve. Hence, the Miles. The real reason they were coming was Janna. Bad as he was, Mr. Miles was her father.

Janna was staying the night and they'd get paid for cleaning up after the party. Since the advent of The New Mrs. Miles and her retinue, Janna didn't mind staying once in a while. And sometimes Maffy stayed at the Miles'. Which was worse—the uncertainty of her house or the predictability of Janna's? The possibility of volatility or the absolute assurance of none? Maybe it was all in what you got used to and eventually even the craziest place seemed normal if that was all you knew.

When the props were organized they loaded them onto trays and moved them into the small, unfinished room off her parents' bedroom. There was a lot of noise coming from the kitchen, fall out from the shrimp dip.

"Time to improvise," her father said, whistling into the kitchen to invent another dip just as good as the shrimp one he'd thrown together an hour ago. How about a dog food dip? A little Miracle Whip, a few liver snaps, and voila, a tasty melange.

She opened the front door and Bosun slipped in. He was like a sea otter with drops of water sliding off his sleek black head. His brown eyes were grateful as he crept into the warmth. Everyone loved coming into this warmth. They flocked here every New Year's.

In summer, it could only be a summer house, sun blinding through sheets of glass, doors thrown open to the wilderness, swirling chintz mingling with the wildflowers. The straw on the floor was woodsy, rustling like dry moss.

Now, it could only be a winter house. Now when the fire roared warming the marble hearth, the straw cradled like in the manger and the wool drapes cocooned. The lamps made pools of light and the cedar walls were like the insides of a strong, sheltering tree.

"Myfanwy, what are you mooning at? We've got twenty people coming. I told you if Janna is coming you've got to pull your weight. It was you who let the dog back in, wasn't it."

"It's sleeting out." If she were pulling the load of a team of Clydesdales would it be enough?

"He's a dog, for heaven's sake. A dog who's eaten the shrimp dip."

"Relax, old girl, I've whipped up a peach of a dip." Her father offered no elaboration as to what had gone into the peach of a dip. He was at his best before a party, her mother at her worst. He'd nudge her along and she'd somehow know to keep the lid on no matter how loosely. The weight of twenty guests kept them in line. And when the front door, ringed in fir boughs and coloured lights, swung open at eight o'clock, what a shining couple they were. They clung to New Year's Eve. In the years since Rossie's birth, her mother especially was determined to carry on as if things were normal.

Maffy and Janna hung around in the kitchen, listening to the radio. KJR Seattle was counting down the top one hundred hits of the decade. The Crew-Cuts were *Sh-Boom Sh-Boom, Ya da da da da da da da-ing,* in combat with her father's *St Louis Blues,* rattling off the piano keys in the living room. He was best at the blues until he moved into boogie woogie. Then he was best at that. When the evening got older he'd take a sentimental journey, and really, nothing could top that. In between times, the hifi blasted out the big bands. Everyone liked it here. Old Mrs. Milburn cried into her gin when her father played *La Vie En Rose.*

They'd convinced Denise that Owen wouldn't be at the party and she'd bought it. It was just too bad they had to plan around Denise now. It was over two years since they'd all become "One Big Happy Family," as The New Mrs. Miles liked to say. She was the kind of ninny who said things like that. There was nothing happy about The New Miles Family. Tolstoy was deluded—there were no happy families. Not even the royal family. Princess Margaret and Anthony Armstrong-Jones were doomed, according to her mother. "He's a Welshman." Nothing more need be said.

She could hear The New Mrs. Miles holding forth in the living room. At any given time the odds of that were good. The Real Mrs. Miles had said very little but Maffy tried to remember it all. The New Mrs. Miles's laugh was like a high-pitched sonar device shaking the walls of the cocoon.

Janna looked like Eeyore, drooping with sadness. New Years could be as bad as Christmas. Since the Miles had become one big happy family ten months after Janna's mother had died, Janna wasn't even supposed to remember her mother, as if it would hurt The New Mrs. Miles's feelings.

Maffy's mother came flying into the kitchen. Good. They needed a job, any job to get them going before Janna went further downhill. Her mother looked regal in her emerald green dress. She was slim again and her hair swept back from her forehead in soft waves that broke shore on the nape of her neck. When her face was thin her nose looked even longer and her eyes were very green in that dress. She had high heels dyed to match. Most mothers wore black patent leather shoes with everything. Her face was flushed and she looked happy. The shrimp dip episode had blown over and if people were eating dog food, they didn't know it.

"Girls, we need to get the rice on, it needs gentle heat for one hour, the curry too. Turn that radio down."

WHAT A DARN GOOD LIFE, WHEN YOU'VE GOT A WIFE LIKE—

"I said down!"

Janna was laughing, at last.

"The Bakers have brought vats of Major Grey's Chutney, bless their hearts." Her father was coming through the door, waving two bottles in the air. They already had vats of Major Grey's chutney ready to go but it felt good when friends knew you well enough to bring exactly what you wanted. The Miles had brought pastel-coloured mints that tasted like toothpaste. The New Mrs. Miles would never make curried lamb with coconut and raisins and pineapple. She would serve roast beef with a green salad. Green salad meant lime Jell-O with miniature marshmallows. Jell-O. One of the Great Food Disappointments. The colours looked so good.

Her parents whirled out again, brimming with the goodwill of a stiff drink. They were like the little girl with the little curl right in the middle of her forehead. Tonight they were very, very good. *Sweet, sweet, the memories you gave to me.*

The rice came to a boil and Maffy turned it to simmer. She turned the curry to low. They had an hour. Dean Martin's voice said he'd had a few too.

"Let's make a tour with the eggnog and see who's the drunkest," Maffy said.

"Okay, but first let's see what Owen's up to. I want to see my stepmother's face when she sees he's here. She'll tell Denise, for sure."

"You feeling up to that?"

"She'll behave in a crowd. Her doting stepmother number. Nobody can gush like she can."

"She makes Old Faithful pale."

"What?"

"Nothing. Let's go get Owen." She knocked three times on his door.

"Who is it?" He sounded preoccupied, probably discovering anti-matter or the Andromeda Spiral. Light reading on this festive occasion.

"C'mon Owen, we're going to take a tour of the zoo. The fauna are in fine form." She heard his chair scrape on the concrete floor. He'd moved into the unfinished room next to the back door. Rossie had been in this room first. There were only three finished bedrooms. They were only supposed to have needed three. When Rossie had turned two and her father still hadn't laid the tile on the floor, Owen had switched rooms with him. Owen wanted this room anyway, he'd said. Now Rossie was in a room with green linoleum tile just like hers. The door opened. He'd made the room look great. He'd painted the floor and the walls dark blue and had mapped in the constellations with careful dots of yellow. He kept two lamps on instead of the overhead light, and like the living room, his room glowed. It was like stepping into outer space.

"C'mon, you don't want to miss New Years."

"The wild life is gearing up, is it?" He grabbed her lightly around her waist and started tickling. Then he beamed his megawatt smile on Janna. "Lead the way, Great White Huntress."

The noise in the house was rising. Luckily, Rossie slept through anything. How long could she go without thinking about him? Tommy Dorsey's trombone was wa-wa-ing hot and exotic—*Night and Day, You Are The One*—turning these tired parents sexy and sophisticated, like people in TV ads watched with envy through glimmering yellow windows. Mrs. Baker spotted them instantly and made her way over. She liked talking to them. You could tell when an adult was just acting. After five seconds their gazes wandered over your head to something—anything—better right behind you.

"Come to watch the oldsters make fools of themselves? If I were you, I'd avoid that old blowhard, George Baker. He's about to tell his famous joke about the farmer with three daughters." No wonder Mrs. Baker was her mother's best friend. You could stop worrying for a while when someone like this liked your mother.

Owen was smiling and shaking hands with their parents' friends. It was hard not to like Owen. It was in the way he acted as if being smart wasn't the most important thing. She felt a claw digging into her waist and looked down at pointed red fingernails. The New Mrs. Miles. The talons on the other hand were wrapped around Janna's waist. The New Mrs. Miles liked to put herself in the middle of things.

"How are the two most beautiful girls at the party?"

We're the only girls and I'm not beautiful. Maffy ran her tongue over her front teeth, straight now, but still, she was nowhere near beautiful.

"How Donna and Denise would have loved to be here tonight." She directed her next remark to Owen. "After all, we're one big family and families stick together." Wrong again, Mrs. Miles, Maffy thought, but what a big knife you have, all the better to slide between the ribs.

"In tribal societies, perhaps, but not in the Uplands in the early sixties," Owen intoned, looking thoughtful.

"Why, Owen—what an interesting person you are." The woman could say something innocent and make it come out pretty biting. "Full of very unique ideas." Something was either unique or it wasn't, Mrs. Miles.

"Not unique, Mrs. Miles, but perhaps ideas unfamiliar to you. Maffo, you need to check the curry. You coming, Janna?" He pulled them firmly in his direction, leaving The New Mrs. Miles staggering. If they really were One Big Happy Family how come Janna's father had no interest in her? What about that, Mrs. Miles?

Maffy remembered that moment, years ago on the Olympic Peninsula, when Mr. Miles had hoisted Janna over his head and sat her on his shoulders so she could try to reach the top of those blue green trees. In that moment, Janna's face had had the desperate look she got when she tried to pretend something was good. Which was worse—to have attention from a father like Mr. Miles or to be ignored?

The dinner was good and eating was easy on a night like this. When midnight was getting close her father warmed up his bagpipes and handed out the song sheets.

"Fall in!" he called.

When everyone had jostled around and formed a sloppy column, he marched them around the house, piping in the New Year with *Scotland the Brave*. Mrs. Milburn was crying again. *Hark! Now the night is falling, Hear hear the pipes are calling.*

On the stroke of twelve they gathered in a circle. With arms reaching out to hold the hand of the person one away, they wove themselves together. *Should old acquaintance be forgot, and never brought to mind . . .* They swayed back and forth and when Mrs. Milburn went the wrong way they crashed into each other, but still it felt good, all of them together, swaying and banging and singing, woven together in an all-is-forgiven oneness, and in that moment of happiness, the house was safe and they were as safe with each other as they'd have been alone. Her father's voice led them, eyes twinkling with tears, smile shining like a star. *We'll drink a cup of kindness yet, for auld lang syne.*

Chapter Twenty-one

---❖·❖---

Which way does the wind come? What way does he go?
He rides over the water, and over the snow.

William Wordsworth

1962

The New Year's party was over. The guests had all gone home.
The only sound now was Janna's breathing. As quiet as Janna's
breath was, she could always hear it. She got up silently and went
into the empty living room. The New Year was four hours old. At
four in the morning in winter, there were no shrouded shapes. It
was inky black.

This was the year Rossie would turn four and they'd send
him away. The English pram, boy oh boy, had the aunts got their
money out of that. He couldn't walk. He couldn't do anything
and they were going to send him away. The lump in her throat
tightened. It wasn't like the fox that made her stomach dance.
The lump sat in her throat like a rock. Rossie couldn't do
anything except grow and he'd get too big to carry, too big for
the pram.

She'd been sitting in the living room for an hour, according
to her glowing Timcx. It was still as black as India Ink. The New

Year was moving at the pace of a turtle. If the year took forever, it wouldn't be long enough. By the end of it, Rossie would be gone. Oh, they'd bring him home for Twin Coves, they said, but how could they? How could they bring him back three weeks a year, then send him away again? Which was worse, sending him away once, or sending him away over and over? When her parents were bad they were horrid.

Every day after school, she walked him, with Bosun running beside the buggy. Rossie loved Bosun. He couldn't talk, but a sound came. "A-a-a-a-a." His left arm flapped on the dog's soft head. She let Bosun jump up, front paws resting on the pram, so he could reach Rossie's face with his purple tongue.

Women looked out their windows, looked up from their *Ladies Home Journal*. Gracious Uplands women. That poor child. Poor retarded boy with his scrawny sister. Why does she let that filthy dog all over him? Don't linger, dearie, just keep walking. The New Mrs. Miles pulled her drapes. Always a good idea, Mrs. Miles. Aren't you glad we're not one big happy family—the kind that takes care of each other even if one's not quite right? A unique idea, Mrs. Miles. Go back to your *Canadian Homemaker's* magazine. Canadian Homewrecker.

Maffy read the dictionary. She loved words, the way they sounded in her mind, the lush feel of them on her tongue. A good word could fill you up with its perfection. Being able to say things that had once been beyond words made those things easier somehow. Being able to write things. Rossie was replete with poignancy. The New Mrs. Miles was repugnant in her perniciousness.

The houses of the Uplands were big. The one at the bottom of Lansdowne hill, where the Lieutenant Governor lived, took up half a block. Over by Willows School, where Joanne lived, there were ten houses to a block. Here it was more private, fewer women leering out their windows.

Janna had joined the tumbling club on Tuesdays and Thursdays after school. Even though Janna was pretty good, Maffy knew she was better. Janna's body was long and graceful, but Maffy could tuck tighter than anyone, and no one could climb the ropes hanging like nooses from the gym ceiling faster than she could. She had reached the foot of Lansdowne Road and was walking along Beach Drive now, past the Chinese house, where the two silent Wong sisters lived their secluded life. Next to it was the Bakers'. These houses were directly on the water, their back front yards sloping down to the beach. Gargantuan boulevard trees shielded everything within. She heard a horn behind her. It was Mrs. Baker in her new Thunderbird with the spare tire in the continental kit.

"Are you kids cold?"

"Not really."

"Come in for hot chocolate."

"No, it's okay."

"Myfanwy, your little brother's cold. Besides, I have a special mug I'd like him to try."

He could hold it in his right hand, if she held his flailing left hand to the side. The cup had a lid on it, and Mrs. Baker showed him how to drink from the little spout, talking to him as if he could understand. Then she turned to Maffy as if she were a grown up.

"So Janna's at the tumbling club. Would you like to join too? Could I take Ross for a walk on Tuesdays and Thursdays?"

"No . . . my mother . . . Thank you, but she doesn't like to have Rossie with other people, much." Mrs. Baker looked calm. You could say things to her and she didn't start blethering about how they weren't true.

*

She and Rossie were the only ones left in the living room, but still, her father had jollied up the fire. Ed Sullivan's star-studded line-up was over, and luckily, Topo Gigio hadn't put in an appearance. She should be finishing her assignment on Cheop's pyramid. It was due tomorrow, but she wouldn't be in school tomorrow. Rossie was restless, his left hand beating against his neck like a moth at a flame. She reached for the book her father used to read.

"How about *Old Mother West Wind, and the Merry Little Breezes?* The little breezes have no bodies to tie them down. They just blow and tumble things around. You can blow too, Rossie. Go like this." She blew gently on his forehead. He looked puzzled.

She did it again on his cheek. "Wind, Rossie. We can't see it but we can feel it." She closed the book and showed him the cover. "This is what the wind looks like." Leaves swirled under a cloud with an O shaped mouth. She pointed to the word "Wind" in the title and blew. She was sighing, like her mother, who had recently introduced a neighing tone, like an old horse shuddering its withers. "Let's forget the Merry Little Breezes." She set Rossie down on the couch and went and got another Burgess Bedtime Book. *Grandfather Frog*, that crabby old chug-a-rummer.

*

Rain pinged on the windshield. The car bounced over the gangplank at the ferry terminal in Tsawwassen, just south of Vancouver, only they weren't going to Vancouver. They were going to New Westminster—the Royal City. It had once been the capital of British Columbia, until that honour had gone to Victoria. Her father was keeping up a steady stream of conversation and conviviality. He'd kept it up since the dining room on the Princess Elaine, that "Old Grandam of the Sea."

"Ships are like women," he'd pointed out. "And like the age of a woman, the age of a ship is not something usually discussed." There were exceptions, he went on. "When she is very young, she does not mind people noticing and commenting, and if she has reached advanced years, with a distinguished life behind her, she can be proud to have her birth year recalled with respect." The ancient, rattling ferry had reached the number of years, he said, when it was permissible to discuss her age. He was trying to distract her, trying to make it easier.

She stared out at grey fields, like swamps now. Some were full-fledged lakes of muddy water. This was the delta, her father's voice was saying, the flat, fertile flood plain of the Fraser River. Those were potato fields. Now they were following the road along the river where it would soon turn into a huge bridge, and once over that they'd be in the Royal City. The houses along the river were tiny and sad looking, but not as sad as the trailers. Could anything be more pathetic than Christmas lights on a trailer? As if outlining the windows of a putty-coloured metal box would make it less depressing. The road wound on, and finally they were over the steel bridge and at their destination. They sat in the car for what seemed like a long time, contemplating the tall grey stone building. The Woodvale School for the Retarded.

Inside everything was okay enough in separate bits. When you put the bits together, it was not okay. The pastel green walls might be okay if the windows had soft curtains. The beige venetian blinds might be okay if the walls were knotty wood. The fireplace in the big playroom, where all the little retarded kids were gathered, would be okay if it had a fire in it, instead of a blue plastic tub filled with towels. Was someone likely to throw up or wet the floor? Very likely, from the looks of the poor little kids. Some were sitting on the floor banging soft toys on the serviceable brown linoleum, or on their noggins. Some were walking around, getting as close to the visitors as they dared. Some had fat stubby fingers. Some had eyes that were slanted and thick tongues that lolled in open mouths. Maffy, her father and the children eddied around for about ten minutes, while a mossy-lipped nurse looked on grimly. She was wearing a light blue uniform and her hair was scrapped back into a bun pulled so tight, her eyes had an amphibian quality. Chug-a-rum. There would be no Burgess bedtimes with this old toad.

Eventually, her father and the nurse went into her office to talk. Without Mossy-lip hanging over her in that annoying shape-up-and-be-a-good-soldier way, Maffy felt free to take it all in. She tried not to hate the smell of the little kids. The problem with this place was it wasn't bad enough. It was just okay enough not to be able to say, kindly of course, that this simply wouldn't do. She could hear a soft thudding. She hunched down beside a child banging a blue velveteen rabbit up and down. She made a note never to read that book to Rossie. Had this little thing ever heard a story? She looked into the full moon face under its shelf of mud-brown hair. The face had a strange sweetness that made Maffy smile.

"Hello, little one." There didn't seem much point in saying more. But she stayed in a squat, waiting for an answering smile. Nothing. The banging went on. She gently took the rabbit out of the small, fat hands and smiled her biggest smile. The full moon clouded over. Couldn't the child see her, barely twelve inches away? Was she blind?

Maffy danced the rabbit slowly across the floor. The little girl watched it go. Maffy brought it slowly up to her face and smiled again. The child finally met her gaze. She wasn't blind. But there was no recognition in her dull blue eyes. Only the sweetness that no longer made Maffy smile. She could feel the rock in her throat. Just a pebble, really, but it was there.

She put the rabbit back in the starfish hand and watched it automatically go up and down again. She looked into other faces. One smiled, some looked away. Were they shy, or scared? She went over to the smiley one, a little blond boy, only his hair wasn't a shiny gold halo, it was a dull yellow. She got down again and smiled widely, then frowned. She stood up, out of his line of vision. He smiled on with a vacancy that left her cold. She wanted to shake some life into the little body that hung off his shoulders like a slack balloon. Rossie was retarded, but he wasn't like these kids. If Rossie was retarded, why wasn't he like these kids?

Her eye caught a glint of metal. A wheelchair was sitting off by itself with a child strapped in it. That appeared to be a good thing, because the little thing writhed like it was inhabited by a cruel snake. Its crop of hair, the colour of an underdone pork chop, gave no clue to its sex. A girl? The sweater had a pink bunny on it. A girl.

"Her name is Bonnie."

Maffy jumped. The nurse had reappeared and her voice was cross, as if Bonnie was an irritating name.

"Hi Bonnie." Maffy spoke quietly, anxious not to get too wordy, in case it provoked a long talk with the bug-eyed nurse. "How are you?" she asked inanely. It was pretty obvious how Bonnie was.

"She can't talk. She can't walk either," the nurse added needlessly, more blame in her voice.

"Why does she move like that?"

"Cerebral palsy, of course. A more severe case." The nurse spun away as the smell of pee wafted toward them.

Rossie had celebral palsy. His left arm and leg moved like Bonnie's whole body did, only not nearly as bad. Imagine him entering this world of smells—clorox, urine, the sickening sweetness of kool aid at lunch. It would be mushy food. Why not let the little blighters choke? Let them go out with more than tapioca on their lips. Fish egg pudding. It was not possible to imagine Rossie, who looked like a Christmas card angel, in this world of smells.

Her father was approaching briskly, taking her hand and saying they'd be off. He looked like he'd been shot at. She felt embarrassed when he held her hand, but pulling away would feel worse. He only did it when he really needed to. He turned to Bug-eyes, giving Maffy just enough time to look at Bonnie.

"Good bye, Bonnie."

The little wraith raised her shaking right arm in a salute. Her eyes looked out intently from her lopsided face.

They were through the door in a few strides. Her father had long legs and he wasn't fooling around, but it wasn't going to be quite that easy, as if any of it had been. They were being led into a different wing, for older boys, Nursey stated flatly. She called herself a nurse, but was she? Or was she just a nasty woman enjoying her petty moment of power? There weren't any Florence Nightingale moments. They followed obediently because it seemed the only route to eventual escape.

"This is the adolescent wing. Of course, by adolescence, they are housed in separate quarters—male and female."

Warehoused, like cattle.

"Yes, of course," her father said, his voice faltering, his grip on her hand convulsing.

"This is where your son will be, when he's older, in a room similar to this." She veered sharply to the right—all her moves were sharp—and flung open a huge pastel blue door, as if presenting a palace that Rossie would someday be lucky enough to inhabit. The sight inside caused the nurse to falter, but only for a second. Six narrow beds were lined up like coffins ready for burial at sea. On one lay a large boy only partially covered by a thin grey blanket. Was he sick? He was moaning in a large way while rubbing his stomach, only lower. Now he was gasping.

"Is he all right? We can't leave him," Maffy said.

But they were leaving him.

"Although retarded, they have natural urges, and are, of course, kept strictly separate from females." The mechanical voice perked up, clearly pleased with the shock value of her charges. This is the world of the retarded, people. Shape up or ship out.

They were moving faster now. Her father dropped her hand and pushed her ahead of him. She saw the glass door at the end of the long corridor and made for it at a trot. She heard her father making vague, obligatory remarks. Thank you for an afternoon in hell, good madam. What fine work you are doing. The padlock on the glass door brought her to a halt. Beyond it, out of reach, was the main door. By the time they caught up with her—the nurse rattling a hundred keys in a self-important way—her father's good-byes were sounding final. At last they were out the doors, sucking in fresh air, unable to speak.

Chapter Twenty-two

And winter's dregs made desolate
The weakening eye of day.

Thomas Hardy

February was pitiless. Just when the early rhododendrons and even some camellias, gulled by warmth, were readying to send forth recruits, the snow hit. The crocus would survive. They grew like weeds in Victoria, but the rhodo buds were brown and wrinkled. Like walnuts. So went his mother's litany. He looked up Lansdowne hill, slick as a bobsled run. What did temperate Victorians know about navigating on ice? Not enough to keep off it. Owen kept a sharp eye out for cars coming down the street sideways.

He ran every day. Two weeks ago, on his sixteenth birthday, he'd run sixteen miles, doing a full circuit around U.Vic. He hadn't planned it, he'd just run until the thinking had stopped and he could drop on his bed and stare at the universe without a thought except going there. Maffo had given him an odometer for his birthday, which was how he knew how far he'd run. That was just like her. She needed to keep track of things. He'd watched her, head down, lips moving, counting squares of straw matting. He'd walked in on her in the bathroom once. She'd have been less embarrassed if she'd been on the throne.

Toothbrush in her mouth, she was pacing out the bathroom tiles. He'd seen her walking Ross in the buggy, eyes in the sidewalk. *Step on a crack, break your mother's back. Step on a line, break your mother's spine.* He strapped the odometer to his wrist in case she saw him, but he didn't set it. The number of miles didn't matter, it was the number of his thoughts.

People were getting killed going over the Berlin wall six months after the Russians had built it. God willing, it was Khrushchhev's last erection. The poster of Dag Hammarskjod, ordered through the *New York Times*, had arrived, six months after Hammarskjod's plane had gone down over the Congo. Maff was counting more since her trip to Woodvale. Counting more and eating less, unless you considered the cupcakes she bought at Woolworths bakery, when she and Janna went shopping downtown

It was Saturday. He usually ran downtown to Government Street, where he bought the weekend edition of the *Seattle Post Intelligencer.* It was pretty good at keeping up with the American space program. Then he'd take the bus home. Today, because of February's moods, he had to take it both ways. Standing at the bus stop in the freezing cold, he hadn't been surprised to hear Denise Green's voice taking a bite out of the quiet. It was amazing the number of times he ran into Denise. For some unknown reason, she was waiting at the bus stop, too.

"Hi, Owen. I got my learner's license last week. I passed the written test on my first try, and as soon as the ice melts, I'm going to take the car out. When are you getting yours? If your parents don't have time you could learn with me in the Cadillac. Then you wouldn't have to run everywhere. Or ride the peasant wagon like a little kid."

Denise started out coyly, but when she sensed how excited he was to see her, she turned nasty. She'd sat at the feet of the best.

"Tell you what," he said. "You learn to drive and get your stepfather to buy you your own Caddie, and if it's black, with decent emission control, then you can teach me yourself. When you're eighteen."

That confused her. Was it an overture? Too bad he never ran into Janna. But she was always with Maff, and he was always the big brother. Janna would be fourteen soon. She was going to be tall, like her father, but in every other way she was getting more and more like her mother.

He opened the back door carefully. His father had drilled the hole for the doorknob too close to the edge of the door so when you turned it you had to grip with half your hand like a twisted arthritic. Maff had learned the hard way, taking the whole knob in her hand and skinning her knuckles. She never made a sound. You had to watch her eyes.

He slid into his universe before anyone knew he was home. Things had settled down since the January wars brought on by the Woodvale trip. He should have gone. Maff was the one with courage. He sat down at his desk, which consisted of a large piece of plywood hinged to the wall and held up with a wooden dowel, the bedroom version of the ironing board in the kitchen. He opened the Seattle paper and did his usual scan. President Kennedy had established an overseas service called the Peace Corps. On the same page was an article on the proposal to begin testing nuclear armaments above ground in Arizona, beginning this April. The copyeditor should watch his layout.

He turned the page. On February fifth, just two days away, there would be a total eclipse of the sun way out in the Pacific. This event would be accompanied by a rare grouping (last one in 1821) of Mercury, Venus, Mars, Jupiter, Saturn and Earth. The next time it would happen would be 2002. Would anyone survive till 2002? If he did, he'd be fifty-six. A space probe would visit Venus in December. Ten months from now. On February twentieth, the first man would go up in space, orbiting the earth three times. Eighty-one thousand miles in four hours and fifty-six minutes.

The next Saturday Owen was downtown by eleven in the morning. The weather had warmed up, the rhodos were trying again, and people were mobbing the streets. He wasn't taking any chances on the paper being sold out. He'd watched television all week, but a Venus probe was too obscure for the nightly news. He picked up the Seattle paper and a copy of *Science Digest*, with an article on John Glenn, then caught the bus for home.

Four more stops and he'd be there. He whistled quietly, and two old Victorian prunes looked at him in irritation. He raised the volume fractionally and gazed out the window. Three more stops. A small figure appeared along the road. Maffo. She was pushing Ross in the pram. For a second, he saw them as others did—Maff too small and Ross too big, even for a buggy that size. The absurdity of it came to him, just as it came to the two boys who had materialized right behind Maff. The bus thundered by. Two stops. Owen looked back as one boy picked up something and arched his arm back to throw. Owen hurried to the front of the bus.

"Could you stop—my sister—I need to get off."

The driver turned a bored face to Owen while the prunes tisked furiously.

"Wait for the stop, young man."

"Young hooligan," the more wrinkled prune said.

Finally the bus stopped Owen shot off and down the street. There had been two of them and at least two minutes had passed. Four minutes worth of bullying. He saw her eyes first—overflowing pools of green. She was trying not to cry but as she got closer to him, pram bouncing ahead of her like something out of a ghoulish cartoon, she let out a howl in spite of herself. Then he heard Ross's frightened puppy yelp as an acorn missile caught him on the face. His outing, his treat, ruined.

"Reeetard!"

Owen saw a fat boy, and another one behind him with a low forehead and pimply skin. Ross was scared but safe. Safe because he didn't understand. But Maff. He saw her stumble. She was pushing that thing and trying not to step on the lines in the sidewalk. Poor messed up kid. His head was pounding, the pain building behind his eyes. The pimply one was laughing. Owen covered the last five feet in one lunge and felt his hands digging into that blotched neck. The boy staggered but didn't go down. Owen pulled back quickly from flailing fists and drove his own into that red knob of a nose. He heard crunching and saw blood, then he turned to face the other one. He brought up his fist and slammed it out again. And again.

The fat one was down now, hands over his head. Behind him the broken nose was crying. Owen was panting, half crying himself. There was blood on his hands. After the first punch, which had felt like ramming his fist into a brick wall, he hadn't felt a thing.

The fat one was trying to get up. Owen started kicking. The world was messing up little kids. Parents, bullies, bus drivers, all of them, too stupid to be allowed to breathe. Fatso was bellowing. One more kick. Another. Owen backed off, stomach churning in panic. What if he couldn't stop? What if the pounding in his head wouldn't stop? Maff was holding him from behind, face pressed into his back. She was so small. Fatso and The Nose were getting away. Ross was crying heartily now, a really good bellow. Owen started to laugh. They were all crazy, messed up for good, probably. So why was he laughing? It went on and on. Maff was looking scared. Finally he stopped, and they walked home.

He'd left his newspaper on the bus, but he told Maffo everything he knew about the Venus probe. They talked about what the spacecraft might learn about the planet. He'd helped her make a model of Venus once. Maybe it was still on exhibit in the elementary school.

Late that night, he went back out into the streets, dark now and perfectly orderly. His fists throbbed and his right knee ached from kicking. He ran, one foot ahead of the other, down the civilized streets.

Chapter Twenty-three

⸰❊⸰

The tender bloom of heart's gone, ere youth itself be past.
George Gordon, Lord Byron

It was the Moron Quartet again, busy trumping their partners' aces. Her mother refused to play with The New Mrs. Miles' bridge club. She and Mrs. Baker played downtown at the University Women's Club, a club the New Mrs. Miles couldn't get into. Into which she couldn't get, her father would say.

A crescendo of laughter rose from the pink and blue living room. Elaborating on party plans and wardrobe enhancement was a laugh fest all right. Were the other three around the bridge table aware of how adept The New Mrs. Miles was at wangling more than her share of the airtime? But it was only fair. She had so many more possessions to talk about, so many more parties to drag everyone through the minutia of planning.

She and Janna were lying on the den couches, listening in. Spying. Janna liked hanging around on bridge day. She still couldn't tell her stepmother off but she'd become adept at The New Mrs. Miles' own game. Never say anything a person could pin down, act innocent at all times, keep smiling at all costs. The New Mrs. Miles prided herself on the self-control of Gandhi, but Janna had observed that calling her stepmother "Daphne" caused that permanent smile to tighten. She'd discovered that calling her "Daphne" irritated her more than calling her nothing at all and now found numerous occasions to address her stepmother and upset the neat order of Daphne's daft little world. It was out of sequence, after all, for a fourteen year old to call a grown up by her first name. It gave the big happy family a bit of a black eye. You had to give Janna credit.

She had turned fourteen before Janna, but you wouldn't know it. She was fourteen and flat. *I've got a gal named Bony Maroni.* Who would want a gal if she were bony? They had sock hops at school the last Friday of each month, but the only hopping she was doing was the Bunny Hop, when the wallflowers finally got their chance. Janna was starting to fill out. When they went to see *To Kill a Mocking Bird,* Owen had wanted to come.

Janna was still reading Little Lulu comics. She wasn't dumb. She just couldn't keep her mind on much, like someone had pulled the plug on her brain. Maffy stretched out on the light blue couch and propped her feet on a cushion the mauvy blue of a varicose vein. Of course no shoes were ever allowed to make contact with the miles of blue carpet. In expiation for this (she loved the "e" words) Maffy made sure her socks were filthy. She rubbed her heels back and forth on the couch, doing what she could. You could pretty much go dead in this house and that wasn't all bad. Like Janna was right now, one languid white arm holding Lulu, the other draped across her forehead. Even when she felt sad, Janna could sleep in this house. Nothing ever happened here, not like last night in Maffy's own house. Which was worse, being sad all the time and knowing nothing was going to change, or being worried all the time because something was always changing?

She listened to the bridge babble. Spying still had the odd pay off and it kept Janna awake. She looked over to the matching blue couch. Little Lulu had slipped noiselessly to the carpet. Janna was asleep.

It had been six months since Owen's fight and he had finally gone to juvenile court the day before yesterday. Their father had gone with him, saying they didn't need a big law firm, the likes of "Dewey, Soakem and Howe." Har Har. Alongside the fat boy and the red faced one, her father and Owen would have wowed the judge even if they hadn't opened their mouths. It had gone their way and all they had to do was pay for the pimply one's nose. They'd offered a lifetime supply of Clearasil as a goodwill gesture. She'd celebrated quietly with a few cupcakes. Owen was sullen now that the worry was over. If only her father hadn't been so proud maybe her parents wouldn't have fought.

The New Mrs. Miles was holding forth again, well into more than her twenty-five percent.

"Winton is just so much fun to be with." Her voice squeaked on "so." "He's got a new interest for us!"

What? Was Mr. Miles taking up wardrobology?

"He's talking about playing golf. He's full of ideas, looking for ways to do new things together. He's still the man of my dreams."

Maffy shot a look at Janna. Still asleep. Good.

"Last week he brought home a book on the perfect golf swing."

"You can do a lot of business on the golf course." That must be Mrs. Tippet, the biggest moron of them all. She didn't have the foggiest about anything, but she was finally making sense.

"Well yes, Nancy, but that's not the point."

Sure it is, Mrs. Miles.

She wasn't eager to go home, but Janna's breathing was getting deeper. The bridge would go on for ages. According to her mother, it took them hours to get through a rubber of bridge. She swung her legs off the couch, remembering to grind the balls of her feet into the blue carpet. She could sneak up the big staircase without being seen from the living room. The room was so huge, the bridge table looked like doll furniture way over by the front window where the morons would catch the breeze. It was the hottest summer she could remember. If she snuck upstairs she couldn't be accused of invading the family's precious privacy, could she? The New Mrs. Miles enjoyed her greatest happiness when people were oohing and aahing over her house.

The doors off the wide hallway upstairs were closed, except for the master bedroom. She looked in on its enormous space and saw the thick pink curtains move slightly, like an unseen hand was getting ready to pull them. Her stomach fluttered. The renovations had reached their zenith here. Maybe Janna wasn't sleeping so well after all, given her proximity to this. It felt wrong to be seeing this, even though the open door invited seeing. The house relied on people seeing it, like a sideshow relied on people gawking in wonder. The maid did a full tour of duty on bridge days.

Back in the den, she found Janna as she'd left her. She would be woken in time to eat dinner in the big dining room with its heavy pink drapes like the ones Maffy had seen upstairs. She wanted to go home. There was something wrong in this house, something worse than the fighting at home. It wasn't true that nothing ever happened here. Besides, she had to get home. All those potatoes.

"Janna, I've gotta go." She shook the milky arm lying over closed eyes. She knew Janna was awake now, but the arm stayed where it was.

"Okay," came her muffled voice.

'I'll see you tomorrow. It's our last day before Twin Coves." Silence. "Janna?" On impulse Maffy blurted, "You could come too. My mother never minds when you come. We could sleep under the stars, like last year. There's plenty of room outside." No response. "Wouldn't it be better to be there?"

"I don't want to be anywhere. I don't want to be."

Could they do without potatoes? Just this once? Maffy sat down on the couch. "Could you . . . why don't you call your uncle?"

"He has to call me. There's no phones on his island."

"What's it like, when you're with him?"

"It's kind of like being with Jesus."

"Jesus?"

"He is so good, so kind. But did Jesus ever laugh?" All through those religious movies, like *Ben Hur,* did Jesus once laugh?"

"Not a lot to laugh about, I guess." Maffy curled up on the couch with her feet in their dirty socks tucked under her. "Have you ever noticed how high Charlton Heston's forehead is? God could have emblazoned the ten commandments right there on Moses's forehead."

Janna laughed. A good sound. She dropped her arm from her forehead and looked over at Maffy. "Uncle Alistair gets this look, like he knows something I don't."

"Is it creepy?"

"No."

"Can you talk to him?"

"Not about everything. Not about my dad. But I can about my mum. All the time. And he buys me things that she would have."

"That's neat."

"Uncle Alistair is like a hammock." Janna was getting into the swing of things. "You know what I mean?"

Maffy shook her head.

Janna looked up at the ceiling now, like it was hard to look at Maffy and talk about this stuff. "A little hard to get into, to find your balance, but once you do, you want to stay there forever. When someone pushes you back and forth, even really high, you know you won't fall out. The hammock wraps around you and holds you in. Being with Uncle Alistair is the closest thing to being with my mother."

"You miss her."

"All day, every day."

"Can you talk to her, up there in heaven?"

"What if there is no heaven," Janna said.

"Don't you believe in God? I mean you should, then you'd know your mother's up there with him."

Janna rolled onto her side, facing away from Maffy. "If there was a God my mother would be down here with me."

Someone had plugged Janna's brain back in. It should have been a relief. "If there is a God, you'll see your mother again. That's worth believing in, isn't it?"

"Maybe."

"But you won't see her for a long time. Janna? Look at me." Cloudy blue eyes slowly turned toward Maffy. "Promise me, Janna. You've got a job to do."

"A job?"

"Yeah. Who else can keep Denise off Owen?" Janna laughed again. Maffy's stomach unknotted. "Do you like him?" Maffy asked. Did she really want to know?

"Who?"

"For crying in the mud, Janna!"

"Of course I like him. He's your brother."

"Does Owen being my brother have anything to do with it anymore?"

"What's wrong, Maffy?"

"I don't know." Now that Janna had perked up, Maffy was feeling different. People were more appealing when they were down.

"Would it be okay if I liked him?" Janna asked.

"Yeah, I guess so."

"I know someone who likes you."

"Don't change the subject."

"Come on, Maffy, guess."

She uncurled her legs and stretched them out in front of her. "How can I? He doesn't exist."

"I'll give you a hint. He's . . . he's younger than you."

"Great."

The New Mrs. Miles's voice broke in. "Janna! No more comics. Come and put the kettle on, please. We're almost ready for tea."

"In a dash, Daph," Janna called. "Got any rat bait, Maff?" she asked in a softer voice.

"How about a dead bird, Baby Jane?"

Maffy left through the den's French doors and sat on a patio chair to put on her shoes. She thought she knew who Janna was thinking of—the boy who liked Maffy—but if she said his name it might not come true.

She headed down the path to the garage where the Cadillacs usually glistened. It was empty. Where was The New Mrs. Miles' car? Maffy thought of the green Chev her father still drove. And Olive, her mother's green Hillman. They'd always have Olive. There'd been a fight when her mother had first seen The New Mrs. Miles' car. What would it be like if she ever saw the bedroom, which of course she would, since there was no reason for The New Mrs. Miles to do something like that bedroom unless everyone saw it.

She was almost at the end of the long driveway. She looked up and saw why The New Mrs. Miles' Cadillac wasn't in the garage. It was gliding down the street with Denise behind the wheel, and she was navigating very close to the wrong side of the road. Maffy ran toward her bike which she'd left lying at the end of the driveway. Too late. Denise got there first, equipped with two tons of car and perfect aim. She managed to drive over the front wheel of the bike, even though the driveway was at least two car widths wide, and the bike was on the very edge of it.

"It's your fault. You should have left it up near the house." Denise leaned out the open window, fat hand gesticulating, black diamond ring mapping an elongated kite on her fat middle finger. Her dark hair made her lipstick even whiter.

"Mr. Miles doesn't like it up there. The kickstand is broken, I'm not allowed to lean it against the house, or lie it on the—"

"You should have left it on the grass!" She was yelling now, a real pro at shifting blame.

"I'm not allowed—he doesn't want tire marks on the grass."

"When are you going to grow up and stop riding a bike, for Petey-eyed sake? Maybe then you wouldn't look ten years old"—her voice lowered—"and retarded." Loud enough for Maffy to hear, low enough to pretend she'd never said it. With that fake innocence, she didn't just look like her mother.

"I guess I'm going to stop riding now, aren't I, lard ass." The last two words achieved the same effect as Denise's. She grabbed her bike and tore herself away from the pleasantries. She needed distance before the lump behind the wheel could park the brute and come after her. The front wheel of her bike looked like she was seeing it in a circus mirror.

It was worse for Janna. Denise would be inside now, maneuvering blame in her direction. It would be Janna's fault for knowing Maffy. Denise had given Janna an autograph book for her birthday and given herself permission to sign the first page. She enjoyed setting a tone. *Roses are red, violets are blue; I remember how repulsive you were when you were two.* Make way, Browning. Denise hadn't known Janna at two, but it was the best she could come up with because now that they were growing up, Janna got the last laugh in the looks department. Finally, somebody else was getting the last laugh. Try as she might to ridicule Janna's hair, Denise could feel it slipping away. Janna was beautiful, with a body that draped like the pear tree along the Morgans' driveway, trained to weep by Maffy's mother. Her hair was the colour of its leaves in autumn. Denise was the pear itself, big hipped and sallow.

Maffy went in the back door. The house was quiet. She walked through the empty rooms and thought about what constituted a master bedroom. A big bedroom with a bathroom attached. The door in the corner of her parents' room opened onto a room that was supposed to be a bathroom. It smelled of raw wood with a mass of tools and plumbing fixtures jumbled on the floor.

Time to get at the potatoes. She went to the kitchen where her mother was sighing and folding Rossie's small T-shirts.

"I'll fold them, mum. The potatoes won't take long."

"It's not the work, it's the worry. The worry of a mother."

Oh I've got heartaches by the number, troubles by the score. Her mother was folding those T-shirts to pack for Twin Coves. Was this the last year Rossie would go with them? Once he was in Woodvale, would it be just as easy to leave him there, even when they went on holiday? Only a few more months. Her mother was clear this was their course of action. Ross wasn't going to suffer, the doctor said. Children like Ross were perfectly content at Woodvale because they didn't know a normal life. "In fact," Dr. Gregson had reasoned, "they're better off away from the cruel stares." Dr. Gregson had been more interested in his upcoming holiday than in Rossie's future. Wouldn't there be cruel stares in Hawaii, when people saw him in his bathing suit? Perhaps the good doctor would be better off staying home.

Her mother was rummaging in the clothesbasket now, looking for Rossie's sun hat. Every summer it was the same. "He must wear his hat, his hair is so fair and thin." Her mother always sewed a piece of soft elastic to either side of the brim, but Rossie still managed to pull it off. Would there be any sun at Woodvale? The rummaging grew frantic. Finally the hat flew out, freed from the tangle of clothes. Maffy picked it up. He was growing so fast, it would be too small this year, anyway.

*

Lying in the top bunk at Twin Coves, she heard the murmur of her parents' voices. They were very, very good tonight, and her mother's laughter bubbled up like warm, fizzy pop. Every summer it was the same. The happiness of the first day, the mustiness of the cabin, like it had no life until they walked in and drank in the sight of the sea, the smell of the sea, the sound of the sea. They never got over that first night, she and Owen on narrow bunks, her parents rolling into each other on the hammock of a double bed and Rossie snuffling in his play pen. Owen's flashlight was bright with new batteries. It skipped over the pages of his new space annual. He'd saved the magazine for the first night so he could have all his good things at once. She'd rather stretch it out. She would save *Gone With the Wind* for a while. Tonight she had all she needed.

The stars were bright through the small bedroom window. Owen loved to tell her about them, and he made it interesting. There were countless numbers of them. *Oh, the night, has a thousand eyes.* Some stars were giants and some were dwarfs. The giant star in Orion was two hundred and fifty million miles across, bigger than the Earth's orbit around the sun. Some were hotter than others, like the white and blue stars. Orange and yellow stars were cooler. Some stars got brighter, some burned out. *Catch a falling star and put it in your pocket, never let it fade away.* Their own sun was a star and not a very bright one. It was a yellow dwarf star that didn't stand out in the big picture. The true searchlight up there was Rigel, with fifty thousand times the luminosity of the sun. The hottest stars burned with over a million sun-power, but even so, their little dwarf would be shining tomorrow, and Rossie had a new navy blue sun hat. Her mother had rushed out and bought it, had sewn in the elastic the last thing before they'd left.

Chapter Twenty-four

Maybe this world is another planet's hell.

Aldous Huxley

Women in print dresses. Owen lowered the binoculars. Women in print dresses all looked alike. The breeze rippled the hem of this print dress like butterflies fluttering at her calves. Her head was hidden under the straw of her hat but he knew the shape of those calves. Beef to the heel, like a Mullingar heifer. His father would describe those legs that way which made it all the odder. His mother's legs weren't thick. There were no better legs than his mother's and his father called himself a leg man. Maff would have those legs, already taking up half her pint-sized body. She looked like the heron picking its way through the crabs in the front cove.

He lowered the binoculars. What were those legs without ankles doing here? He'd brought the binoculars to watch for seals but now he pinned them on the shore again. The print dress was disappearing into the brush behind the arbutus tree that stood sentinel over Smuggler's Bay Beach half a mile up the coast from Twin Coves. The kayak took a wave of water and his view veered to the left. Owen saw the patch of white. A figure moved through the scrub just ahead of the woman, then was gone. Sunlight played on the yellow dress patterned with dark

spots like a Monarch butterfly—a scene from Cezanne, except
Cezanne painted the sharp, smug green of spring. His mother
had a calendar of the impressionists and at the beginning of
each month gave a little lecture over dinner. Now the grass was
dry. Bone dry. The cougar alert would be sounding all down the
length of Vancouver Island. They crept out of the wilderness
when things got really dry and there was no water to be found.
Now the woman in the dress had disappeared too.

He grasped the paddle with his left hand and slipped the
binoculars back into the plastic bag with his right. He pulled hard
on the paddle, turning his head side to side to watch the muscles
of his forearms, stroke after stroke. The kayak slid through the
green water of the second cove, stroke after stroke, and touched
shore, the bow anchoring itself in the mud-coloured sand, the
stern still afloat, willowing gently. Owen pulled himself out,
barely noticing Henry, anxiously waiting for a turn. Henry lived
in an anxious state. Owen turned his gaze on him, relieved by his
presence.

"Got a life jacket?"

"I can swim."

"You know the rules." The kid reminded him of Maff. Looking
to him always with the same dumb hope. She read to Ross in her
patient voice, pointing out words, willing him to understand. If
she weren't so hopeful he could have taken it. He reached down
for his binoculars and headed up the path toward the first cove,
looking over his shoulder to see Henry struggling with the long
paddle. He needed the shorter one like Maff did.

Beyond the pathetic scene in the kayak lay his father's boat.
The *Pleiades* pulled at her moorings, bow pointing out to sea. She
was longing to go. She'd sat so long in the driveway, and now she
sat at anchor in the cove, serving the same purpose—providing
a burrow for his father. His parents had found a bigger audience
to embarrass their kids in front of. In front of which to embarrass
their children. Owen considered the precision with which his
father would have said it. His parents liked to snipe at each other
in public, where it was safe. Like at the campfire. You could make
it sound innocent, a casual quip, not enough to give the other
cause to have at it. There was greater impact too. Public exposure
of each other's inadequacies had more effect. "Hasn't he rigged

a perfect spit over the fire? He's good with the primitive—you should see our house." "You're a riot, Alice," said with none of Ralph Kramden's blundering affection. Later, when they could wake up their kids and put the finishing touches on a summer day, they'd dredge up the rough stuff. At two in the morning, the party would begin in earnest. Now, when the fighting got bad at Twin Coves, his father slept on the boat, rowing out to her lonely mooring at three in the morning. What were those thick calves doing there . . . and what about that patch of white?

He carried on to the first cove. They'd all be there except Maff and Ross, who were waiting for him in the cabin. Ever since the incident with Fatso and The Nose, she wasn't that confident with Ross around people. Ross didn't embarrass her. She wasn't like that. Not like him and their mother. He'd heard things. "Yes, retarded, so ironic, in a family like that." It was the pity he hated. He was like his mother that way. Maff was like their father. It didn't matter to her what people thought, it only mattered that she wasn't confident anymore, like it was her job to take care of Ross and she couldn't be sure she'd do it right.

The front cove was full of them. Did Paige Lindell ever get tired of holding in her stomach so her chest swelled like twin spinnakers? She was listening to her transistor, so the whole beach got in on, *Tears on my pillow.*

"Hi Owen. We're having a sleep out on the point tonight. Wanna come?"

"I'm babysitting my little brother," Owen lied, "Wanna come?"

"Sure!" Her guileless face shamed him. She smiled. "Your little brother is the most beautiful kid I've ever seen. He looks like you."

The usual overture, but she really seemed easy about Ross. "Tell you what, let's go get Ross and Maff and babysit him now."

Paige fell into step, spinnakers luffing. As they neared the cabin, Owen recognized the whistling first, then caught a glimpse of the white T-shirt bustling around. They went in.

"Owen lad, shake a leg. The Chev's groaning with groceries, we're going to feast tonight!"

He'd been to the farmer's market, then down to Smuggler's Bay wharf for shrimp. The clams were squirting their last on the porch. The life of a clam was a straightforward one. Owen looked intently at his father, whose childish blue eyes beamed.

"Herself is coming in on the four o'clock. Finish unloading the car and I'll run down and meet her ferry. Step lively, lad!"

His mother had been in Seattle for her annual two-day getaway. She'd stayed overnight at the Mayflower Hotel and if history could be trusted, she'd come home in a good mood. His father was whistling *Men of Harlech*. How had he gotten home so fast? Was it possible? Leave it alone.

"I'll help," cooed Paige.

He'd forgotten she was there. Maff came out of the bunkroom lugging Ross, who'd just woken up.

"See what I mean?" Paige went on obliquely.

Ross was flushed, his eyes wide, his frieze of hair haloing his remarkable face. The grimace that shuddered down his left cheek was still after a rest. In fact it wasn't as pronounced even when he was tired anymore.

"Hi Maffy," said Paige. She didn't dig like she usually did. They convoyed out to the beaten down Chev and began the great unload. The campfire might be fun. A stolen beer, a midnight swim, and maybe he would sleep out with all the little campers.

The moss was five inches thick under the big fir tree on the Point. This year they didn't need tarps under their sleeping bags. It hadn't rained for eighteen days, each one counted like a litany. They were hypnotized with heat. Each day of their three weeks so far had opened on a cloudless dawn and closed on a pink dusk. Around day ten security had set in, and they'd become languid—beautiful people living lives of privilege and certainty. Warmth could do that.

The rustle of his mossy mattress was the only sound. Even Paige had finally given in and gone to sleep. He rolled out of his bag and got lightly to his feet. Out from under the trees he looked for Ursa Major, standing on its head in the northern sky. Off its handle the Pole Star was bright. The moonless night highlighted the meteorites, and as always, when he looked up, he dreamed of going there. Up to the stratosphere, silent and dark, its void of humanity its greatest lure. Kennedy had promised they'd get there this decade. They had to, before the communists did. The Russians weren't coming, they were going—to the moon.

Kennedy vowed they'd get there first. He'd got them through the missile crisis; maybe he'd be good for this too. *I believe this nation should commit itself to achieving the goal, before this decade is out, of landing a man on the Moon and returning him safely to Earth.*

The moon was one thing but it was the planets that held the promise. If there was life on earth there had to be life somewhere else in one of the solar systems, in one of the galaxies. The Venus probe would be launched on August twenty-seventh, looking for life behind the planet's cover of clouds. Another meteorite shot by. The air was hot even at this hour. The fir tree smelled sweet, like spice. His legs ached. He'd run ten miles up the coast road before dinner, but he didn't want to sleep. He wanted sit in the quiet and listen to the waves lap against the rocks. The air was still enough to balance an egg on end, but the waves lapped on, powered by a thousand miles of water. He lay back in the prickle of dead leaves. Were there oceans on other planets? The Venus probe was only the first. Although Venus was Earth's twin, Mars was more likely to have life, from what they knew so far. The mystery of Venus would soon be explained. Then Mars. Oceans meant life, the beginning of it all. There must be life out there, life that wasn't in danger of being blown to bits or being whittled away in little ways that made a person want to get off this planet. Marilyn Monroe had decided to get off. On the plus side, they'd got Eichmann off too, hanged in an Israeli prison.

John Glenn had gone into orbit and had circled the globe three times. The beautiful blue-green planet, he'd called it. "Just like your eyes, Owen," Maff had said. "All bluey-green, like the earth seen from way out in space." Why would a man like Glenn want to go into space? Owen knew all about his life and wondered how much he'd risk if he had that perfect life. The print dress danced before his eyes, dark dots flickering on a yellow background. The universe was the negative of that dress—yellow stars dotting navy skies stretching forever.

His mother had come back from Seattle flushed with shopping. His father had insisted on her trip. Owen felt pain snaking through his right temple. Soon it would slither behind his right eye. He'd been holding it off since the kayak ride, but it was no use. The headache would go on for twenty-four hours.

*

His classes were being beefed up again for his last year at Oak Bay High. The teachers ran around trying to find something to challenge him. Did they think they were going to find a new theory of lineal algebra in the staff room? What they didn't get was that he didn't want to be challenged. School was a chance to rest. Where he went when high school was over was his choice, in theory. He wanted MIT, his mother, Harvard of course. The Kennedy tradition. What kind of astronaut went to Harvard? Leaving Maff and Ross behind to balance the challenges on their narrow shoulders was something he didn't think about. The sweat ran down under his arms. His hair was wet, as if he'd been standing in a shower instead of pounding up Lansdowne Road. He'd done 15.7 miles. He kept track of the miles now. He'd read how far the long distance teams ran at the universities and wherever he ended up, he'd be ready for them.

The heat had gone on and on and a cougar had been spotted near Mount Douglas Park, looking for water. There were other warnings, other sightings. Someone had seen something in Uplands Park—probably just Charlie, the Turners' golden lab—but Maff and Janna weren't allowed to walk home from school through the park anymore. No one could remember heat like this. His parents were muffled by it, too hot to fight. The brooding was worse. When they fought, he dealt with it. When they didn't, he waited, knowing it was only a matter of time. One more year and he'd be gone. He pushed Ross's puckered face out of his mind. Maffy's staring eyes belonged to someone else's sister.

He'd gone 15.9 miles when the house loomed. Bosun was at the bottom of the driveway, waiting with his snaggle-toothed grin. He was too old to keep up now.

"Bosun Boy, how are you, doggle?"

His tail thumped like a metronome against Owen's calf, eyes opening and closing slowly, crocodilelike.

His bedroom was dark. How long had he been asleep? He kicked off his blanket. They had to sleep with windows shut, due to the cougar warning. A cramp was starting in his left calf and he struggled to stretch his leg, heel down, toes up. Then he heard them.

"You think I can't tell? I knew immediately, the minute you walked in! How dare you?"

"For pity's sake, woman, I—"

"Don't you dare! Don't you defend yourself."

"Goddamn it, Eleanor!"

"I won't take this from you, not anymore."

She was beside herself. Again. Their fighting was like a separate entity. Like there were three of them—him, her, and this thing they became together, a thing that neither of them could stop. He covered his ears but couldn't block a new sound—the shattering of glass. He moved silently out his door and into the living room, eyes squinting in the light. The glass door to her china cabinet was open, and one by one she picked up each exquisite Royal Dalton figurine, looked at it, then hurled it at the marble hearth. She studied each victim with eerie control, but the hand that held the little figure in the red coat shook. She looked up as if she'd smelled him, eyes like a baited animal. He backed away, down the hall, toward the whimpering coming from Ross's room. Maff had him in her arms. She looked like she'd fallen from a great height, cheeks hollowed out, her eyes wide and staring.

He lay awake until the first of dawn. He'd heard the reports. He knew it was out there. Why wouldn't it be? There was no better place than Uplands Park. They'd found a cougar downtown once, strolling up Government Street way back in 1913. There wouldn't have been much of a city then, but even so, it was no place for a big cat. In the park a cougar could feel a part of things, creeping tawnily through the first fallen oak leaves, bedding down in a den of moss. The wild park should belong to him. In the absence of coexistence, advantage to the cat.

Bosun's breath was hot. The dog always could sense when Owen was about to make a move and he wanted in on it.

"No, Bosun, not this time. Stay. Good doggle." He put out his hand in the early morning light and dug in under the soft ears, kneeding the silken neck. The dog licked his face. All Bosun needed was here in this moment. Owen rose and the dog began to whine. When he slipped through his bedroom window, the whining grew worried.

"No, Bosun. Stay."

He shut the window behind him, with Bosun scrabbling at it with his front paws. The whining grew fainter.

He ran down the path that led into the middle of the park. At the big oak tree he turned and headed through the thick brush, dense with hawthorns and broom, into the clearing. The land was usually sunken and marshy here where the rain gathered itself into a pond. In winter they skated on it. Now it was dry as bones, dead bull rushes forming stiff spikes. The air was flat and hot. The park was dying of thirst but even now there would be a hint of moisture from an underground spring.

Uplands Park was the perfect place for a cougar. He climbed the tallest oak in the clearing to watch and wait.

The light was pale and the oak leaves were the slightest silver. The sun was creaking through the trees, revving up for another day.

What would a cougar feed on? Mice, rabbits, the quail quivering in her nest? Ground nesters were vulnerable and each year they saw fewer quail, their white topknots bobbing through the grass. He could hear them talking to one another, Bob Whites beginning their neighbourly day.

Sunlight was gilding the leaves of the oak and the view from Owen's perch was growing. He could sit here all day. Let them worry. No one would find him up in this nest of leaves. From up here, maybe he'd see what he'd come for.

The air grew quiet. Slowly, gradually, the birds stopped singing. One family of robins alerted the next, a quail hushed her noisy neighbour. Owen held still. The rough bark of the oak tree dug into his hands.

It appeared out of nowhere, pawing at the ground, smelling the unseen water, growling a low, rumbling growl. The skin on Owen's arms tingled and his legs trembled beneath him. The cougar lifted its head, looking tired and hot. Its dull, amber pelt hung loosely. Owen met its gold eyes head on. He smelled its wild, musky odor. A smell like nothing he'd ever known.

The cat sauntered to the tree and pawed at the rippled grey bark. The low-pitched rumbling grew. Owen reached for the branch above him. His movement enticed the cougar, who decided not to climb the tree. It leapt.

A huge paw swiped at him. He yanked his leg up, trying to reach the higher branch. The cougar leapt again, effortlessly. This time its paw grazed the branch. Vomit rose in Owen's throat. He was going to wet his pants, or worse.

The cat dropped back to the ground. Its paws looked soft, like a stuffed toy. It sprang again. Owen held on, kicking and thrashing, choking on his screams. His arms were weakening. The cougar looked calm as it readied itself to leap again. One more swipe, this one hitting home. A jolt of pain shot through his leg and his grip on the branch was gone. His head knocked the lower branch on his way down to the warm earth. He landed heavily on his torn leg.

The cougar took its time, watching as Owen scrambled toward the trunk of the oak tree. Its breath, like steam from a kettle, hissed at his flesh. The cat batted playfully at his bleeding left leg before taking his ankle, almost gently, into its mouth. As its jaws closed, Owen heard the pop, like stepping on a kelp head. Blood soaked the ground. He kicked wildly with his other foot, screaming full out, pain like white-hot fire. The cougar was twisting its big head, alerted to a noise behind it. Another sound was coming through the bush, getting closer. The cougar let go of Owen's ankle and turned to face the frantic growling of another animal. This growl was familiar. And the bark, the high-pitched yodeling, the way he got when he wanted to bark and growl and cry all at once. The way he got when he was beside himself.

"Bosun! No! Go home. Go home!"

The light was dimming, the sounds of growling softening. His throat was sour and swollen. Water would help. The pond was near. It lapped at his feet, cradled his body, washed coolly over his lips. It was dark now. There were no stars. The pain was fading, floating away, into the darkness.

Chapter Twenty-five

——— ·⊰⊱· ———

All heaven and earth are still—though not in sleep,
But breathless, as we grow when feeling most.

George Gordon, Lord Byron

The feeling was not like waking. Waking was remembering the familiar. Familiar hands tucked into armpits, familiar legs wrapped in a snarl of sheets, familiar mouth gummed with sleep. This was not waking. This numbness was more comforting than waking could ever be again. This absence of all thought for a few blissful seconds. Then came awareness and memory and certainty that nothing would ever be familiar again. The way things were, she didn't want to feel familiar with life now.

Bosun was gone. Owen too, in his own way. In his Owen way. When they'd found out he would live, nothing else had mattered. After the doctors had pumped all that blood into him, sewn up his tendon, and told them he would live, that was all that mattered. Now things were sinking in, like cougar's teeth into Owen's ankle. That had taken a second. The real sinking in would go on forever. It was sinking in that Owen would never run again. That Bosun would never lick her face again. That she would never see his good brown eyes again. Sometimes his eyes had been too much. Sometimes she couldn't bear to see in his eyes how much he loved her. Now she would never see that too much again. Now she would never see him at the foot of the driveway again, all those times, left at the foot of the driveway, giving his heart for a pat on the head. She had crawled under the Holly tree, and found his treasures. His secret bone and his special throwing stick were with him now, along with a new treasure. A pair of rolled up socks. She had kept his ball, now hidden in her bottom drawer.

Owen's left foot. The Achilles tendon was bit in two. They were their own Greek tragedy now.

He was coming home from the hospital today. Would life feel familiar when he was back in his universe? Would he be the same? The day went slowly and when he finally limped through the front door with her mother clucking around him and her father looking stricken, Owen was white and quiet.

He slept the rest of the day and had dinner in bed. She was afraid to talk to him, afraid to find out he might not be Owen anymore. Everyone was quiet that night and it wasn't the malevolent quiet of waiting for her parents to erupt. It was a hushed, sad quiet, like the family didn't know how to be anymore.

When it was dark her father lit a fire in the living room. It had started raining the day after it happened and the air was cold. Her father helped Owen into the living room and her mother made him take up the whole couch, draping the green afghan over his legs. She sat on the arm of the couch at Owen's feet. Maffy sat on the marble hearth in front of the fire. The marble was green. Looking into the hearth, she could see the deep water at Twin Coves. Way out in the kayak, she'd look down and see the green water swirling beneath her, with strands of seaweed waving in the ocean's deep silent wind.

Her father opened the book that was once Owen's favourite. Owen didn't seem to remember that and was too old for stories. They all were but her father insisted. It wasn't like Christmas Eve when everyone knew her father would end up crying. He was beyond that now. They sat there listening, all except Rossie, who was asleep. The family could only deal with one wrecked kid at a time. Would Rossie ever hear their father read *The Wind in the Willows*?

Her father went straight to Owen's favourite chapter; *The Piper at the Gates of Dawn*. Suddenly, something was familiar again. The tears were in his voice as he read about the Otter family who had lost their son. Little Portly had been gone for days and was feared drowned in the river. Rat and Mole watched the Otter father . . . *the lonely heart-sore animal, crouched by the ford, watching and waiting—on the chance.*

Rat and Mole sculled their small craft through the long night, looking, listening for a sign. Suddenly, it came to them in . . . *the thin, clear, happy call of the distant piping.* It was Mole who saw the vision, Mole who *looked in the very eyes of the Friend and Helper . . . saw the backward sweep of the horns . . . saw the stern, hooked nose between the kindly eyes . . . saw the long supple hand still holding the pan-pipes only just fallen away from the parted lips; saw the splendid curves of the shaggy limbs disposed in majestic ease . . . saw last of all, nestling between his very hooves, the sleeping form of the baby otter.*

They sat in the deepening evening with the vision of the half-human, half-stag "Friend and Helper", the God of the Animals, who looked on his kingdom with amused love, who watched over Little Portly, who eased the hearts of his family. The sound of the pan-pipes danced in the darkening room as they listened.

*

She spent much of that long, empty fall writing her own stories. No matter how bad she could make them, she was always in charge of a happy ending. Then she'd disappear into the park, making her way to the clearing at its centre. She had climbed the tree thirty times or more, getting faster and better, fingers fitting into the grooved bark. Owen had taught her to climb trees. She could get well past the first branch which held signs of Owen's scrabbling grip. She dropped down easily to the brush below. The ground was still broken and trampled. But the blood was gone, lashed away by rain. The earth had waited a long time for the rain that now fell steadily. She lay in the hollow where they had found them, Bosun lying over Owen's body. He'd known to do that. When they'd found the big orange cougar it was clear how hard Bosun had fought. They'd barely needed to shoot it. Today, lying in the hollow where Owen had lived and Bosun had died she remembered the cougar too. It had been nearly seven feet long from the tip of its nose to the tip of its tail, one of the biggest ever seen on the island. Dying for water.

After a while she left the clearing. Her back was wet from lying on the ground and she was cold. Would the pond freeze this year? Would Owen ever get a skate on his left foot again? She wandered back, noticing the leaves were almost all down now, and the trees' personalities were coming to life.

She looked up and saw her father, just off the path, leaning against the big tree that marked where to turn off for the clearing. He looked like he'd been there a while and like he wasn't in a hurry to be going anywhere else. Just leaning against a tree in the dead middle of Uplands Park, *hooked nose between the kindly eyes.*

"Hello, Nuffer."

They stood in silence.

"He was an old soldier, Myfanwy," her father finally said, "and he went out fighting, in a blaze of glory. He had his three score and ten. He won't have to creep through old age, sad and incontinent." His hand was heavy on her head. "You have it in you to love a dog. That's a good thing, and worth even this." They stood through more sad silence until her father picked up again. "Because of him, we have Owen. When you let Bosun out, you set him free. Without Owen, he wouldn't have lived. Not like he was alive."

Her father's hand moved gently down her head. He lifted her chin. She looked into his damp, red eyes. "Bosun loved you too, Myfanwy. I believe he loved you best. Our steadfast Bosun. He asked nothing but to live at our feet, desired only the comfort of our hands. We'll miss his honest heart, as fine a dog, as fine a friend as we'll ever have. And when his noble heart gave out, he knew that Owen's beat still. He knew. He died with what he loved—living, breathing—under his faithful head. He died with pride in his heart. He did not die in vain, Myfanwy, or alone.

> "But the poor dog, in life the firmest friend,
> The first to welcome, foremost to defend,
> Whose honest heart is still his master's own,
> Who labors, fights, lives, breathes for him alone.

"Lord Byron. It was his tribute to another dog named Bosun, "Boatswain," as it's spelled on the monument where the tribute is inscribed. That stone remembrance sits in the garden of Newstead Abbey. England. Our Bosun was named for that dog. He lived up to the honour."

They walked back slowly. He knew she was too old to hold his hand so he rested his lightly on her shoulder, and gradually the house came into sight, sitting in its own hollow in its own clearing in Uplands Park. It looked like a house that no one lived in anymore. There were a few lights on, but that only emphasized the lack of movement within. The garden hadn't had its fall clean up. The roses, those slavering heavy feeders that her mother usually topped up with blood meal just before the first frost, had gone hungry, gone leggy too, their thorny fangs drooping in the weak fall light. The wall flowers scraggled brownly around the patio door and the iris hadn't been cut back from around the bird bath, full of syrupy water the colour of the drapes. What gave it away as occupied was the music, weaving its way through the broom, stirring up the dead oak leaves, coming to meet them as they made their joyless way home. You could hear it a long way off, the air was that still.

They didn't go in, but walked down to the foot of the driveway where Bosun was buried under the oak where he'd sat and waited. Now he would be at the foot of the driveway forever, surrounded by his treasures.

"Our Bosun will have his own headstone," her father said.

She already knew. She'd seen Owen working on it, carving the beautiful piece of oak that would be put on Bosun's grave. Her father was the woodcarver but he knew to let Owen do it.

"What will it say? It's taking a long time and Owen won't show me until it's done."

"You'll see, Little One, when Owen is done."

They walked toward the house. The music was sad.

"Debussy. *Clair de Lune*. She'll be in a quiet frame of mind. What we have to pray for, Nuffer, is no Fauve—no *Apres un Reve*."

After a dream. She looked up and caught his quick smile. Whatever mood took hold of her mother held them hostage until the next one hit. They went through the back door. Her father pinched his hand between the doorknob and the doorframe. He couldn't remember anything anymore. *Clair de Lune* was filling each nook and cranny with its heartbreaking sweetness. The Rachmaninoff moods were easier somehow, the music rolling down hallways, roaring out pain. Easier than tiptoeing Debussy, so terribly, terribly sad.

Chapter Twenty-six

---·❧·❦·---

These pleasures, Melancholy give,
And I with thee will choose to live.

John Milton

The last orange would last a lifetime at this rate. Everyone had to eat oranges, according to Nadine Smyth. If only oranges would help.

Eleanor found she could not take her eyes off the minutia of their daily lives. She could study the cat's bowl—square—such an odd shape for a cat dish, or any dish for that matter. The colour of it, Wedgwood, was probably the only blue thing in the house. The cat dish was positioned prominently now, where the dog's had once been. Don't think about the dog. Don't think about his gentle eyes. There would be no more dogs. They couldn't go through that pain again. The cat's dish had tiny white puppies running ironically around its rim.

Eventually she came up with another blue item. It was navy actually, not the medium blue of the cat bowl, but blue nonetheless. The pram, of course. It was in Ross's room. It didn't get out much. Now they had a stroller for him. Easier to push, easier to get Ross in and out of. He was getting bigger all the time, growing like the garden, enthusiastic, untamed, out of control. But he wasn't heavy, Myfanwy stubbornly maintained.

He had all that energy pulsing through him, all that sweet cheer about him, bouncing into your arms, his wiry excitement making him lightweight, really.

She watched Myfanwy peeling each segment of her orange with religious intensity, pulling off each piece of white filament from the orange flesh. Was there a name for those white threads that clung to an orange? Myfanwy pulled off each offending bit until the segment was perfectly skinned. Then she'd start on the next one until she'd lined up all the perfectly prepared pieces, like misshapen kumquats. Then, and only then, would she allow herself to eat. Myfanwy didn't know she was being watched. Eleanor watched whatever she could, whenever she could.

Nadine had taken to dropping by. Sometimes Jean came with her. They thought she was crazy. Too bad she wasn't. She wasn't going to be allowed the relief of finally slipping her cog. She might fool others but not herself. This wouldn't do it. She knew what would finally make her snap and how fine the balance was. Ross would be staying put for a while. Now that Owen was handicapped too, it didn't seem the ideal time to be sending Ross off. They thought she didn't care about Ross and for the most part it was easier to let them think that.

Her eyes swept the room for something to focus on. The clock. The Electric Moonbeam Clock. She had brought it out of the bedroom to where it now sat on the end of the kitchen counter. It gave her comfort to watch time go by. What a marvel, folks! The Moonbeam Clock. Let the silently blinking light awaken you at the appointed hour, and the rest of the household sleeps in peace. The post war miracle clock Hugh's mother had bought them in 1949 had been humming all these years but Eleanor had never really looked at it before. Now she couldn't take her eyes off it. And how did it work? If you were asleep, how would you see a blinking moonbeam? "Well," Hugh's mother had explained, "If the flashing light doesn't get you, a cheerful alarm eventually sounds off." Cheerful? She watched the minute hand steadily eating up the seconds around and around its cheerless face. It was restful because it didn't tick. Just the quiet hum of post war progress.

Myfanwy's robin alarm clock really was cheerful, and like the ubiquitous Moonbeam, it kept on going. Sometimes she went into Myfanwy's room and watched the seconds go by. It was a true marvel, a bucolic garden scene painted with unlikely beauty onto the clock's face in the middle of which a robin appeared, moving independently, back and forth, tick tock, on its own spring. Three-D folks! In its beak was a worm, also on a spring. On the tick, the robin pulled the worm out of the earth, on the tock, the worm pulled back to earth. Tick tock, back and forth. The alarm on this clock sounded loud and clear, with the power to wake the whole family, and when it did, the robin prevailed, pulling the worm full out. Yes, folks, the early bird gets the worm.

Time marched slowly all that fall and Eleanor watched it. It would take time they said, Jean and Nadine hovering nervously. Alistair phoned, his voice soft with concern. He understood suffering. It seemed he cared not just for Janna but for all of them. They were his link to Lily.

Eleanor memorized every detail of the house that fall, planning a thousand interior decoration schemes. Some were all green, some all white, others a wild nightmare of colour. Broadloom roamed from room to room. She memorized every detail of those living in the house too. They were all watching her, but they didn't know she was watching them too. Hugh—wandering like a ghost in his white Welsh skin. He wasn't small and dark like so many of the Welsh. Someone had kissed an Englishman way back when. Owen, distant and calm—almost peaceful? Ross, alive with energy. Could he intuit they had two of him now? And Myfanwy—the little savior, thorns so heavy on her furrowed brow.

Chapter Twenty-seven

By the pricking of my thumbs,
Something wicked this way comes.

William Shakespeare

"I'm not perfect anymore."

"I never was."

"Once you know a person a certain way, what's it like to see them differently? I mean, how do you see me now?"

"You walk different but you're still perfect in the ways that count. You still act the same, that's not something the accident changed. You're in charge of that."

"I don't know, Maff, are people in charge of how they act?"

"Well, if they're not, who is?"

"Maybe it's the world that does it to people."

"Too easy. Are you going to tell me that people like, well, like Denise, aren't responsible for the way they act? I mean she can't change her looks, not in any significant way, but she could change her personality."

"If that were true, wouldn't she have? She'd have to be crazy not to. Maybe that's the point. Maybe she's crazy. Maybe we all are."

"Am I?"

"A little. Normal most of the time."

"I'm average. I look average."

"You're lucky. Besides, you don't. Average people don't have eyes like new moss. Hand me the paper, would you?"

She reached for the Seattle paper that their father brought home every day now, detouring to Government Street, so Owen could keep up with Mariner II. The Venus probe was speeding along brilliantly. Venus was thirty-six million miles from earth but on December fourteenth Mariner would be only twenty-one thousand, five hundred and ninety-four miles from Venus, all instruments on high alert.

"By the way, you still look the same. Just because you don't walk the same doesn't mean you get to go crazy."

"Don't worry, Maffo. I'm not perfect so now I don't have to go all out crazy, just a little, like everyone else."

He was getting more and more like himself but did they take astronauts who couldn't run? All they did up there was float around in the absence of gravity. The one place it wouldn't show. He'd been quiet for a while, reading intently, but now he looked up.

"Kennedy is launching something other than spaceships. The First International Program of Fellowships To Train The Handicapped is being launched in New York. In the United States, the number of retrained handicapped persons finding jobs has reached a new high, it says here, for the seventh year in a row."

"You're not handicapped."

He raised his right forefinger, signaling that he was God and would continue their conversation when he was good and ready. Eventually he read aloud. "*A President's panel of leaders in education, medicine, psychology and social work have campaigned to get the word "Physically" dropped from the title of the President's Committee on Employment of the Physically Handicapped.*"

"So what? You're not handicapped."

"Clue in, Maff. If they're not just talking about the physically handicapped, who are they talking about?"

She stared at him, shaking her head.

He carried on. "They mean the mentally handicapped. They want to talk about employment for the physically and mentally handicapped."

"Rossie."

There was hope for Rossie, maybe for those kids in Woodvale too. Not all, but some. She'd like to grab them out from under Mossy-Lip's nose. Time to get to work, kids! It had been ten months since she'd seen them but she thought about them and the nurse who regimented their days into efficient sameness. Day after day of subtle bullying. The kind that masquerades as concern.

She and Janna were taking Rossie out for Halloween—give him a chance at normal, average things. He would be a ghost. Uninspired and definitely not up to her standards, but there was a plethora of white bed sheets at Janna's these days, due to the fact that The New Mrs. Miles had rampaged through the house and made everything new. The house was burgeoning with colour—coloured sheets, coloured serviettes, coloured toilet paper—while the Morgans were making do with plain white. Except the telephone. There they were making do with plain black. White offended The New Mrs. Miles' "flair." The flair that said I'm not afraid of colour. Too bad. A little fear was a good thing. Janna had been allowed to choose her own colour of bed sheets and had done well to contain her excitement. She'd chosen yellow, of course. Her room was the only place yellow existed anymore. Everything else was rioting shades of pink and blue with purple "accents." Looking into the living room was like witnessing abdominal surgery, according to Maffy's mother, and she hadn't seen anything yet. Wait'll she got a load of the master bedroom.

Janna's bedroom was perfect. It was pale blue with white eyelet curtains and an eyelet bedspread that looked perfect over her yellow blanket. Her uncle Alistair had sent these things from Seattle along with her yellow rug shaped like a daisy that lay over the blue wall to wall carpet. Her mother's picture was on her wall. Mrs. Miles was wearing her blue pedal pushers and her hair clouded around, filling the picture with a kind of glow. Maffy's father had taken that picture at Twin Coves with the first colour film he'd ever bought. He'd seen to the eight by ten enlargement and sometimes, looking at it, you could still hear her laugh.

Yes, it was easy to abscond with a white bed sheet. She took it home to her own room, imperfect in all the right ways. The closet was unpainted inside, the cedar shelves smooth and sweet, holding onto the faint smell of the forest. The moldings that her father hadn't gotten around to were stacked in the corner. The ceiling was cedar two by sixes, like her bed, snug as a ship's cabin. Her desk was homemade and could fold down, making the room bigger, which had been important once. The room had been her private ballet studio with a barre mounted above the desk. She'd quit dancing years ago, the night her aunts had been there and her mother had called out to her to come and dance.

"We're waiting, Myfanwy. Make your grand entrance!"

After that night she just couldn't dance any more. In spite of those dying swan arms, she wasn't headed for Swan Lake. No one ever knew how much she'd wanted to be a dancer so it didn't matter now that she wouldn't be one.

She would be a writer. She'd already filled seven of the blank books that Grandmaf kept on giving her. She wrote at her desk which was painted the same leafy green as the floor tiles. Her walls were the lightest green paint you could mix and still have it come out green, like the first bite of a Granny Smith.

Rossie did pretty well on his first foray into an average life. He couldn't see everything from under his sheet, but that turned out to be a good thing. He missed two boys throwing firecrackers at a dog who would think twice about bounding toward strangers again in trusting anticipation. The boys looked familiar even in the dark. Picking on animals now. Maybe those Middle-eastern women in *National Geographic,* the religious ones flapping through life in black bed-sheets, weren't so badly off. There was a lot about the world they missed.

Without Rossie in tow, she and Janna would have been too old for Halloween, although it occurred to her that the whole Morgan family could stroll through the Uplands on Halloween, sans costume. Wouldn't that be scary? They could stroll straight into the looney bin and it would be understood.

They were too old for Halloween but there were still times, off on their bikes, when they hung on to being kids again. Once they let go it would be gone for good. She was riding Owen's bike now and once she'd gotten the hang of swinging her leg over the bar, it was faster than hers had ever been. Getting off was the tricky part.

Now they had an excuse for spending hours on a Saturday off on their bikes. Mr. Cartwright had assigned rock collecting in grade nine science. Mr. Cartwright was a big man and wasn't much enjoying living up to his nickname, but the fact that he knew what it was recommended him. He was the kind of teacher you could horse around with to the point of letting on what the students called him. You couldn't clue pointy-nosed Miss Ferris or hairy Mr. Petrochuk in on My Ferret Lady or Goat Face.

Hoss had sent his students in search of fourteen different kinds of rocks. Maffy and Janna had already found eleven and had accepted that there were some that no one would find. No one but Mr. Miles had ever found Fool's Gold. It looked like the real thing until you looked a little closer.

They went to Janna's to mount their rocks. They would finish off at Maffy's, using Owen's typewriter to produce the labels. Janna was chewing on a Macintosh toffee left over from Halloween when The New Mrs. Miles, clutching her tiny, wizened poodle, appeared in the den doorway. Two inches of cadaver blue pile carpet could muffle the most aggressive footsteps. Janna looked up guiltily, teeth glued together, hands glued to the cardboard from one of her father's dry cleaned shirts that she was rubber-cementing rocks onto. There'd be no such thing at Maffy's house. The New Mrs. Miles was too busy to iron shirts.

"Janna, I've asked you not to eat in the den, or anywhere in this house except at the dining table. This is expensive broadloom, not straw. Oh, hello Myfanwy, you're here again."

What The New Mrs. Miles wanted to say was, You're always here. Why don't you go back to your barn? But she wouldn't. She'd never give you an in.

"You girls take this mess out of here. This is my home, not a geology lab. And by the way, Janna, your uncle called while you were out. What a shame you missed him."

The studied sweetness didn't waver but even a moron wouldn't be taken in by that smile. Not even the three sitting in the "drawing room" right now, waiting for The New Mrs. Miles to sit back down in her last-forever orlon blouse and bid. Or maybe she was the dummy. How could that foursome distinguish the dummy?

The way it peeled away in layers made mica the most interesting rock in their collections. The top layer was thin and shiny, easy to chip off. Underneath, another layer would chip off, and so on and so on, until there was nothing left but a hard little stone.

Chapter Twenty-eight

I will drain him dry as hay;
Sleep shall neither night nor day
Hang upon his pent-house lid;
He shall live a man forbid.

William Shakepeare

"I'm not going into the Twilight Zone without you. Pull yourself together and buy a new dress."

"You would suggest a party. A party thrown by Daphne."

"It'll make you or break you. Think about it. Will you allow the likes of Daphne to break you?"

"I won't leave myself open to pity. This is where I draw the line."

"She'll pity you more if you don't go. How much fodder can you afford to give her?"

"You underestimate her, Jean. She sets my teeth on edge. I can lose enamel just being in the same room with her."

"Make you or break you."

"I'm not fit to be around anyone let alone Daphne."

"It's time you made a start. You'll feel better when you do."

"It's taken all I've got . . . I'm like that old joke—I feel much better now that I've given up all hope. I'll be one of those women who just keep busy."

"Snap out of it! Don't make me slap you. I will, you know I will, and it'll hurt me more than it'll hurt you."

Eleanor's laugh pealed out, rusty, like church bells in Russia.

"Come to this party, Eleanor. It'll make you feel better. Trust me."

Jean ended up buying the dress. A Christmas present, she insisted, traipsing in unannounced and out of breath.

"We're going for elegance and drama, none of the predictability of black. You're ahead of your time. It'll be gorgeous on you." She drew the dress out of its bag with her own inimitable drama. "What's wrong, Eleanor? Don't you like it? Just try it on."

"Oh Jean. Of course I like it. It's beautiful . . . I don't know what comes over me these days."

Jean put her arm around Eleanor. "It's okay. Have a little cry. But only a little—I want to see this dress on you."

Brown velvet, liquid chocolate, flowed around her, clinging to her narrow hips, flaring out like a mermaid at her knees. Scoop necked and long sleeved, its bias cut achieved fluid elegance. She would never have twigged to brown. God knew she needed help, thin as a needle, face like a horse, as Alice had once put it, in a sisterly moment.

"Jean." Eleanor reached for her hand. "How can I thank you?"

"Just don't get tears stains on it. Having you at this party is my reward." She looked critically at the hemline. "Should it be shorter?"

"It's perfect, Jean. Do you know, I'm starting to look forward to this!"

"That's my girl. Now what about Myfanwy? What will she wear?"

"Daphne wants the girls decked out in holiday aprons over white blouses and blue skirts. She's got it all arranged. They'll be passing food around."

"That figures. Shoulders to the wheel for the big happy family."

Owen had announced in his way that brooked no discussion that he was staying home. No one would argue with him. Her own attendance was reliant on brown velvet and Hugh would go based on his apparent need to Try At All Costs.

Jean was an organized person and the brown velvet hung expectantly in Eleanor's closet days before the party. Just knowing it was there cheered her and she found herself in the car again, at the store again, at the meat locker, moving through the days with a semblance of normalcy. Back in gear, just in time for the Christmas rush. All those mincemeat tarts to bake. All those presents to buy. There would be no last minute dash to the pet store for the red mesh stocking full of liver treats and a new rubber ball. The plight of animals was their utter dependence on the people they arbitrarily belonged to.

Ross's plight. What arbitrary law of the universe governed that this cherub had limbs that couldn't function, a brain that couldn't reason? Next year he'd have to go. It was all very well for Hugh, who wasn't the one sitting home, watching Ross, thinking about what the future offered a retarded child. If there were places like Woodvale, wasn't it right that children like Ross went there?

What did they want for Christmas? Maybe Myfanwy should have a new dress. She and Lily used to shop together, topping it off with tea at the Empress Hotel. Lily would never again ponder Janna's wants. But Alistair did, phoning to discuss the perfect gift. He was thoughtful, phoning when he knew Ross would be asleep and she'd be alone with her thoughts. Asking about the children, giving her an ear. He'd asked what she wanted for Christmas, and Eleanor was deeply touched. How about a new life, Alistair?

"I'm thinking of a puppy for Janna," he had said. "She needs something to love."

"Are you mad?"

"Why not? A little Golden Retriever."

"The perfect breed. Long yellow hairs all over Daphne's pink house. How bad do you want it to be for her?"

*

The house that she couldn't leave for months was now a prison, and on Saturday she headed out. She didn't care if Olive broke down. The car was something they had an off chance of fixing.

Driving along Willows Beach, she imagined Owen as he was now. Slightly lopsided but improving, the doctor said. The limp would lessen but there would be no more distance running. He couldn't race but he could dance and dodge about with the precision of a prize-fighter, hopping nimbly on his right foot, the left one building in strength, while he jabbed with his fists at a pillow he had nailed—nailed!—to his bedroom wall.

The car was trundling down Fort Street. Where would she find them? Did sedate Victorian sporting goods stores carry boxing gloves? A memory of buying Owen's track shoes came out of nowhere and she veered sharply onto Blanshard Street, Olive meeting the challenge with surprising vehicular agility. She usually geared down on the corners, with Olive screaming in protest, but this time they shot around without a pause. "Double clutch," Hugh was always moaning, whatever that meant. Owen would have trouble with a clutch now. Just get to the sporting goods store. Owen had long fine fingers, like her father's, so the gloves were man-sized in butter soft black leather with white laces up the palm. Even Hugh wouldn't have thought of this.

She drove quickly down Fort Street, turned left and parked in front of Munro's Books. There was no point in buying Ross a book, but there were illustrations on the walls of the children's section—Robin Hood and His Merry Men, Long John Silver stumping along the deck of his trusty ship—but not what she was looking for. Her eyes swept the walls. There it was. Four little forest creatures sat around a toadstool, enjoying afternoon tea. Mr. Toad's open-topped car sat off to the side of their resplendent picnic and Moley was caught stealing a covetous glance at it. Ross would love it. Rat, Mole and Mr. Toad of Toad Hall, and, of course, the Otter. The detail would enchant him for hours. They didn't have a print in stock and were reluctant to part with the framed one on the wall.

It just fit into Olive's trunk. Back up Fort Street onto Douglas Street heading towards Eaton's parking lot. Myfanwy could use a sweater, a navy cardigan, and maybe a pair of white rabbit's fur pompoms on a velvet cord. The car was zooming—zooming!—past Eaton's, out of the city, past Goldstream Park, and up the Island Highway. The afternoon was grey and the oak trees were stark and lonely without their leaves.

The weather was comforting. Sunny days expected so much from a person.

She was approaching the little town of Duncan with enough money left, if Olive didn't whine for gas. The car rolled to a stop in front of the Indian Crafts store. It was more like an open-air lean-to, built on the highway, with Indian sweaters displayed on coat hangers hung from its roof. They were knit in thick cream-coloured wool and patterned with brown bears on the front and back. Her knitter's eye saw they were perfect, quite spectacular really. She found a smallish one that Myfanwy would get at least two years out of. Maybe more. Would she ever grow? Stop thinking. Buy the sweater and get back on the road. She approached the old woman sitting on a stool in the centre of the lean to in front of a pot-bellied stove. The stool was invisible but for its spindly legs sprouting under her bulk. Her round face broke into a sweet smile.

"Welcome, lady. A sweater for you today?"

"It's for my daughter. She's fourteen, but small. I'd like her to get a few years wear—" Eleanor stopped. Her eye caught the lush white rabbit's fur on a pair of beaded moccasins the old woman was working on. The suede was butternut brown, the beadwork blue and white.

"You like the moccasins? I'm finished, just a few more beads."

"No, the sweater is what I came for. She's still a bit of a tomboy. She'll love it."

"For your daughter, take the sweater and the slippers. They're small, they'll fit."

"I can't, it wouldn't be fair. She has two brothers, I need to be fair." How easy it was to carry on like they were a normal family, kids with nothing more than sibling rivalry on their minds.

"Only one daughter? Then she's special. Get her both. You can come back with the money." She was watching Eleanor fumbling with her purse.

"No," Eleanor's voice was firm. "She needs a sweater. That will do."

Their eyes met. Eleanor saw nothing but kindness in those brown almonds, and wondered what the old woman was seeing in hers.

*

The first sight that assailed their eyes was Daphne, assembled in pink and blue to match her house.

"All that meat and no potatoes?" Hugh muttered.

Daphne's bosom was no match for her ample hips. Her full length skirt, a deep sea blue, bunched in the way only taffeta could. Her pale pink organza blouse was cut to feature the sapphires winking around her neck. They couldn't possibly be real, could they?

The party was in high gear by the time they arrived and Jean Baker was by her side within minutes.

"Good God, Eleanor, you look brilliant."

"I know . . . I can't take my eyes off myself!"

Jean herself was toned down in the predictable black. She would always go the extra mile to let Eleanor shine, although what could outshine Daphne's house? The renovations were complete and Daphne and Winton's Annual Christmas Crush did double duty as an exhibition. The house had been systematically stripped over the years and bore no resemblance to the home Janna had shared with her mother. It would have been easier if they'd started fresh with a brand new house but Daphne couldn't outdo Lily if it wasn't Lily's home she was sacking.

This had been the Year of the Kitchen and Daphne lost no time corralling them into it. Florescent light glared off stark white counters and frigid blue walls. No shoes left under the white formica table framed by sterile chrome chairs, no collection of unpaid bills cluttering the counter by the blue phone, no greasy prints on the gleaming white fridge.

They were herded back to the living room where Daphne had set an altogether different tone. Uvula-coloured drapes yawned from the walls. Pink and mauve accent pillows shouted from the quilted floral chesterfield. Blue and white striped wing chairs flanked the fireplace, in front of which was a low blue-velvet bench.

They were being driven on, into the dining room, where a ten-foot rosewood table groaned under the weight of food for forty. "The forty people we party with, just our closest friends." The table was further laden with two silver candelabra, each with six pink candles. Then Eleanor spotted the Christmas tree standing senatorially in the massive front hall and there were no words. Jean was right by her side again, and they stared in mute awe. The laws of nature were being written anew. The tree had once been green, though they knew that by logic alone. This one was now ice blue and was lit entirely by white lights. Had Daphne bought fifty strings of lights, unscrewed all the white ones, and reunited them on four strings in an obsessive tour de force? Or was the world ready for Daphne and did lights now come in uniform colours?

Jean found her voice. "A country Christmas, this isn't."

"My God, Jean, where are the Styrofoam balls covered in red and green crepe paper? Aren't mothers compelled to hang them forever?"

The tree was covered in blue and white glass balls and glittering silver stars. In its cold perfection, it belonged on the same ice floe as the kitchen.

"Shall we adjourn to the upstairs?"

"Well—it can't get worse."

"You underestimate her, Eleanor."

They slipped up the staircase and into the master bedroom.

"Well," Eleanor said. "Well."

Jean was close to overcome, though she'd seen it before. "*Methinks she doth protest too much.*"

A fainting couch languished in the far corner of the twenty-foot square room. Pink marble glinted from the ensuite. Best not to look further in that direction. Flames licked in yet another marble fireplace. A fireplace in a bedroom. The dog's satin bed lay in front of it. The main exhibit, done up in rose silk, was the mahogany bed, its four posters rising suggestively.

"Romantic, aren't they?" Eleanor muttered.

"Like two wolverines in a rumble seat."

Eleanor looked at Jean. "You realize this could have gone either way. You know how close to the edge I've been." She fingered the brown velvet. "What if all this splendor sent me over?"

"I was willing to risk it."

They went downstairs in search of a drink. The loaded dining table gave no hint of Daphne's former life. A life of margarine in a tub. Melmac dishes. Plastic glasses with daisies on them. Daphne had been raised by her grandmother. A grandmother who didn't love her. Nadine had grown up in the same duplex.

Eleanor sipped her gin. There was Nancy Tippet, giving them a wide berth. Jean's husband, George was bellowing by the fire and Edith Milburn was looking weepy. She and Roy were celebrating their fiftieth wedding anniversary.

Winton, grandiosity itself in a navy blue tuxedo, was announcing speeches. Daphne prodded them back to the living room and launched in.

"Christmas is our opportunity to greet our friends and to wish you a joy-filled holiday. Winton and I want for each of you all the happiness that we have. God has smiled on us."

Daphne. Reveling in the roundness of her life. The life she would drag everybody in on it, like it was a national pastime. Daphne's focus in life was simply her life—a brilliant streamlining of energy.

"What has she done to deserve all this happiness?"

"It doesn't work that way, Eleanor. As your husband has been known to point out, life isn't fair. If happiness came to those who deserve it, you and I would be euphoric. They'd have to medicate us."

"Reminds me of a birthday card I once gave Hugh. A down trodden man bleats, *All I want in life is a place to live, enough to eat and clothes on my back.* Inside it says, *AND I WANT TO BE HAPPY ALL THE TIME!*"

"You could give that card to Daphne and she wouldn't get it."

Daphne was calling for order again as the hubbub of their happiness simmered down. "And now, as is my tradition at Christmas, I want to say a few words about my Winton."

"Is it my imagination or does Winton wear a hunted look? And what is it about Daphne's joy that smells just a bit of desperation? What a burden to keep that all-important happiness alive." Jean's voice was soft, audible only to Eleanor over Daphne's proud one.

"—and I want to take this opportunity to announce that Winton has received an award from the Victoria Club, for adding to the happiness of so many families this year." Daphne turned to her husband and put her arm through his. "An award for enhancing Victoria's landscape with new housing opportunities and—"

What was Winton thinking, allowing Daphne this egotistical egg-laying? But of course, he would be loving it. And what was George Baker doing, stepping forward with a purple Seagram's bag in his hand? The draw string sack looked heavy.

"As a self-appointed representative of the people of Victoria," George began, "who have watched your developments creep like a cancer—" He paused till he had everyone's attention. Hugh appeared beside her, an expectant air about him. "On behalf of those who have watched house after house go up, on behalf of everyone, I offer you a token of our esteem, Winton. Thirty pieces of silver."

Jean was absolutely right. This party had made her feel much better. Living with Jean was finally having the desired effect on George.

George had cooled the festivities and the party was over. They made their thank yous and tromped out the door.

"For pity's sake, Eleanor, give us your arm." What a relief to hear Hugh's voice slipping around her. He'd taken a drink for the first time in a long time. And then another. What did it mean to welcome that? Don't think about it. She was feeling good. Even the sight of Winton's new car left in the driveway to impress his friends couldn't dull Eleanor's glow. The car was a Bricklin this time, shining in the beam of the spotlight trained on it. No one had ever heard of a Bricklin until Winton soared through Victoria in his car of the future. Its gull wing doors opened upward and arched over the car, like a bird of prey. He'd managed to be one of the first ever to drive the Bricklin, treading in the hoof prints of Chaucer again, on that pilgrimage to Canterbury, when what you were riding said it all. The Prioress on her palfrey and the Monk astride his hunter could get in line.

Jean was volunteering for New Year's. "Let me throw the party, you're not up to it this year. We can't miss Daphne's goal setting gala—the amusement goals alone provide mileage for months."

"We'll talk about it in the morning, Jean, when we're sober."

Chapter Twenty-nine

Buy a pup and your money will buy
Love unflinching that cannot lie—

Rudyard Kipling

Fifteen paper doors opened onto cheerful Christmas scenes. Ten doors to go on the Advent calendar. Some days Maffy was excited, some days those Seventh Day Adventists looked pretty good. They missed a lot, not celebrating Christmast—the holiday fights, the black feeling you got when you knew you should be feeling white, the knowing that everybody else's Christmas was a Pat Boone sing-a-long and yours an Edgar Allan Poe marathon.

It was hard to say what her parents were better at—the hollering or the House of Usher silences, a creepy new act in their holiday repertoire. Still, there were one or two satisfying curves this year. Like the dog, which Owen maintained would change the status quo in the house. A dog would bark the house down and give them something new to fight over. They couldn't lose, Owen said.

A dog for Rossie was Owen's master plan. When he had gone back to school in November, he'd learned Joe Murphy's dog had delivered her pups. Just in time. By Christmas, they'd be eight weeks old and ready to leave their mother. Owen was feeling pretty warm about Joe, who'd broken up with Denise, who was mad as a weasel in a sack.

They walked through the park to Joe's house, four blocks over from Joanne's. Owen still couldn't ride his bike and hers still hadn't been fixed after Denise ran over it. They wouldn't bring the dog home until Christmas Eve but they went over to visit her, taking one of Rossie's undershirts each time, so she'd know his smell. The dog had gone through four so far. Black Labs chewed everything, according to Mrs. Murphy. Bosun had been half lab, half border collie and he'd done a job on their mother's horsehair sofa. Best to lay in a supply of rawhide bones. Her mother was confounded on laundry day now. Where were those undershirts?

They'd chosen the runt and Mrs. Murphy wouldn't charge for her. "It's hard enough to get rid of a runt, they're better off culled." They named her Bess and visited often, anxious to prove themselves and avoid a culling spree.

Going home through the park, Maffy thought of that eager puppy face, domed head shiny and new. They were nearing the clearing where the rain had organized itself into a pool, glinting in the fragile light. Did they think Bosun would be so easily replaced? The oak leaves were brown mush, like Chokies left too long in milk. It wouldn't snow this year, they said. It was going to be a mild winter with lots of rain. Lots of rain after the summer of none. Which was worse—the crackling heat that cost them Bosun or the silent wet gloom that sent their mother to another place? As they got closer to the house, she saw Bosun rushing to meet them. Other times she saw him lying in his sunny spot under the oak tree, groaning his satisfaction when someone reached down to give him an offhand pat.

That night they sat in Owen's universe while he read his Seattle paper. The music was Spanish that night, flamboyant and haughty, clicking its heels aggressively across the linoleum. Their mother was coming out of the shadows.

Just being in Owen's room was enough; they didn't have to say a word. But tonight he was talking. It was December 15 and the first news of Mariner II was in the paper. Yesterday it had been closest to Venus, but its mission had been nearly doomed when the timers on board failed to operate. Miraculously, a precisely timed radio command was sped to the spacecraft and thirty-six million miles away, Mariner heard it and responded! The experiments were done. Earth's twin in mass, Venus was also Earth's closest neighbour, but the planet was shrouded in clouds, its surface invisible. It would take months for the information to be decoded, but they had it. In time they would know.

Christmas Eve finally arrived. They'd been late getting the tree up this year and Maffy hadn't had time to coordinate the lights yet. There were two green ones in a row. Still, it looked good. The coloured bulbs twinkled in nests of swirling angel hair. She rubbed the sliver of raw, red flesh on her forefinger. Angel hair was deceptive in its shimmery beauty. The spun glass could slice like a knife. Like family. Sometimes they could be so beautiful. Sometimes you got cut.

After her father read *The Pied Piper*, she and Owen snuck out to where Mrs. Murphy was waiting, her black Austin spluttering and coughing in the dark.

"It's too cold for the car," Mrs. Murphy said. "The damp air is no good for her lungs. She makes a bad stealthmobile, she gives everything away. Here's your pup, with a starter bag of food, but I imagine you've got some lying around." She caught their eyes in the streetlight and smiled apologetically. Would people ever be unapologetic around them again? "You've got a good dog here; she'll be a loyal pet. The runts always are—full of gratitude."

The black car wheezed off, making Olive sound good in comparison. Maffy hugged Bess to her chest. Owen went first to see if the coast was clear. Quick as a flash they were in his room, but they hadn't bargained for the dog's crying.

"She misses her mother," Owen reasoned. "She'll get used to this, but we've got to keep her quiet tonight. It's critical she start out on a good note."

They were in active defiance of their mother's wishes. After Bosun, she'd said, "No more."

They slept in shifts till four, when the dog gave in and fell asleep on another of Rossie's undershirts. When the time came, Owen was ready with his speech about Bess's role in Rossie's life. Maffy had put a green bow around her neck and before long their mother was rummaging on her hands and knees in the ironing cupboard. Ancient clothes were in use again. Owen's grade eight parka with its furry lining was the critical item. Along with an old blanket and a cardboard box, her mother and father made Bess a bed.

"She'll be sleeping in the back hall," her mother announced.

Owen threw Maffy a look that said, play along, we're on a roll. And they were. The dog knew Rossie at once—another runt in the litter.

In the afternoon, Owen heaved Rossie onto his shoulders, Maffy put Bess on Bosun's old leash and they headed out. At the end of the driveway they stopped at the oak tree by Bosun's wooden plaque. It had taken Owen over a month and was as good as anything their father could have done. The lettering was small and perfect.

> *His heart is still his master's own,*
> *He laboured, fought, drew breath for him alone.*

Bess strained at her leash, and they headed into the park. Rossie clasped his hands around Owen's neck and gazed on the world like a little Maharajah. Their golden heads lit up the dark day, two shining birds in a nest of winter bracken. Maffy was wearing her new Indian sweater that took on her shape like it had been knit around her. When they had opened their gifts, her mother's smile had been a beautiful thing. She knew she'd done well. Owen, laced in his boxing gloves, had held his mother in a bear hug, "Just like boxers, locked in mortal combat!" Maffy had hugged her mother too. It was like wrapping your arms around an oak tree. You knew what it was going to feel like, but you did it anyway.

The Bakers had their big party on Boxing Day. Mrs. Baker's house was everything The New Mrs. Miles's wasn't. They were serving at her party too but they weren't wearing matching aprons like circus monkeys and they were getting paid.

"It's less interesting when everything matches, girls. Mother Nature is never that orderly and who can improve on her?"

The Bakers' tree looked like Mother Nature had decorated it. For starters, it was green. Joanne's family had a metallic tree that came apart and went into a box the second day of January so they had the comfort of knowing Christmas would look the same every year. The thing about the Bakers' tree was the decorations. The tree was so bushy it didn't need many. Pinecones tied with green and red plain ribbons hung from its branches. Sprigs of snowberries and mulberries lay on the boughs, as if Mrs. Baker had tossed them with her eyes closed. Maffy and Janna had strung cranberries that looked like braided ropes cordoning off the waiting lines at the Royal Theatre. There were no lights, just white candles flickering in wooden candleholders from Austria. The tree looked like it had just stepped in from the Alps. Beside this vision of a tree stood Owen and Janna, and the picture was complete. Somewhere a flash bulb went off. Next year they would be in a frame.

There were pictures everywhere in the Baker's house—of places they'd been, of friends, of family, of other people's children in white, ruffled clothing. And there were things. A carved chest from the Orient, a wall hanging from India, a footstool covered in leopard skin, a family of black elephants parading across the coffee table in front of the fireplace. Best of all was the giant clamshell with wavy lips that sat on the marble hearth. Imagine the sea that had given that up. Nothing matched in this house. The sofa was the blue of sapphires and each of the cushions scattered on it was a different jewel colour. Red and blue carpets from the east covered the floor. You could curl up in this house and go anywhere in the world.

Maffy would have served at Mrs. Baker's party without getting paid. People who felt you deserved to be paid were people you didn't need anything more from. And serving gave her and Janna a chance to spy. Donna and Denise were stationed in the front hall, failing in their attempts to look decorative. Donna sensed her failure and slithered into the library to look at books from everywhere in the world. She was thinner even than Maffy. Denise was taking another stab at Owen, now that Joe had clued in. She would never twig to the obvious hopelessness of this cause, seeing as Owen was twice as smart as Joe.

"Hi, Owen. Did you read about the expedition to Venus?" Denise had been doing her reading, coached no doubt by her mother. Two barracudas in the goldfish bowl.

Owen was ready for her. "They want to launch a woman next. They're calling for volunteers."

Maffy headed toward the library in search of Donna, who looked like she could use a crab puff. She had that mongrel look about her in a family of poodles. Maffy stopped at the entrance to the library where Donna was no longer alone. A large man in a party hat—a paper crown from the inside of one of the Christmas crackers the partygoers had so recently torn into—was standing beside her. Donna's dull brown hair hung in a limp pageboy with no festive headgear to pep it up. Maffy stepped into the shadow of the breakfront in the hall. Donna hadn't seen her, and something told Maffy she wouldn't want to be seen. Her eyes had a look of fear when she darted them around. The man spoke in a honey voice.

"All dressed up for the party? Even so, you're homely, aren't you? Just like your father."

Donna looked down.

"Won't fight back? You don't just look like your cuckold of a father." The man was mad all of a sudden. He gripped Donna's arm and her white nylon blouse gaped at her bony neck. Donna squeaked softly and the man laughed. Maffy backed away. She knew that meaty hand and the dark red hair under the paper crown. She knew that slippery voice, sliding in and out of anger.

She lurched into the kitchen, crab puffs piling into each other at one end of the tray. She knew what cuckold meant. Did Donna? Like every good family, the Miles had a dictionary, bent on doing their best for their young. She went from room to room looking for Janna who was in charge of the cheese balls. Why wasn't she doing her job? There she was, coming out of the emerald green bathroom like she'd just seen Oz. Maffy tried to speak but her throat was dry. She stared into Janna's deep sapphire eyes, just like her father's. She'd blend right in on that sofa. Was there any hint in those blue eyes of what Maffy had seen in Donna's mouse brown ones? Janna stared back.

"Are there ghosts in this huge house?" she asked.

Worse, Maffy thought. Janna began to laugh. Maffy had never seen her look like Donna had, backed up against a wall of books that in a different world than this would have held everything she'd ever need to know.

Chapter Thirty

Ring out, ring out my mournful rhymes
But ring the fuller minstrel in.

Alfred, Lord Tennyson

1963

They'd sung in another New Year, her father crying as usual, and the waiting went on. She and Janna, both of them waiting. Janna was waiting to be free. She could walk away. When she was old enough she could just walk away. There was nothing in her house to hold her.

Maffy was waiting to fill out, like other fourteen-year olds. She was three inches taller than last January, but still thin as a rail. Owen was waiting to go to university, and Rossie didn't know what he was waiting for or what was waiting for him. And everyone was waiting for Owen to limp less. Everyone watched Owen. The less attention from parents, the better off a kid was.

Maffy was also waiting for the day when she stopped wondering what her mother would be like when she walked in the back door from school. It was the never knowing.

She lay in bed waiting for dawn, another year bearing down. She'd given Rossie a broomstick horse for Christmas. Trigger had a yellow cloth head and a mane of lamb's wool. A brown leather rein looped through its mouth. She'd hoped he would straddle it and get on with walking, but he couldn't. His left leg wouldn't hold him and his left arm wasn't too steady either. He was lucky, they said, because his cerebral palsy was nothing like Bonnie's. Would that please Mossy-Lip? He'd turned four in November, but no one talked fondly about the day he was born.

She turned on the light and looked at her clock. It was four, of course. She tried to think of something good, like her father's voice when she'd first heard him sing *Myfanwy* like it was a hymn. She shivered again. *Maaavaunwhee.* Grandmaf had found the record for her, for Christmas. The choir from the Rhonda Valley was famous for singing her name but it wasn't the same as when her father did.

She thought back to the Christmas visit from her other grandmother and the aunts. Grandmaf had been there too, and her grandmother and the aunts from Vancouver had that perfectly polite way about them around Grandmaf. So polite you'd have to be a moron not to smell a rat. Grandmaf wasn't a moron but she had this terrible habit of only seeing the good in people. Her other grandmother was just the opposite, critical of everything, especially Grandmaf's clothes and hair. Who did she think she was impressing with her perfect cream blouse and her perfect rose suit with the diamond broach on its collar and the three stranded Queen Mother pearls around her neck? Whatever the Vancouver relatives said, Grandmaf was beautiful in a black and white way, the kind of old lady who would be proud to have her birth year recalled with respect. Her white hair was rolled into an old fashioned bun with the sides all loose and half undone. She had a shapeless black hat held on with a hatpin with a blob of Baltic amber on the end. Her dresses were black, in serviceable material, and large black lace up shoes completed her wardrobe. Her soft white face had large folds in it. Not the papery skin and finely wrinkled eyes of the other grandmother, but great crevices bisecting her forehead and paving her face from nose to jaw. The only colour in Grandmaf was in her eyes. Though she was nearly eighty, they were still bright blue.

Maffy's thoughts drifted on. It must be four-thirty by now. Why hadn't Donna gone to university? No one ever asked. She was another person putting up with the thinly veiled contempt of others. She was invisible in that family. Maffy could hardly recall her voice. The New Mrs. Miles and Denise did all the talking. Did Donna talk to her mother? What would she say and how would she say it?

*

She was walking Rossie in the January drizzle. He still fit in his stroller, but for how long? Bess clung to the stroller's side, her little trotters almost caught in the wheels. The dog slept at the foot of Rossie's cedar bed and Rossie loved her almost as much as he loved Maffy. She wasn't being conceited. Everyone saw the way Rossie loved her, the way his eyes followed her around, and the way he called her, "Ma-a-a-a." He could say things and she was convinced he could understand. She read to him, pointing to words, sounding them out slowly. *Old Mother West Wind* was still his favourite.

She turned the stroller onto Beach Drive with the really big houses. The Bakers' was two blocks down, sort of, since the freewheeling Uplands didn't have regular blocks. Streets wound and twisted any way they wanted in the Uppity Uplands. She had passed the Bakers, Bess showing forbearance as a cat sauntered by on the other side of the street, when she heard panting behind her. Her heart jumped, but it was only Mrs. Baker, looking like she belonged on the street where Joanne and the Murphys lived. Her hair was in rollers, which surprised Maffy. It always looked like it was done at the beauty parlour, all waved around her face. It was silver but she seemed younger than Maffy's mother, whose hair was brown. Mrs. Baker was overweight, the flesh around her eyes too fat for wrinkles, and she was out of breath, short legs fighting with the leopard print caftan snarling around her ankles. Maffy liked her as much as she'd ever liked anyone.

"Myfanwy, I'm glad I caught you, I was just taking out the garbage. Will you and Ross come in for hot chocolate? George is away for the weekend and I'd love the company."

"Thank you, Mrs. Baker, but Bess won't leave Rossie. She'd put on a panic show."

"Bess can come too and Ross can play with the elephants."

Mrs. Baker bustled around laying out a book for Rossie, as well as the elephants. It was a book on animals. She opened it to a giraffe.

"They call these animals 'twiga' where they live in Tanzania. Isn't that logical? The Swahili language makes sense."

Bess ended up peeing on the carpet, the really beautiful one, right in front of the fireplace. Mrs. Baker just laughed.

"In Turkey, where this came from, people put their rugs in the street for trucks to drive over. Carpets are only beautiful when they're broken in. The older the rug, the more valuable it is. Things are better when they are not perfect. That goes for people too. We can relax when things aren't perfect."

"Owen's not perfect anymore."

"And Ross," Mrs. Baker said.

No one ever talked about Ross but he wasn't invisible like Donna. Maffy wasn't sure she wanted to talk about him now. She didn't want to start bawling. Mrs. Baker was content with silence, but eventually, she started in.

"When I was a young woman I always knew I'd have lots of children, like my mother, and like her mother before her. That's what good Clarke girls did, you see. Besides, I'd wanted children ever since I was Ross's age and the last of my sisters was born. The last of seven. We were a big happy family, one of the few I knew, one of the few I've ever known." Mrs. Baker was watching Rossie from some place far off. "For a long time, I thought it was my fault. I thought God was punishing me for some unnamed, unremembered sin. I thought I'd done something wrong, but it doesn't work that way. Things happen. Ross is retarded. It's not your fault, Myfanwy."

She could feel the rock in her throat and the live thing in her stomach. Apart from the fighting in the night, no one talked about Rossie. The rock was getting bigger and she was making an odd mewing noise. Mrs. Baker's arm was light around her shoulder, pulling her ever so gently toward her big chest and the smell of cigarettes and perfume.

"Do you think you're the reason? If you hadn't been there, he might not have lived."

What if her mother thought it was her fault Rossie had lived? The mewing was a bawl now, and it went on for a long time, back and forth in that soft chest. Finally she stopped and met Rossie's anxious eyes. She smiled at him and his smile in return was like the sun. He sat by the wet spot on the carpet with Bess at his side. He turned back to the book. He was staring at elephants now. When had Mrs. Baker turned it to that page?

Chapter Thirty-one

Where the apple reddens,
Never pry—
Lest we lose our Edens,
Eve and I.

Robert Browning

Spring could be counted on in Victoria, could be celebrated with arrogant fervor while the rest of the country froze. Daffodils on Saint David's Day, patron saint of the Welsh. Eleanor turned off the music. It had seemed a good idea, thematic, but *The Rites of Spring* was too close to the bone today. The mood in the house was malignant enough without the crashing chords of Stravinsky heralding growth. She went to the piano and picked through the *Minute Waltz*. Lily had played it perfectly. It took Eleanor ten minutes.

Ross was still asleep. She wandered out to the garden with Jean's newest home decorating book. Once she'd wanted to teach; now she dreamed of decorating. Colours, space, accents, themes. Each time she entered a room, she saw it differently.

Owen had pitched the old tent on the patch of grass that bordered the park. The canvas window flaps ruffled in the breeze. Spring wasn't that dependable after all and she debated going back for her jacket. Sure as she set the spring pansies out, there would be a northern front. The kind that made you forget you'd ever been warm. Each year the garden had the power to excite her. Each year promised a new chance for the pink dogwood, the Japanese maple and the purple hyacinth. *If I had but two pence . . . was it the Koran? . . . I'd spend one for bread to feed the body, one for a hyacinth to feed the soul.*

The wisteria would cover the carport with a fall of lavender and they should get a decent number of pears. The peach tree, well, if they got even one, it was a victory. Counting success on the strength of a peach tree reduced life to a manageable point. Maybe Jean was right. "Get a grip, Eleanor!" The thought of Jean brought a smile. She'd done a good job on the Christmas tree, taking each of Eleanor's suggestions to heart. Jean swore Eleanor's talents were wasted on her stodgy Tudor bunker. It had been a challenge, introducing just the right hint of order to the eclectic chaos Jean loved, coaching her over the years on how to give each treasure a place to shine. And wouldn't they shine, anchored by Persian carpets? Wouldn't an original Emily Carr buck up any room?

The phone rang. She ran back into the house. It might be Alistair. He would let it ring long enough. He knew she would be home.

"Hello."

"Eleanor, it's Alistair."

"I thought it might be you. How are you?"

"Fine, how are you all?"

"Doing well enough. Janna's holding her own in the hornets' nest. All is well, Alistair."

"Is she okay?"

"Actually, quite okay."

"The horse has made a difference, hasn't she?"

"Janna loves that animal. It was stroke of genius, Alistair." He had leased a gentle grey mare for her and provided riding lessons for Christmas. "Janna bikes up to the stables any chance she gets, according to Myfanwy, who goes along too."

"I took a chance. Not everyone loves horses the way I do."

"Because you do, she does."

"Thank you, Eleanor. I'm getting her a riding habit for her birthday. She's going to enter the odd show."

"We'll find her a black velvet riding helmet. Myfanwy and Owen would love to help with that."

"That's very kind. How is Ross?"

"He's growing, he's happy, he's beautiful." It was all true but it didn't add up the way it should.

"Beautiful. That stands to reason. Are you okay?"

"I'm okay." He knew when not to push.

"And everyone else?" He wouldn't ask the question but Eleanor knew what he meant.

"Winton has been subdued since the Christmas party."

"I wonder how he spent his thirty coins."

"Perhaps Daphne spent them."

"I wonder if that is about out of steam. I think it's only a matter of time."

"He does seem stressed. Cheeks flaming; high blood pressure by the looks of it. It can't be any good, but you'd never guess it from Daphne."

"Janna is coming down to Seattle for her birthday. It's on Easter this year. She'll be out of the fray for a bit."

"Just don't plan an Easter egg hunt. Too many memories."

It was a relief to touch on things that had changed their lives forever. Not talk, not yet. But acknowledgement. After fifteen minutes they said good bye and Eleanor put on her new green jacket and headed back to her green Cape Cod chair. The wool was the colour of her eyes. Where had Hugh found something so beautiful? Why this lavish gift for Valentine's of all things? There was a time when they'd been of one mind. Valentine's Day was for fools pressing their ardor lest it came up wanting. She stared into the park and marveled as she did every year at the disorganized glory of the wild flowers beginning their brief tenure.

The wind picked up and the tent shuddered as if it would collapse. Owen slept in it on weekends though it was cold.

It had been years since she'd known the inside of that tent. Years since she'd smelled its stale air and felt its still heat. Hugh had pitched it next to two small arbutus trees just starting out in life.

"It's so hot, let's sleep under the stars."

"Do you know any?"

"Well, there's Polaris, off the Big Dipper."

"Everybody knows that," he teased.

"Do you know any?" What did she know about what he knew?

"Let me show you the Pleiades, Eleanor."

Her name floated on his lips, into the layers of the night choir, joining the tiny buzz of the mosquitoes—the sopranos—and the rumble of the frog—the bass. The owl was the alto, and the closest sound, so beautifully close, was the tenor, singing the language of lullaby.

"Myfanwy, booed yr oll o'th fywyd
Dan heulwen ddisglair canol dydd
A boed I rosyn gwidog iechyd
I ddawnsio ganmlwydd ar dy rudd
Anghofia'r off o'th addewidion
A wnest I rywun, eneth ddel
A dyro'th law, Myfanwy dirion
I ddim oud dweud y gair "Ffarwell!"

"What does it mean?"

"Myfanwy, may you spend your life long
under a midday sunshine bright
And may the blushing red rose of health
Dance a hundred years upon your cheeks
Forget all the promises
Made to someone, pretty girl
And give me your hand, gentle Myfanwy
If only to utter the word, "Farewell".

"Such haunting sweetness." She reached for his hand. "Why are the Welsh so sad?"

"The world is sad, the Welsh aren't afraid of it. It's where poetry comes from. *Our sweetest songs are those that tell of saddest thought.*"

"Shelley," she whispered.

He drew her closer.

Later, when his breath settled like mist on her brow, she lay in his musky warmth and listened. The wind in the fir trees took up the song. The smell of heat enveloped her. The moon rose, and in its pool of light, the two young arbutus trees glowed. They were growing from a single trunk, arching out in mirror image, twisting as only arbutus could, like the rust velvet antlers of a young stag. The beauty of their harmony stilled her breath. Could they maintain their perfect, careless symmetry?

Chapter Thirty-two

—— ·◈·◈· ——

Can a mother sit and hear
An infant groan, an infant fear?

William Blake

She brushed her hand over the stubble of her eyebrows. Fewer today than yesterday. Throwing off her quilt, she headed for Rossie's room. There was comfort in the sound of his able breath. Mrs. Baker was right, she did feel responsible for him, but beyond that, she just loved him. The shadow of his hair wisped around his head like duckling down. She tucked his quilt around his neck, then headed for the living room. Her bangs were in her eyes as she tried to make out the shape of things. She needed them long. Her eyebrows had always been faint, no one noticed they were hardly there at all now. She found one, pulled, and felt the bright dot of pain.

Morning came and she got Rossie dressed in his good clothes. "We're leaving, Mum."

No answer. It was hard to tell what was registering on her mother's radar these days. She was always quiet. Not a calm quiet, but a quiet that felt like she was building a fire inside that could suddenly burst into flames. The house was quiet too, and when she came home through the park, Maffy didn't hear it belching out music anymore. They were beyond music.

Mrs. Baker had asked her and Rossie to tea this morning. He was wearing the royal blue knitted leggings and sweater Mrs. Baker had bought him on Government Street. He looked like Shirley Temple.

"Okay, Mum, we're going now." Still no answer as the stroller clattered through the front door with Bess leaping around the wheels.

Mrs. Baker was wearing her leopard print caftan with a matching turban wrapped tightly around her silver hair. She looked like no one else in the world.

"Come in, dear. Hello, Rossie, and here's our Bess. Come in you lot."

"Hello, Mrs. Baker." Maffy moved into her warm arms.

"We'll go into the living room. I've laid a fire and there's someone I'd like you to meet."

She led the way with Rossie straddling her hip. There was never any question that Bess wouldn't be darting along in Mrs. Baker's big wake, her little otter head sniffing furiously at every exciting thing. Maffy sighed. She didn't want to meet anyone. She'd spent more time getting Rossie ready than she had herself. Standing by the fire was a Chinese man. Maffy was sure she'd seen him before.

"Arthur, I'd like you to meet the Morgans. Myfanwy, Ross and Bess." She announced them as if they were as important as he must be. A dark blue suit on a Saturday morning. "Children, this is my neighbour, Dr. Wong."

The father of the two beautiful Chinese girls, Shirley and Stella. The waist on her slacks was too tight and her stomach hurt. Dr. Wong's daughters never wore slacks.

"Hello, Me Von Way, hello Ross." Mrs. Baker pronounced her name the Welsh way and Dr. Wong was having trouble following suit. He seemed awkward, like he didn't have those slap-you-on-the-back comments ready to rush out of his mouth. His voice had an accent. Rossie started to cry. Her Indian sweater pricked the back of her neck, but she didn't take it off. Her blouse had a stain.

"Dr. Wong is a children's doctor. He's helped children like Ross."

If he wanted to help Rossie, why was he staring at her? Her bottom lip tasted of blood.

"Myfanwy, Dr. Wong is here just as a friend of mine."

"Mevonway." He was getting the hang at it. "Interesting name." He was very small and very calm and his voice was gentle. He took Rossie carefully from Mrs. Baker's arms and Rossie stopped crying. "Mrs. Baker tells me you have been to Woodvale School, Mevonway. I understand your concern." He seemed to like saying her name and was talking to her like she was Rossie's mother.

"Your young brother has Cerebral palsy, this we know, but each case is unique. Sometimes it is not easy to make a responsible prognosis until a baby has developed into a young child."

They might be different, but they were all retarded. Right now Bonnie was in her wheelchair in the playroom that smelled of vomit and pee.

"What is a responsible prognosis?"

"Each child is different. I wanted to meet you and Ross, and would like to meet your parents too."

He sat down on the carpet. Amazingly, he didn't seem much bigger than Rossie. He took each of Rossie's hands in his own and began lightly clapping them together. Then he got out a gold watch on a long chain and swung it like a hypnotist in front of Rossie, who laughed and followed it methodically with his eyes, while the little Chinese man watched intently.

"Myfanwy, will you help me with tea, please?"

She followed Mrs. Baker into the huge kitchen crammed with copper tubs and straw baskets from Africa. Mrs. Baker was the only person she knew who grew plants inside the house. The Real Mrs. Miles had grown orchids but they had lived in the green house for the most part. The round kitchen table was large enough to hold all the gardening books and cook books that lay scattered on it. In the midst this welcoming mess was a tea set in the lightest green imaginable, with delicate blue birds flying blithely around the cups that had no handles and no matching saucers. The teapot had a wicker handle that looped over the top.

"They're cranes—bringers of good luck." Mrs. Baker was smiling a smile that worried Maffy. She didn't want to start crying now, for crying in the mud.

"What does he mean, *Each child is different?*"

"It means he can't make promises, but he's kind and a wonderful doctor. He's interested in exploring with your parents—gently of course—why Ross hasn't been through a thorough assessment. Dear Dr. Gregson has one foot on the sands of Waikiki. The old fool."

Explore? Gently? Mrs. Baker knew better than that. Her mother wasn't an explorer; she was a search and destroyer. The weight of the tea set dragged at her shoulders, as she backed her way through the swinging door leading into the dining room. Mrs. Baker followed with the tea pot in one hand and in the other, a dark blue glass plate loaded with tea-cakes from the Golden Sheaf Bakery, a full dozen. She was lavish with food and was so relaxed you could actually enjoy eating it. There were no silver serving platters and armies of pink candles in silver candlesticks.

Dr. Wong left right after tea, saying it had been an honour to meet them, like they'd done him a favour. What if all adults were like him and Mrs. Baker? Would kids end up talking back and getting fresh? Was that what all grown ups were so sure would happen if they throttled back and treated kids like they treated each other?

*

The librarian looked up suspiciously. Dark moles were sprouting little forests on her face. They matched her brown cotton dress and her brown hair. She had a high, wide forehead, down which her pageboy bangs fell halfway. How now, brown cow? Maffy pulled on her own bangs.

"Can I help you?"

"I, um, I'm writing a school report."

"School is out."

She was usually pretty smooth when it came to lying, but the librarian unnerved her. There was something about that hairy face that reminded her of Woodvale. "I like to give myself plenty of time . . . a head start."

She sidled off toward the reference room, feeling Miss Brown's eyes boring into her back. She pulled *The World Book, Volume C,* off the shelf and found an empty chair at a long wooden table. Actually, they were all empty. Strangely enough, there were no other eager beavers getting a head start. She found four and a half pages of babble on ceramics and not a word on Cerebral palsy. This was no more helpful than *The Book of Knowledge* at home. How complicated could ceramics be?

She carried the book back to the shelf and put it carefully into its spot. Pulling out *The Encyclopedia Americanna, Volume C,* and opening it where she stood, she stared briefly at the two pages of information. She then took the same volume of *The Encyclopedia Britannica* off its shelf and returned to her seat with the heavy volumes. She opened her school binder, got out her pen and paper and began to write.

Two hours later, hand cramped from writing, she put the books back. Too bad she couldn't bring Owen's typewriter here. He let her take it to her bedroom and she was getting pretty good, pecking at those keys. Typing had to be perfect. If it wasn't, it wouldn't achieve the desired effect. What she really wanted to do with the books was steal them. Just for a day. Would Owen believe this without reading it himself? But she didn't dare in case the librarian found out and took away her library card.

"Is it allowed, could I borrow these books, just overnight?"

"Those are reference books, they cannot be loaned. But there should be a non-fiction section for the topic you are researching."

"I'm looking up, ah, researching childhood illnesses." It was getting easier.

"For school?"

Maffy met her eyes. "Just for my own interest."

"Would you like to be a doctor?"

"I'm a girl."

"Well, what illness in particular?"

"Cerebral palsy."

"I'm not too familiar with that but the medical section is in the Dewey Decimal six hundreds and there is a good resource there specifically for neurological issues."

"Maybe I'll be a librarian."

Miss Brown smiled and offered to come and help.

"I, uh, I've got enough for today, but thank you very much. I'll be back for more information. Thank you." She wanted to get home to see Owen.

She knocked on his door. There was no answer. "Owen, open up, I've got news!" There was no sound from inside. He must be in there. "Owen!"

"Okay, okay. Come in."

She turned the doorknob and went in. The sun was shining in his window, making his universe oddly small.

"I've been to the library!" She couldn't contain her excitement. "Let me show you what I've copied. I found two encyclopedias with more on their minds than ceramics."

"What?"

"Look, Owen, I've got seven pages of notes! On Cerebral palsy." What if Owen didn't think it was important? She pressed on. "Let me read it, I've copied it exactly." She looked at him closely for the first time since she'd entered his room. He was lying on his bed, propped up on his left elbow. "What's wrong?"

"I just got the Seattle paper." He took the bus downtown on Saturdays now. "The Venus probe has been decoded." His voice was flat.

"What did they find?" She'd let him go first.

"Nothing. They found nothing. Venus, our closest neighbour in the solar system, in the galaxy, in the whole damn universe—"

"Owen!"

"There's nothing there, Maff. Nothing but poisonous gases, temperatures up to six hundred degrees, no possibility of life." He slumped backward on his pillow. "No possibility of neighbours. They thought the clouds might have protected her from the heat of the sun, allowed for life, but all those swirling clouds are poisonous. It's like a hell, with deadly gases that—"

"Owen! For God's sake, there's life here on earth. Could we talk about that, for crying in the mud!"

He sat upright and stared at her. Had she ever sounded so much like their mother?

"What's going on?"

"I have been to the library." She enunciated each word like she was teaching English. "I'm sorry about Venus," she added, with fleeting contrition, "but this might be important, Owen. Important for Rossie." She stopped. She couldn't bear for this not to be important for Rossie.

"Okay, what have you found?"

She began to read, slowly at first, then faster, stopping to breathe only when breathless, picking through her notes for the most important parts.

> "*It is estimated that there are probably more than half a million cases of Cerebral palsy in the United States. In every six new cases . . . roughly two are feebleminded, four have normal intelligence . . . does not necessarily imply mental retardation; many children grow to be mentally competent adults . . . children may be perceptive and intelligent; however, because of involuntary movements and dysarthia, they may be unable to communicate and so may appear mentally retarded. The child should be exposed to the normal demands . . . speech therapy is often indicated . . . many drugs have been used to relieve spasticity . . . in some cases surgery is used . . . functioning may be improved by the application of braces . . .*

She stopped. Her papers were scattered around her feet with the Seattle paper, replete with bad news for Venus. She looked at Owen, who was sitting up now, elbows on his knees, hands propping up his serious face. He didn't say a word. She waited for what seemed like a long time.

"Well? Owen, what do you think?" she pleaded.

"Maybe you're right; maybe this is important for Ross."

"What if he's not retarded, Owen?"

"How can they find out? If a kid can't talk, doesn't that mean he's retarded?"

Owen wasn't sounding all that convinced though, like suddenly he was seeing through a different lens. Maffy scrambled through her notes and read the part about speech therapy again. Eventually, Owen stirred himself.

"Let's go get him, take him out to the park."

"Yeah, he loves the park. You climb the big oak, and I'll pass him up!"

"No, you climb, and I'll pass him to you. He's getting heavy." Owen's voice was strange, like he was afraid. Hope could do that to you.

Chapter Thirty-three

————— ·◈◈· —————

There may be a heaven; there must be a hell;
Meanwhile, there is our earth here—well!

Robert Browning

His limp had been less noticeable when he'd walked across the stage to accept the silver medal for scholarship. Owen had won all the Oak Bay High School awards including the Premier's Award for the top student in the province of British Columbia. That was in June. Now it was August, and his walk was even smoother. Eleanor had studied his progress. She knew that looking healed and being healed were different. He would never run like he had. He would never be the same. None of them would. High school was over for Owen. Could he hardly wait to be somewhere else? August, and he still hadn't made a decision, but she knew he'd go. That she knew. Ross too. When he was five. Don't think about it.

Eleanor sat listlessly in the garden chair, drinking in the heat, listening to the phone jangling on and on. It wouldn't be Alistair. He had called yesterday. She wouldn't get up. She talked to few people now. Even Jean was a problem with her constant cheerfulness, her certainty that Eleanor ought to stiffen her lip and get on with it. Jean with all her advice. Unwanted advice about the children and in particular, what they should be doing about Ross. Had Jean ever known what it was like to worry about a child? Had she ever felt the weight of certainty that life wasn't going to work out after all, that all the energy poured into it was wasted?

The phone had stopped ringing. She sat in the stillness and indulged in her favourite fantasy. The one where she wasn't anymore . . . she was just gone, vapourized. No more pain, or worry, or anger. No more thinking. No more calls from her mother, no more remembering Lily, no more agonizing over Owen, no more despairing over Ross, and most of all, no more watching over Hugh. Watching for the signs that were there all the time now. Why was he late? Where had he been? No more of that.

The phone was ringing again, and this time it wouldn't stop. After three minutes, she got to her feet and headed in. It was amazing the phone hadn't woken Ross.

"I knew you were home, Eleanor," Jean said. You're always home. I'm coming over. Put the kettle on. Forget that, I'll bring the gin."

Eleanor smiled. Gin would go down well. Ross was awake now. He didn't need much of an afternoon nap and he woke as sweetly as he did everything. Don't think. Just put the kettle on, put Ross's blue shirt on and soon you'll be swilling gin.

Jean huffed in, out of breath. She handed over a full bottle of Tanqueray. Only the best.

"I'll trade you, give him to me. Hello, little trouper. The shirt is a good fit. That was thoughtful of you, Eleanor, I knew it would be perfect on him."

Eleanor passed Ross over. When he was in someone else's arms she could take him in. He was heartbreaking. Don't look.

"Pour us a drink, Eleanor. I'll be in the garden."

She loaded the old wicker tray with the kettle of hot water, two large gin and tonics and one small apple juice in Ross's special cup. She threw on a couple of arrowroots and headed for the battered cape cod chairs. She set the tray down on the low round patio table. After handing Jean her drink, she lifted the kettle.

"It warms the water in his wading pool," she explained. "I filled it two hours ago, so the sun would warm it too." She poured the full kettle into the blue plastic pool with yellow fish swimming

on its inflated tubes. She tested the water with her hand. It was
the right temperature, the temperature that could soothe his
shuddering, but still bring on that delicious intake of breath
on a scorching day. She took Ross from Jean's arms and began
to remove the blue shirt and the red shorts. When all that was
left was the brown hat that had been part of Myfanwy's brownie
uniform, she lowered him gently into the pool. Immediately,
Ross began his birdcall of joy. Bess crept in too, trying to disguise
herself as a water toy. When had she gotten so big? Her brown
eyes were trained on Eleanor.

"It's all right, girl, you can stay."

Bess stood behind Ross, up to her knees in water, an
unwavering black sentinel bolstering his back. Ross kept up his
examination of the blade of grass he held in his right hand.
Eleanor felt Jean's eyes on her. Neither spoke until Jean broke
the silence.

"You're a good person, Eleanor. That may not be your goal,
but you are all the same."

Jean opened her silver cigarette case and tapped one smartly
on its end. She snapped her slim silver lighter, and drew lovingly
on the cigarette.

"Give me one. Please."

"Atta girl—want something. Anything."

Eleanor lit her cigarette and almost began to enjoy herself.
The smoke wafted in the hot, still air. "What's new in the world,
Jean? I'm afraid I'm loosing touch."

"You're not missing much. Let's see . . . The University
Women's Club has voted to disband, Nancy Tippet needs a
hysterectomy, Winton Miles has invested in Mount Tolmie. He'll
turn that pristine wilderness into a housing development. Lily's
money is his ticket to all that raw land. He's let George know that
his investment dollars aren't welcome anymore." Jean's laugh bit
the air. "Says he won't touch George's money with a ten foot pole.
Says we'll never make another dime off his 'genius'."

"What a blow! How will George go on?" Eleanor laughed in
spite of herself.

"Apparently Winton got stuck in the parking lot at Mount
Tolmie." Jean stubbed out her cigarette in the portable ashtray

she always carried and lit another. "Well, not really stuck, but he couldn't get into his car."

Eleanor looked at Jean, who offered her another cigarette. "No, but thank you. One was just right. What's this about Winton's car?"

"Those narrow diagonal parking spaces. When he drove in, he had the parking lot to himself, it seems. Then when he returned from his scouting—always scouting—two cars had parked on either side—too close apparently—and Winton couldn't get the door of the Bricklin open. You know those wings on that car. There wasn't enough room between the cars to, you know, open the doors! Apparently he was apoplectic. Red as a beet. It does my heart good to picture it."

"Winton and his Car of the Future. Worse than the Edsel, if you ask me. The annoying thing is; he'll just buy something else. He can afford a collector's item, and get another Cadillac too. A newer model. His must be at least two years old by now."

"But who would want a Cadillac, Eleanor? I mean really, I wouldn't touch one of those bourgeois land yachts with a ten foot pole. In fact, there isn't a pole long enough."

"Daphne seems to be enjoying hers."

"A prime example of the bourgeois. I rest my case."

"You do me good, Jean."

"Okay, out with it. How is everything with you? How are the children?" Jean waited until she had Eleanor's eye. "How is Hugh?"

Eleanor looked down at the jagged edge of her thumb nail. Gardening without gloves again. She heard the patio door open and Myfawnwy called, "I'm home mum."

"Myfanwy!" Eleanor called back, with enthusiasm. "Come and tell us about your day, dear."

Jean gave Eleanor a knowing look and held out her arms to Myfanwy.

That night Hugh did not come home. Finally she heard the back door open. She sprang out of bed and raced to the back hall.

"Where have you been? It's midnight!"

"I told you when I called. I've been working."

"Working! Until midnight? I don't believe you. What kind of projects have you got that need that amount of work? I've been worried sick, contending with these kids."

"They're contending with you."

"Now you listen to me. You're the one who's never home, anymore, I'm the one who cares for them, all day, every day, I can't believe—"

"It's a harsh kind of care. What kind of care sends kids off to find cougars, off to sit in oak trees, off to Woodvale?"

"You blame me? You—off with your secretary, that's what's really going on, that's what this is all about. Let's talk about that!"

"Still got that bee in your bonnet, Eleanor? We're not going to talk about my secretary, but we could talk about Ross. About why you're so set on sending him off."

"He's retarded." She felt her throat thicken and she turned away.

"What if he's only mildly retarded? That's the term they're using now. What does that useless Gregson know?"

"He can't walk. Or talk. And wouldn't it be worse to know he was mildly retarded? My God, Hugh, then he'd know what he was missing. He's missing his life! 'Mildly retarded'. What a cruelty of God. To allow him just enough intelligence to know what he lacks. Kennedy's sister, his older sister, they keep it hushed up. That was her fate in that family of over-achievers. What little hope she may have had, killed by those golden siblings. Are any bells going off, Hugh?"

"You would take a chance on giving him no chance?" He was shaking his head, wearily, getting ready to head out the back door again. The boat was in the water, where would he go?

"Don't you dare leave. You have no right coming in at midnight, saying you've been working. Working!" She tried to grab his arm and he shook her off violently. "If you were working, we wouldn't be like this. You have no right—"

"Eleanor." He paused. "The Great Adjudicator of Human Rights." He shook his head. "We're forever off course."

"What do you mean?"

"It's not that complicated."

"I love you, Hugh. I do." Did she?

"Then it's a voracious love."

"Can we, can we get back on course?" Her voice was croaking like a frog's.

"No."

"But, Hugh, we . . . we were happy once. How did it turn out like this?"

"Does any marriage turn out like you thought it would? If you knew, would you do it again? Looking back on these nineteen years, Eleanor. Would you choose this again?"

"That's hardly the point. For God's sake, Hugh! We did choose it! Now what do we do with that? Don't think you can walk away from this. We've got to talk, we've got—"

"It's all been said." His face was sad. "Once the milk has soured can it be sweetened again?" He turned through the back door and was gone.

Chapter Thirty-four

—◈◈◈—

"The merry bubble and joy,
the thin, clear, happy call of the distant piping!
Kenneth Grahame

It was how she'd imagined the sound. When her father read about the piper in *The Wind in the Willows*—the piper who was the God of the little animals, standing by, keeping watch, the God of Rat and Mole and the Otter family—it was how she imagined the fluty caroling. Wisps of sound came to her now. Was it real? Was it possible she was hearing pipes at five in the morning?

The light was still weak. There! She heard it again. She got up from the couch, leaving her quilt in a heap. The patio door was ajar. Had it been open all night? Now the doors were always locked and the windows had been screened. 'The horse is out of the barn, Eleanor.' As if the danger was coming from outside. Through the open door she heard it again, a sad sweet drone.

The ground under her bare feet was already warm and the day had barely begun. Would they have another Indian Summer like last year, another September when it got so dry the cougars would be starved for water? She heard it again and this time the notes went on without pause. She ran into the park, stumbling as the flesh of her instep hit a stone. The rest of her foot was hard as rock from months of going barefoot. The path was brittle with heat and the smell of broom hung in the air. The tang of it filled her nostrils, sharp as the ocean. It was getting lighter and the birds were chiming in with the piping. It filled all the air. She slowed down as the music grew stronger, and began to slip from tree to tree.

His back was to her. All the fullness of a Scottish kilt lay in the back, and the muted tartan was in gentle swing as he marched slowly across the clearing. The highland wear had been her grandfather's, who'd joined the Scots Guards and died in the Great War. He'd wanted to play the pipes and they'd taken him, because although he was Welsh, he wasn't English. The cracked broom pods pricked her hands as she crouched and watched him begin his precise military turn. He'd been in the army too. He moved in slow motion, pivoting on one foot, at last revealing his face. Her chest was hammering and she wanted to run.

"Daddy?"

The sun was coming. Another day was starting. She felt his warm hand on her shoulder.

"It's all right, Nuffer. Go home now. Put on the porridge, Goldilocks!" He was drunk. She'd seen that before. But this was different—a brokendowness, a dying-animal-creeping-off-to-die drunk.

"Come on, Daddy. Please. Next week is Twin Coves. It'll be better there. It's your vacation, your three weeks." He met her eyes and she watched his giving in. He'd have to keep going, they said.

"I'll be along. No, don't look at me like that. Great Jupiter, I'll be along." He leaned against an oak tree, the pipes discarded and quiet. "I'm tired of being seen as a failure."

Where was the God of the little animals now? How could someone who knew poetry, who could play any instrument by ear, be a failure? Someone who could build a house and a boat and who knew the stars. How could a father who loved Rossie like he did be a failure? It was in the way he held Rossie's perfect head up to his temple, basking in that golden nimbus without even knowing he was doing it, the way he bounced him on his knee, and when he caught her watching, asked, "Do you remember when you were this child?"

She had planned on waiting until Twin Coves to confront her mother about Rossie. But if she couldn't count on her father, then what? As the days passed, he was different. Different than when she'd found him piping in the clearing. He was no longer crying, just distant and quiet, like he was already somewhere else.

They'd leave tomorrow morning, travelling in two cars. It was unspoken but understood that this was Rossie's last year. She heard the sigh escape her mouth. Janna would be here in a minute. They'd spend their last afternoon together for three weeks in the park. Her thoughts wandered to Donna. There was another lost cause, just like Rossie. She had given up her goals for university and was working for the telephone company. She was learning to be an operator. People could be as rude as they wanted to the operator, and they'd be rudest to someone whose voice had been reduced to a plea, a tentative questioning in every word she uttered. "Operator?" she'd say, in her begging voice. Yes Donna, you are the operator. It's not a question, for crying in the mud.

When Janna knocked on the back door, Owen was already out of his room. He could hear her coming and was there to open the door before she could pinch her fingers. They'd let her in on Rossie's brace, and she was helping, urging Rossie on from in front, while Maffy stood behind him holding both his arms. Owen watched their slow progress from all angles. The make shift brace could stand to be smaller, he had said last week, and then they'd see if it was just the ankle that needed support. Miss Brown, the librarian, had found her a new book, and she'd read that if a child with Cerebral palsy wasn't walking by the time he was four, he never would. Rossie would be five in the fall.

It was too hot for the stables so she and Janna headed for the park and lolled in the branches of the big oak tree, like leopards, those big dappled cats of the Serengeti. Janna was golden again, getting her summer sun, just like when the real Mrs. Miles had been alive.

*

Settling in at Twin Coves had none of the usual excitement. The three weeks stretched before them like a prison sentence, one that would go too fast for Rossie. They unpacked in glacial silence. Waiting for the storm to hit was worse than the storm itself. When her parents fought, it was like a wild animal took over, one that would give them no peace. But this was worse somehow. Now the animal was dead.

The first week went quietly enough. At night Maffy lay curled up on the top bunk with Rossie below her. Owen was out in his tent. It was better that way. The farther away he was, the less he heard, and maybe the longer he'd stay. Maybe he wouldn't leave this fall after all. He hadn't made plans yet. The cabin was quiet as a tomb and she couldn't even hear waves on the sandstone rocks. Was everything in this heat soaked world asleep except her?

She lay awake long into the still night, enjoying the experience of thinking about something other than the family. She thought about the change in Henry Johns. Henry no longer followed her like a puppy. His face no longer lit up when he saw her or darkened when she went left him. Now his face was guarded, except for his eyes, which followed her intently. Her stomach fluttered. He was fourteen now, and suddenly tall. He looked like his mother, with dark hair and brown eyes, almost black. The Johns had Spanish blood, her mother said. Black Irish. Whatever that meant, Henry was handsome. She thought about her own brown hair and her strange green eyes. Her nose was too big and she was poker thin. It made no sense. Liking someone like Janna made sense. Was there something other than beauty? "Your face has bones," the real Mrs. Miles had said.

In two nights it would be the Saturday night campfire. The first one of the holiday. It was mid August. The days were getting shorter. Tonight it would be dark by eight-thirty and Henry would find a way to sit beside her at the fire, find a way to lean against her, their bodies touching from their shoulders all the way down to where they sank into the sand. Henry meant she could forget for a few more days that she was going to have to talk to her mother. In the middle of next week, they'd be halfway through the holiday.

Her opportunity came sooner than she expected. She was in the water with Rossie, her hand under his stomach as he lay in the warm, shallow water. Green seaweed caught between his pink fingers. He could almost swim now, and she looked down at his straight back, marveling at how his body moved in the water. He was graceful and coordinated, arms paddling evenly, feet kicking strongly. He was almost five and small still, but then she'd always been small and now she was growing. His being small had made it easier. Easier to carry his light, airy body, easier to believe he was much too young to send away. But that back would stretch out and those legs would get longer. Her mother sat with the other mothers in the shade of the big arbutus that arched over the beach.

"Ross is such an exceptional child," Mrs. McLean said suddenly.

Even though Rossie was laughing his loon laugh, Maffy could still hear Mrs. McLean. You could tell she meant it. She wasn't smart or mean enough to play around with double entendre, like The New Mrs. Miles.

Mrs. McLean thought Rossie was exceptional and she was too oblivious to stop herself from explaining why. She didn't notice Maffy's mother's face tighten and her mouth thin to a disapproving line.

"He's beautiful, but it's more than that. His sweetness and his . . . well, it's a kind of courage, isn't it? Courage to face life. I can see it, the way he looks directly at me. It's hard to explain."

"Well, then perhaps you stop trying." her mother said.

Maffy followed her mother, who toiled up to the cabin with Rossie. It was late afternoon, time to give him a rest before Maffy would help him with his dinner. He could handle his spoon beautifully in his right hand. Should she bring that up?

"Mum, I've been working with Rossie. Don't you recognize when he saying Bess's name, or Owen's? Those are the easy ones. Mine's too hard, but—"

"What are you talking about?" Her mother's voice was cranky and disbelieving.

"He can talk—I think he can learn. He loves to listen to stories, I'm sure he knows what's going on. What if he's not retarded?"

"Well of course I know he can say the odd thing. I'm with him all the time. Do you think I don't know that? It doesn't mean he's not retarded." Her voice was wavery, and not nearly as convinced as her words sounded. "Why is everyone so determined on thwarting me? Of second guessing, and musing on things that don't have nearly the effect on them as they have on me!"

"I'm not talking about you, I'm talking about Rossie."

Her mother put her hand to her eyes. Was she crying? Maffy's throat tightened. Her mother never cried.

That night it got worse than her mother crying. They were fighting again and this time the world was slipping out from under them. Nothing would be the same after this time. Their voices oozed throughout the dark cabin, leaving a stain in every cranny. There was no moon and the blackness felt evil. She covered her ears and began to hum. She could hear their noise but not their words. After an eon of crooning to herself, she sensed silence. She slowly lowered her hands from her ears. Too soon.

"All right, it's true!" her father hissed. "Nessie has a heart, a soul, she's—"

"Nessie? How dare you call her by that name? So you finally admit it. Well then go to her. Go to your precious secretary. Go!"

"No, Eleanor. I'm not leaving. This is their holiday. I'm not leaving them with you. We'll talk about what to do in the morning." His voice was firm, final. Strong in a way it hadn't been before.

The bed springs creaked and the front door opened, then clicked shut again. Who had gone? Who was left in the double bed on the other side of the curtain?

The families that gathered at Twin Coves every August had seen their share and no family was spared its moment in the spotlight. They all had their good times and bad. But the Morgans' bad was different and the other families' happiness made their own unhappiness worse.

"She's gone to Seattle . . . her annual shopping trip," her father maintained quietly. Who was buying that? Now that her mother wasn't there, Maffy had the first glimmer of what it had been like for her, with their father drinking and being the sadder for it. He had himself under control, but not without help from the bottle. And without her mother there to bash himself against, he drifted, relieved, but somehow confused and not at all cheerful.

She took the binoculars off the nail by the cabin's back door and looked through the wrong end. It was better to see things made smaller rather than bigger. She stared down at the beach and saw all the mothers sitting on their blankets, colorful dots with no faces. This way, she couldn't see any expressions of shock and excitement replacing customary boredom. What shocked Maffy was that Rossie missed his mother who'd never been away for more than one night in Seattle each summer. One night a year for nearly five years. She'd been gone now for two. Was she really in Seattle? Would she stay away forever? Be careful what you wish for. Where had she heard that haunting bit of know-it-all-itis?

She put the binoculars back and got ready to take Rossie to the beach, down to the sympathetic clucking and the watchful eyes. No matter what, Rossie needed to squirrel away sun for the winter, and the water was where he was free. She couldn't deny him that, but she'd take him to the lagoon where it was hushed and still. In the lagoon she'd set him down in the water and he would walk. The buoyancy of the salt water helped and he held on to her tightly, but he walked.

Too bad they were too stubborn to just go home. Home, where she wouldn't have to avoid Henry's sympathetic eyes. Home, where she could talk to Mrs. Baker. But there was also The New Mrs. Miles at home, and good old Denise. Maybe it was better here. Maybe it would be the same anywhere. The same shame and embarrassment wherever they went.

Chapter Thirty-five

And I shall have some peace there, for peace comes dropping slow

William Butler Yeats

The ferry slid effortlessly through the choppy channel. All things considered, hanging over the ship's rail was the place to be. If the nausea rising steadily in her stomach won out, she was in the right place. The wind knifed through her scanty hair.

The ferry churned past the Puget Sound islands that sprouted like weeds through asphalt. Nothing could stop volcanic progress. Nothing could stop hot, furious lava boiling up through the earth's wounds, forging its way up through thousands of feet of ocean, to create these rocky outcroppings dotting the Sound. The island she was headed to, her final destination, wasn't even served by a ferry. It was that small.

How dare he? After all they had gone through! But under the boiling rage an icicle of fear poked at her. What if she lost him? Lost them all? Which of them would choose her?

What was she doing on this ferry? What had she been thinking? It was the memory of those hands, those eyes. That concerned voice. Would he even be there? He was one of those people whose life meant he'd never be anywhere else. Few led lives like that. Was she idealizing him, like she'd once idealized Hugh—all beauty and extreme ideas?

Olive did her standard job of nearly giving Eleanor a stroke, but somehow the car's old heart turned over at last, just when Eleanor was about to be towed off the ferry. She had no sense of embarrassment left. A broken down algae-coloured car blocking lines of hot summer motorists was chicken feed. She joined the stream of sleek cars humming off the ferry, big German cars fuelled by hundreds of horsepower. Hugh would love the sight of the pompous ass in the Mercedes glaring impotently at her.

Would she be able to find his cabin? He'd described it to her over the years. Most people knew very little about Alistair. Daphne made a pathology of his remoteness. If he wanted to steer clear of Winton and her, there was something wrong with him. Ever since Lily's death and then the wedding when he witnessed the worst first hand, Alistair had disappeared. Slipped into a world so private he'd almost ceased to exit. But Janna hadn't forgotten him. And he was there for her, sending parcels and calling regularly, just like he called Eleanor.

Olive was climbing the steep hill leading away from the ferry terminal. She was headed across the island to the little bay where the water taxi waited. Eleanor had called from the terminal in Seattle, where she'd ferried to from Victoria, in order to get this ferry. The huge charts of ferry routes resembled Churchill's war room during Bismark days. These islands were Washington's treasure, making them accessible an obsession. She'd found the name of a water taxi from a ragged list pinned to a bulletin board and had liked its prosaic optimism. It would take her to the island where Alistair had lived as a recluse for five years. He'd sold his ranch and ended up on tiny Telescope Island. She felt sick to her stomach and willed Olive to break down. One single thing to focus on. A useless car on a remote island. Let Olive collapse so she wouldn't have to think about what she was doing heading towards Alistair's island. But Olive, contrary as always, was running smoothly.

It was time to turn back. She pulled into a little general store; the kind that aims to look like it's been there a hundred years. The telephone booth outside put the lie to that. Was this the phone booth Alistair used? She would call the captain of the *Even Keel*, explain that it was all off, and give Olive her head.

She let the number ring, gazing at the Indian craft table set up outside the store. There were the usual sweaters. Were there beaded moccasins with rabbit fur linings? He didn't answer. She'd have to go to the little bay and tell him. Or could she just fade away? How long would he wait? He'd sounded so important when she'd made the arrangements, like he was taking her trip very seriously. Did she have the heart to let him hang there, expectantly? She sagged against the hot glass of the phone booth and caught a glimpse of herself in the smudged pane. Her hair looked like she'd stepped out of a wind tunnel. If she didn't go to the island, where would she go? She dialed the Bakers' number, not knowing what she would say.

"Hello."

Jean had a way of saying it with the emphasis on the "lo," that always meant business.

"Jean, it's Eleanor."

"Eleanor! How did you know to call? Have you already heard? You will go off to that swamp by the sea with no phones."

"What are you talking about? I phoned to tell you my life is over."

"Well then, you and Winton will have to get together. You suddenly have a lot in common . . . Seriously, Eleanor." Jean slowed down a bit. "What's the matter? You go first."

"What's going on in Victoria? What am I missing?" She wanted back in the fold of daily gossip, to pretend for the duration of this call that nothing had changed.

"Is everything all right, Eleanor? Why did you call? I mean I'm thrilled to hear from you, but if you don't know what's going on here, what made you call?"

"I'm fine. Really. You know I get tired over here in the swamp. I needed to hear your voice, that's all."

"Sure? What's this about the termination of your life?"

"My blackberry pie lost out to Midge Lindell's in the annual Twin Coves Bake-off. I'll be finishing myself off tomorrow. Nothing to worry about."

"Well, as long as it's not till tomorrow. You sound quasi normal again, given that normal with you remains undefined. Are there really women in this world named Midge?"

"Jean! It's a long distance call!"

"All right, I've got news."

"Will it cheer me up?" It had become a feeble joke between them. Like Jean could monitor the world for favourable news. Somewhere, something good was happening.

"No. Well, maybe."

"Did it cheer you up?"

Jean cawed. "Listen to this. Winton Miles has had a stroke."

"Good God, a stroke? Did Daphne do it?"

"Daphne couldn't 'do' a stroke, Eleanor, it's a brain thing."

"She did Lloyd." Silence from Jean. For once. Eleanor went on, "Is he all right, I mean, how bad is it?"

"Pretty bad. He has no mobility, no speech. But he's conscious. He knows what shape he's in. It's pitiable. Worse than dying, really."

"It's unbelievable. I wouldn't wish this on anyone—even him."

She was rolling down the hill to the miniscule wharf, thinking of Winton and of Daphne. What a shock for her, and he would be in the nether regions of hell. And what about Janna? This would affect her, but how? How would she feel? From observations of Janna and her father, the obvious could not be assumed. And whatever she felt, Janna would need her uncle more than ever. Eleanor braked as she reached the wharf. It was just as well she was going to call off this ill-conceived trip. Would Alistair know about his brother yet? He might even be on his way to Janna by now. She spotted a short, rotund figure hauling on the stern line of a flat-bottomed boat. Diesel fumes struck her full in the face through the car's open window. She pulled on Olive's hand brake and leapt out, hoping to forestall any further preparations for the now unwanted trip.

"Ah, hello. I'm Eleanor Morgan, and I'm sorry, but I've—"

"Hop aboard, Miss. I'll have you to Telescope in a twinkling." A smile split his face. His eyes were small and round, deep-set like currents in a plum pudding. His hair fringed his head in a mass of white curls. He had a full beard to match. "Come along then,

Missy. Hop aboard." How many times had his Scottish brogue welcomed strangers?

"No—I've changed my mind. I'm sorry but I won't need the water taxi."

His face clouded.

"I'll pay you anyway. I'll just go get my purse, I'm very sorry."

"She' a worthy craft, you'll be safe. I've a wee bite on board fer you, a sluice a' tea." He was studying her intently. "You're looking a mite peaked lass. Jist get aboard now. Dinna fass yourself. Collect your kit and come aboard."

What was it about him that made her obey? His earnest effort to provide a little tea? His sweetness, so like Hugh's? Kindness always at the ready. She walked with resignation back to the car, got her purse and her small overnight bag. Maybe Alistair would be there. The stroke had just happened, after all. She might be the one to tell him. She rolled up the window, taking care to pull on the left side of the window where it stuck, locked up and headed back to the boat. She grasped his outstretched hand. Was this filthy hand the one that had prepared her bite? Just be grateful for once in life. He had laid out a surprisingly decent cake, neatly sliced, with two pears on the side. She'd choke it down, somehow. How long since anyone had cared if she looked "peaked" or since he'd had a paying customer? It didn't seem to be a matter of money, he just seemed to need to be useful, to be a part of the world of people interacting and helping each other. He jumped off the boat and onto the wharf again. The boat lurched and she grabbed the pears before they were on the oily floor boards. In ten seconds he was back on board, having cast off the bowline. The engine was roaring. He hollered above it, as if it had only just occurred to him.

"Who would be meeting you then?"

"Ah, a friend, an old friend."

"An' her name would be?"

"Well, ah, it's a man, just a friend. Alistair Miles."

"Does he know you'll be arriving, then, lass?"

"Well, yes . . . no, but we're good friends. My, um, closet friend was married to his twin brother, and I'm just . . . visiting."

He was looking at her closely. She tried her best to smile. At last he said, "It may be that he'll be glad of your face. It'll be about thirty minutes, lassie. The wind's fresh, we'll take it slow, so's you can enjoy yourself and have a cup."

"Call me Eleanor. Please. You've been very kind."

"Well then, I'm Captain McPherson, but call me Hamish."

Her smile was genuine now. Hamish. A quintessential little Scottish seaman, bearing tea.

"There's something about a thermos," he declared, happily.

The tea would be sweet and milky. She settled into the rotting cushions that lined the taffrail. His boat had seen better days, but cosmetics aside, it was sturdy enough. All the effort had gone into the hull and she could see it was shipshape. The afternoon sun beat down on her bare head and she leaned back into the mustiness. Her cup was indeed sweet and she sipped it slowly as Hamish, glad of company, told her of his years in the mines in Scotland. Years of coal dust, of sun only in memory.

Hamish set her on the rocky beach of Telescope Island. She walked purposefully to the little dirt road that ran along the waterfront. She'd insisted Hamish cast off again, and his stumpy little arm was waving in the distance. He'd be back the next day, he said, at noon. There were no cars on the island. The few inhabitants ran their small boats over to the neighbouring island she'd just come from, where their cars were parked and ready for the obligatory trips to the grocery. It was a rare life for a rare type of person. As isolated as Alistair had been on his ranch, he was even more so now. The island was only a few miles long and a half a mile wide. She'd find him in less than an hour. She had an excuse. Janna needed him. Whatever happened, Janna needed Alistair. She'd show Hugh.

She tramped along the track by the beach. There wasn't a sound except the irrepressible crickets and the wind whispering through the arbutus boughs. She'd seen it all, as islands went, but this was different, primeval in its separateness. It was utterly still, a sanctuary inaccessible except by extreme intention. Years ago Winton had described his brother's latest whim in disdainful detail. Good cocktail hour fodder. Poor Winton. Finally, it was a cocktail too far. She walked on. This wasn't a whim. It was an escape.

She startled a doe with a fawn by her side. They bounded away from her. She walked on in a westerly direction and noticed the sun getting lower. Another summer of their lives gone, taking so much with it. Taking everything she should have loved, had tried to love.

She must have fallen asleep. She'd sat down to watch the sun sliding into the arms of the sea. Now it was dark. A bat streaked by her head. She started to trot down the path, for that's all it seemed to be now. The track had narrowed on either side. Something sharp tore at her bare arm. Blackberries. She took time to pull on her sweater, then squatted behind a cedar tree. All that tea.

The moonless sky was quilted with stars. She stared at the vast tapestry, stitched into patterns Hugh could name. She walked on and the path widened again.

A light appeared in the distance and she quickened her pace. It was a tent flickering from within, like a fat candle whose wick has burned down its centre. Better keep going. Who knew, maybe it was teen-aged boys.

She walked through the soft darkness, no longer a part of the world, but floating somewhere above it. She looked down on her sad, puppet body plodding forward. Sagging, angular shoulders, long, gaunt form, shapeless after three kids. Legs moving like a robot's, one foot ahead of the other for the rest of her life. Her face was thin, eyes shadowed underneath with matching blue circles.

Another light appeared and a good-sized cottage took shape, a soft glow wafting from its two large front windows. The dim light showed a garden lush with late summer's riches. There couldn't be more than a few cottages on the island. Perhaps this was Alistair's. He'd done well on the ranch and could live anywhere he chose. He might as well have been on the moon.

She knocked. After a long moment the door opened. She didn't recognize the thin face. Only the eyes.

"Hello, Alistair."

"Eleanor?"

"Yes, it's me. I'm sorry . . ." Would the rest of her life start with an apology?

"Come in, for God's sake. What in the name of—" His face was more familiar with each word. He reached out to pull her inside, pulling her into his arms. Her heart was racing. His body was welcoming, and his hands had an oddly familiar warmth, softening her stiff, cold back.

"I'm so sorry to invade you like this." She held on to his bony hand. "I had to go somewhere, had to talk to someone. I needed to get away, a long way away. But only for a bit. You must think I'm mad. Maybe I am. I'm . . . I'm at my wit's end."

He held her close. "It's wonderful to see you. My God, you're cold, have you been traveling all day? How did you get to the island?"

"A little Scotsman. Looks like Santa Claus."

"Hamish. Sit by the fire, Eleanor. I'll get you a drink."

"I must look terrible."

"You look wonderful."

"We've both changed, haven't we?"

"The world has changed."

She stepped into the generous, open room and sank into a wicker chair. Soft and unexpectedly feminine. The fire simmered in its stone fireplace, giving out just the right warmth on a late August night. The room was serene with the right amount of clutter. Another room led off darkly to the left and Eleanor could just make out a round oak table surrounded by more wicker chairs with green cushions. An open book lay on the rough driftwood table, among a dozen others. She couldn't see the title. Bookshelves filled with volumes lined one whole wall of his home.

He was across the cedar-lined room in five long strides, reaching into an antique armoire for a bottle. He poured thick amber liquid into an unexpectedly delicate glass.

"Here. Drink this. Put your feet up." He dragged a hassock over. "You're exhausted."

"It's Hugh. He's, he's . . ." She had yet to say the words out loud.

Alistair waited. He had all the time in the world. After a few hefty swallows of brandy, she began again.

"Hugh is having an affair. It's been going on for some time. Going on while the rest of our life has been going on. It's the betrayal—the horrible knowledge that's it's been going on while we've been going on." She gulped her drink. "How can a person carry on two going's on?"

"I'm sorry, Eleanor. So very sorry. The last time we talked, you said everything was fine."

"I lied. You've been worried about Janna, we all have, you needed to talk. She's—oh my God, Alistair! Have you heard about Winton? He's had a stroke. He's in the hospital."

"Good Lord. When? Is he all right?"

"He's not in good shape. I just found out today. I phoned my friend, I phoned Jean from the store on the big island. It's just happened. I don't know more details, just that he's immobile, without speech."

Alistair's face was ashen. "I've lived with the hope of Winton's death for a long time." His voice was calm but his face revealed the pain of wanting a brother's death. "His arrogance, the ruthlessness. I knew it when I was five. I got away from it as soon as I could. That poor family next door, their little boy. That poor devastated family. They had to move, had to get away from the sight of their swimming pool." He shook himself out of dark catacombs where memories had lain for forty years. What had life been like, twinned to Winton? He went on, voice flat with shock. "He should be dead. I nearly killed him myself, after Lily. He should never have taken her out in those waters. One way or another, he was responsible for her death."

"One way or another?"

Alistair looked at her bleakly.

"How is it possible? He's your brother, your twin."

"I ask myself that every day. I've read everything I could put on hands on." He slumped into the sofa, head buried in those hands.

"Where's the brandy? No, sit still. I'll find it."

"I've got to get to her. She can't go on in that mad house."

"Let us take her away for a while. We've still got some time at Twin Coves." She spoke as if they were still a "we." "She needs to be with young people, with Myfanwy. And Owen."

"Ah yes. Owen." He smiled. "We were young once, weren't we Eleanor?"

"For a few weeks."

"Come, join me Ellie, and tell me what you've been enduring."

"If you call me Ellie, I'm going to cry."

"We can't have that, Mrs. Morgan. Come and tell me."

"What is this about Winton and a swimming pool?"

"Ancient history, Eleanor. Some other time. For now, tell me."

His arm was warm and heavy around her shoulders and she cried into his gaunt chest. Finally, gently, he spoke.

"Is it irretrievable, Eleanor?"

"How can it not be? How can I accept this?"

"We accept the unacceptable all the time. Tell me what's happened. Hugh, the children, everything."

She let go for the first time in a long time.

The fire was embers and he got up stiffly for more bark. He brought the bottle over and filled her glass, then his. Bark burned hot but with very little flame.

"Perhaps it's not irretrievable. I think it's up to you, Eleanor."

"Me?" She was crying again.

"I saw the way he looked at you. At the wedding. He looked like he wished you were someone else. Someone he could fall out of love with."

"That's how I feel about him."

"I don't think he can do anything but love you. It's not duty. I saw in that moment he'd have loved not to love you. But he did then and still does, I bet."

"Then why this? Why an affair?"

"Disaster relief? When the disaster's over, a man goes back to his life. When your anger's over, will he come back to his life?"

Eleanor stared into the orange coals. She'd been angry all her life. One thing after another.

"How are your children doing in all this? How is Ross?"

Ross. No one understood how she felt about Ross. She rarely allowed herself to think about it, let alone talk about it. She sat in silence. Alistair waited, all the time in the world.

"What if Ross is what finally unhinges me? Seeing him day after day, seeing him with no life. I can't bear it. I can't bear to think about it. I can't bear to watch him year after year without a life. I'm afraid . . . afraid I'll finally go crazy. I mean really crazy. Insane. I simply cannot bear that beautiful face." She turned into that starved chest again. Anger was easier than this pain. "I have . . . I have to believe it'll be easier for him somewhere else. Somewhere safe from cruelty, from seeing others live a life he can't. Can you imagine what it's like to feel like a freak, to be unacceptable? People stare at him, Alistair."

"It is hard to imagine how he would cope, isn't it?"

"I never let myself."

"Hard to imagine how we've coped.

The silence between them was easy, the slight scent of brandy heady and sweet.

"Alistair. Are you asleep? I've kept you up."

"No, just thinking, like you."

"Hamish—Captain McPherson will be here at noon. We'll have time in the morning to talk about Janna . . . and Winton. I'm so sorry, Alistair. He's your brother."

He got off the sofa and pulled her up. "There's a warm bed for you in the guest wing." He smiled. "Just let me clear it out a bit. And you're not going back with Hamish, I'll run you over."

"No, Alistair. You've done enough. Besides, Hamish needs to take me. He'll have made a spot of tea. Just as long as we have time for a walk. I want to see your island, and there's more to talk about." She sank back on the sofa while Alistair disappeared into the 'guest wing'. She was too tired to brush her teeth. The taste of brandy was sweet and comforting.

He reappeared, stuffing odds and ends into a pillowcase. "I've just cleared some room. It's a cozy space."

She followed him, looking hungrily at the wood frame double bed laden with pillows and an old patchwork quilt. Otherwise, the room was quite bare and spacious, with nothing but a matching dressing table on which sat a yellow flashlight and an old-fashioned pitcher and basin in blue and white. The curtains were eyelet, airy and dreamlike.

"Sleep well, Ellie. I'm sorry, there's nothing but an outhouse, just through this door when you need. The guestroom has its own door onto the back garden."

"Don't worry, I'm like a camel. Besides, I like an outhouse. I'll acquaint myself with it about four this morning, I expect. Don't worry about me, Alistair. I'm so tired and so grateful. Thank you."

He put his arms around her and said good night.

The expected trip to the outhouse did indeed occur at four o'clock. After that, Eleanor fell immediately back to sleep. It wasn't until the sun shone in her face that she woke again and remembered why she was in this strange bed with its worn quilt. She slid out of bed, still in her clothes from yesterday, and walked to the window. Her room was at the back of the cottage and looked out onto a mass of flowers growing out of everything imaginable. An old rowboat was a flower bed for anemones. Clay planters held rose bushes, most past blooming. But one bush promised the last rose of summer—a perfect yellow bud getting ready to burst. The morning sun was reflecting off something, sending sharp points of light into her eyes. It was very small, but yes, there it was, way in the back of the garden . . . a greenhouse.

She jammed her feet into her old running shoes and opened the bedroom door. The living room was shaded. The cottage faced west. The sun would stream in here in late afternoon. Alistair was pouring coffee. Toast and orange slices were ready. The plates he set out were yellow. Exactly what Lily would have chosen. The garden, the greenhouse, the eyelet curtains—all what Lily would have chosen.

"Alistair." Her voice cracked with mourning. "The greenhouse—are there orchids growing in there?"

"Yes, amazingly enough. I've learned the secret of how much moisture. It's one of the ways I cope." He put the coffee pot back on the stove. "Janna will feel at home here someday—a place where she can remember her mother. Someday she'll visit, when she's older and Winton can no longer object." He shrugged. "Maybe that day has come." He handed her a cup of coffee. "Let's walk in Lily's garden."

The garden was perfect in its imperfection. Lily had always known the importance of that. The too manicured yard, the military precision of neatly bordered flowerbeds were not for her. It felt like Lily could step out of that greenhouse at any minute, black ribbon holding back Botticelli hair, hands carrying a fragile orchid, delicate feet stepping through the tiny ice flowers twinkling between the rough stones of the path. It was almost possible to hear her laugh.

The natural growth of salal and ferns mingled with fading lilies, larkspur and hollyhocks. A collection of shells were arranged under a wild rose bush. From the end of the path, Eleanor looked back and saw the sign above the front door, carved in greying driftwood. Perihelion, it read.

"Pear-a-he-leon?" she asked.

"Yes. You got it right."

"What does it mean?"

"The point of the earth's orbit nearest the sun."

"It's perfect, Alistair. You've even got vegetables."

"Potatoes, tomatoes and bean rows."

"Nine bean rows?"

"Nine? No, only six."

Eleanor laughed. "*Nine bean rows will I have there, a hive for the honey bee, And live alone in the bee-loud glade. And I shall have some peace there.*"

"That's beautiful, Eleanor. Lily always said you were a poet."

"That's Yeats. Have you had any peace here, Alistair?"

"Of a kind. I couldn't seem to do much else. Now I'll go to her. To him." His voice trailed off and he wandered toward the sounds of the waves and sat in the grassy sand facing the sea.

"Alistair." She sat beside him, pulling his head gently down to her lap. "No, don't try to talk. He's your brother. Let it out now."

She stroked his thinning hair, his lined forehead. She listened to the mystery of the waves, breaking forever. Perhaps peace would come, *dropping from the veils of morning.*

Alistair had gone to meet Hamish at noon and invited him to stay a while. Eleanor wasn't quite ready to leave, and this Hamish had accepted with magnanimity. He'd make sure she got back to the ferry terminal in time for the four o'clock to Seattle, he said, very much a part of things. She would need time to visit the country store in order to make a call. She needed a hotel in Seattle for the night.

When the time came, they walked back to the little cove where the *Even Keel* was anchored. Hamish was discreet, walking ahead, giving them a chance to talk in private.

"Forgive me in advance, Alistair, but somehow it would help to know. Did you and Lily ever . . ." She looked up at his face. "I'm sorry, I've gone too far. I'll never ask—"

He held up his hand. "It's all right, Eleanor, it's a relief to finally talk about it." His arm dropped easily over her shoulder. "I met Lily on the day she was married, a marriage that should never have happened. In other families it might have been stopped. She was a child, twenty years old. She was only thirty-six, with a ten-year old daughter, when she died. In another family, she might have had a voice, the look of panic on that day . . . but not in this family. Not with Winton. Who would cross him? It would have been worse for Lily if she had spoken up, allowed herself some morsel of self-awareness. You saw what happened when she finally did." Alistair paused, seeming exhausted by memories. "Lily married Winton. We saw each other every year at Mother's infernal birthday, her June birthday. And there were other occasional gatherings—a cousin's wedding, a funeral—the usual family things—but it was mainly the birthday. Why mother kept it up, I don't know. She knew how Winton and I felt about each other." He glanced up. Hamish was a safe distance ahead. "Lily and I were very careful, barely exchanging a word with each other, counting ourselves lucky with a quick look and the simple joy of each other's presence. That was all. Six years went by." His voice took on a heavy cadence, as if the only way he could tell it was like a robot. "And then our chance came. We'd been so careful, never to look too long, never to speak too softly, so Winton never suspected, and of course there was his ego. How could anyone be as important to her as he was? Our chance came. Mother's birthday celebration was postponed till August one year, June being consumed by a world cruise. Lily came down without Winton. She took the early ferry to Seattle to shop. He'd join her later, he said. He would drive down after a meeting in Vancouver. He never came. He missed Mother's birthday because his car failed him. Winton and his cars. It was our chance. They always stayed at the Mayflower."

Eleanor shivered. She would be there tonight.

"After dinner at the Seattle Club, I went to her. She was waiting in the hotel lobby. Not a word had been said at dinner. We had barely looked at each other while Mother toasted her precious birthday and displayed pictures of her trip. Lily just knew I'd find her there. We walked to the elevator—I looked more like Winton in those days—and no one ever knew. Until now. I wondered how I'd go on after that night, but knew I'd have to. Winton would never let Lily go. I knew it was too dangerous to risk."

"Dangerous?"

"Yes, Winton is dangerous."

"Six years?"

"I know what you're thinking. Janna was born the following April."

"After all those years of hoping for a child, she finally had one." She turned to him. "Alistair, you can tell me. You know I'll never tell a soul."

"I don't know the answer, Eleanor. I'll never know."

"But Lily—"

"Whatever she knew, or suspected, she never said. She knew Winton too well." He kicked fiercely at an old weathered bottle lying on the beach. "She knew me too well."

"It doesn't matter, you're Janna's blood. Her only blood, now that Winton . . . he's not dangerous now, Alistair."

"And she'll need me, won't she?"

"She's always needed you." She took his arm in hers. "Children make you vulnerable."

"Like nothing else can.

"And it goes on forever."

Suddenly Alistair was smiling. "Isn't it wonderful?"

"Where's my cigar?"

Hamish was making a casting off noises.

"There are places near Victoria. Wild acreage with room for what you need. But closer. Closer than this."

"Thank God you came, Eleanor." His arms enfolded her. "Will you be all right in Seattle?"

"Of course. I go every year to shop. I have new things to shop for this time, a few stops along the way, but I'll be fine. I can take care of myself."

"I never doubted it. Take care of them too."

Chapter Thirty-six

·⟨3⊹⟩·

Counting the Beats
Counting the slow heart beats,
The bleeding to death of time in slow heart beats.

Robert Graves

He could see. He could hear. He'd heard them all along. He'd heard the prognosis. "Extreme stress. Far too much on his plate. Like his father before him. Very little we can do."

The room was empty, except for the machines that loomed and hummed. He'd made his decision. He refused to live like this. Now he needed a plan.

Daphne's face was hanging over him. Smiling in satisfaction. Hard to remember what he'd once felt for her. She'd made him feel important and she would never leave him. Once that had been important. It had been of the utmost importance.

They'd lit a match in front of him, rung a bell, so now they knew he could see and hear. Still Daphne talked loudly. If he couldn't talk, he couldn't hear, she would reason. The days were sliding into each other. How long would he have to listen? He tried to ward her off with his eyes. He still had his eyes. They still had the power to frighten. He could see it in other people's eyes. If only he could plan.

A wolf caught in a trap can free itself. Gnaw off its leg. He couldn't move. But they were going to move him, back to the family home. He'd heard the mutterings as he slipped in and out of sleep. "It'll be the best thing for him."

He had to plan. He'd hire someone. But how could he pay them? Could he ask a friend? Who were his friends? Why couldn't he remember? A man like him would have a lot of friends. Powerful, influential people attracted to their like. Who were they? Would anyone do him a favour? The only one he'd ever ask for, the only one he'd ever need.

How long till his arms began to atrophy? He'd never thought he'd need that word. His fingers curled into his palm. He was shrinking. How long had it been? His world had shrunk to an endless round of nurses lifting flaccid limbs.

His relief should have been sleep, but nightmares came. His mother came to him at night. He'd been her favourite. The kind of mother who could choose a favourite was a dangerous thing.

The boy down the street. The boy named Donald. He'd loved to swim. Alistair had been Donald's favourite. Alistair had been their father's favourite. Donald was there, watching, like his mother watched him. The sound. The exquisite crunch. The sound of the cat's skull when the rock crushed it. He'd trapped it in an empty garbage can. It was small, still a kitten. Too bad the kid was a spy. Too bad he hadn't waited an hour after eating. Isabelle watched him like a hawk after that.

He'd found his chance. He'd gotten away. Out from under her nose. Sometimes he could fool his mother, hide from her slate eyes. Other times she was just like him, watching like a hawk. Lily had been his way out. Lily and her land.

Alistair came to him at night. Alistair who was never fooled, who robbed him of his pride. Would Alistair help him now, at the end? Make an end! The first and final act of brotherly love. Give me the one thing left to me. You robbed me of my life long before this. Robbed me of Lily.

He was dancing with her, drinking in her beauty, her elegance, her mystery. She was a sylph in his powerful arms. Her hair floated gently down his chest, smelling of gardenias.

He started awake. The room was never dark. There was always a light. Always the fetor of medical smells seeping through his skin. The hum of machinery monitoring breath that went on and on.

Chapter Thirty-seven

Deep as first love, and wild with all regret.
Alfred, Lord Tennyson

The bell hop had given her a hard look when she'd walked into the Mayflower. She'd cleaned up as best she could in her good navy slacks, but what did those city faces at that big marble reception counter think? Good thing she and her pride had parted company or she might have turned back. Maybe her state-of-mind had been an advantage. Did her stark eyes look artistic? Or just plain crazy? However she looked, they'd taken her cheque and given her a bed.

The few days she'd been gone seemed like eons. Ross was never out of her thoughts but Myfanwy was so capable with him and these few days had been worth it. Her business in Seattle had gone quite well. And Alistair. Fragments of memories blew through her mind.

The ferry was docking on Gabriola. The steering wheel was slippery as Olive trundled onto the island. Eleanor wiped her sweating hands on her slacks. Her gaze strayed to the brown paper bag on the floor of Olive's passenger side.

The road into Twin Coves was quiet. It was late afternoon. Would they be on the beach getting the last of the sun? Or under the big arbutus tree? Or in the cabin, flaked out on their bunks?

Sometimes they put Ross on the cool patch of clover right outside the cabin's front door. He loved to study the little triad of leaves. She pulled up behind the Chev.

The children roasted hot dogs on the beach. They drank Orange Crush from the can. For Hugh and herself, she'd bought steaks. Good ones, better after sizzling on the fire. And a bottle of red wine. Not the best, but decent. Again her cheque had been honoured. One look at Eleanor's face and the clerk must have just been grateful she wasn't carrying a gun.

Hugh was grim. But he was going along. She had counted on him going along, for the kids. The family was being watched. Each little cabin had a line of eyes trained on the the beach, watching the Morgans' impromptu roner weist.

She pulled aside the curtain of the little bedroom. He was lying on the bed, fully clothed. Getting ready to leave?

"I've done a lot today, Hugh. A lot in the past few days. Don't let me fail now. Listen to me. Please." She sat down beside him and took his reluctant hand. The wine had worn off for both of them. She needed all her courage to say, "Please, Hugh, hear me out."

He stiffened. How many times had she stiffened at his touch?

"Do you love her?"

He continued staring up at the knot-holed ceiling. His answer came slowly.

"Yes."

She hadn't expected it. Hadn't thought there could ever be anyone who could tamper with them.

"My God, Hugh, what does this mean? Will you . . . will you keep on loving her?"

"I don't know. The heart is a capricious thing. It beats along for years, steady as she goes, then in a single beat, veers off course."

"Will you keep on loving her?" Her voice was frail, cobwebby.

"I said I don't know. I ask myself what it is I really feel for her and will it last? Or will it become a burden of guilt and ultimately lack the glue of all those things quite apart from love? I can't trust love. All those things I feel for her, I've felt for you. Only this is different. Easier."

She kept still.

"Men have been disappointing women for thousands of years," he said. "More to the point, would her feelings last?"

"Her feelings?" Stay calm.

Hugh carried on, scarcely aware of her presence. "We build attachments in life. Some make us ardent, alive, others make us miserable. I've learned all attachments are potential for both."

She pulled him back to her. "Can you . . . could you love me again?" Her neck muscles were tighter than violin strings.

"You're a minefield, Eleanor." He pulled his hand out of hers and turned away on the bed. "A minefield that's sometimes the Elysian Fields. A bloody free fall with a temperamental parachute. I've tried to think of you as just a wife. A wife in the ordinary sense is many things apart from love."

"What? What kinds of things is a wife?" For God's sake, stay calm.

"History. Familiarity. Having the rules down pat. No more disappointments, you convince yourself you've had them all. No more surprises. But with you there is nothing but surprises. I tried to do it. Really, I did. Then I surprised myself by feeling love again. A different kind of love. Loving someone out of choice, not out of some irrevocable rootedness, some form of madness."

A strange, serene voice asked, "So you love her out of choice? What does that mean?"

"It means I have some control! When I look at you I feel trapped and wonder if I'll ever be free of feeling for you. The way I feel for Ness—for Agnes—is different. She's peaceful, predictable. She's different in a way that makes me want to love her."

"Is wanting to love her the same as loving her?"

"You make my point. She'd never come out with that kind of double talk. It's easier with her."

"Easier?"

"Yes, Eleanor. It's easier. It's possible to have it easy, but you wouldn't know that."

"Is easy enough?"

"There are worse things than boredom."

"Be careful what you wish for, Hugh."

"She makes me happy, Eleanor. I know I'm a fatuous fool, but there you have it."

"I think I've outgrown my need to be happy. I've learned more from unhappiness. I've learned neither last forever. I've learned about what I really want. And I don't think it's just happiness."

"For pity's sake, what do you want?"

"I thought I wanted holidays and new cars. A typical house. A normal child. To have you stop drinking. To not have this paralyzing fear!" She breathed in and went on, quietly now. "That's still part of it and maybe always would be, but I wonder if having those things would make much difference. Do they stand the test of time? There's more that I want."

"There's always more with you, Eleanor."

"Maybe that's a good thing."

"Tell me, what is it you want?"

"First, I want you to love me again. Even though we're not always happy."

"Does what you want have that much to do with me?"

She had no reply. At last Hugh turned to face her again.

"Really, Eleanor, what would make this right? Make us right? Can we ever recapture, *That first fine careless rapture?*"

"*. . . Though the fields look rough with hoary dew, All will be gay when noontide wakes anew.*" She finished his quote with the old careless ease. "We can set a new course, Hugh. Does any marriage end up like you think it will, after two decades? Can anyone say it went off without a hitch? You were the first one to ask these questions. All right. The answer is no. But don't people find a way to go on?" She reached out her hand. When he didn't respond she dropped it listlessly. "Why did you marry me, Hugh?"

"I can't remember."

"Try."

"You don't bore me."

"I thought that was a bad thing."

"Why did you marry me?"

"I've asked myself that. God knows." She slid him her smile. "I had no choice. You quote Browning. Your hands are warm . . . you're my father all over." Lily would have had a Freudian field day with this. "I'll tell you what I want. I want Ross to stay. He needs what you've all been saying. It wouldn't always make me happy. How could watching his life make me happy all the time? But it seems I want that more than an easeful life."

"Do you mean this?" Five years of pain on his face.

"Yes, I mean it." She studied her long fingers, nails dirty from building the campfire. "I could never have sent him away. I was fooling myself that it would be easier. Easeful." She pulled at a loose thread on the faded quilt. "Could I ever have done that to Myfanwy and Owen? They've never wavered with Ross. Maybe people stare at him because he's beautiful. When you hold him . . . it's like seeing double. Maybe that's what people are staring at. Whatever it is, I'm willing to face it. Forgive me, Hugh . . . all these years, living in anger and fear." She was unraveling a square of the quilt. She dropped the thread. "And there's another thing."

"There would be."

"I can't just make pies."

"What?"

"Because this family is my whole life, my only life, I expect too much. For everyone's sake, I need more."

"Other women don't. Their children, their homes, their husbands—yes, their husbands—are enough for them."

"Would it be enough for you?"

"It's not the same. That's not the point."

"You make my point. Listen to yourself, Hugh. Is that the kind of woman you want? I can't make it easy for you like she can."

"But what does this say about me? That you're not content with my children, in my home?"

"Nothing, Hugh. It has nothing to do with you. Can you cope with that?"

"I'm only trying to reason this out!"

"Yes. It's what you do."

"It's all I can do, Eleanor." His pale face was blanched now. "I've never been unfaithful, you know. I've tried to reason out that paradox, but there reason fails me."

"What do you mean," she asked cautiously, "'never been unfaithful'?"

"I couldn't bring myself. I talk, she listens. She talks, I listen. Nothing more. There is no rhyme or reason. I love her because she listens—like a friend. A wonderful loving friend."

Something dropped away inside her. "You couldn't bring yourself?"

"I won't lie, I wanted to, but I couldn't do it."

She looked into his white face. Her throat was tight. "I haven't been easy. I know that."

"You've been difficult, so have I."

Her mind was racing. He couldn't bring himself. What if . . . "What if Ross is able to go to a school, a special school, or a therapist or something. Myfanwy has been trying to get through to me—everyone has—but would I listen? But the minute we're back in Victoria I'm calling Dr. Wong." She shook her head. "I've been a coward, focusing on my feelings, my fears. What about theirs?" She looked at Hugh. "And yours?" His eyes were intense. "Do we really think we're good enough, strong enough to be parents? Is anyone? The worry, the self-sacrifice. Why don't we choose to be careless and free?"

Hugh shrugged. "The Higher Good? The Elysian Fields, elusive though they be?"

Her smile was rueful. "Raising Ross will make me unhappy sometimes. Unhappy for him, afraid for him. But he doesn't seem to feel any of that. He seems happy."

"He wasn't as happy these past few days."

"What?"

"You weren't here."

"He missed me?"

"Strangely, I think we all did."

An unfamiliar hope was springing, uninvited, unexpected, but insistent. "If I can make Ross happy—and Owen and Myfanwy—even some of the time—"

"But we have to be happy, too, Eleanor. With each other."

"We were once. We've got nothing to lose by trying again, and maybe if we're not looking for so much from each other . . ." Her back was stiff and sore. She arched it like a cat, and heard the click in her neck. She needed to walk more.

"If Ross could go to a school, one where he's never humiliated, I would want to go too. Not to Ross' school—to my own. I want to go back and learn how to be an interior decorator. There's a decorator in Seattle who might help me. A very good decorator. I've seen his work in magazines, and Lily—" would saying her name always feel like this?—"Lily told me about Winton's mother's palace. This designer did everything."

"And he will help you?"

"I pushed my way into his office. This morning." She could feel the smile on her face. "I pretended I wanted to hire him, then told him about my ideas . . . you know what I'm like." She took his hand again, willing him into their private world.

"For pity's sake, Eleanor, you wanted to teach. With your brain you could be bringing literature to the heathen masses."

"And you wanted to be a doctor. We both had dreams. Life has disappointed you too. They weeded you out, Hugh, for good reasons. The suffering would have broken you."

"My father would have made a doctor, if he'd survived the war. But you, Eleanor, you could still teach."

"Maybe someday. I need more education, not to mention patience. Decorating is what I want right now—the creativity, the freedom. A world of colour, of shape, of no people. It's art, Hugh, and I want it."

"In order to decorate for people, you'd have to listen to them."

"I'd need your help."

"No one could have done what you've done with that house."

"I've got ideas. I drew the decorator some quick sketches, showed him a photo of the house, the one in my wallet with the kids in front of the patio. He was more interested in your architecture than my design. *Modernist planes with lightness and grace, serenity, beautifully framed views anchored to the landscape.* Those were some of his thoughts. I'm not as articulate. I just see it as poetry." She stood up and began to pace.

"I'd be gone a bit, a couple days in Seattle every few months to show him my designs, get his feedback. And there are lectures I would need to go to. Books to buy. It would cost a bit. I'd have to pay him for his time. I guess I am hiring him. You and I could work together. You're ahead of your time, Hugh. Your architecture will break ground." She grinned. "I never wanted a different house. A different furnace perhaps . . . sea-green broadloom, a pink marble ensuite."

Was his mouth twitching, just a little?

"Lightness and grace?"

"Those were his words."

Chapter Thirty-eight

—◈◈◈—

Come away, O human child
To the waters and the wild
With a faery, hand in hand,
For the world's more full of weeping
than you can understand.

William Butler Yeats

The lagoon was a different planet at four in the morning. The laws of gravity were different here. Her body was lighter. The water silked around her, draping tiny fronds of seaweed around her legs. Soft as spider webs. She reached her toe out in the still, dark water. She couldn't see them, but she'd give the crabs time to scuttle. Further out in the cove the swell of the seal's head glistened above the flat calm surface.

She drifted on her back, watching the morning star disappear. Venus. The sky was green with earliest dawn. It would be another hot day. Another surreal day. She was up to s's in the dictionary again. Since her mother had come back the days had been surreal, like Cezanne had dropped by, painting their days in strange new colours.

The incoming tide bore her over the sandstone rocks that bordered the lagoon. She felt the bite of the barnacles, white and ridged like molars that smothered the rounded rocks. The limpets, like miniature Chinese hats, fought for space. The salty smell was overpowering. Four more days at Twin Coves. Everything was changing. For the better. She tried to dampen the happiness that flipped back and forth in her chest. What if things changed again for the worse? The main thing she knew about her mother was that she never knew. She kept waiting for the day when she would know her mother.

But for now, her parents were going away again for three whole days. There was that flipper of excitement. She looked down at her chest, expecting to see it pulsing. The sky was getting lighter. The softest light of the day. She could see her chest now—see that it was finally taking shape. Two small points showed through her turquoise Janzen bathing suit and broke the surface of the water, like limpets on a slowly curving rock. Still on her back, she frog kicked out to where the water was deeper green, where a large log jutted out from shore. It was jammed between two rocks and likely would be forever. She swam around the log to where it hid her from shore and stood up in the thick, quaggy sand. The water was up to her new chest and under its cover she peeled the turquoise tube of elastic down her body and hooked it on a snag in the log. Naked as the seal, she dove under, cool water wrapping around her like a cocoon.

Rossie wouldn't be going to Woodvale and her parents wouldn't be talking about a divorce. For now. She remembered their private campfire with everybody watching them from their cabins, like secret agents behind incongruous yellow gingham curtains. Her mother had noticed too, but for once hadn't cared about what everyone must be thinking. Her mother hadn't noticed that she ate four hot dogs. Owen had. "Making hay, Maff?" Her mother had pulled Rossie onto her lap and wrapped her arms around him. "*There was Rossie, Rossie, Being very saucy, in the sto-o-ore, in the sto-o-ore!*" She looked at Rossie now, like she could take the time. Was her mother looking at her more too? Good thing she was growing her eyebrows back, making hay while the sun shone.

Grandmaf was coming today to take care of things while her parents were gone. Janna was coming with her. It was complicated because there was no one left in Janna's house who could drive them to the ferry in Naniamo. They'd be having bags of fun in the Miles house. Mr. Miles was sick and no one knew whether he'd live for very long. Maffy prayed he wouldn't. What did God do with prayers like that? The New Mrs. Miles wasn't the type who would drive you anywhere. Donna and Denise could drive and would be eyeing that Bricklin, but on this chauffeuring option Grandmaf drew the line. She would be levering herself into Mrs. Baker's car right about now. Donna could crack up the Bricklin and the Cadillac and still not be even with Mr. Miles.

Coming off the ferry, Janna looked pale, but she was smiling like she was walking out of prison. She was carrying her portable record player that looked just like a regular suitcase with all her 45's packed inside. She was going slowly, keeping pace with Grandmaf, but her feet were schottisching under her like a marionette's. Owen's were doing the same. Maffy glanced at his blank face. He reminded her of Henry. She sighed and answered Janna's wild waving. Grandmaf's face broke into a million creases.

*

She was reading *The Wind in the Willows* to Rossie, savoring the comings and goings, the joys and sorrows, the messing about of Ratty and Mole and Mr. Toad. After the first chapter—Mole on the river bank, spring cleaning his humble home—she let Rossie look at the pictures, hoping his eyes would droop in sleep before their parents left. He would miss his mother. For the first time her mother had agreed to boating, back to someplace they'd been when they were young. She used to moan about Hawaii, now she was content to see a pair of arbutus trees.

His bright eyes were intent on the book. She leaned back and heard the low tinkle of Janna's laugh like glass wind chimes from Chinatown. Her mother had laughed just like that. Owen was making Janna laugh. They were playing her records on the porch, *Oh Angel Eeeeyes, I'm so in love with you,* and he'd be telling her about his plans. He'd finally made up his mind. He was going to the University of California. It sounded important and far away but Owen assured her, just as he was assuring Janna right now, that it was closer than any place in the east and that he'd come back the same as he'd left. He'd explained it carefully so they'd understand. Somebody at the university, a physics prof, had won a peace prize. A Dr. Edwin M. McMillan to be exact. Seventy-five thousand dollars for his work on peaceful uses of atomic energy. The 1963 Atoms for Peace Award to be exact, and Owen had been, so they'd understand. It all added up. Owen would go, but he'd come back. He'd come back to Janna. It added up to a perfect even number. The universe had thumped them around but they still shone with matching magnitudes, equal brightness. Two cool stars, one red, one yellow, drawn inexorably toward each other. Maffy's sigh ruffled Ross's fluff of hair lying against her chest. *My Venus, in blue jeans.*

"Not sleepy yet?" She reached down for another book. "How about *Old Mother West Wind and the Merry Little Breezes?*"

"Whoo Whoo." Rossie was looking at the cover and blowing, like a snowy topped owl.

She heard laughing from the porch. The *Theme from a Summer Place* was settling over them like a benediction, promising everything. She heard Grandmaf rustling in the tiny alcove that was the kitchen, getting up a batch of Welsh cakes, no doubt. Having her grandkids to herself was the mountaintop for Grandmaf.

"Shall we read the chapter about Sammy Blue Jay, Rossie? Pretend we can fly in the wind too?"

"Myfanwy!" Her grandmothers voice rang out from the kitchen. Is there a baking sheet, dear?"

"Just a sec, Grandmaf." She moved him off her lap. "Here, you hold the book till I get back?"

There wasn't a baking sheet. How did her mother make all those oatmeal cookies? But grandma could improvise anything. The Welsh cakes would take form in a roasting pan. "It'll work," she said, in her cheery lilt.

Rossie hadn't missed her, it seemed. He could hold the book pretty steady now and had found a page he liked. "What is it? What have you found?" It was Sammy Blue Jay, flying over the corn crib, looking for a way in. "You found Sammy. Good boy."

"Saaam," he said

Another new word. What else would he learn?

The little rowboat sat in the front cove while the *Pleiades* waited at anchor farther out. A northeasterly blew, tingeing the water indigo. She focused the binoculars on her father and mother walking down the beach with their last load. Her father's arms would be cradling his rum. What had her mother armed herself with? The bow was loaded down with camping gear. She stepped into the rowboat, arm reaching out for her father's support. He grasped her hand and settled her in the stern, then pushed out the bow and hopped in, still nimble. He fitted the wooden oars into the oarlocks. Maffy followed them with her binoculars, every details in sharp focus. Her mother's shoulders slumped and her head looked down at her fingers, trailing lightly in the water. Was she sighing? Her father's shoulders tightened then eased, tightened then eased, and the small boat surged across the cove toward the *Pleiades*. Tonight Maffy would sneak down to the cove with Henry and swim down the path of the moon. Henry. The only one who would go to the Milky Way with her, arms reaching before him like sparklers on Halloween.

She watched the oars dip and glide, breaking the water with a cascade of drops. It had been a lot of years, but her parents were both in the same rocky boat again. Her mother's head lifted and turned slowly, eyes finding the cabin's porch. Her eyes were brighter these days, like sea lettuce under an inch of tide. Maffy lowered the binoculars and raised her hand in a tentative salute. Her mother smiled.

It wasn't till late that night that she found it. Lying on the top bunk, she almost missed the brown paper bag wedged between her mattress and the knot-holed wall. Janna was breathing lightly below her. Owen was sleeping under his stars. Rossie was curled around Grandmaf in the big bed, breathing in the smell of earth and lavender soap.

She switched on her flashlight. No one would wake. Everyone was so exhausted with relief they might sleep forever. The bag was rumpled like it had seen a lot of use. She reached in. Her hand touched warmth. She pulled out something feather soft. A moccasin in toffee-coloured suede with white rabbit's fur lining. Soft on her cheek, smelling of cedar woods. She pulled out the other, lined them up evenly on the bed and held the flashlight on them; saw the beaded patterns of blue and green. Swirling patterns, like the ocean's deep, silent wind. Like Owen's still fathomless eyes. Like the earth seen from far in space, silently turning into tomorrow.

Margot Griffiths was born in Victoria BC where her story is set. She has a masters degree in psychology and has worked at universities in the US, Canada and Tanzania. She now lives in Point Roberts Washington where she is a freelance journalist

Edwards Brothers Malloy
Thorofare, NJ USA
May 23, 2014